The Picador Book of the Beach

Robert Drewe was born in Melbourne in 1943, grew up on the Indian Ocean coast of Western Australia and has lived on the Pacific coasts of New South Wales and California. His novels *The Savage Crows*, *A Cry in the Jungle Bar* and *Our Sunshine* have received wide critical praise and *Fortune* won the National Book Council fiction prize. One book of stories, *The Bay of Contented Men*, won a Commonwealth Writers' Prize, while another, *The Bodysurfers*, became a best seller and was adapted for film, television, radio and the stage. He is also a film critic and the author of several screenplays. His stage drama, *South American Barbecue*, was first performed in 1991. He was awarded an Australian Creative Artists Fellowship by the Prime Minister of Australia in 1992.

Also by Robert Drewe in Picador

The Bay of Contented Men

THE PICADOR BOOK OF THE
BEACH

Edited by ROBERT DREWE

PICADOR

First published 1993 by Pan Macmillan Publishers Australia

First published in Great Britain 1994 by Picador
a division of Pan Macmillan Publishers Limited
Cavaye Place, London SW10 9PG
and Basingstoke

Associated companies throughout the world

ISBN 0 330 33621 5

1 3 5 7 9 8 6 4 2

A CIP catalogue record for this book is available from
the British Library

Typeset by Midland Typesetters
Printed and bound in Great Britain by
Cox & Wyman Ltd, Reading, Berkshire

For
Dinny O'Hearn

joyful bodysurfer of Lorne, Portsea, Wye River,
Trigg and Noosa

CONTENTS

INTRODUCTION   1

LEARNING TO SWIM
Graham Swift   9

THE CLIFF
Charles Baxter   37

THE HOTTEST NIGHT OF THE CENTURY
Glenda Adams   43

BIG FISH, LITTLE FISH
Italo Calvino   57

SPINDRIFT
Candida Baker   71

LAST DAY OF SUMMER
Ian McEwan   95

ACROSS THE PLAINS, OVER THE MOUNTAINS
AND DOWN TO THE SEA
Frank Moorhouse   121

PAGES FROM COLD POINT
Paul Bowles   127

THE FISH-SCALE SHIRT
Ruth Fainlight   163

RADIANT HEAT
Robert Drewe   173

UNNAMED ISLANDS IN THE UNKNOWN SEA
Keri Hulme   193

GETTING READY
Barry Hannah   205

THE WATER WAS DARK AND IT WENT FOREVER
DOWN
Tim Winton   221

REDFISH
Rick Bass   229

POSTCARDS FROM SURFERS
Helen Garner   243

SO MUCH WATER SO CLOSE TO HOME
Raymond Carver   265

THE HANDSOMEST DROWNED MAN IN THE WORLD
Gabriel García Márquez   277

THE CATCH
Nadine Gordimer   287

GREAT BARRIER REEF
Diane Johnson   309

THE SEASIDE HOUSES
John Cheever   341

A CHANGE OF SCENE
David Malouf   357

THE MIDNIGHT LOVE FEAST
Michel Tournier   393

LIFEGUARD
John Updike   415

BLUEGILL
Jayne Anne Phillips   425

THE BEACH
Alain Robbe-Grillet   437

NOTES ON THE AUTHORS   447

ACKNOWLEDGEMENTS   457

INTRODUCTION

THE LYRIC POET, critic and masochist Algernon Charles Swinburne so adored vigorous surf swimming that the French philosopher and psychologist Gaston Bachelard named a complex after him. For Swinburne, 'the sea my nursing mother' had a 'goodlier breast' than his own mother. It was Swinburne who said to a wave: *My lips will feast on the foam of thy lips . . . /Thy sweet hard kisses are strong like wine/Thy large embraces are keen like pain.*

Those neurotics with the Swinburne Complex not only desire the physical struggle against the elements, and the ambivalence of pleasure and pain ('each wave hurts, each one cuts like a whip'), but delight in the dramatic moment—presumably around the time that the body's circulation finally triumphs over the cold water—when the good and evil of a whole universe seem to come together in the swimmer's/poet's heart.

Swinburne had it bad, but Byron would have known what he was on about. And those two body-surfing extremists were, to use a suitably littoral Australian colloquialism, *not Robinson Crusoe*. They were not alone: other literary figures with exceptional hydrous psyches included Shelley; Walt Whitman; Jack London; Paul Valery; Virginia Woolf and Rupert Brooke, swimming naked together, the dark water 'smelling of mint and mud'; Coleridge, surrendering to the sea's dreamy seduction ('my whole Being is filled with waves, as it were, that roll and stumble, one this way, and one that way, like things that have no common master.'); the erotically likeminded Flaubert, who longed to be littorally transformed, with the sea's 'thousand liquid nipples' travelling all over his body; Edgar Allan Poe, prone to long, lone, mysterious swims; Hart Crane, who swallow-dived to his death off the stern of the *Orizaba* into the Bay of Mexico; Tennessee Williams, who had a surprising passion for long swims off Nantucket with Carson McCullers; and the impulsive divers Zelda and Scott Fitzgerald, whose habit enlivened many a La Garoupe cocktail party and gave a name to *Tender is the Night*'s Dick Diver. Indeed, it was

Fitzgerald, in *The Crackup*, who described 'all good writing' as 'swimming underwater and holding your breath'.

Flaubert's and Shelley's most profound erotic experiences were related to the beach, and for Valery, swimming was, simply, a *'fornication avec l'onde'*. Despite their ardour, however, it is Byron whom one generally associates with coastal/lyrical/physical release. It is also Byron, of course, who features in literature's most melodramatic seaside event, the aftermath of non-swimmer water-worshipper Shelley's drowning in Italy—itself a compulsive act of myth fulfilment. When the body of Shelley's boating companion Williams was being cremated on the beach, his face having been nibbled by fish to a 'livid mass of shapeless flesh', Byron shouted, 'Are we all to resemble that?', stripped off and plunged into the Gulf of Spezia to challenge the surf that had drowned his friends. Only after swimming more than a mile from shore and spending an hour in the surf, did he swim back. Later, when Shelley's corpse broke open on the pyre, exposing the heart, and the brain 'visibly seethed, bubbled and boiled as in a cauldron', Byron again dived into the sea and swam two miles out to his yacht, and back again, while the sea and sun turned him into 'one large continuous blister' and peeled all the skin from his body.

Such scene-stealing and romantic events did nothing to diminish the beach's influence, whether creative, psychological, sensual, Byronic—or even Swinburnian —on poets and, later, on novelists and writers of short stories. Given the power such watery myths as that of Charon, the ferryman of the dead, and Ophelia, Shakespeare's beautiful creature born to die in water (and their related psychological impulses), have always wielded over artists of all kinds (Virginia Woolf, for one), this is hardly surprising. It is fascinating that variations of these myths constantly crop up in the twenty-five very different modern stories selected for this anthology.

I am someone who prefers to live where I can catch a glimpse of the sea at least in my mind's eye, but I chose these particular stories for more than just their setting; not only because I think they represent the best of contemporary shorter fiction writing about the beach—the coasts, ocean shores, bays, dunes, lagoons and rivers—but because each of them has the extra dimension of what Gerard Manley Hopkins called 'deep down things'. They share a concern with pressing personal, social and political questions, their satiric, humorous or fantastic sidelong glance often revealing more than direct realistic examination. All of these stories truly plumb the depths.

The role of the beach in contemporary fiction (and perhaps in modern life, too) may be literally gauged by the stories' subject matter. The vast majority are to do with escape, often from the next most popular

category—family and sexual relationships. These are
followed in popularity by drowning, growing up and
the mysterious voyage/journey to the Apocalypse. It
will not surprise fishermen and beachgoers—or students
of literary symbolism—that fish and fishing are a
constant symbol throughout the stories. Fish are rather
special things, being themselves symbolic of the world
of symbols, of spirituality, in contrast to the material-
istic, earthbound approach to life. The products of
emotion and intuition, they symbolize the psyche in
contrast to the body, the unconscious to the conscious.
The fisherman, whether the Fisher King of the Grail
legends or the New Testament's leader of the apostles,
was the wise man who could bring up the treasures
of the deep from the depths of the mind.

Interestingly, many of the stories, especially those
by the Australians and Americans, are evidence of 'the
unconquerable summer' of Albert Camus and the
enduring influence of *The Stranger*, an influence that
rests less in its sense of existential absurdity than in
the salty heat and glare of the beach and Camus's
evocation of sensual happiness. Camus, of course, grew
up in a working class district of Algiers where poverty
and a colonial culture were redeemed by the riches
heaped on his senses by sea and sun. 'Poverty prevented
me from thinking that all is well under the sun and
in history; the sun taught me that history is not
everything.'

The greatest pleasure in compiling this collection of fine beach stories, apart from the joy of being able to choose the fiction of my favourite authors, has been to match the old European artistic preoccupation with the ancient sea and water myths to the modern intuitive and sensual appreciation of the coast felt by the world's great beachgoers, the Australians. It has been exciting to discover new writers and an honour to absorb myself in the work of our era's most illustrious ones, whose alacrity at agreeing to be included in this collection was both generous and welcome. May Hughie, the Australian god of surf, send 'em up for Glenda Adams, Candida Baker, Rick Bass, Charles Baxter, Paul Bowles, Ruth Fainlight, Gabriel García Márquez, Helen Garner, Nadine Gordimer, Barry Hannah, Keri Hulme, Diane Johnson, David Malouf, Ian McEwan, Frank Moorhouse, Jayne Anne Phillips, Alain Robbe-Grillet, Graham Swift, Michel Tournier, John Updike and Tim Winton, for those beloved of the late Italo Calvino, Raymond Carver and John Cheever, and, finally, for Jane Palfreyman, for helping to acquire such illustrious contributions, and for guiding this book through the reefs.

ROBERT DREWE

HARDY'S BAY, NEW SOUTH WALES

LEARNING TO SWIM
Graham Swift

MRS SINGLETON HAD THREE times thought of leaving her husband. The first time was before they were married, on a charter plane coming back from a holiday in Greece. They were students who had just graduated. They had rucksacks and faded jeans. In Greece they had stayed part of the time by a beach on an island. The island was dry and rocky with great grey and vermilion coloured rocks and when you lay on the beach it seemed that you too became a hot, basking rock. Behind the beach there were eucalyptus trees like dry, leafy bones, old men with mules and gold teeth, a fragrance of thyme, and a café with melon pips on the floor and a jukebox which played bouzouki music and songs by Cliff Richard. All this Mr Singleton failed to appreciate. He'd only liked the milk-warm, clear-blue sea, in which he'd stayed most of the time as if afraid of foreign soil. On the plane she'd thought: he hadn't enjoyed the holiday, hadn't liked Greece at all. All that sunshine. Then she'd thought she ought not to marry him.

Though she had, a year later.

The second time was about a year after Mr Singleton, who was a civil engineer, had begun his first big job. He became a junior partner in a firm with a growing reputation. She ought to have been pleased by this. It brought money and comfort; it enabled them to move to a house with a large garden, to live well, to think about raising a family. They spent weekends in country hotels. But Mr Singleton seemed untouched by this. He became withdrawn and incommunicative. He went to his work austere-faced. She thought: he likes his bridges and tunnels better than me.

The third time, which was really a phase; not a single moment, was when she began to calculate how often Mr Singleton made love to her. When she started this it was about once every fortnight on average. Then it became every three weeks. The interval had been widening for some time. This was not a predicament Mrs Singleton viewed selfishly. Love-making had been a problem before, in their earliest days together, which, thanks to her patience and initiative, had been overcome. It was Mr Singleton's unhappiness, not her own, that she saw in their present plight. He was distrustful of happiness as some people fear heights or open spaces. She would reassure him, encourage him again. But the averages seemed to defy her personal effort: once every three weeks, once every month . . . She thought: things go back to as they were.

But then, by sheer chance, she became pregnant.

Now she lay on her back, eyes closed, on the coarse sand of the beach in Cornwall. It was hot and, if she opened her eyes, the sky was clear blue. This and the previous summer had been fine enough to make her husband's refusal to go abroad for holidays tolerable. If you kept your eyes closed it could be Greece or Italy or Ibiza. She wore a chocolate-brown bikini, sunglasses, and her skin, which seldom suffered from sunburn, was already beginning to tan. She let her arms trail idly by her side, scooping up little handfuls of sand. If she turned her head to the right and looked towards the sea she could see Mr Singleton and their son Paul standing in the shallow water. Mr Singleton was teaching Paul to swim. 'Kick!' he was saying. From here, against the gentle waves, they looked like no more than two rippling silhouettes.

'Kick!' said Mr Singleton, 'Kick!' He was like a punisher, administering lashes.

She turned her head away to face upwards. If you

shut your eyes you could imagine you were the only one on the beach; if you held them shut you could be part of the beach. Mrs Singleton imagined that in order to acquire a tan you had to let the sun make love to you.

She dug her heels in the sand and smiled involuntarily.

When she was a thin, flat-chested, studious girl in a grey school uniform Mrs Singleton had assuaged her fear and desperation about sex with fantasies which took away from men the brute physicality she expected of them. All her lovers would be artists. Poets would write poems to her, composers would dedicate their works to her. She would even pose, naked and immaculate, for painters, who having committed her true, her eternal form to canvas, would make love to her in an impalpable, ethereal way, under the power of which her bodily and temporal self would melt away, perhaps for ever. These fantasies (for she had never entirely renounced them) had crystallized for her in the image of a sculptor, who from a cold intractable piece of stone would fashion her very essence—which would be vibrant and full of sunlight, like the statues they had seen in Greece.

At university she had worked on the assumption that all men lusted uncontrollably and insatiably after women. She had not yet encountered a man who, whilst prone to the usual instincts, possessing moreover a

magnificent body with which to fulfil them, yet had
scruples about doing so, seemed ashamed of his own
capacities. It did not matter that Mr Singleton was
reading engineering, was scarcely artistic at all, or that
his powerful physique was unlike the nebulous creatures
of her dreams. She found she loved this solid man-
flesh. Mrs Singleton had thought she was the shy,
inexperienced, timid girl. Overnight she discovered that
she wasn't this at all. He wore tough denim shirts,
spoke and smiled very little and had a way of standing
very straight and upright as if he didn't need any help
from anyone. She had to educate him into moments
of passion, of self-forgetfulness which made her glow
with her own achievement. She was happy because she
had not thought she was happy and she believed she
could make someone else happy. At the university girls
were starting to wear jeans, record-players played the
Rolling Stones and in the hush of the Modern Languages
Library she read Leopardi and Verlaine. She seemed
to float with confidence in a swirling, buoyant element
she had never suspected would be her own.

'Kick!' she heard again from the water.

Mr Singleton had twice thought of leaving his wife.
Once was after a symphony concert they had gone to
in London when they had not known each other very
long and she still tried to get him to read books, to
listen to music, to take an interest in art. She would
buy concert or theatre tickets, and he had to seem

pleased. At this concert a visiting orchestra was playing some titanic, large-scale work by a late nineteenth-century composer. A note in the programme said it represented the triumph of life over death. He had sat on his plush seat amidst the swirling barrage of sound. He had no idea what he had to do with it or the triumph of life over death. He had thought the same thought about the rapt girl on his left, the future Mrs Singleton, who now and then bobbed, swayed or rose in her seat as if the music physically lifted her. There were at least seventy musicians on the platform. As the piece worked to its final crescendo the conductor, whose arms were flailing frantically so that his white shirt back appeared under his flying tails, looked so absurd Mr Singleton thought he would laugh. When the music stopped and was immediately supplanted by wild cheering and clapping he thought the world had gone mad. He had struck his own hands together so as to appear to be sharing the ecstasy. Then, as they filed out, he had almost wept because he felt like an insect. He even thought she had arranged the whole business so as to humiliate him.

He thought he would not marry her.

The second time was after they had been married some years. He was one of a team of engineers working on a suspension bridge over an estuary in Ireland. They took it in turns to stay on the site and to inspect the construction work personally. Once he had to go to

the very top of one of the two piers of the bridge
to examine work on the bearings and housing for the
main overhead cables. A lift ran up between the twin
towers of the pier amidst a network of scaffolding and
power cables to where a working platform was
positioned. The engineer, with the supervisor and the
foreman, had only to stay on the platform from where
all the main features of construction were visible. The
men at work on the upper sections of the towers,
specialists in their trade, earning up to two hundred
pounds a week—who balanced on precarious cat-walks
and walked along exposed reinforcing girders—often
jibed at the engineers who never left the platform. He
thought he would show them. He walked out on to
one of the cat-walks on the outer face of the pier where
they were fitting huge grip-bolts. This was quite safe
if you held on to the rails but still took some nerve.
He wore a check cheese-cloth shirt and his white safety
helmet. It was a grey, humid August day. The cat-
walk hung over greyness. The water of the estuary
was the colour of dead fish. A dredger was chugging
near the base of the pier. He thought, I could swim
the estuary; but there is a bridge. Below him the yellow
helmets of workers moved over the girders for the
roadway like beetles. He took his hands from the rail.
He wasn't at all afraid. He had been away from his
wife all week. He thought: she knows nothing of this.
If he were to step out now into the grey air he would

be quite by himself, no harm would come to him . . .

Now Mr Singleton stood in the water, teaching his son to swim. They were doing the water-wings exercise. The boy wore a pair of water-wings, red underneath, yellow on top, which ballooned up under his arms and chin. With this to support him, he would splutter and splash towards his father who stood facing him some feet away. After a while at this they would try the same procedure, his father moving a little nearer, but without the water-wings, and this the boy dreaded. 'Kick!' said Mr Singleton, 'Use your legs!' He watched his son draw painfully towards him. The boy had not yet grasped that the body naturally floated and that if you added to this certain mechanical effects, you swam. He thought that in order to swim you had to make as much frantic movement as possible. As he struggled towards Mr Singleton his head, which was too high out of the water, jerked messily from side to side, and his eyes which were half closed swivelled in every direction but straight ahead. 'Towards me!' shouted Mr Singleton. He held out his arms in front of him for Paul to grasp. As his son was on the point of clutching them he would step back a little, pulling his hands away, in the hope that the last desperate lunge to reach his father might really teach the boy the art of propelling himself in water. But he sometimes wondered if this were his only motive.

'Good boy. Now again.'

At school Mr Singleton had been an excellent swimmer. He had won various school titles, broken numerous records and competed successfully in ASA championships. There was a period between the age of about thirteen and seventeen which he remembered as the happiest in his life. It wasn't the medals and trophies that made him glad, but the knowledge that he didn't have to bother about anything else. Swimming vindicated him. He would get up every morning at six and train for two hours in the baths, and again before lunch; and when he fell asleep, exhausted, in French and English periods in the afternoon, he didn't have to bother about the indignation of the masters— lank, ill-conditioned creatures—for he had his excuse. He didn't have to bother about the physics teacher who complained to the headmaster that he would never get the exam results he needed if he didn't cut down his swimming, for the headmaster (who was an advocate of sport) came to his aid and told the physics teacher not to interfere with a boy who was a credit to the school. Nor did he have to bother about a host of other things which were supposed 'to be going on inside him, which made the question of what to do in the evening, at week-ends, fraught and tantalizing, which drove other boys to moodiness and recklessness. For once in the cool water of the baths, his arms reaching, his eyes fixed on the blue marker line on the bottom, his ears full so that he could hear nothing around him, he would feel quite by himself, quite sufficient. At the end of races, when for one brief instant he clung panting alone like a survivor to the finishing rail which his rivals had yet to touch, he felt an infinite peace. He went to bed early, slept soundly, kept to his training regimen; and he enjoyed this Spartan purity which disdained pleasure and disorder. Some of his school mates mocked him—for not going to dances on Saturdays or to pubs, under age, or the Expresso after school. But he did not mind. He didn't need them. He knew they were weak. None of them could hold out, depend on themselves, spurn comfort if they had to. Some of them would go under in life. And none of them could cleave the water as he did or possessed a hard, streamlined, perfectly tuned body like he did.

Then, when he was nearly seventeen all this changed. His father, who was an engineer, though proud of his son's trophies, suddenly pressed him to different forms of success. The headmaster no longer shielded him from the physics master. He said: 'You can't swim into your future.' Out of spite perhaps or an odd consistency of self-denial, he dropped swimming altogether rather than cut it down. For a year and a half he worked at his maths and physics with the same single-mindedness with which he had perfected his sport. He knew about mechanics and engineering because he knew how to make his body move through water. His work was not merely competent but good. He got to university where he might have had the leisure, if he wished, to resume his swimming. But he did not. Two years are a long gap in a swimmer's training; two years when you are near your peak can mean you will never get back to your true form. Sometimes he went for a dip in the university pool and swam slowly up and down amongst practising members of the university team, whom perhaps he could still have beaten, as a kind of relief.

Often, Mr Singleton dreamt about swimming. He would be moving through vast expanses of water, an ocean. As he moved it did not require any effort at all. Sometimes he would go for long distances under water, but he did not have to bother about breathing. The water would be silvery-grey. And always it seemed that as he swam he was really trying to get beyond the water, to put it behind him, as if it were a veil he were parting and he would emerge on the other side of it at last, on to some pristine shore, where he would step where no one else had stepped before.

When he made love to his wife her body got in the way; he wanted to swim through her.

Mrs Singleton raised herself, pushed her sun-glasses up over her dark hair and sat with her arms stretched straight behind her back. A trickle of sweat ran between her breasts. They had developed to a good size since her schoolgirl days. Her skinniness in youth had stood her in good stead against the filling out of middle age, and her body was probably more mellow, more lithe and better proportioned now than it had ever been. She looked at Paul and Mr Singleton half immersed in the shallows. It seemed to her that her husband was the real boy, standing stubbornly upright with his hands before him, and that Paul was some toy being pulled and swung relentlessly around him and towards him as though on some string. They had seen her sit up. Her husband waved, holding the boy's hand, as though for the two of them. Paul did not wave; he seemed more concerned with the water in his eyes. Mrs Singleton did not wave back. She would have done if her son had waved. When they had left for their holiday Mr Singleton had said to Paul, 'You'll learn to swim this time. In salt water, you know, it's easier.' Mrs Singleton hoped her son wouldn't swim; so that she could wrap him, still, in the big yellow towel when he came out, rub him dry and warm, and watch her husband stand apart, his hands empty.

She watched Mr Singleton drop his arm back to his side. 'If you wouldn't splash it wouldn't go in your eyes,' she just caught him say.

The night before, in their hotel room, they had argued. They always argued about half way through their holidays. It was symbolic, perhaps, of that first trip to Greece, when he had somehow refused to enjoy himself. They had to incur injuries so that they could then appreciate their leisure, like convalescents. For the first four days or so of their holiday Mr Singleton would tend to be moody, on edge. He would excuse this as 'winding down', the not-to-be-hurried process of dispelling the pressures of work. Mrs Singleton would be patient. On about the fifth day Mrs Singleton would begin to suspect that the winding down would never end and indeed (which she had known all along) that it was not winding down at all—he was clinging, as to a defence, to his bridges and tunnels; and she would show her resentment. At this point Mr Singleton would retaliate by an attack upon her indolence.

Last night he had called her 'flabby'. He could not mean, of course, 'flabby-bodied' (she could glance down, now, at her still flat belly), though such a sensual attack would have been simpler, almost heartening, from him. He meant 'flabby of attitude'. And what he meant by this, or what he wanted to mean, was that *he* was not flabby; that he worked, facing the real world, erecting great solid things on the face of the land, and that, whilst he worked, he disdained work's rewards—money, pleasure, rich food, holidays abroad —that he hadn't 'gone soft', as she had done since they graduated eleven years ago, with their credentials for the future and their plane tickets to Greece. She knew this toughness of her husband was only a cover for his own failure to relax and his need to keep his distance. She knew that he found no particular virtue in his bridges and tunnels (it was the last thing he wanted to do really—build); it didn't matter if they were right or wrong, they were there, he could point to them as if it vindicated him—just as when he made his infrequent, if seismic love to her it was not a case of enjoyment or satisfaction; he just did it.

It was hot in their hotel room. Mr Singleton stood in his blue pyjama bottoms, feet apart, like a PT instructor.

'Flabby? What do you mean—"flabby"!?' she had said, looking daunted.

But Mrs Singleton had the advantage whenever Mr Singleton accused her in this way of complacency, of weakness. She knew he only did it to hurt her, and so to feel guilty, and so to feel the remorse which would release his own affection for her, his vulnerability, his own need to be loved. Mrs Singleton was used to this process, to the tenderness that was the tenderness of successively opened and reopened wounds. And she was used to being the nurse who took care of the healing scars. For though Mr Singleton inflicted the first blow he would always make himself more guilty than he made her suffer, and Mrs Singleton, though in pain herself, could not resist wanting to clasp and cherish her husband, wanting to wrap him up safe when his own weakness and submissiveness showed and his body became liquid and soft against her; could not resist the old spur that her husband was unhappy and it was for her to make him happy. Mr Singleton was extraordinarily lovable when he was guilty. She would even have yielded indefinitely, foregoing her own grievance, to this extreme of comforting him for the pain he caused her, had she not discovered, in time, that this only pushed the process a stage further. Her forgiveness of him became only another level of comfort, of softness he must reject. His flesh shrank from her restoring touch.

She thought: men go round in circles, women don't move.

She kept to her side of the hotel bed, he, with his face turned, to his. He lay like a person washed up on a beach. She reached out her hand and stroked the nape of his neck. She felt him tense. All this was a pattern.

'I'm sorry,' he said, 'I didn't mean —'

'It's all right, it doesn't matter.'

'Doesn't it matter?' he said.

When they reached this point they were like miners racing each other for deeper and deeper seams of guilt and recrimination.

But Mrs Singleton had given up delving to rock bottom. Perhaps it was five years ago when she had thought for the third time of leaving her husband, perhaps long before that. When they were students she'd made allowances for his constraints, his reluctances. An unhappy childhood perhaps, a strict upbringing. She thought his inhibition might be lifted by the sanction of marriage. She'd thought, after all, it would be a good thing if he married her. She had not thought what would be good for her. They stood outside Gatwick Airport, back from Greece, in the grey, wet August light. Their tanned skin had seemed to glow. Yet she'd known this mood of promise would pass. She watched him kick against contentment, against ease, against the long, glittering life-line she threw to him; and, after a while, she ceased to try to haul him in. She began to imagine again her phantom artists. She thought: people slip off the shores of the real world, back into dreams. She hadn't 'gone soft', only gone back to herself. Hidden inside her like treasure there were lines of Leopardi, of Verlaine her husband would never appreciate. She thought, he doesn't need me, things run off him, like water. She even thought that her husband's neglect in making love to her was not a problem he had but a deliberate scheme to deny her. When Mrs Singleton desired her husband she could not help herself. She would stretch back on the bed with the sheets pulled off like a blissful nude in a Modigliani. She thought this ought to gladden a man. Mr Singleton would stand at the foot of the bed and gaze down at her. He looked like some strong, chaste knight in the legend of the Grail. He would respond to her invitation, but before he did so there would be this expression, half stern, half innocent, in his eyes. It was the sort of expression that good men in books and films are supposed to make to prostitutes. It would ensure that their love-making was marred and that afterwards it would seem as if he had performed something out of duty that only she wanted. Her body would feel like stone. It was at such times, when she felt the cold, dead-weight feel of abused happiness, that Mrs Singleton most thought she was through with Mr Singleton. She would watch his strong, compact torso already lifting itself off the bed. She would think: he thinks he is tough, contained in himself, but he won't see what I offer him, he doesn't see how it is I who can help him.

Mrs Singleton lay back on her striped towel on the sand. Once again she became part of the beach. The careless sounds of the seaside, of excited children's voices, of languid grownups', of wooden bats on balls, fluttered over her as she shut her eyes. She thought: it is the sort of day on which someone suddenly shouts, 'Someone is drowning.'

When Mrs Singleton became pregnant she felt she had outmanoeuvred her husband. He did not really want a child (it was the last thing he wanted, Mrs Singleton thought, a child) but he was jealous of her condition, as of some achievement he himself could attain. He was excluded from the little circle of herself and her womb, and, as though to puncture it, he began for the first time to make love to her of a kind where he took the insistent initiative. Mrs Singleton was not greatly pleased. She seemed buoyed up by her own bigness. She noticed that her husband began to do exercises in the morning, in his underpants, press-ups, squat-jumps, as if he were getting in training for something. He was like a boy. He even became, as the term of her pregnancy drew near its end, resilient and detached again, the virile father waiting to receive the son (Mr Singleton knew it would be a son, so did Mrs Singleton) that she, at the appointed time, would deliver him. When the moment arrived he insisted on being present so as to prove he wasn't squeamish and to make sure he wouldn't be tricked in the transaction. Mrs Singleton was not daunted. When the pains became frequent she wasn't at all afraid. There were big, watery lights clawing down from the ceiling of the delivery room like the lights in dentists' surgeries. She could just see her husband looking down at her. His face was white and clammy. It was his fault for wanting to be there. She had to push, as though away from him. Then she knew it was happening. She stretched back. She was a great surface of warm, splitting rock and Paul was struggling bravely up into the sunlight. She had to coax him with her cries. She felt him emerge like a trapped survivor. The doctor groped with rubber gloves. 'There we are,' he said. She managed to look at Mr Singleton. She wanted suddenly to put him back inside for good where Paul had come from. With a fleeting pity she saw that this was what Mr Singleton wanted too. His eyes were half closed. She kept hers on him. He seemed to wilt under her gaze. All his toughness and control were draining from him and she was glad. She lay back triumphant and glad. The doctor was holding Paul; but she looked, beyond, at Mr Singleton. He was far away like an insect. She knew he couldn't hold out. He was going to faint. He was looking where her legs were spread. His eyes went out of focus. He was going to faint, keel over, right there on the spot.

Mrs Singleton grew restless, though she lay unmoving on the beach. Wasps were buzzing close to her head, round their picnic bag. She thought that Mr Singleton and Paul had been too long at their swimming lesson. They should come out. It never struck her, hot as she was, to get up and join her husband and son in the sea. Whenever Mrs Singleton wanted a swim she would wait until there was an opportunity to go in by herself; then she would wade out, dip her shoulders under suddenly and paddle about contentedly, keeping her hair dry, as though she were soaking herself in a large bath. They did not bathe as a family; nor did Mrs Singleton swim with Mr Singleton—who now and then, too, would get up by himself and enter the sea, swim at once about fifty yards out, then cruise for long stretches, with a powerful crawl or butterfly, back and forth across the bay. When this happened Mrs Singleton would engage her son in talk so he would not watch his father. Mrs Singleton did not swim with Paul either. He was too old, now, to cradle between her knees in the very shallow water, and she was somehow afraid that while Paul splashed and kicked around her he would suddenly learn how to swim. She had this feeling that Paul would only swim while she was in the sea, too. She did not want this to happen, but it reassured her and gave her sufficient confidence to let Mr Singleton continue his swimming lessons with Paul. These lessons were obsessive, indefatigable. Every Sunday morning at seven, when they were at home, Mr Singleton would take Paul to the baths for yet another attempt. Part of this, of course, was that Mr Singleton was determined that his son should swim; but it enabled him also to avoid the Sunday morning languor: extra hours in bed, leisurely love-making.

Once, in a room at college, Mr Singleton had told Mrs Singleton about his swimming, about his training sessions, races; about what it felt like when you could swim really well. She had run her fingers over his long, naked back.

Mrs Singleton sat up and rubbed sun-tan lotion on to her thighs. Down near the water's edge, Mr Singleton was standing about waist deep, supporting Paul who, gripped by his father's hands, water-wings still on, was flailing, face down, at the surface. Mr Singleton kept saying, 'No, keep still.' He was trying to get Paul to hold his body straight and relaxed so he would float. But each time as Paul nearly succeeded he would panic, fearing his father would let go, and thrash wildly. When he calmed down and Mr Singleton held him, Mrs

Singleton could see the water running off his face like tears.

Mrs Singleton did not alarm herself at this distress of her son. It was a guarantee against Mr Singleton's influence, an assurance that Paul was not going to swim; nor was he to be imbued with any of his father's sullen hardiness. When Mrs Singleton saw her son suffer, it pleased her and she felt loving towards him. She felt that an invisible thread ran between her and the boy which commanded him not to swim, and she felt that Mr Singleton knew that it was because of her that his efforts with Paul were in vain. Even now, as Mr Singleton prepared for another attempt, the boy was looking at her smoothing the sun-tan oil on to her legs.

'Come on, Paul,' said Mr Singleton. His wet shoulders shone like metal.

When Paul was born it seemed to Mrs Singleton that her life with her husband was dissolved, as a mirage dissolves, and that she could return again to what she was before she knew him. She let her staved-off hunger for happiness and her old suppressed dreams revive. But then they were not dreams, because they had a physical object and she knew she needed them in order to live. She did not disguise from herself what she needed. She knew that she wanted the kind of close, even erotic relationship with her son that women who have rejected their husbands have been known to have. The kind of relationship in which the son must hurt the mother, the mother the son. But she willed it, as if there would be no pain. Mrs Singleton waited for her son to grow. She trembled when she thought of him at eighteen or twenty. When he was grown he would be slim and light and slender, like a boy even though he was a man. He would not need a strong body because all his power would be inside. He would be all fire and life in essence. He would become an artist, a sculptor. She would pose for him naked (she would keep her body trim for this), and he would sculpt her. He would hold the chisel. His hands would guide the cold metal over the stone and its blows would strike sunlight.

Mrs Singleton thought: all the best statues they had seen in Greece seemed to have been dredged up from the sea.

She finished rubbing the lotion on to her insteps and put the cap back on the tube. As she did so she heard something that made her truly alarmed. It was Mr Singleton saying, 'That's it, that's the way! At last! Now keep it going!' She looked up. Paul was in the same position as before but he had learnt to make slower, regular motions with his limbs and his body no longer sagged in the middle. Though he still wore the water-wings he was moving, somewhat laboriously, forwards so that Mr Singleton had to walk along with him; and at one point Mr Singleton removed one of his hands from under the boy's ribs and simultaneously looked at his wife and smiled. His shoulders flashed. It was not a smile meant for her. She could see that. And it was not one of her husband's usual, infrequent, rather mechanical smiles. It was the smile a person makes about some joy inside, hidden and incommunicable.

'That's enough,' thought Mrs Singleton, getting to her feet, pretending not to have noticed, behind her sun-glasses, what had happened in the water. It *was* enough: they had been in the water for what seemed like an hour. He was only doing it because of their row last night, to make her feel he was not outmatched by using the reserve weapon of Paul. And, she added with relief to herself, Paul still had the water-wings and one hand to support him.

'That's enough now!' she shouted aloud, as if she were slightly, but not ill-humouredly, peeved at being neglected. 'Come on in now!' She had picked up her purse as a quickly conceived ruse as she got up and as she walked towards the water's edge she waved it above her head. 'Who wants an ice-cream?'

Mr Singleton ignored his wife. 'Well done, Paul,' he said. 'Let's try that again.'

Mrs Singleton knew he would do this. She stood on the little ridge of sand just above where the beach, becoming fine shingle, shelved into the sea. She replaced a loose strap of her bikini over her shoulder and with a finger of each hand pulled the bottom half down over her buttocks. She stood feet apart, slightly on her toes, like a gymnast. She knew other eyes on the beach would be on her. It flattered her that she—and her husband, too—received admiring glances from those around. She thought, with relish for the irony: perhaps they think we are happy, beautiful people. For all her girlhood diffidence, Mrs Singleton enjoyed displaying her attractions, and she liked to see other people's pleasure. When she lay sunbathing she imagined making love to all the moody, pubescent boys on holiday with their parents, with their slim waists and their quick heels.

'See if you can do it without me holding you,' said Mr Singleton. 'I'll help you at first.' He stooped over Paul. He looked like a mechanic making final adjustments to some prototype machine.

'Don't you want an ice-cream then, Paul?' said Mrs Singleton. 'They've got those chocolate ones.'

Paul looked up. His short wet hair stood up in spikes. He looked like a prisoner offered a chance of escape, but the plastic water-wings, like some absurd pillory, kept him fixed.

Mrs Singleton thought: he crawled out of me; now I have to lure him back with ice-cream.

'Can't you see he was getting the hang of it?' Mr Singleton said. 'If he comes out now he'll —'

'Hang of it! It was you. You were holding him all the time.'

She thought: perhaps I am hurting my son.

Mr Singleton glared at Mrs Singleton. He gripped Paul's shoulders. 'You don't want to get out now, do you Paul?' He looked suddenly as if he really might drown Paul rather than let him come out.

Mrs Singleton's heart raced. She wasn't good at rescues, at resuscitations. She knew this because of her life with her husband.

'Come on, you can go back in later,' she said.

Paul was a hostage. She was playing for time, not wanting to harm the innocent.

She stood on the sand like a marooned woman watching for ships. The sea, in the sheltered bay, was almost flat calm. A few, glassy waves idled in but were smoothed out before they could break. On the headlands there were outcrops of scaly rocks like basking lizards. The island in Greece had been where Theseus left Ariadne. Out over the blue water, beyond the heads of bobbing swimmers, seagulls flapped like scraps of paper.

Mr Singleton looked at Mrs Singleton. She was a fussy mother daubed with Ambre Solaire, trying to bribe her son with silly ice-creams; though if you forgot this she was a beautiful, tanned girl, like the girls men imagine on desert islands. But then, in Mr Singleton's dreams, there was no one else on the untouched shore he ceaselessly swam to.

He thought, if Paul could swim, then I could leave her.

Mrs Singleton looked at her husband. She felt afraid. The water's edge was like a dividing line between them which marked off the territory in which each existed. Perhaps they could never cross over.

'Well, I'm getting the ice-creams: you'd better get out.'

She turned and paced up the sand. Behind the beach was an ice-cream van painted like a fairground.

Paul Singleton looked at his mother. He thought: she is deserting me—or I am deserting her. He wanted to get out to follow her. Her feet made puffs of sand which stuck to her ankles, and you could see all her body as she strode up the beach. But he was afraid of his father and his gripping hands. And he was afraid of his mother, too. How she would wrap him, if he came out, in the big yellow towel like egg yolk, how she would want him to get close to her smooth, sticky body, like a mouth that would swallow him. He thought: the yellow towel humiliated him, his father's hands humiliated him. The water-wings humiliated him: you put them on and became a puppet. So much of life is humiliation. It was how you won love. His father was taking off the water-wings like a man unlocking a chastity belt. He said: 'Now try the same, coming towards me.' His father stood some feet away from him. He was a huge, straight man, like the pier of a bridge. 'Try.' Paul Singleton was six. He was terrified of water. Every time he entered it he had to fight

34

down fear. His father never realized this. He thought it was simple; you said: 'Only water, no need to be afraid.' His father did not know what fear was; the same as he did not know what fun was. Paul Singleton hated water. He hated it in his mouth and in his eyes. He hated the chlorine smell of the swimming baths, the wet, slippery tiles, the echoing whoops and screams. He hated it when his father read to him from *The Water Babies*. It was the only story his father read, because, since he didn't know fear or fun, he was really sentimental. His mother read lots of stories. 'Come on then. I'll catch you.' Paul Singleton held out his arms and raised one leg. This was the worst moment. Perhaps having no help was most humiliating. If you did not swim you sank like a statue. They would drag him out, his skin streaming. His father would say: 'I didn't mean . . .' But if he swam his mother would be forsaken. She would stand on the beach with chocolate ice-cream running down her arm. There was no way out; there were all these things to be afraid of and no weapons. But then, perhaps he was not afraid of his mother nor his father, nor of water, but of something else. He had felt it just now—when he'd struck out with rhythmic, reaching strokes and his feet had come off the bottom and his father's hand had slipped from under his chest: as if he had mistaken what his fear was; as if he had been unconsciously pretending, even to himself, so as to execute some plan. He lowered his chin into the water. 'Come on!' said Mr Singleton. He launched himself forward and felt the sand leave his feet and his legs wriggle like cut ropes. 'There,' said his father as he realized. 'There!' His father stood like a man waiting to clasp a lover; there was a gleam on his face. 'Towards me! Towards me!' said his father suddenly. But he kicked and struck, half in panic, half in pride, away from his father, away from the shore, away, in this strange new element that seemed all his own.

THE CLIFF

Charles Baxter

ON THE WAY OUT to the cliff, the old man kept one hand on the wheel. He smoked with the other hand. The inside of the car smelled of wine and cigarette ashes. He coughed constantly. His voice sounded like a version of the cough.

'I used to smoke Camels unfiltered,' he told the boy. The dirt road, rutted, dipped hard, and the car bounced. 'But I switched brands. Camels interfered with my eating. I couldn't taste what the Duchess cooked up. Meat, salad, Jell-O: it all tasted the same. So I went to low tar. You don't smoke, do you, boy?'

The boy stared at the road and shook his head.

'Not after what I've taught you, I hope not. You got to keep the body pure for the stuff we're doing.'

'You don't keep it pure,' the boy said.

'I don't have to. It's *been* pure. And, like I say, nobody is ever pure twice.'

The California pines seemed brittle and did not sway as they drove past. The boy thought he could hear the crash of the waves in front of them. 'Are we almost there?'

'Kind of impatient, aren't you?' the old man said, suppressing his cough. 'Look, boy, I told you a hundred times: you got to train your will to do this. You get impatient, and you —'

'— I know, I know. "You die."' The boy was wearing a jacket and a New York Mets cap. 'I know all that. You taught me. I'm only asking if we're there yet.'

'You got a woman, boy?' The old man looked suspicious. 'You got a woman?'

'I'm only fifteen,' the boy said nervously.

'That's not too old for it, especially around here.'

'I've been kissed,' the boy said. 'Is that the ocean?'

'That's her,' the old man said. 'Sometimes I think I know everything about you, and then sometimes I don't think I know anything. I hate to take chances like this. You could be hiding something out on me. The magic's no damn good if you're hiding something out on me.'

38

'It'll be good,' the boy said, seeing the long line of blue water through the trees. He pulled the visor down lower, so he wouldn't squint. 'It'll be real good.'

'Faith, hope, charity, and love,' the old man recited. 'And the spells. Now I admit I have fallen from the path of righteousness at times. But I never forget the spells. You forget them, you die.'

'I would not forget them,' the boy said.

'You better not be lying to me. You been thieving, sleeping with whores, you been carrying on in the bad way, well, we'll find out soon enough.' He stopped the car at a clearing. He turned the key off in the ignition and reached under his seat for a wine bottle. His hands were shaking. The old man unscrewed the cap and took a long swig. He recapped it and breathed out the sweet aroma in the boy's direction. 'Something for my nerves,' he said. 'I don't do this every day.'

'You don't believe in the spells anymore,' the boy said.

'I *am* the spells,' the old man shouted. 'I invented them. I just hate to see a fresh kid like you crash on the rocks on account of *you* don't believe in them.'

'Don't worry,' the boy said. 'Don't worry about me.'

They got out of the car together, and the old man reached around into the back seat for his coil of rope.

'I don't need it,' the boy said. 'I don't need the rope.'

'Kid, we do it my way or we don't do it.'

The boy took off his shoes. His bare feet stepped over pine needles and stones. He was wearing faded blue jeans and a sweatshirt, with a stain from the old man's wine bottle on it. He had taken off his jacket in the car, but he was still wearing the cap. They walked over a stretch of burnt grass and came to the edge of the cliff.

'Look at those sea gulls down there,' the old man pointed. 'Must be a hundred.' His voice was trembling with nervousness.

'I know about the sea gulls.' The boy had to raise his voice to be heard above the surf. 'I've seen them.'

'You're so smart, huh?' the old man coughed. He drew a cigarette out of his shirt and lit it with his Zippo lighter. 'All right, I'm tired of telling you what to do, Mr. Know-It-All. Take off the sweatshirt.' The boy took it off. 'Now make a circle in the dirt.'

'With what?'

'With your foot.'

'There isn't any dirt.'

'Do like I tell you.'

The boy extended his foot and drew a magic circle around himself. It could not be seen, but he knew it was there.

'Now look out at the horizon and tell it what I told you to tell it.'

The boy did as he was told.

'Now take this rope, take this end.' The old man handed it to him. 'God, I don't know sometimes.' The old man bent down for another swig of wine. 'Is your mind clear?'

'Yeah,' the boy said.

'Are you scared?'

'Naw.'

'Do you see anybody?'

'Nope.'

'You got any last questions?'

'Do I hold my arms out?'

'They do that in the Soviet Union,' the old man said, 'but they also do it sitting on pigs. That's the kind of people they are. You don't have to hold your arms out. Are you ready? Jump!'

The boy felt the edge of the cliff with his feet, jumped, and felt the magic and the horizon lifting him up and then out over the water, his body parallel to the ground. He took it into his mind to swoop down toward the cliffs, and then to veer away suddenly, and whatever he thought, he did. At first he held on to the rope, but even the old man could see that it was unnecessary, and reeled it in. In his jeans and cap, the boy lifted himself upward, then dove down toward the sea gulls, then just as easily lifted himself up again, rushing over the old man's head before flying out over the water.

He shouted with happiness.

The old man reached down again for his wine.

'The sun!' the old man shouted. 'The ocean! The land! That's how to do it!' And he laughed suddenly, his cough all gone. 'The sky!' he said at last.

The boy flew in great soaring circles. He tumbled in the air, dove, flipped, and sailed. His eyes were dazzled with the blue also, and like the old man he smelled the sea salt.

But of course he was a teen-ager. He was grateful to the old man for teaching him the spells. But this— the cliffs, the sea, the blue sky, and the sweet wine— this was the old man's style, not his. He loved the old man for sharing the spells. He would think of him always, for that.

But even as he flew, he was getting ideas. It isn't the style of teen-agers to fly in broad daylight, on sunny days, even in California. What the boy wanted was something else: to fly low, near the ground, in the cities, speeding in smooth arcs between the buildings, late at night. Very late: at the time the girls are hanging up their clothes and sighing, sighing out their windows to the stagnant air, as the clocks strike midnight. The idea of the pig interested the boy. He grinned far down at the old man, who waved, who had long ago forgotten the dirty purposes of flight.

THE HOTTEST NIGHT
OF THE CENTURY
Glenda Adams

I WAS BORN within the sound of the waves, in a house on a sandstone cliff. It was the hottest night of the century.

The night I was born my father went swimming. It was the last time he ever went willingly into the water.

My father put on his bathing trunks and climbed down the cliff path to the rocks below the house and dived into the sea. He was used to swimming in the ocean, and some mornings he even swam around the headland to the next beach.

While he could not clearly remember having decided

to make such a swim that night, he assumed when he found himself in the water that he was heading south around the headland. When he had swum for some time and the familiar cliff and rock shelf had not appeared on his right, he stopped swimming and took stock of his surroundings. To his great surprise he found himself far out to sea, heading away from the land towards the horizon. He was even more surprised, when he resumed swimming, that it was not back to land that he directed himself, but along the course he had begun, towards the horizon.

After he had swum for several miles a small fishing boat spotted him and pulled him aboard, against his objections. He told the fishermen that he was not at all tired and intended to continue his swim. When they asked him where he thought he was going, he replied New Zealand, north island, and if possible Chile.

The men brought him back to the bay and handed him over to the police. He was placed under observation at the hospital for one day and then released.

After that, my father would go only to the water's edge. He refused to wear, or even own, a bathing suit, nor would he wear shorts or go without a shirt on hot summer days. Sometimes he took off his shoes and socks and rolled his trousers above his ankles and walked along the beach or around the rocks, letting the sea lap at his feet.

I never saw any part of his body except his head, his hands and his feet.

From three sides of our house we could see the ocean.

By the end of the day the windows were always clouded with salt, in spite of the fact that I took great care to wipe them clean every morning.

The ocean spray also corroded the gutterings and caused the window frames and doors to swell and stick.

The house was old and shabby, but very beautiful.

My father often stood by the window and watched the sea. Some mornings he went to the phone box at the terminus down at the bay and called his office to say he was sick. Then he would stay by the window all day watching the sea, frowning.

I, too, watched the sea, and I was able to stay very still beside the window for long periods of time.

My father never liked me to come near him, especially when he stood by the window. I had to choose a window in another room for myself. If I refused to leave him alone, he would slam out of the room and often right out of the house, leaving rattling floors and doors behind him.

On occasion, however, he became so consumed with watching that I was able to move quietly into the room and remain near him for hours without his hearing or feeling me.

People often remarked that it was most unusual for a child to be able to stay still and quiet for more than a minute or two. People said I was an unusual child, and they were always very glad to turn to my little brother.

Everyone admired him.

He had good brown skin and very beautiful brown eyes and good, strong white teeth. He laughed often and was good-natured.

My father loved him greatly. He often said that the son would do all the things the father was prevented from doing.

My skin was pale and the veins showed through. I was obliged to wear a large sunhat and something covering my arms and legs whenever I was on the beach.

I did not care for swimming. I hated the way the waves tossed me about against my will. I preferred to sit at the water's edge, on the sand or on the rocks at the foot of the cliff.

I sat just out of reach of the waves and they had to strain to touch me. They had to keep jumping up and falling back and jumping up again.

Sometimes, on calm days, I lay in a shallow rock pool.

My little brother loved to swim. He loved to dive and splash and laugh in the water all day.

In summer we went down to the beach every day, even during heatwaves. For protection from the white sun I wrapped an old cotton bedspread about my shoulders and legs. My brother played on the sand beside me, his skin and body welcoming the sunrays. Now and then he started up and dashed into the water and splashed about until he was cool.

'How long do you think the longest story is?' I asked him once.

'As long as "The Nose",' he said.

'Not how long a distance, but how long a time?' I said.

'One whole hour,' he said. 'Or perhaps even two.'

'I know a story that lasts until the sun goes down,' I said.

'No you don't,' he said.

I only smiled.

'Do you really?' he said.

I nodded.

'Tell it to me,' he said.

'You could never listen that long,' I said. 'It is only just after breakfast and the sun won't go down for a whole day. You are too young and can't stay still longer than a second.'

'I could so,' he said.

I said nothing. He got up on his knees and pulled at my bedspread.

'Please tell it to me,' he begged.

'It is a most important story,' I said. 'How can I be sure that you will stay still and listen?'

'I promise I'll listen, I promise,' he said.

I said nothing.

'Please,' he said. 'Cross my heart and spit my death.'

I waited for him to do so.

'Since you have sworn,' I said, 'I shall tell you. But I must warn you. If you stop listening, even for a moment, you will suffer untold tortures and great pain, and you may die.'

He lay down on the sand beside me on his stomach. He lay rigid and attentive.

And I closed my eyes and told a story that contained one sentence for every grain of salt in the sea.

I opened my eyes when my father grabbed my shoulders and shook me and slapped me many times over the head.

'You've gone and killed your little brother,' he said. 'Is no one safe with you?'

The shadow of my sunhat stretched out in front of me and was long enough almost to be touched by the water. The sun was on its way behind the houses on the hill behind the beach.

My brother lay on the sand beside me. His body was swollen and had changed from nut brown to deep red. His mouth had fallen open and sand was clinging to his lips and tongue. But he was not dead.

For two weeks my brother lay on his stomach in bed. The doctor came every day to treat him for sunstroke and dress the burns on his back.

When the wounds began to heal, it became clear that the sun had left behind dark brown spots and scars, all over his beautiful back.

I was kept away from his room for the first week. When they allowed me to visit him he turned his face to the wall.

I reminded him of the warning I had given him that day on the beach.

'You must have stopped listening,' I said. 'Otherwise you would not be suffering this great pain.'

'I never stopped listening,' he said.

But when I asked him to prove it by recounting something of what I had told, he could say nothing.

After he recovered he did not care to play with me.

Even when he was much older he refused to go anywhere with me alone and if we happened to walk down to the terminus at the same time, he would make sure there was always six feet at least between us, and he would warn me to keep my distance.

For company my brother talked to his cat.

He kept the cat away from the house as much as possible. In the winter he allowed it into the basement, but during the warmer months the cat roamed all over the headland, coming to the house once every evening to seek him out. After it had eaten, it would sit on my brother's knee to be searched for ticks, of which there were three or four every day buried in its skin.

Once the cat did not appear for four evenings in a row, and we assumed that it had wandered off. The following week, however, as I danced in the remotest corner of our yard, I found the cat lying in the undergrowth, beneath a eucalyptus. It was dead. I knelt beside it and counted seventy-two ticks hanging from its skin.

My brother brought home a new kitten, still very young and stupid. I was dancing among the hydrangea bushes and the nasturtiums when the kitten sprang out in front of my feet, and I kicked it. The kitten went flying across the ground and fell in the long grass. I knelt beside it. A colourless substance ran from its nose and from one ear, and it breathed noisily and with difficulty. I lay in the grass and placed the kitten under my shirt, against my nipple. But it did not revive.

I took it to the edge of the cliff and threw it over.

'You are a murderer,' said my brother, who had watched me throw the kitten away.

And then he suddenly started searching all over the yard, until he found the other cat under the eucalyptus.

'You murderer,' he said.

As soon as he was fifteen my brother left school, against the wishes of my parents, and went off on his own. Now and then he sent a postcard to say he was all right.

My father took me on a ferry ride across the harbour and back.

We stood at the back of the green and yellow ferry. I watched the foam churned up by the propeller. The agitated water was a pale, sickly green beside the dark bottle green of the calm. I had sweets, and I dropped the wrappers into the foam and watched them sucked under.

My father stood back, several paces behind me. When I turned around he was watching the sky rather than the water. His chin was lifted and his gaze passed over my head.

I went and stood beside him and took his hand, startling him. He shook his hand out of my grasp.

'I love ferries,' I told him. 'Just us and the water all around, and everything quiet and smooth.'

He turned and walked inside, jerking his head for me to follow. We leant against the wooden rail in the centre of the ferry and watched the engine.

The pistons, thick with grease, slid up and down, and as I looked down into the dark of the engine, I saw that every surface seemed to be coated with the same thick, dark grease, even the catwalks and ladders that the crew used.

'I hate it in here,' I said, and I screwed up my nose. 'How smelly and noisy and dirty.'

I watched the engineer checking the different parts of the engine and expected him to slip on the grease. The rag that he carried was black with engine dirt, and when he mopped his forehead or wiped his hands with it he merely redistributed the patterns of the oil slicks that coated him. He was filthy from head to foot. My father talked with him about the engine and work, while I held my nose.

When we got back to the quay it was almost dark. All those on board, having taken their Sunday trip across the harbour, crowded to one side. They pressed forward and waited for the men on the wharf to set the gangplank in place.

The ferry was a small craft, and with everyone standing on one side, the deck inclined towards the wharf.

It was low tide and the deck was two or three feet below the wharf. After the engine was turned off it took a couple of minutes for the ferry to nudge its way into position.

Some of the passengers were impatient to be off, for they had connections to make with the buses or the train. Some men, their coats over their shoulders, jumped on to the wharf before the gangplank had been fixed in place, and then they turned around and leant back toward their girls, with outstretched arms, and called to them to jump.

Then there was a shout. One man had attempted to jump, but he had stubbed his toe on the edge of the wharf as he landed. He lost his balance and fell back into the water.

Someone quickly sat on the edge of the wharf and

pushed at the ferry railing with both legs to keep it from bumping against the wharf, while the passengers on board fished the man out of the water.

He stood on the deck, covered with the slime of the tide, laughing.

I could take either a tram or a ferry to school. The tram went across the bridge and stopped almost at the gate of the school. The ferry stopped at the quay beside the docks. From the docks to the school were many stairs leading up the hill to a tunnel under the approach to the bridge.

One morning in the tunnel I met an old man. He had left the fly of his trousers open.

At home I watched for my father to come. I waited for him to put on his slippers and go to his chair by the window. I sat on his knee, quickly, before he could stop me. I put my arms around his neck and told him about the old man in the tunnel.

He pushed me off his knee and jumped up and raced from the house without bothering to change his slippers. When he came back several hours later his slippers and his trouser cuffs were soaking wet and had sand all over them. He would not talk to me or even look at me.

I told my mother about the old man in the tunnel. She sat down and wrote a note to my teacher. The next day the teacher took me aside and told me that it must have been a shock but I should try to forget what I had seen.

The headmaster announced that it was against the rules for any pupil to walk through the tunnel. Although he gave no reason for the new rule, the whole school seemed to know that it was because of what I had seen in the tunnel.

During class I received a note from some of the boys saying they wanted to meet me behind the observatory after school. I said I would meet them.

When school was over I went to the headmaster's office and showed him the note. He and another teacher went to the observatory and rounded up the eight boys who were waiting for me.

The boys were caned and the headmaster sent notes to their parents warning them that their sons were a danger.

My father said I should go away to the mountains for a month for a change. I begged not to be sent away. But both my parents and the doctor said it would do me good after my experience.

I stayed at a holiday home for children. Since it was winter there were only two of us at the home, a very fat girl and myself.

The woman who cared for us made the fat girl and myself take a bath together every day. She stood over us to make sure we washed ourselves thoroughly.

Then she supervised our drying, saying that she didn't want us breaking out in rashes and sores through leaving any part wet while we were under her care. She also said she would allow us to get into bed with her, since it was so cold at night.

I wrote and asked to be brought home. My father wrote back and said that I had to stay the full month. Nevertheless, the following Saturday he came in the train and brought me home, against his better judgment, he said.

The building inspector paid us a visit and condemned our house. He told us that the water falling from the leaks in the gutterings had split the foundations, and since the house was so old it might well collapse.

My father decided we should move to a new house, inland. He found a little house in a flat street that always smelled dusty, even in winter and when it rained. My mother liked the house. She said it could never deteriorate since it was made of cement blocks.

It was an ugly, horrible house. Its windows were large. But there was nothing to watch through them but the flat backyard and the tall, grey paling fence.

The sea was twenty miles away.

Every second Saturday I rode my bicycle to the sea, and often I did not get back home until nearly midnight.

I made a point of checking my father's shoes and trouser cuffs every night, without his noticing, but only rarely did I find traces of sand or the smell of the sea.

I met a boy with a car, and I was easily able to prevail upon him to drive me to the sea every Saturday.

Once, I stayed by the sea a particularly long time, and I did not arrive home until well after midnight. I knew that my father was not asleep.

Very early the next morning—I had only been asleep for an hour or two—my father came into my room.

'What do you think you're doing,' he screamed, 'staying out till all hours?'

I said nothing.

'You should be thinking of your studies and your exams,' he said, 'not boys.'

I smiled at him.

He strode over to my bed and shook me.

I only smiled.

He kept on holding my shoulders.

'You're enough to drive a man out of his mind,' he said.

He moved his hands to my neck. He touched my ears and my head. Then he put his hands over his face.

'I don't know why I try to keep on living,' he cried.

'So why do you?' I asked.

He drowned three weeks later.

BIG FISH, LITTLE FISH
Italo Calvino

ZEFFIRINO'S FATHER NEVER got into bathing-dress. He stayed in rolled-up trousers and vest, with a white linen cap on his head, and never moved away from the rocks. He had a passion for limpets, the flat clams which stick to rocks and become with their very hard shells almost part of the stone. To prise them off Zeffirino's father used a knife, and every Sunday he would scrutinize the rocks on the headland one by one through his spectacled eyes. On he would go until his little basket was full of limpets; some he ate as soon as gathered, sucking the damp bitter pulp as if from a spoon; the rest he put into his basket. Every now and again he would raise his eyes, let them meander over the smooth sea and call out: 'Zeffirino! Where are you?'

Zeffirino spent whole afternoons in the water. They would go together as far as the point, then his father left him there and went straight off after his clams. Limpets were no attraction to Zeffirino, they were so motionless and stubborn; what interested him most were crabs, then octopuses, jelly-fish, and then eventually any kind of fish. In summer his hunts became ever more arduous and resourceful; and now there was not a boy of his age who was so good with an underwater gun as he. In water the types that go best are rather stocky, all lungs and muscle; and Zeffirino was growing up like that. Seen on land, holding his father's hand, he was one of those crop-haired, open-mouthed boys who need clouting to drive along; but in water he outdid everyone; underwater better still.

That day Zeffirino had managed to put together a complete gear for underwater fishing. The mask he already had from the year before, a present from his grandmother; a girl cousin with small feet lent him the flippers; the gun he had taken from his uncle's home without saying anything and told his father they had lent it. Anyway he was a careful little boy, who knew how to use and take care of everything and could be trusted with a loan of them.

The sea was lovely, so clear. Zeffirino said 'Yes, dad' to all his father's advice and went into the water. With that glass snout and that breathing tube, his legs ending like a fish's, his hands gripping that weapon, part spear, part gun, and part fork, he no longer looked like a human being. But as soon as he was in the sea, though he slipped along half-submerged, one could see it was him at once; from the shove he gave with his flippers, the way his gun jutted under his arm, the care he took to move along with head down on the surface of the water.

At first the sea-bed was of pebbles, then of rocks, some bare and corroded, others bearded with thick brown seaweed. From every fold of rock, or between the quivering beards of weed poised in the current, there might suddenly appear a big fish; behind the glass of his mask Zeffirino moved around anxious attentive eyes.

A sea-bed is lovely the first time when one discovers it; but it's lovelier afterwards like everything else, when one gets to learn all about it, stroke by stroke. One seems to be drinking them, these marine landscapes; on and on, one goes and might go on for ever. The glass of the mask is a huge single eye to swallow up shadows and colours. Now the dark ended and he was out of that boulder-strewn part; on the sand of the bottom could be made out fine crinkles drawn by the movement of the sea. The sun's rays reached right down with peering gleams amid twinkling shoals of tiny fish swimming along in a straight line then suddenly all turning together at a right angle.

A little cloud of sand went up from the blow of a sea-bream's tail on the bottom. It had not noticed that harpoon pointing at it. Zeffirino was now swimming right under water; and the bream, after a few distracted movements of its striped sides, all of a sudden rushed away closer to the surface. Fish and fisherman went swimming off between rocks bristling with sea-urchins until they reached a cove of porous, almost bare rock. 'Here it won't give me the slip,' thought Zeffirino; and at that moment the bream vanished. From holes and cavities rose a row of air bubbles which quickly stopped and started again elsewhere; sea-anemones gleamed in expectation. The bream peeped out of one hole, vanished into another and reappeared again at once from a distant aperture. It tacked along a spur of rock, headed down and Zeffirino saw a patch of luminous green towards the sea-bed. The fish lost itself in that light, and Zeffirino went after it.

He crossed a low arch at the foot of the rock and again had above him high sea and sky. Shadows of clear stone surrounded the sea-bed all round lowering into a half-submerged rock towards the open sea. With a thrust of his loins and a shove at his flippers Zeffirino re-emerged to breathe. The air-tube surfaced, away blew some drops filtered into the mask; but the boy's head stayed in the water. He had found the sea-bream again; in fact two! Just as he was aiming he saw a whole squadron of them navigating calmly to the left, and another shoal gleaming to his right. The place was swarming with fish, almost an enclosed lake, and wherever Zeffirino looked he met a frisking of narrow fins and a gleaming of scales. Between amazement and delight he did not let off a single shot.

He must not hurry, must calculate the best shots without sowing terror around. Zeffirino, still with head under water, moved towards the nearest rock; and in the water, along the wall, he saw a white hand dangling. The sea was motionless; concentric circles were widening as if from a drop of rain on the tense, terse surface. The boy raised his head and looked. Face downwards on the edge of the rock was a fat woman in a bathing-dress taking the sun. And crying. The drops came down her cheeks one after the other and fell into the sea.

Zeffirino raised his mask onto his forehead and said 'Excuse me.'

The fat woman said, 'Of course, boy,' and went on crying. 'Do please go on fishing.'

'It's full of fish, this place is,' he explained. 'Have you seen how many there are?'

The fat woman lay with face raised, her eyes staring ahead full of tears. 'I haven't really looked. How can I? I just can't manage to stop crying.'

Zeffirino was at his best in matters of sea and fishes; but in the presence of people he took on that stuttering open-mouthed air of his again.

'I'm sorry, signora . . .' and he would have turned back to his breams; but a fat woman crying was such an unusual sight that he stayed there spellbound, gazing at her in spite of himself.

'I'm not a signora, boy,' said the fat woman in that noble rather nasal voice of hers. 'Call me Signorina. Signorina De Magistris. And what's your name?'

'Zeffirino.'

'Fine, Zeffirino. Have you had a good fish? Or a good hunt? What do they call it?'

'I don't know what they call it. I haven't caught anything yet. But this is a good place here.'

'Be careful with that gun, though. Not for my sake, poor little me. But for your own, not to hurt yourself.'

Zeffirino assured her that she need not worry. He sat down on the rock next to her and watched her crying for a bit. There were moments in which she seemed to be stopping; then she would breathe through her reddened nose, raising and shaking her head. But meanwhile in the corners of her eyes and under her lids a bubble of tears seemed to be swelling up and her eye quickly overflowed.

Zeffirino didn't know quite what to think. To see a signorina crying like that wrung his heart. But how could one be sad facing that marine pen brim-full of every variety of fish, and filling his heart with joy and longing? As to plunging into that green water and going after the fish, how could one do that with a grown-up in tears nearby? At the same moment, at the same place, coexisted two opposite, irreconcilable urges. Zeffirino could not manage to think of both together; nor of letting himself go to one or the other.

'Signorina,' he asked.

'Yes?'

'Why are you crying?'

'Because I'm crossed in love.'

'Ah!'

'You can't understand, you're only a boy.'

'Would you like to try and swim with the mask?'

'Thank you, I'd love to. Is is nice?'

'It's the nicest thing ever.'

Signorina De Magistris got up and buttoned the straps of her bathing-dress on her back. Zeffirino gave her the mask and explained carefully how to put it on. She moved her head a little with the mask over her face, part-joking and part-coy, but through the glass could be seen her eyes which never stopped crying. She went into the sea gracelessly, like a seal, and began to hold her face down gaspingly.

Zeffirino, gun under arm, jumped in and swam too.

'Tell me when you see a fish,' he called to Signorina De Magistris. In water he never joked; coming to fish with him was a privilege he rarely conceded.

But the signorina raised her head and shook it. The glass had gone opaque and her features were not to be seen anymore. She took off the mask. 'I can't see a thing,' she said, 'the tears are dulling the glass. I can't do it. Sorry.' And she remained there in the water, weeping.

'What a mess,' said Zeffirino. He had no half-potato with him to rub on the glass and make it come clear again, but did the best he could with a little saliva, then put on the mask himself. 'Watch how I do it,' he said to the fat woman. And they moved on together over that sea, he all flippers with his head down, she swimming sidestroke, with one arm out and the other folded, and her head bitterly erect and inconsolable.

She swam badly, did Signorina De Magistris, all on one side, with clumsy sweeping strokes. And beneath her for yards and yards fishes coursed the sea, starfish and cuttlefish navigated, the mouths of sea-anemones opened. Now Zeffirino's eyes met seascapes that were quite bewildering. The tide was high and the sandy bottom was scattered with little rocks among which swayed clumps of seaweed moving to the faint movement of the sea. But looked at from above on that uniform stretch of sand it was the rocks that seemed to be waving about amid the still water dense with seaweed.

Suddenly Signorina De Magistris saw him vanish with head down, surface a second with his behind, then

64

with the flippers, and then his clear shadow was under water, swooping down towards the sea-bed. When the bass noticed the danger it was too late; the loosed harpoon had already hit it aslant and the middle prong was stuck near its tail, piercing right through. The bass straightened its spiky fins and rushed off beating the water, the other prongs of the harpoon had not hit it and it still hoped to escape at the cost of shedding its tail. But all it gained was to impale a fin on one of the free prongs, and it was lost. The reel was already pulling in its cord, and the pink, pleased shadow of Zeffirino was above.

The harpoon appeared out of the water with the bass skewered on it, then the boy's arm, then his masked head and a gurgle of water from the barrel. And Zeffirino uncovered his face. 'D'you see what a fine one? D'you see, signorina?' The bass was a big silvery black one. But the woman went on crying.

Zeffirino clambered on to the top of a rock; Signorina De Magistris followed with some difficulty. To keep the fish fresh the boy chose a little rock-pool full of water, and they crouched down by it. Zeffirino watched the changing colours of the bass, stroked its scales and wanted Signorina De Magistris to imitate him.

'D'you see what a fine one? D'you see how it pricks?' When he thought that there was a faint interest in the fish leavening the fat woman's misery, he said, 'I'll just try a moment and see if I can catch another.' In full harness he dived.

The woman stayed with the fish. And she discovered that never had a fish been so unhappy. She began passing her fingers on its ring-like mouth, its gills, its tail; and now all over its lovely silvery body she saw thousands of tiny perforations. Water fleas, minute parasites of fish, had become masters of the bass for some time and were gnawing their way into its flesh.

Ignorant of all this, Zeffirino now re-emerged with a sea-perch on his harpoon, and proffered it to Signorina De Magistris. So the two had already divided tasks; she took the fish from the harpoon and put it to keep cool in the rock-pool; and Zeffirino again plunged in head-first to catch another. Before he did so he looked every time to see if Signorina De Magistris had stopped crying; if she did not stop at sight of a bass or a sea-perch, what on earth could ever console her?

Golden stripes went across the sides of the sea-perch. Two rows of fins went up its back. And in the gap between these fins the signorina saw a deep narrow wound that had been there before the harpoon's. A seagull's beak must have bitten into the fish's back so sharply that she could not understand why it had not been killed. Who knows how long the perch had taken this agony about with it?

Faster than Zeffirino's harpoon, a bream fell on a shoal of little uncertain whitebait. It was just in time to swallow a whitebait before the harpoon was embedded in its throat. Never had Zeffirino made such a good shot.

'It's an outsize dentex!' he cried, taking off his mask. 'I was following the whitebait! It'd swallowed one and I . . .' and he explained the scene, showing his excitement by his stutter. No bigger or finer fish was possible to catch; and Zeffirino would have liked Signorina De Magistris to take part in his pleasure at last. She looked at the plump silvery body, that throat which had just a moment before swallowed the greenish little fish and been in its turn torn to shreds by the harpoon's teeth. Such was life in the entire sea.

Zeffirino fished out yet a grey rock-fish and a red rock-fish, a bream with yellow stripes, a fat dory and a flat bogue; even a hairy and prickly flying fish. But in each of them, apart from harpoon wounds, Signorina De Magistris found the pricks of fleas that had gnawed at them, or the mark of an unknown disease, or a fish-hook stuck in its gullet some time ago. That cove discovered by the boy, where every sort of fish met, was perhaps a refuge for creatures condemned to a long death agony, a marine hospital, an arena for desperate duels.

Zeffirino was now manoeuvring among the rocks. Octopuses! He had discovered a colony hidden at the foot of a boulder. The harpoon had already surfaced a big lilac octopus, its wounds dripping with liquid like watered ink; and a strange anguish now came over Signorina De Magistris. To hold the octopus a separate rock-pool was found and Zeffirino felt like staying there for ever, lost in admiration of the grey-pink skin slowly changing colour. It was also late and the boy was beginning to get a little goose-flesh, his bathe had been so long. But Zeffirino was certainly not one to renounce a family of octopuses already discovered.

The signorina was examining the octopus, its slimy flesh, the mouths of the suckers, the reddish almost liquid eye. And the octopus seemed to her the only one among the creatures fished up to be without a mark or sign of torment. Its tentacles of almost human pink, so soft and sinuous and full of secret suckers, made her think of health and life; some torpid contraction was still making them turn with a slight dilation of the suckers. Signorina De Magistris's hand sketched a caress above the coils of the octopus and she moved her fingers imitating its contractions, getting closer and closer until she grazed it.

Evening was coming down, a wave beginning to beat in the sea. The tentacles vibrated in the air like whips, and suddenly the octopus was clinging tight with all its strength to Signorina De Magistris's arm. Standing on the rock as if trying to escape from her own imprisoned arm, she let out a cry which sounded like, 'The octopus! He's tearing me to bits!'

Zeffirino, who had just that second managed to dislodge a cuttlefish, put his head out of the water and saw the fat woman with one of the octopus's tentacles reaching from her arm to take her by the throat. He heard the end of her cry too; it was a high and continuous howl but—so the boy thought—without a sob.

Up rushed a man armed with a knife and began slashing blows down on the octopus's eye; he cut off its head almost clean. It was Zeffirino's father, who had filled his basket with clams and was coming along the rocks to look for his son. Hearing the shout, and adjusting his spectacles, he had seen the woman and rushed to her help with the knife he used for clams. The tentacles went flabby at once; Signorina De Magistris swooned.

When she came to herself she found the octopus cut in pieces: Zeffirino and his father gave it to her to fry. It was evening and Zeffirino had put on his vest. The father explained with precise gestures how to make a good fry-up of octopus. Zeffirino looked at her and a number of times thought she was on the very point of starting again; but no, not even one tear came out.

SPINDRIFT

Candida Baker

IT IS NOT UNTIL the auction is over that Rosemary Tarrant realises the full implications of what she has just done.

What she has just done is to sell the house her husband had presumed she would live in for the rest of her life; not only presumed but taken into account when he was making his final plans, after they had both come to terms—as much as they could—with the idea of his death.

'It'll be just the place for you, love,' he'd said, on one of his increasingly rare visits home from the hospital. She can see him now, sitting on the verandah in the old steamer chair he'd bought her years before, a blanket wrapped around his knees. She'd patted his hand and shushed him, but he waved her off.

'No,' he said, 'it's all right. I like to think of you here—I'll know exactly where you are.'

Rosemary finds she is having trouble breathing. Her daughter-in-law had suggested that holding the auction in the house could be distressing but the real estate agent had been firm. 'Beach views, Mrs Tarrant,' he'd stressed. 'You know the first three rules of real estate: position, position, position . . . Let your buyers see this place and it'll soon get snapped up.'

Rosemary stands up and walks outside, excusing herself through the crowd until she reaches the verandah. She sits on the steps and puts her head in her hands. She is not surprised when she feels Timothy's touch on her shoulder.

'Mum? Are you all right?'

She nods.

Timothy sits down beside her and puts his arm around her. He gives her tiny ineffectual pats, as a baby might to a kitten, but she can feel his good intention, his own pain. He's doing his best, she thinks.

She doesn't speak. There is no need. Timothy is sure he is on his mother's wavelength and Rosemary certainly isn't going to disillusion him. But it isn't despair flooding through her body, it is exultation— exultation at the thought that soon, she, Rosemary

Tarrant, will never in her life have to look at the beach again.

In England it was every child's dream to go to the seaside. Rosemary and her younger sister Angela would pester their mother until she told them they were driving her crazy with their nagging.

'I've never been to the seaside and I'm ten,' said Rosie early on in the summer holidays. 'You never take us to the seaside.'

'Darling, you'd hate it,' her mother told her. 'The English seaside is horrible, all pebbly and grey. Wait until we can take you to the south of France.'

'I don't want to go to south France,' Angela said. 'I want to go to the seaside.'

For many years Rosemary has had a recurring nightmare. She dreams she is trapped in a landscape of primary colours—Australian colours. In her nightmare this landscape is simply a fine, sunny day but for Rosemary there is nowhere to escape from the sunshine or the sand. For her, her nightmare landscape is a beach; a beach on a bright, hot day without a cloud in the sky. Waves pound the sand with monotonous regularity, the sand itself is hot and sticky underfoot. Sometimes there are people on the beach, sometimes it is just Rosemary. But always there is the suggestion, no, the certainty that she is caught there, her skin frying, her eyes sore and tired and longing for shade; her whole body aching to be placed somewhere cool, to be clothed in wool and drinking a hot cup of tea. Invariably Rosemary wakes from this nightmare drenched in sweat.

A few weeks into the summer holidays, their mother called Rosemary and Angela into the living room to give them what was, to Rosemary at least, a startling piece of news.

'Guess what?' their mother said. 'We've decided to let you go to the seaside. Granny's going to take you to Butlin's. You'll love it there!' She clapped her hands and smiled at her two daughters. 'Isn't that splendid, darlings? Your very own holiday by the sea. How I wish I was coming with you.'

Peter, Rosemary's husband, was an urban Australian who had turned his back on the bush and wholeheartedly embraced the coast, where as he often used to say, ninety per cent of the population lived anyway. Rosemary misses him desperately. He was her antithesis: darkness to her light, light to her darkness. He was gregarious and extroverted, he liked beer, r meat pies and the surf. He had witnessed Australia's coming of age and was fiercely nationalistic, unfettered by any loyalty to old Europe. As an architect he designed houses that suited both his personality and the personality of his country. No cramped dark rooms or wasted space, just gracious lines of timber and tin, always with that all important 'view' in mind. Rosemary, who usually went on site at some point towards the completion of a project, never failed to be impressed by his imagination. She thought of his architecture as art and was always surprised by his dismissal of his own talent. 'Functional,' he used to say, 'that's what an architect should be.' But functional, in his case, was art, and over the years she had come to rely on him as an internal barometer of simple good taste—from him she had learned that less is more.

'I hate England,' Peter would say morosely on their biannual trip to visit the family. 'All those small windows. Why do all the houses have such small windows?'

But although Rosemary would murmur sympathetically, those visits to England were essential to her survival. For six weeks she could live in a landscape of shade and muted colours, she could walk along English lanes and imagine herself the owner of a dozen tiny cottages. In her fantasies these cottages were always surrounded by fields full of quietly grazing horses; there would be a river nearby, perhaps a small wood or copse, and always they would be as far as possible from the sea.

Butlin's had small windows, Rosemary remembers. The rooms were tiny and built of grey concrete. Inside there were two sets of grey iron bunks and on the floor was a grey rug.

Whenever they went out for Sunday drives with their father he would sing them silly ditties to keep them amused. Rosemary's

*grandmother didn't believe in rhymes. She called them 'whimsy'
and suggested the children read a book.*

'I can't read in the car,' said Rosemary. 'I'll be sick.'

'I'll be sick too,' said Angela.

'Sickness is all in the mind,' their grandmother said firmly,
but she was wrong.

When Rosemary and Peter bought their block of land
on the coast, Rosemary had still not quite relinquished
her fantasy of somewhere in the country, she had merely
shunted it to one side. She could not bring herself to
believe that her dream of a farm had become a tree-
studded half-acre with water views, noisy neighbours
and weekend chainsaws. The beauty of it did not escape
her and she always joined in enthusiastically with their
visitors' praise of the house and its bush garden, but
it was not what she had imagined for herself.

They had bought the block when Timothy was five,
they'd camped on it for almost a year, and from the
time he was seven it was firmly the 'beach house'. The
thing was, Rosemary thought, it was convenient and
not far from the city, and anyway, Timothy loved the
coast just as much as his father did. He was, and always
would be, an Australian through and through. He
seemed almost to have an instinctive dislike of England,
even of anything vaguely connected with Rosemary's
childhood.

The first time he was put on a pony he cried and

cried until he was taken off, the second time he screamed it was running away with him.

'But, darling, I've got my hand on the reins,' said Rosemary, calmly, patting her son gently. 'He's only walking, that's all.'

'He's not. He's not,' Timothy sobbed. 'He's running away and I will fall off.'

On the whole it seemed better not to pursue the career path she'd mapped out for him as a member of the Olympic equestrian team. On the whole it seemed better not to upset the apple cart by trying to explain her vague yearnings for something different, for somewhere else. Occasionally when her husband and son were both out—swimming, fishing, sailboarding, surfing —Rosemary would allow herself the luxury of tears. She would hide in her studio, lock the door and cry.

'I bags the top bunk,' shrieked Angela as soon as they were in their room. When Rosemary pointed out to their grandmother that at home she always had the top bunk in case Angela fell out, her grandmother sided with her younger sister.

'She's not going to fall out, are you, precious?'

'No, I am not, Granny.'

'There you are, Rosie,' said her grandmother. 'She's not going to fall out.'

But it was dinner that caused Rosemary to decide she would ring her mother the next morning and ask her to come and collect her.

'I don't think Mummy would want us to eat this,' Rosemary whispered to her grandmother. 'She doesn't approve of overcooked food.'

'Nonsense. The trouble with your mother is she's a snob—always has been, always will be.' Her grandmother held her fork triumphantly over the grey gelatinous mass on her plate. 'I don't know where she gets it from.'

But Rosemary couldn't eat. She sat and watched in amazement as Angela tucked into these strange substances with gusto, and as the room filled up with noisy, jolly people she wondered if perhaps she was dreaming. But no matter how hard she pinched herself, she stayed right where she was and even the one thing that might have made it all right seemed not to be mentioned, as though its very existence were somehow in doubt.

'What about the sea, Granny?' she asked. 'Why can't we go for a walk and see the sea? I've never been to the sea.'

'We'll go tomorrow, love,' said her grandmother. 'Let's just relax and enjoy ourselves.'

Rosemary decided to be magnanimous—after all, in the morning her mother would come and get her.

For as long as Rosemary has lived in Australia, she has made a lucrative living from her rock painting. She takes river rocks and turns them into animals. They were never Peter's taste, but she enjoys them, and sells them faster than she can paint them.

After their house, designed by them both, was built, it took Peter several years to work out what was wrong with her studio.

One morning he appeared at her door with a cup of coffee. 'Christ!' he said, 'you can't see the sea! How on earth did we manage that? You poor thing.'

But Rosemary, looking through her large window onto the small courtyard full of jasmine and honeysuckle, just smiled at him.

It was hard watching Peter die. It was the hardest thing Rosemary had ever done in her whole life. To be unable to help a loved one was a terrible, terrible thing, something for which she had been quite unprepared, for which, she now understands, there can be no preparation. Yet despite her grief and loss she still finds it impossible to understand that she is now a widow. Even the word widow seems to belong to somebody much older. She had always thought of widows as being at least in their sixties and here she is in her early fifties.

When Peter had first started getting sick she had even thought it was because he wanted her attention. Her menopause had begun a year or so before and had been playing havoc with her mind and body. She had thought getting sick was his way of telling her that he needed her to come back to him, body and soul; for her to leave the strange twilight zone she had begun to inhabit, the limbo between middle age and what she saw as old age. She reluctantly dragged herself away from self-obsession only to discover that his crisis had nothing to to with her—his body was failing him in a way that made her menopause seem trivial. For a while she had been angry about it. It seemed as if he had to beat her at her own game, as if he had done it on purpose. She is still not sure if this is a natural reaction to a loved one's death or just another sign of what her mother used to call her 'selfish' nature.

But perhaps the worst thing of all had been having to watch Peter try to adapt to this sickness. Both he and Rosemary were post-war babies, born and brought up 12,000 miles apart. She had, still has, an English attitude to life. Clothes are bought for best and put in the back of the cupboard for years before Rosemary can wear them guilt-free. Peter bought clothes, wore them and chucked them out. Rosemary would buy treats and store them away. For what? For a rainy day, for the next world war, the next inevitable catastrophe. It was Peter's job to hunt down the treats or if he had done the shopping to dive head-first into them— he could finish a packet of cashews in minutes.

'But there'll be none left,' Rosemary would wail.

'For what?' her husband would laugh at her.

'For *later*,' was her constant reply.

But as the cancer ate away at him, nothing could tempt his appetite. He would want to be hungry but after just a mouthful or two he would look sadly at her and say, 'I'm sorry, love. I don't seem to feel like eating today, maybe tomorrow.'

And she would nod, an eager accomplice in this fantasy. 'Yes. Maybe tomorrow.'

In a way it was as if their positions had been reversed. She began to eat and drink everything he had always enjoyed as if in some magic way she could osmosis it through to him, while he saved things for later. At the beach it was Rosemary who swam while Peter sat in the car gazing at his beloved ocean and his wife tried desperately to control her feeling that this time, this time for certain she would drown.

In the morning her grandmother wouldn't allow her to call her mother.

'There's no point, Rosie,' she said. 'She won't even be there.'

'Yes, she will,' Rosemary insisted. 'She's working hard on the house. She told me.'

Her grandmother looked vague. 'Yes, well she's not going to be there today. Anyway, you'll love it here when you get used to it, just you wait and see.'

Realising there was going to be no grown-up capitulation, Rosemary made a last-ditch attempt at compromise. 'Well,' she said, 'if I can't speak to Mummy, can we go to the seaside?'

'We'll go tomorrow,' her grandmother said. 'I promise.'

And where did her son fit into all this? The son who had lost his father. He had always been a good child. 'Mummy's good boy,' Rosemary used to call him when he was a child—so much so that he used to compliment her in the same vein. 'Good *boy*, Mummy,' he would say if she bought him a present or fed him a sticky sweet. 'Good boy.'

But at the time of her menopause, at the beginning of Peter's sickness, while they were both keeping secrets from one another, their son had married. And it was not, as Rosemary had always fondly imagined it would be, a woman whom they all loved, so that in the fullness of time she might feel she had gained a daughter, as the saying went, it was a woman who felt it was her right to keep *their* son entirely to herself. Was it fair, Rosemary railed to Peter, that their usual Christmas celebration should be cut off quite so abruptly? 'Christ,' she had said, 'she could have waited one year, just one year.'

Peter thought it was all what he referred to scathingly as 'female stuff'. 'She's a nice girl, Rosie,' he chided. 'And he's happy.'

Rosemary found it hard to stomach, her son being happy with a woman she didn't like. She was conscious that since Peter had died she had been using Tim far beyond her real need of him, simply to score marks off Jan and to assuage her own loneliness.

As if he could read her mind, Tim tightened his

hold on her shoulder. 'Don't you worry, Mum,' he said. 'We'll find you something near us. At least you'll still be near the sea—and the family. I'm sure that's what Dad would have wanted.'

The next day there was still no beach, but there was fancy dress and there was no getting out of it. One of the red-coated jolly people came bearing down on the three of them. 'Now then,' she said, her lipstick creasing around her mouth. 'Who have we here?' She looked at their compulsory name-tags. 'Rosemary and Angela. How lovely. Well, kiddies, it's fancy dress this morning, won't that be fun?'

'It was fancy dress last night,' said Rosie.

'It was too,' said the woman, smiling harder than ever. 'And it is again today—aren't you lucky?'

Rosie tugged at her grandmother's sleeve. 'Granny,' she said, 'remember what you promised? You promised we could go to the beach.'

Her grandmother chucked her under the chin. 'Did I?' she said. 'Never mind, darling, you just run along and have a good time.'

Gradually the strangers leave. Last to go are the new owners and the real estate agent. He presses a card into her hand. 'I know it's a bit soon for you,' he says in what he obviously imagines is a tactfully low voice, 'but you'll be needing somewhere else, of course. If we can be of any help . . . any help at all . . .'

The new owners try to contain their excitement but it oozes through their pores. The husband runs an already proprietorial hand along the top of the bookshelves; the wife glances at the windows, and Rosemary can tell she is sizing up—already measuring for her curtains and blinds, her furniture.

Tim waits on the verandah with Jan. 'We'll have to go, Mum,' he says. 'Are you sure you'll be all right?'

Rosemary nods. 'I'll be fine.'

Jan says, 'Look after yourself, Mum.'

One day, thinks Rosemary, one day I'll tell her I don't want her to call me Mum. I'm not her Mum, and I never will be.

Behind her the new owners are almost playful. 'You'll have to tell us all about the area,' says the wife, locking her arm through her husband's.

'All about it,' echoes her husband.

'I don't want to be Little Bo-Peep,' Rosemary said to the red-coated woman who was trying to force a dress over her head. 'This is a stupid costume and I don't want to be in any fancy dress.'

The woman, whose tune had changed as soon as their grandmother was out of sight, was short with her. 'I know your sort,' she said. 'You're a trouble-maker. Everybody loves the fancy dress. Now stand still! Look at your sister—doesn't she look as pretty as a picture?'

Rosemary glanced at Angela, who was dancing around the

stage in her Robin Hood costume. 'Well,' she said, 'she's a tomboy—that's why she likes it.'

Rosemary is unsurprised when Peter appears in front of her while she is eating dinner. She has been expecting him in some form or other, although perhaps not in as insubstantial a guise as this grey hovering shape. She can tell immediately he is unhappy.

'I'm sorry,' she says. 'I really am. I just don't like the beach. I never have. I could never tell you because you loved it so, and I didn't want to hurt you but I can't live here without you and that's that.'

The spirit trembles around the edges like a thin cloud, and Rosemary seems to sense a question mark over its head. 'I don't know,' she says. 'I don't know where I'll go. Tim wants me to live near him, but I couldn't bear that. I didn't want to be a widow and I don't want to be a mother-in-law.'

Peter bends himself towards her and then shrinks back when Rosemary recoils from him.

'Don't go,' she says. 'I didn't mean it—it's just that well, you know, you look different.' She pauses. 'You could come with me. I mean, you've lived by the beach all these years, you could come wherever I go.' The spirit quivered with what Rosemary understood was indignation, and began to fade away.

'All right,' she shouts after it, 'I'm sorry, but you tell me—why can't I cry? Why can't I cry? You tell me that.'

'Did you have to look so sullen?' asked her grandmother. 'You looked as if you hated every minute of it.'

'Well, I did,' said Rosemary.

'I didn't,' said Angela. 'I enjoyed myself.'

'You like showing off, that's why,' Rosemary spat at her. 'That's the only reason you won—because you did all that stupid dancing and showing off. I hate you!' She ran into the cabin and threw herself on her bed. 'I just want to go home,' she bawled. 'You said we were going to the seaside and we haven't even got there yet.'

Her grandmother bent down to pat her. 'I'm sorry, pet,' she said. 'That's true. I tell you what—we'll go this afternoon, just the three of us.'

After dinner Rosemary decides to go for a walk along the beach. If she has a favourite time, this is it, when the crowds have gone home and the only people are locals jogging or walking their dogs. The evening is fine; the air a soft misty pink and the tide right out. She walks along briskly, swinging her arms. The headlands are bathed in the last golden glow of the day and Rosemary is surprised to find herself gazing at them as if she has never seen them before. A sea eagle wheels above the cliffs and the stunted eucalypts hold the silver sheen of an olive grove.

'But it's beautiful,' she says to herself, 'it really is beautiful.'

As the sea air fills her lungs she shakes her arms to rid

herself of the day's tension, but her body seems to be craving more. The heat of the day, the crowds, the handshakes with strangers—her every muscle is crying out for relief, insisting that this day be gone from her. Rosemary feels her whole life bearing down on her as heavy as lead, and, suddenly, as if to lighten the load, she finds herself stripping down to her T-shirt and under-pants and striding out towards the waves. 'I'm going to be baptised,' she thinks in surprise. She feels as if forces outside her control have overtaken her senses. She can taste the air, pierce the sea's surface with her eyes. She looks down at her legs and notices that they need waxing—she hasn't done them since Peter died; there didn't seem much point. The thought gives way to others, equally disjointed and bizarre. How hard, she wonders, would it be to drown herself? To walk on into infinity.

The seaside was not what Rosemary expected. To begin with, it was crowded, thronged with people and somehow they looked wrong—they looked what her mother would call 'common'. The children were wearing luridly frilly costumes, the grown-ups were fat and pale. There were even some men wearing handkerchiefs on their heads.

As usual Angela was unperturbed by her surroundings and Rosemary felt a surge of familiar jealousy at her sister's ability to adapt. While Rosemary surveyed the beach with anxious displeasure Angela had already taken off her clothes and put on her costume—right in front of everybody.

'You'll catch cold.'

'I won't.' Angela headed for the water's edge, shrieking loudly for good measure, until finally, curiosity overcoming her shyness, Rosemary gave in to her grandmother's cajolings and joined her sister.

Waist deep, Rosemary gazes at the beach which has been her home for twenty years. She is hardly surprised to find it is full of visitors. She can see Tim and Jan walking along, deep in conversation; how they must have looked when they were still trying each other out for size. Their old dog, who had died several years before, is trotting behind Tim, an old plastic juice container swinging from her mouth.

'Perhaps my life is flashing before my eyes,' Rosemary thinks. There are others too, and she squints her eyes to see them better. The whole beach seems to be full of family and friends. She can see Colin and Carol—The Two C's—as she and Peter called them. They had been close as a foursome but since Peter had died they had hardly been in touch. She feels betrayed, although she understands it is because they too felt the loss of him so keenly.

'Hi!' she shouts out to them and waves, but they do not respond. She shrugs her shoulders and turns towards the sea again. She dives under the first wave and comes up, as she always does, gasping and spluttering for breath.

Their grandmother read a book on the beach while Angela almost drowned. In front of their grandmother's nose Angela went in further and further.

'Watch out,' said Rosie. 'Remember we can't swim.'

'I can too swim,' said Angela, putting her head right under the water and laughing at the stricken expression on her sister's face. 'You can't swim. You're a scaredy-cat.'

'I am not.'

So silly now, to think that was why she joined her sister, why she too put her head into the bitterly cold English Channel and, elated by her bravery, went on and on and on until she lifted her head from the water and glanced around for Angela's naughty laughing face, only to find it was not there. There was a feeling she would never forget in her bones, a feeling of doom and disaster which has lived with her ever since. She screamed—'Angie!'—and then saw her sister's body.

In the water Rosemary suddenly begins to shiver uncontrollably. The waves, small as they are, seem not cleansing but full of death. But this time, Rosemary knows, she must not leave the water. She must catch another wave. She must do what she has never done before—wait and see if her number is up. She sees the swell out the back, it seems massive: the sort of wave Peter and Tim used to pray for. She positions herself to catch it and as it rears up behind her, she pushes off, straight into it. It takes her a split-second to realise that she has misjudged it; the wave is breaking on top of her, around her, sucking her under. She is being dumped, swirled this way and that. She can feel her underpants and T-shirt being sucked away from her body by the force of the water. As panic sets in she still has just enough presence of mind to feel furious with God for letting her down. Now she realises she didn't really believe her number was up, and the irony is that it is.

In the Butlin's sick bay Angela revelled in her status as an almost drowned person, and Rosemary quickly forgot what she had realised with surprise—that she loved her sister and would miss her if she were no longer there.

That night, while Angela slept, her grandmother gave Rosie her interpretation of events. 'We don't want to worry Mummy and Daddy,' she said, kept on saying. 'We'll simply tell them Angela had a bit of dunking, that she caught a bit of a cold. Angela will soon forget. It wouldn't be good for her to make a thing of it—okay, Rosie love? All right by you?'

'I suppose so,' said Rosie. 'All right.'

Without warning, the wave gives up its hold on her, spews her into the shallows and leaves her floundering belly up. Gingerly Rosemary pats herself, notices the great red weals down her thighs from the sand. 'I'm alive!' she shouts out. *'I am alive!'* As she sits there a small gust of wind blows the last of a wave back on itself. The spindrift sprays her face, and she rubs it into her skin, pressing hard into her cheeks, her neck, her breasts.

She picks herself up and heads out for the surf again. In the last five minutes it has shrunk. It seems insignificant beside her. She has always wondered how Tim and Peter could be so cavalier with the surf, how they could laugh about their dumpings, compare notes over dinner. Now she understands. It is almost sexual, the thrill of being caught and turned over and over. She wouldn't even care if she felt it again. For the first time since Peter's death she feels randy, electric with desire. She dives again and again, waiting for the right wave. Feeling the power of it between her legs.

She shrieks like a child as she catches wave after wave, speeding in to the beach. Her body is beginning to ache with tiredness. The sun is slipping away fast but still she goes on and on as if to erase every memory from her body. She wants only to be cleansed, to be washed up on a new shore, given one more chance to start again.

As the shadows lengthen on the beach, Rosemary sees Peter. He puts his towel down and walks into the water to join her. This time he is no longer grey and insubstantial but youthful and strong, as muscly and bronzed as he was the first day she met him. As he comes towards her through the waves Rosemary suddenly and without warning begins to cry.

'Why did you leave me?' she shouts at him. 'Why did you leave me?'

But Peter has no answer for her. He simply grins and waits for a wave. He beckons to her to ride it with him and she does.

When they got home their mother couldn't stop hugging them.

'Gosh, I missed you,' she said. 'I missed you so much.'

Rosemary noticed that her mother was a great deal browner than she had been a week before, and on the hat stand was a new hat. 'Where did you get that?' she asked.

'We got it in Nice, kiddo,' said her father, swinging by with Angela on his back.

Her mother looked shocked. 'Jim,' she said, 'we weren't going to say.'

'Oh, come on.' Her father ruffled her hair. 'She didn't really think you were staying here to clean house for a week, did you, darling? She knows what side's up.'

'Where's Nice?'

'Don't they teach you anything at school?' her father said. 'Nice is in the south of France.'

'I want to go to south France,' said Angela.

'And so you shall, my pretty,' said her father, putting on his stupid pirate voice. 'And so you shall.'

'We went to the seaside,' Rosie told them. 'I didn't like it. Granny read a book and Angela almost drowned.'

'I did not,' said Angela. 'I put my head under and got a dunking.'

'You mustn't tell fibs, Rosie,' her mother said. 'I've told you about that before.'

Sometime in the few seconds it takes to ride the wave Peter disappears again.

'Bastard,' screams Rosemary, while the tears fall and fall. She runs out of the water and grabs her towel from the sand, hugging it close to her, rocking and caressing it.

'I have no one left,' she says, wiping her eyes. 'My husband is dead and my son is married and my family live on the other side of the world. I belong with nobody and I belong nowhere.'

She picks up her things and wraps the towel around her. The evening is turning moody, thunder clouds are building up. Soon there will be a storm.

'I must get home,' Rosemary says. She laughs. 'Of course, I must go home.'

On the way back to the car she wonders if it is too late to catch the estate agent. He won't be best pleased, she thinks. But there it is. She knows what side's up.

LAST DAY OF SUMMER

Ian McEwan

I AM TWELVE and lying near-naked on my belly out on the back lawn in the sun when for the first time I hear her laugh. I don't know, I don't move, I just close my eyes. It's a girl's laugh, a young woman's, short and nervous like laughing at nothing funny. I got half my face in the grass I cut an hour before and I can smell the cold soil beneath it. There's a faint breeze coming off the river, the late afternoon sun stinging my back and that laugh jabbing at me like it's all one thing, one taste in my head. The laughing stops and all I can hear is the breeze flapping the pages of my comic, Alice crying somewhere upstairs and a kind of summer heaviness all over the garden. Then I hear them walking across the lawn towards me and I sit up so quickly it makes me dizzy, and the colours have gone out of everything. And there's this fat woman, or girl, walking towards me with my brother. She's so fat her arms can't hang right from her shoulders. She's got rubber tyres round her neck. They're both looking at me and talking about me, and when they get really close I stand up and she shakes my hand and still looking right at me she makes a kind of yelping noise like a polite horse. It's the noise I heard just now, her laugh. Her hand is hot and wet and pink like a sponge, with dimples at the base of each finger. My brother introduces her as Jenny. She's going to take the attic bedroom. She's got a very large face, round like a red moon, and thick glasses which make her eyes as big as golf balls. When she lets go of my hand I can't think of one thing to say. But my brother Peter talks on and on, he tells her what vegetables we are growing and what flowers, he makes her stand where she can get a view of the river between the trees and then he leads her back to the house. My brother is exactly twice my age and he's good at that sort of thing, just talking.

Jenny takes the attic. I've been up there a few times looking for things in the old boxes, or watching the river out of the small window. There's nothing much in the boxes really, just cloth scraps and dressmaking patterns. Perhaps some of them actually belonged to my mother. In one corner there's a pile of picture frames without pictures. Once I was up there because it was raining outside, and downstairs there was a row going on between Peter and some of the others. I helped José clear out the place ready for a bedroom. José used to be Kate's boyfriend and then last spring he moved his things out of Kate's bedroom and moved into the spare room next to mine. We carried the boxes and frames to the garage, we stained the wooden floor black and put down rugs. We took apart the extra bed in my room and carried it up. With that, a table and a chair, a small cupboard and the sloping ceiling, there is just room for two people standing up. All Jenny has for luggage is a small suitcase and a carrier bag. I take them up to her room for her and she follows, breathing harder and harder and stopping half way up the third set of stairs to get a rest. My brother Peter comes up behind and we squeeze in as if we are all going to be living there and we're seeing it for the first time. I point out the window for her so she can see the river. Jenny sits with her big elbows on the table. Sometimes she dabs at her damp red face with a large white handkerchief while she's listening to some story of Peter's. I'm sitting on the bed behind her looking at how immense her back is, and under her chair I can see her thick pink legs, how they taper away and squeeze into tiny shoes at the bottom. Everywhere she's pink.

The smell of her sweat fills the room. It smells like the new cut grass outside, and I get this idea that I mustn't breathe it in too deeply or I'll get fat too. We stand up to go so she can get on with her unpacking and she's saying thank you for everything, and as I go through the door she makes her little yelp, her nervous laugh. Without meaning to I glance back at her through the doorway and she's looking right at me with her magnified golf-balls eyes.

'You don't say much, do you?' she says. Which sort of makes it even harder to think of something to say. So I just smile at her and carry on down the stairs.

Downstairs it's my turn to help Kate cook the supper. Kate is tall and slim and sad. Really the opposite of Jenny. When I have girl friends I'm going to have them like Kate. She's very pale, though, even at this time in the summer. She has strange-coloured hair. Once I heard Sam say it was the colour of a brown envelope. Sam is one of Peter's friends who also lives here and who wanted to move his things into Kate's bedroom when José moved his out. But Kate is sort of haughty and she doesn't like Sam because he's too noisy. If Sam moved into Kate's room he'd always be waking up Alice, Kate's little girl. When Kate and José are in the same room I always watch them to see if they ever look at each other, and they never do. Last April I went into Kate's room one afternoon to borrow something and she and José were in bed asleep. José's parents come

IAN MCEWAN

from Spain and his skin is very dark. Kate was lying on her back with one arm stretched out, and José was lying on her arm, snuggling up to her side. They didn't have pyjamas on, and the sheet came up to their waists. They were so black and so white. I stood at the foot of the bed a long time, watching them. It was like some secret I'd found out. Then Kate opened her eyes and saw me there and told me very softly to get out. It seems pretty strange to me that they were lying there like that and now they don't even look at each other. That wouldn't happen with me if I was lying on some girl's arm. Kate doesn't like cooking. She has to spend a lot of time making sure Alice doesn't put knives in her mouth or pull boiling pots off the stove. Kate prefers dressing-up and going out, or talking for hours on the telephone, which is what I would rather do if I was a girl. Once she stayed out late and my brother Peter had to put Alice to bed. Kate always looks sad when she speaks to Alice, when she's telling her what to do she speaks very softly as if she doesn't really want to be speaking to Alice at all. And it's the same when she talks to me, as if it's not really talking at all. When she sees my back in the kitchen she takes me through to the downstairs bathroom and dabs calamine lotion over me with a piece of cotton wool. I can see her in the mirror, she doesn't seem to have any particular expression on her face. She makes a sound between her teeth, half a whistle and half a sigh, and when she wants a different part of my back towards the light she pushes or pulls me about by my arm. She asks me quickly and quietly what the girl upstairs is like, and when I tell her, 'She's very fat and she's got a funny laugh,' she doesn't make any reply. I cut up vegetables for Kate and lay the table. Then I walk down to the river to look at my boat. I bought it with some money I got when my parents died. By the time I get to the jetty it's past sunset and the river is black with scraps of red like the cloth scraps that used to be in the attic. Tonight the river is slow and the air is warm and smooth. I don't untie the boat, my back is too sore from the sun to row. Instead I climb in and sit with the quiet rise and fall of the river, watching the red cloth sink in the black water and wondering if I breathed in too much of Jenny's smell.

When I get back they are about to start eating. Jenny is sitting next to Peter and when I come in she doesn't look up from her plate even when I sit down on the other side of her. She's so big beside me, and yet so bowed down over her plate, looking as if she doesn't really want to exist, that I feel sorry for her in a way and I want to speak to her. But I can't think of anything to say. In fact no one has anything to say this meal, they're all just pushing their knives and forks backwards and forwards over their plates, and now and then someone murmurs for something to be passed. It doesn't usually happen like this when we're eating, there's usually something going on. But Jenny's here, more silent than any of us, and bigger, too, and not looking up from her plate. Sam clears his throat and looks down our end of the table at Jenny, and everyone else looks up too, except for her, waiting for something. Sam clears his throat again and says,

'Where were you living before, Jenny?' Because no one's been speaking it comes out flat, as if Sam's in an office filling in a form for her. And Jenny, still looking down at her plate, says,

'Manchester.' Then she looks at Sam. 'In a flat.' And she gives a little yelp of a laugh, probably because we're all listening and looking at her, and then she sinks back into her plate while Sam's saying something like, 'Ah, I see,' and thinking of the next thing to say. Upstairs, Alice starts crying so Kate goes and brings her down and lets her sit on her lap. When she stops crying she points at each one of us in turn and shouts, 'UH, UH, UH,' and so on right round the table while we all sit there eating and not speaking. It's like she's telling us off for not thinking of things to say. Kate tells her to be quiet in the sad way she always has when she's with Alice. Sometimes I think she's like that because Alice doesn't have a father. She doesn't look at all like Kate, she has very fair hair and ears that are too large for her head. A year or two ago when Alice was very little I used to think that José was her father. But his hair is black, and he never pays much attention to Alice. When everybody's finished the first course and I'm helping Kate collect the dishes, Jenny offers to have Alice on her lap. Alice is still shouting and pointing at different things in the room, but once she's on Jenny's lap she goes very quiet. Probably because it's the biggest lap she's ever seen. Kate and I bring in fruit and tea, and when we are peeling oranges and bananas, eating the apples from our tree in the garden, pouring tea and passing cups with milk and sugar round, everyone starts talking and laughing like they usually do, like there never was anything holding them back. And Jenny is giving Alice a really good time on her lap, making her knees gallop like a horse, making her hand swoop down like a bird on to Alice's belly, showing her tricks with her fingers, so that all the time Alice is shouting for more. It's the first time I've heard her laugh like that. And then Jenny glances down the table at Kate who's been watching them play with the same kind of look she might have on her face if she was watching the telly. Jenny carries Alice to her mother like she's suddenly feeling guilty about having Alice on her lap for such a long time and having so much fun. Alice is shouting, 'More, more, more,' when she's back at the other end of the table, and she's still shouting it five minutes later when her mother carries her up to bed.

Because my brother asks me to, I take coffee up to Jenny's room early next morning. When I go in she's already up, sitting at her table putting stamps on letters. She looks smaller than she did last night. She has her window wide open and her room is full of morning air, it feels like she's been up for a long time. Out of her window I can see the river stretching between the trees, light and quiet in the sun. I want to get outside, I want to see my boat before breakfast. But Jenny wants to talk. She makes me sit on her bed and tell her about myself. She doesn't ask me any questions and since I'm not sure how to start off telling someone about myself I sit there and watch while she writes addresses on her letters and sips her coffee. But I don't mind, it's all right in Jenny's room. She's put two pictures on the wall. One is a framed photograph taken in a zoo of a monkey walking upside down along a branch with its baby hanging on to its stomach. You can tell it is a zoo because in the bottom corner there's a zoo-keeper's cap and part of his face. The other is a colour picture taken out of a magazine of two children running along the sea shore holding hands. The sun is setting and everything in the picture is deep red, even the children. It's a very good picture. She finishes with her letters and asks me where I go to school. I tell her about the new school I'm going to when the holidays are over, the big comprehensive in Reading. But I haven't been there yet, so there isn't much I can tell her about it. She sees me looking out the window again.

'Are you going down to the river?'

'Yes, I have to see my boat.'

'Can I come with you? Will you show me the river?' I wait for her by the door, watching her squeeze her round, pink feet into small, flat shoes and brush her very short hair with a brush which has a mirror on the back. We walk across the lawn to the kissing gate at the bottom of the garden and along the path through the high ferns. Half way down I stop to listen to a yellow-hammer, and she tells me that she doesn't know the song of one bird. Most grown-up people will never tell you that they don't know things. So farther on down the path just before it opens out on to the jetty we stop under an old oak tree so she can hear a blackbird. I know there's one up there, it's always up there singing this time in the morning. Just as we get there it stops and we have to wait quietly for it to begin again. Standing by that half-dead old trunk I can hear other birds in other trees and the river just round the corner washing under the jetty. But our bird is taking a rest. Something about waiting in silence makes Jenny nervous and she pinches her nose tight to stop her yelp of a laugh getting out. I want her to hear the blackbird so much I put my hand on her arm, and when I do that she takes her hand away from her nose and smiles. Just a few seconds after that the blackbird sets out on its long complicated song. It was waiting all the time for us to get settled. We walk out on to the jetty and

I show her my boat tied up at the end. It's a rowing boat, green on the outside and red on the inside like a fruit. I've been down here every day all this summer to row it, paint it, wipe it down, and sometimes just to look at it. Once I rowed it seven miles upstream and spent the rest of the day drifting back down. We sit on the edge of the jetty looking at my boat, the river and the trees on the other side. Then Jenny looks downstream and says,

'London's down there.' London is a terrible secret I try to keep from the river. It doesn't know about it yet while it's flowing past our house. So I just nod and say nothing. Jenny asks me if she can sit in the boat. It worries me at first that she's going to be too heavy. But of course I cannot tell her that. I lean over the jetty and hold the painter rope for her to climb in. She does it with a lot of grunting and rocking around. And since the boat doesn't look any lower now than it usually does, I get in too and we watch the river from this new level where you can see how strong and old it really is. We sit talking for a long time. First I tell her about how my parents died two years ago in a car crash and how my brother had ideas for turning the house into a kind of commune. At first he was going to have over twenty people living here. But now I think he wants to keep it down to about eight. Then Jenny tells me about the time she was a teacher in a big school in Manchester where all the children were always laughing at her because she was fat. She doesn't seem to mind talking about it, though. She has some funny stories of her time there. When she's telling me of the time when the children locked her in a book cupboard we both laugh so much the boat rocks from side to side and pushes small waves out into the river. This time Jenny's laugh is easy and kind of rhythmic, not hard and yelping like before. On the way back she recognises two blackbirds by their songs, and when we're crossing the lawn she points out another. I just nod. It's a song-thrush really, but I'm too hungry to tell her the difference.

Three days later I hear Jenny singing. I'm in the back yard trying to put together a bicycle out of bits and pieces and I hear her through the open kitchen window. She's in there cooking lunch and looking after Alice while Kate visits friends. It's a song she doesn't know the words for, half way between happy and sad, and she's singing like an old croaky Negress to Alice. New morning man la-la, la-la-la-, l'la, new morning man la-la-la, la-la, l'la, new morning man take me 'way from here. That afternoon I row her out on the river and she has another song with the same kind of tune, but this time with no words at all. Ya-la-la, ya-laaa, ya-eeeee. She spreads her hands out and rolls her big magnified eyes around like it's a serenade especially for me. A week later Jenny's songs are all over the house, sometimes with a line or two if she can remember it, most often with no words at all. She spends a lot of her time in the kitchen and that's where she does most of her singing. Somehow she makes more space in there. She scrapes paint off the north window to let in more light. No one can think why it was painted over in the first place. She carries out an old table, and when it's out everyone realizes that it was always in the way. One afternoon she paints the whole of one wall white to make the kitchen look bigger, and she arranges the pots and plates so that you always know where they are and even I can reach them. She makes it into the kind of kitchen you can sit around in when you've got nothing else to do. Jenny makes her own bread and bakes cakes, things we usually go to the shop for. On the third day she's here I find clean sheets on my bed. She takes the sheets I've been using all summer and most of my clothes away for washing. She spends all of one afternoon making a curry, and that night I eat the best meal in two years. When the others tell her how good they think it is Jenny gets nervous and does her yelping laugh. I can see the others are still bothered when she does it, they sort of look away as if it is something disgusting that would be rude to look at. But it doesn't worry me at all when she does that laugh, I don't even hear it except when the others are there at the table looking away. Most afternoons we go out on the river together and I try to teach her to row, and listen to her stories of when she was teaching, and when she was working in a supermarket, how she used to watch old people come in each day to shoplift bacon and butter. I teach her some more birdsongs, but the only one she can really remember is the first one, the blackbird. In her room she shows me pictures of her parents and her brother and she says,

'I'm the only fat one.' I show her some pictures of my parents, too. One of them was taken a month before they died, and in it they are walking down some steps holding hands and laughing at something outside the picture. They were laughing at my brother who was fooling around to make them laugh for the picture I was taking. I had just got the camera for my tenth birthday and that was one of the first pictures I took with it. Jenny looks at it for a long time and says something about her looking like a very nice woman, and suddenly I see my mother as just a woman in a picture, it could be any woman, and for the first time she's far off, not in my head looking out, but outside my head being looked at by me, Jenny or anyone who picks up the photo. Jenny takes it out of my hand and puts it away with the others in the shoe box. As we go downstairs she starts off on a long story about a friend of hers who was producing a play which ended strangely and quietly. The friend wanted Jenny to start off the clapping at the end but Jenny got it all wrong somehow and started everyone clapping fifteen minutes before the end during a quiet bit so that the last part of the play was lost and the clapping was all the louder because no one knew what the play was about. All this, I suppose, is to make me stop thinking about my mother, which it does.

Kate spends more time with her friends in Reading. One morning I'm in the kitchen when she comes in very smartly dressed in a kind of leather suit and high leather boots. She sits down opposite me to wait for Jenny to come down so she can tell her what food to give Alice that day, and what time she'll be back. It reminds me of another morning almost two years ago when Kate came into the kitchen in the same kind of suit. She sat down at the table, undid her blouse and started to knead with her fingers blueish-white milk into a bottle from one tit and then the other. She didn't seem to notice me sitting there.

'What are you doing that for?' I asked her.

She said, 'It's for Janet to give to Alice later on today. I've got to go out.' Janet was a black girl who used to be living here. It was strange watching Kate milk herself into a bottle. It made me think how we're just animals with clothes on doing very peculiar things, like monkeys at a tea party. But we get so used to each other most of the time. I wonder if Kate is thinking of that time now, sitting with me in the kitchen first thing in the morning. She's got orange lipstick on and her hair tied back and that makes her look even thinner than usual. Her lipstick is sort of fluorescent, like a road sign. Every minute she looks at her watch and her leather creaks. She looks like some beautiful woman from outer space. Then Jenny comes down, wearing a huge old dressing-gown made out of patches and yawning because she's just got out of bed, and Kate speaks to her very quickly and quietly about Alice's food for the day. It's as if it makes her sad, talking about that sort of thing. She picks up her bag and runs out of the kitchen and calls, "Bye,' over her shoulder. Jenny sits down at the table and drinks tea and it's like she really is the big mama left behind at home to look after the rich lady's daughter. Yo' daddy's rich and yo' mama's goodlookin', lah la-la-la la-la don' yo' cry. And there's something in the way the others treat Jenny. Like she's outside things, and not really a person like they are. They've got used to her cooking big meals and making cakes. No one says anything about it now. Sometimes in the evenings Peter, Kate, José and Sam sit around and smoke hashish in Peter's homemade water-pipe and listen to the stereo turned up loud. When they do that Jenny usually goes up to her room, she doesn't like to be with them when they're doing that, and I can see they sort of resent it. And though she's a girl she's not beautiful like Kate or Sharon, my brother's girlfriend. She doesn't wear jeans and Indian shirts like they do, either, probably because she can't find any to fit her. She wears dresses with flowers on and ordinary things like my mother or the lady in the post office wears. And when she gets nervous about something and does her laugh I can tell they think of her like some sort of mental patient, I know that by the way they turn their eyes away. And they still think about how fat she is. Sometimes when she's not there Sam calls her Slim Jim, and it always makes the others laugh. It's not that they're unfriendly to her or anything like that, it's just that in some way that's hard to describe they keep her apart from themselves. One time we're out on the river she asks me about hashish.

'What do you think about it all?' she says, and I tell her my brother won't let me try it till I'm fifteen. I know she's dead against it, but she doesn't mention it again. It's that same afternoon I take a photograph of her leaning by the kitchen door holding Alice and squinting a little into the sun. She takes mine too, riding no-hands round the back yard on the bicycle I put together out of bits and pieces.

It's hard to say exactly when Jenny becomes Alice's mother. At first she's just looking after her while Kate visits friends. Then the visits get more often till they are almost every day. So the three of us, Jenny, Alice and me, spend a lot of time together by the river. By the jetty there's a grass bank which slopes down on to a tiny sand beach about six feet across. Jenny sits on the bank playing with Alice while I do things to my boat. When we first put Alice in the boat she squeals like a baby pig. She doesn't trust the water. It's a long time before she'll stand on the small beach, and when she does at last she never takes her eyes off the water's edge to make sure it doesn't creep up on her. But when she sees Jenny waving to her from the boat, and quite safe, she changes her mind and we make a trip to the other side of the river. Alice doesn't mind about Kate being away because she likes Jenny, who sings her the bits of songs she knows and talks to her all the time when they are sitting on the grass bank by the river. Alice does not understand a word of it but she likes the sound of Jenny's voice going on and on. Sometimes Alice points up to Jenny's mouth and says, 'More, more.' Kate is always so quiet and sad with her she doesn't hear many voices speaking right at her. One night Kate stays away and doesn't come back till the next morning. Alice is sitting on Jenny's knee spreading her breakfast across the kitchen table when Kate comes running in, scoops her up, hugs her and asks over and over again without giving anyone time to reply,

'Has she been all right? Has she been all right? Has she been all right?' The same afternoon Alice is back with Jenny because Kate has to go off somewhere again. I'm in the hall outside the kitchen when I hear her tell Jenny she'll be back in the early evening, and a few minutes later I see her walking down the drive carrying a small suitcase. When she gets back two days later she just puts her head round the door to see if Alice is still there, and then she goes up to her room. It's not always such a good thing having Alice with us all the time. We can't go very far in the boat. After twenty minutes Alice gets suspicious of the water again and wants to be back on the shore. And if we want to walk somewhere Alice has to be carried most of the way. It means I can't show Jenny some of my special places along the river. By the end of the day Alice gets pretty miserable, moaning and crying about nothing because she's tired. I get fed up spending so much time with Alice. Kate stays up in her room most of the day. One afternoon I take her up some tea and she's sitting in a chair asleep. With Alice there so much of the time Jenny and I don't talk together as much as we did when she first came. Not because Alice is listening, but because all Jenny's time is taken up with her. She doesn't think of anything else, really, it seems like she doesn't want to talk with anyone but Alice. One evening we are all sitting around in the front room after supper. Kate is in the hall having a long argument with someone on the telephone. She finishes, comes in, sits down in a noisy kind of way and carries on reading. But I can see she's angry and not really reading at all. No one speaks for a while, then Alice starts crying upstairs and shouting for Jenny. Jenny and Kate both look up at once and stare at each other for a moment. Then Kate gets up and leaves the room. We all pretend to go on reading but really we are listening to Kate's footsteps on the stairs. We hear her walk into Alice's room, which is right over this one, and we hear Alice shout louder and louder for Jenny to come up. Kate comes back down the stairs, this time quickly. When she comes in the room Jenny looks up and they stare at each other again. And all the time Alice goes on shouting for Jenny. Jenny gets up and squeezes past Kate at the door. They don't speak. The rest of us, Peter, Sam, José and me, we carry on with our pretend reading and listen to Jenny's footsteps upstairs. The crying stops and she stays up there a long time. When she comes down Kate is back in her chair with her magazine. Jenny sits down and no one looks up, no one speaks.

Suddenly the summer is over. Jenny comes into my room early one morning to drag the sheets off my bed and all the clothes she can find in the room. Everything has to be washed before I go to school. Then she gets me to clean out my room, all the old comics and plates and cups which have been collecting under my bed all summer, all the dust and the pots of paint I've been using on my boat. She finds a small table in the garage and I help her carry it to my room. It's going to be my desk for doing homework on. She takes me into the village for a treat, and she won't tell me what it is. When we get there it turns out to be a haircut. I'm about to walk away when she puts her hand on my shoulder.

'Don't be silly,' she says. 'You can't go to school looking like that, you won't last a day.' So I sit still for the barber and let him cut away my whole summer while Jenny sits behind me, laughing at me scowling at her in the mirror. She gets some money from my brother Peter and takes me on the bus into town to buy a school uniform. It's strange having her tell me what to do all of a sudden after our times out on the river. But I don't mind, really, I can't think of any good reasons for not doing the things she says. She steers me through the main shopping streets, into shoe shops and outfitters, she buys me a red blazer and a cap, two pairs of black leather shoes, six pairs of grey socks, two pairs of grey trousers and five grey shirts, and all the time she's saying, 'Do you like these ones? Do you like this?' and since I don't have any special feeling for one particular shade of grey, I agree with whatever she thinks is the best. It's all over in an hour. That evening she empties my drawers of my rock collection to make room for the new clothes, and she gets me to put on the whole uniform. They all laugh downstairs, especially when I put the red cap on. Sam says I look like an inter-galactic postman. For three nights in a row she has me scrubbing my knees with a nail-brush to get the dirt out from under the skin.

Then on Sunday, the day before I start back at school, I go down to the boat with Jenny and Alice for the last time. In the evening I'm going to help Peter and

Sam drag my boat up the path and across the lawn into the garage for the winter. Then we're going to build another jetty, a stronger one. It's the last boat trip of the summer. Jenny lifts Alice in and climbs in herself while I hold the boat steady from the jetty. As I'm pushing us off with an oar, Jenny starts one of her songs. Jeeesus won't you come on down, Jeeesus won't you come on down, Jeeesus won't you come on down, lah, la-la-la-lah, la-la. Alice stands between Jenny's knees watching me row. She thinks it's funny, the way I strain backwards and forwards. She thinks it's a game I'm playing with her, moving close up to her face and away again. It's strange, our last day on the river. When Jenny's finished her song no one speaks for a long time. Just Alice laughing at me. It's so still on the river, her laugh carries across the water to nowhere. The sun is a kind of pale yellow like it's burnt out at the end of summer, there's no wind in the trees on the banks, and no birdsong. Even the oars make no sound in the water. I row upstream with the sun on my back, but it's too pale to feel it, it's too pale to make shadows, even. Up ahead there's an old man standing under an oak tree, fishing. When we are level with him he looks up and stares at us in our boat and we stare back at him on the bank. His face does not change when he's looking at us. Our faces do not change, either, no one says hello. He has a long piece of grass in his mouth and when we've passed he takes it out and spits quietly into the river. Jenny trails her hand in the thick water and watches the bank as if it's something she's only seeing in her mind. It makes me think she doesn't really want to be out there on the river with me. She only came because of all the other times we've been rowing together, and because this is the last time this summer. It sort of makes me sad, thinking that, it makes it harder to row. Then after we've been going for about half an hour she looks at me and smiles and I can tell it's all in my head about her not wanting to be on the river because she starts talking about the summer, about all the things we've been doing. She makes it sound really great, much better than it was really. About the long walks we went on, and paddling at the edge of the river with Alice, how I tried to teach her to row and remember different birdsongs, and the times we used to get up while the others were still asleep and row on the river before breakfast. She gets me going too, remembering all the things we did, like the time we thought we saw a waxwing, and another time we waited one evening behind a bush for a badger to come out of its hole. Pretty soon we get really excited about what a summer it's been and the things we're going to do next year, shouting and laughing into the dead air. And then Jenny says,

'And tomorrow you put on your red cap and go to school.' There's something in the way she says it, pretending to be serious and telling me off with one finger wagging in the air, that makes it the funniest thing I ever heard. And the idea of it too, of doing all those things in the summer and then at the end of it putting on a red cap and going to school. We start laughing and it seems like we're never going to stop. I have to put down the oars. Our hooting and cackling gets louder and louder because the still air doesn't carry it across the water and the noise of it stays with us in the boat. Each time we catch the other's eye we laugh harder and louder till it begins to hurt down my sides, and more than anything I want to stop. Alice starts to cry because she doesn't know what's happening, and that makes us laugh more. Jenny leans over the side of the boat so she can't see me. But her laugh is getting tighter and drier, little hard yelps like pieces of stone from her throat. Her big pink face and her big pink arms are shaking and straining to catch a mouthful of air, but it's all going out of her in little pieces of stone. She leans back into the boat. Her mouth is laughing but her eyes look kind of scared and dry. She drops to her knees, holding her stomach with the pain of laughing, and knocks Alice down with her. And the boat tips over. It tips over because Jenny falls against the side, because Jenny is big and my boat is small. It goes over quickly, like the click of my camera shutter, and suddenly I'm at the deep green bottom of the river touching the cold soft mud with the back of my hand

and feeling the reeds on my face. I can hear laughter like sinking pieces of stone by my ear. But when I push upwards to the surface I feel no one near me. When I come up it's dark on the river. I've been down a long time. Something touches my head and I realize I'm inside the upturned boat. I go down again and up on the other side. It takes me a long time to get my breath. I work my way round the boat shouting over and over for Jenny and Alice. I put my mouth in the water and shout their names. But no one answers, nothing breaks the surface. I'm the only one on the river. So I hang on to the side of the boat and wait for them to come up. I wait a long time, drifting along with the boat with the laughter still in my head, watching the river and the yellow patches on it from the sun getting low. Sometimes great shivers run through my legs and back, but mostly I'm calm, hanging on to the green shell with nothing in my mind, nothing at all, just watching the river, waiting for the surface to break and the yellow patches to scatter. I drift past the place where the old man was fishing and it seems like a very long time ago. He's gone now, there's just a paper bag in the place where he was standing. I get so tired I close my eyes and it feels like I'm at home in bed and it's winter and my mother's coming into my room to say goodnight. She turns out the light and I slip off the boat into the river. Then I remember and I shout for Jenny and Alice and watch the river again and my eyes start to close and my mother comes into my room and says goodnight and turns out the light and I sink back into the water again. After a long time I forget to shout for Jenny and Alice, I just hang there and drift down. I'm looking at a place on the bank I used to know very well a long time ago. There's a patch of sand and a grass bank by the jetty. The yellow patches are sinking into the river when I push away from the boat. I let it drift on down to London and I swim slowly through the black water to the jetty.

Across the Plains, Over the Mountains and Down to the Sea

Frank Moorhouse

'It was the road on which Cindy and I had driven. We drove from a long way inland on a hot day to the coast. We drove the car on to the beach and swam naked. It was that road in the dream.'

'Was this trip of special importance to the affair? What was its significance?'

'Oh yes. Yes, it was a climax. It symbolised everything. It symbolised the leaving of a hot, dusty and choking marriage for the clean, free sea.'

'I want you to describe the trip and I want you to free-associate on the dream.'

How do you describe to a psychiatrist when you

are blocked by overlapping grief and jubilation. Grief from having lost perfection, and the jubilation from having had it. God, we loved then. It may have been neurotically doomed but god it felt right. I feel tears about it now. But I do not want to cry. Cindy released me. I don't mean from marriage—I had left that myself—but from a living numbness. She was coming alive out of childhood and I was coming alive out of this numbness from an anaesthetised marriage.

The marriage wasn't bad in the hostile yelling way. I've told you about the marriage. We could never admit to each other that there was anything wrong with the marriage because we were supposed to be perfectly suited and had to live out all our private proclamations about how superior our marriage was to those around us. We had to live out our marriage propaganda. And I left my wife then, not understanding why, and Cindy left me later not understanding why.

At the time of the trip Cindy and I had been together a month. We had to go inland, where a friend's book was being launched.

'You use the word "inland".'

'Yes.'

In-land. Within-land.

'Oh yes—I see.'

Well, at the launching we drank champagne, toasted, danced and cheered and sang. It was the first book by the first of our friends to publish a book. I remember holding Cindy and feeling the fire coming from her hot body. Everything was hot and delirious. It was a raging 'inland' heat during the day and like the heat of the hot coals at night.

'Tomorrow we go home. We'll drive that 360 miles straight to the sea,' I said.

'Yes. Please. Let's do that,' she said. She could be as bright-eyed as a child.

'We will rise early at daylight and drive to the sea, across the plains, over the mountains, and down to the sea. I know a road over the mountains off the highway which is shorter.'

'Yes, we'll do that. We'll swim naked.'

Drunk, we made love in the motel. I tasted the salty sea juices which came from her. I sucked them from her to my parched river bed. Those juices left a taste that I can never swallow away. They were of the whole world.

We rose to a squinting hot sun. We had fruit juices, grilled lambs fry and bacon, and very cold milk. We ate in bed. I saw Cindy's teeth against the milk. Very white, perfect. Then we showered together and we made love in the shower under water, standing up.

The day was very hot and we sweated as we packed the car. With bad love the packing of the car is the greatest irritation of all. For us it was the best of all games.

We drove then along the blue highway. There was

a shimmer by ten. The bush had that screech of hot insects, as though burning to death. And there was a smell of scorched foliage and drying mould. Cindy looked at the shimmer of the highway and said, 'The road is dancing with us.' She said the sticking bitumen was a-kissing at our tyres.

We talked about how love was not our word. Not the word we would use. We would escape its fouled-up connotations. We wanted a new word for what we had. We celebrated our feelings by eating peanut butter sandwiches from a country store. They tasted as no other sandwiches have ever tasted to me. And we had a can of cold beer.

We reached the mountains by two. They were cooler but still the sun was hot. They had more moisture. I supposed they were protected by the thicker growth. It was cooler because of the moisture. I drove on the winding road over the mountains. Further on I knew the shorter road which went to the coast. It was a stony and unsealed road with trees which touched overhead. The road jumped the car about because of the speed we drove over the stones—we were impatient for the sea. It is not a well-known road, no other cars passed us. It was our road. We saw the sea from the top of a rise in the stony road. Cindy squealed and pointed and hugged me. For all the driving she smelled as clean as the shower.

We drove down the last of the stony road with

the dust choking up through the car. Bouncing, we came to the sealed road and the coast.

The car sang along after the stones. We drove fast to the sea, across the grass and on to the deserted beach. It was about four. We pulled the clothes off each other. Damp with sweat. Her body was just out of adolescence. Breasts only slightly larger than my own. We ran naked into the sea. Holding hands, into the cold sea. I remember the sea, cold and swirling around my penis. I felt enlivened.

It was as if the journey had been a *passing through*— 360 miles across the hot plains, over the moist mountains, through the tunnel of trees, and down to the sea. We had been together a month then. It was the leaving of my stultifying marriage for the clean free sea.

But do you know something—and it is this which upset me so much since I saw you last. Cindy and I have only been separated two years. The other night I was talking to her at a party and I told her that I had dreamed of the trip. She smoked in her new careless way and said, 'What trip?' I said the trip from inland, over the mountains, and down to the sea. We made it. Remember?

'No,' she said, 'I don't remember it.'

I went out of the party and on to the balcony of the house and wept.

I'm crying now.

'That's all right. When you're ready, we'll analyse the dream.'

PAGES FROM COLD POINT
Paul Bowles

OUR CIVILIZATION IS doomed to a short life: its component parts are too heterogeneous. I personally am content to see everything in the process of decay. The bigger the bombs, the quicker it will be done. The world is visually too hideous for one to make the attempt to preserve it. Let it go. Perhaps some day another form of life will come along. Either way, it is of no consequence. At the same time, I am still a part of life, and I am bound by this to protect myself to whatever extent I am able. And so I am here. Here in the Islands vegetation still has the upper hand, and man has to fight even to make his presence seen at all. It is beautiful here, the trade winds blow all year, and I suspect that bombs are extremely unlikely to be wasted on this unfrequented side of the island, if indeed on any part of it.

I was loath to give up the house after Hope's death. But it was the obvious move to make. My university career always having been an utter farce (since I believe no reason inducing a man to 'teach' can possibly be a valid one), I was elated by the idea of resigning, and as soon as her affairs had been settled and the money properly invested, I lost no time in doing so.

I think that week was the first time since childhood that I had managed to recapture the feeling of there being a content in existence. I went from one pleasant house to the next, making my adieux to the English quacks, the Philosophy fakirs, and so on—even to those colleagues with whom I was merely on speaking terms. I watched the envy in their faces when I announced my departure by Pan American on Saturday morning; and the greatest pleasure I felt in all this was in being able to answer, 'Nothing', when I was asked, as invariably I was, what I intended to 'do'.

When I was a boy people used to refer to Charles as 'Big Brother C', although he is only a scant year older than I. To me now he is merely 'Fat Brother C', a successful lawyer. His thick red face and hands, his back-slapping joviality, and his fathomless hypocritical prudery, these are the qualities which make him truly repulsive to me. There is also the fact that he once looked not unlike the way Racky does now. And after all, he is still my big brother, and disapproves openly of everything I do. The loathing I feel for him is so strong that for years I have not been able to swallow a morsel of food or a drop of liquid in his presence without making a prodigious effort. No one knows this but me—certainly not Charles, who would be the last one I should tell about it. He came up on the late train two nights before I left. He got quickly to the point— as soon as he was settled with a highball.

'So you're off for the wilds,' he said, sitting forward in his chair like a salesman.

'If you can call it the wilds,' I replied. 'Certainly it's not wild like Mitichi.' (He has a lodge in northern Quebec.) 'I consider it really civilized.'

He drank and smacked his lips together stiffly, bringing the glass down hard on his knee.

'And Racky. You're taking him along?'

'Of course.'

'Out of school. Away. So he'll see nobody but you. You think that's good.'

I looked at him. 'I do,' I said.

'By God, if I could stop you legally, I would!' he cried, jumping up and putting his glass on the mantel. I was trembling inwardly with excitement, but I merely sat and watched him. He went on. 'You're not fit to have custody of the kid!' he shouted. He shot a stern glance at me over his spectacles.

'You think not?' I said gently.

Again he looked sharply at me. 'D'ye think I've forgotten?'

I was understandably eager to get him out of the house as soon as I could. As I piled and sorted letters and magazines on the desk, I said: 'Is that all you came to tell me? I have a good deal to do tomorrow and I must get some sleep. I probably shan't see you at breakfast. Agnes'll see that you eat in time to make the early train.'

All he said was: 'God! Wake up! Get wise to yourself! You're not fooling anybody, you know.'

That kind of talk is typical of Charles. His mind is slow and obtuse; he constantly imagines that everyone he meets is playing some private game of deception with him. He is so utterly incapable of following the functioning of even a moderately evolved intellect that he finds the will to secretiveness and duplicity everywhere.

'I haven't time to listen to that sort of nonsense,' I said, preparing to leave the room.

But he shouted: 'You don't want to listen! No! Of course not! You just want to do what you want to do. You just want to go on off down there and live as you've a mind to, and to hell with the consequences!' At this point I heard Racky coming downstairs. C. obviously heard nothing, and he raved on. 'But just remember, I've got your number all right, and if there's any trouble with the boy I'll know who's to blame.'

I hurried across the room and opened the door so he could see that Racky was there in the hallway. That stopped his tirade. It was hard to know whether Racky had heard any of it or not. Although he is not a quiet young person, he is the soul of discretion, and it is almost never possible to know any more about what goes on inside his head than he intends one to know.

I was annoyed that C. should have been bellowing at me in my own house. To be sure, he is the only one from whom I would accept such behavior, but then, no father likes to have his son see him take criticism meekly. Racky simply stood there in his bathrobe, his angelic face quite devoid of expression, saying: 'Tell Uncle Charley good night for me, will you? I forgot.'

I said I would, and quickly shut the door. When I thought Racky was back upstairs in his room, I bade Charles good night. I have never been able to get out of his presence fast enough. The effect he has on me dates from an early period of our lives, from days I dislike to recall.

Racky is a wonderful boy. After we arrived, when we found it impossible to secure a proper house near any town where he might have the company of English boys and girls his own age, he showed no sign of chagrin, although he must have been disappointed. Instead, as we went out of the renting office into the glare of the street, he grinned and said: 'Well, I guess we'll have to get bikes, that's all.'

The few available houses near what Charles would have called 'civilization' turned out to be so ugly and so impossibly confining in atmosphere that we decided immediately on Cold Point, even though it was across the island and quite isolated on its seaside cliff. It was beyond a doubt one of the most desirable properties on the island, and Racky was as enthusiastic about its splendors as I.

'You'll get tired of being alone out there, just with me,' I said to him as we walked back to the hotel.

'Aw, I'll get along all right. When do we look for the bikes?'

At his insistence we bought two the next morning. I was sure I should not make much use of mine, but I reflected that an extra bicycle might be convenient to have around the house. It turned out that all the servants had their own bicycles, without which they would not have been able to get to and from the village of Orange Walk, eight miles down the shore. So for a while I was forced to get astride mine each morning before breakfast and pedal madly along beside Racky for a half hour. We would ride through the cool early air, under the towering silk-cotton trees near the house, and out to the great curve in the shoreline where the waving palms bend landward in the stiff breeze that always blows there. Then we would make a wide turn and race back to the house, loudly discussing the degrees of our desires for the various items of breakfast we knew were awaiting us there on the terrace. Back home we would eat in the wind, looking out over the Caribbean, and talk about the news in yesterday's local paper, brought to us by Isiah each morning from Orange Walk. Then Racky would disappear for the whole morning on his bicycle, riding furiously along the road in one direction or the other until he had discovered an unfamiliar strip of sand along the shore that he could consider a new beach. At lunch he would describe it in detail to me, along with a recounting of all the physical hazards involved in hiding the bicycle among the trees (so that natives passing along the road on foot would not spot it), or in climbing down unscalable cliffs that turned out to be much higher than they had appeared at first sight, or in measuring the depth of the water preparatory to diving from the rocks, or in judging the efficacy of the reef in barring sharks and barracuda.

There is never any element of braggadocio in Racky's relating of his exploits—only the joyous excitement he derives from telling how he satisfies his inexhaustible curiosity. And his mind shows its alertness in all directions at once. I do not mean to say that I expect him to be an 'intellectual'. That is no affair of mine, nor do I have any particular interest in whether or not he turns out to be a thinking man. I know he will always have a certain boldness of manner and a great purity of spirit in judging values. The former will prevent his becoming what I call a 'victim': he never will be brutalized by realities. And his unerring sense of balance in ethical considerations will shield him from the paralyzing effects of present-day materialism.

For a boy of sixteen Racky has an extraordinary innocence of vision. I do not say that as a doting father, although God knows I can never even think of the boy without that familiar overwhelming sensation of delight and gratitude for being vouchsafed the privilege of sharing my life with him. What he takes so completely as a matter of course, our daily life here together, is a source of never-ending wonder to me; and I reflect upon it a good part of each day, just sitting here being conscious of my great good fortune in having him all to myself, beyond the reach of prying eyes and malicious tongues. (I suppose I am really thinking of C. when I write that.) And I believe that a part of the charm in sharing Racky's life with him consists precisely in his taking it all so utterly for granted. I have never asked him whether he likes being here—it is so patent that he does, very much. I think if he were to turn to me one day and tell me how happy he is here, that somehow, perhaps, the spell might be broken. Yet if he were to be thoughtless and inconsiderate, or even unkind to me, I feel that I should be able only to love him the more for it.

I have reread that last sentence. What does it mean? And why should I even imagine it could mean anything more than it says?

Still, much as I may try, I can never believe in the gratuitous, isolated fact. What I must mean is that I feel that Racky already has been in some way inconsiderate. But in what way? Surely I cannot resent his bicycle treks; I cannot expect him to want to stay and sit talking with me all day. And I never worry about his being in danger; I know he is more capable than most adults of taking care of himself, and that he is no more likely than any native to come to harm crawling over the cliffs or swimming in the bays. At the same time there is no doubt in my mind that something about our existence annoys me. I must resent some detail in the pattern, whatever that pattern may be. Perhaps it is just his youth, and I am envious of the lithe body, the smooth skin, the animal energy and grace.

For a long time this morning I sat looking out to sea, trying to solve that small puzzle. Two white herons came and perched on a dead stump, east of the garden. They stayed a long time there without stirring. I would turn my head away and accustom my eyes to the bright sea-horizon, then I would look suddenly at them to see if they had shifted position, but they would always be in the same attitude. I tried to imagine the black

stump without them—a purely vegetable landscape—
but it was impossible. All the while I was slowly forcing
myself to accept a ridiculous explanation of my
annoyance with Racky. It had made itself manifest to
me only yesterday, when instead of appearing for lunch,
he had sent a young colored boy from Orange Walk
to say that he would be lunching in the village. I could
not help noticing that the boy was riding Racky's
bicycle. I had been waiting lunch a good half hour
for him, and I had Gloria serve immediately as the
boy rode off, back to the village. I was curious to know
in what sort of place and with whom Racky could be
eating, since Orange Walk, as far as I know, is inhabited
exclusively by Negroes, and I was sure Gloria would
be able to shed some light on the matter, but I could
scarcely ask her. However, as she brought on the dessert,
I said: 'Who was that boy that brought the message
from Mister Racky?'

She shrugged her shoulders. 'A young lad of Orange
Walk. He's named Wilmot.'

When Racky returned at dusk, flushed from his
exertion (for he never rides casually), I watched him
closely. His behavior struck my already suspicious eyes
as being one of false heartiness and a rather forced
good humor. He went to his room early and read for
quite a while before turning off his light. I took a long
walk in the almost day-bright moonlight, listening to
the songs of the night insects in the trees. And I sat

for a while in the dark on the stone railing of the bridge across Black River. (It is really only a brook that rushes down over the rocks from the mountain a few miles inland, to the beach near the house.) In the night it always sounds louder and more important than it does in the daytime. The music of the water over the stones relaxed my nerves, although why I had need of such a thing I find it difficult to understand, unless I was really upset by Racky's not having come home to lunch. But if that were true it would be absurd, and moreover, dangerous—just the sort of thing the parent of an adolescent has to beware of and fight against, unless he is indifferent to the prospect of losing the trust and affection of his offspring permanently. Racky must stay out whenever he likes, with whom he likes, and for as long as he likes, and I must not think twice about it, much less mention it to him, or in any way give the impression of prying. Lack of confidence on the part of a parent is the one unforgivable sin.

Although we still take our morning dip together on arising, it is three weeks since we have been for the early spin. One morning I found that Racky had jumped onto his bicycle in his wet trunks while I was still swimming, and gone by himself, and since then there has been an unspoken agreement between us that such is to be the procedure: he will go alone. Perhaps I held him back; he likes to ride so fast.

Young Peter, the smiling gardener from Saint Ives

Cove, is Racky's special friend. It is amusing to see them together among the bushes, crouched over an ant-hill or rushing about trying to catch a lizard, almost of an age the two, yet so disparate—Racky with his tan skin looking nearly white in contrast to the glistening black of the other. Today I know I shall be alone for lunch, since it is Peter's day off. On such days they usually go together on their bicycles into Saint Ives Cove, where Peter keeps a small rowboat. They fish along the coast there, but they have never returned with anything so far.

Meanwhile I am here alone, sitting on the rocks in the sun, from time to time climbing down to cool myself in the water, always conscious of the house behind me under the high palms, like a large glass boat filled with orchids and lilies. The servants are clean and quiet, and the work seems to be accomplished almost automatically. The good, black servants are another blessing of the islands; the British, born here in this paradise, have no conception of how fortunate they are. In fact, they do nothing but complain. One must have lived in the United States to appreciate the wonder of this place. Still, even here ideas are changing each day. Soon the people will decide that they want their land to be a part of today's monstrous world, and once that happens, it will be all over. As soon as you have that desire, you are infected with the deadly virus, and you begin to show the symptoms of the disease. You

live in terms of time and money, and you think in terms
of society and progress. Then all that is left for you
is to kill the other people who think the same way,
along with a good many of those who do not, since
that is the final manifestation of the malady. Here for
the moment at any rate, one has a feeling of staticity—
existence ceases to be like those last few seconds in
the hour-glass when what is left of the sand suddenly
begins to rush through to the bottom all at once. For
the moment, it seems suspended. And if it seems, it
is. Each wave at my feet, each bird-call in the forest
at my back, does *not* carry me one step nearer the final
disaster. The disaster is certain, but it will suddenly
have happened, that is all. Until then, time stays still.

I am upset by a letter in this morning's mail: the Royal
Bank of Canada requests that I call in person at its
central office to sign the deposit slips and other papers
for a sum that was cabled from the bank in Boston.
Since the central office is on the other side of the island,
fifty miles away, I shall have to spend the night over
there and return the following day. There is no point
in taking Racky along. The sight of 'civilization' might
awaken a longing for it in him; one never knows. I
am sure it would have done in me when I was his
age. And if that should once start, he would merely
be unhappy, since there is nothing for him but to stay

here with me, at least for the next two years, when I hope to renew the lease, or, if things in New York pick up, buy the place. I am sending word by Isiah, when he goes home into Orange Walk this evening, to have the McCoigh car call for me at seven-thirty tomorrow morning. It is an enormous old open Packard, and Isiah can save the ride out to work here by piling his bicycle into the back and riding with McCoigh.

The trip across the island was beautiful, and would have been highly enjoyable if my imagination had not played me a strange trick at the very outset. We stopped in Orange Walk for gasoline, and while that was being seen to, I got out and went to the corner store for some cigarettes. Since it was not yet eight o'clock, the store was still closed, and I hurried up the side street to the other little shop which I thought might be open. It was, and I bought my cigarettes. On the way back to the corner I noticed a large black woman leaning with her arms on the gate in front of her tiny house, staring into the street. As I passed by her, she looked straight into my face and said something with the strange accent of the island. It was said in what seemed an unfriendly tone, and ostensibly was directed at me, but I had no notion of what it was. I got back into the car and the driver started it. The sound of the words had stayed in my head, however, as a bright shape

140

outlined by darkness is likely to stay in the mind's eye, in such a way that when one shuts one's eyes one can see the exact contour of the shape. The car was already roaring up the hill toward the overland road when I suddenly reheard the very words. And they were: 'Keep your boy at home, mahn.' I sat perfectly rigid for a moment as the open countryside rushed past. Why should I think she had said that? Immediately I decided that I was giving an arbitrary sense to a phrase I could not have understood even if I had been paying strict attention. And then I wondered why my subconscious should have chosen that sense, since now that I whispered the words over to myself they failed to connect with any anxiety to which my mind might have been disposed. Actually I have never given a thought to Racky's wanderings about Orange Walk. I can find no such preoccupation no matter how I put the question to myself. Then, could she really have said those words? All the way through the mountains I pondered the question, even though it was obviously a waste of energy. And soon I could no longer hear the sound of her voice in my memory: I had played the record over too many times, and worn it out.

Here in the hotel, a gala dance is in progress. The abominable orchestra, comprising two saxophones and one sour violin, is playing directly under my window in the garden, and the serious-looking couples slide about on the waxed concrete floor of the terrace, in the light of strings of paper lanterns. I suppose it is meant to look Japanese.

At this moment I wonder what Racky is doing there in the house with only Peter and Ernest the watchman to keep him company. I wonder if he is asleep. The house, which I am accustomed to think of as smiling and benevolent in its airiness, could just as well be in the most sinister and remote regions of the globe, now that I am here. Sitting with the absurd orchestra bleating downstairs, I picture it to myself, and it strikes me as terribly vulnerable in its isolation. In my mind's eye I see the moonlit point with its tall palms waving restlessly in the wind, its dark cliffs licked by the waves below. Suddenly, although I struggle against the sensation, I am inexpressibly glad to be away from the house, helpless there, far on its point of land, in the silence of the night. Then I remember that the night is seldom silent. There are the occasional cries of the night birds, the droning of the thousands of insects, the loud sea at the base of the rocks—all the familiar noises that make sleep so sound. And Racky is there surrounded by them as usual, not even hearing them. But I feel profoundly guilty for having left him, unutterably tender and sad at the thought of him, lying there alone in the house with the two Negroes the only human beings within miles. If I keep thinking of Cold Point I shall be more and more nervous.

I am not going to bed yet. They are all screaming

with laughter down there, the idiots; I could never sleep anyway. The bar is still open. Fortunately it is on the street side of the hotel. For once I need a few drinks.

Much later, but I feel no better; I may be a little drunk. The dance is over and it is quiet in the garden, but the room is too hot.

As I was falling asleep last night, all dressed, and with the overhead light shining sordidly in my face, I heard the black woman's voice again, more clearly even than I did in the car yesterday. For some reason this morning there is no doubt in my mind that the words I heard are the words she said. I accept that and go on from there. Suppose she did tell me to keep Racky home. It could only mean that she, or someone else in Orange Walk, has had a childish altercation with him; although I must say it is hard to conceive of Racky's entering into any sort of argument or feud with those people. To set my mind at rest (for I do seem to be taking the whole thing with great seriousness), I am going to stop in the village this afternoon before going home, and try to see the woman. I am extremely curious to know what she could have meant.

I had not been conscious until this evening when I came back to Cold Point how powerful they are, all those physical elements that go to make up its atmosphere: the sea and wind sounds that isolate the house from the road, the brilliancy of the water, sky and sun, the bright colors and strong odors of the flowers, the feeling of space both outside and within the house. One naturally accepts these things when one is living here. This afternoon when I returned I was conscious of them all over again, of their existence and their strength. All of them together are like a powerful drug; coming back made me feel as though I had been disintoxicated and were returning to the scene of my former indulgences. Now at eleven it is as if I had never been absent an hour. Everything is the same as always, even to the dry palm branch that scrapes against the window screen by my night table. And indeed, it is only thirty-six hours since I was here; but I always expect my absence from a place to bring about irremediable changes.

Strangely enough, now that I think of it, I feel that something *has* changed since I left yesterday morning, and that is the general attitude of the servants—their collective aura, so to speak. I noticed that difference immediately upon arriving back, but was unable to define it. Now I see it clearly. The network of common understanding which slowly spreads itself through a well-run household has been destroyed. Each person is by himself now. No unfriendliness, however, that I can see. They all behave with the utmost courtesy, excepting possibly Peter, who struck me as looking unaccustomedly glum when I encountered him in the kitchen after dinner. I meant to ask Racky if he had noticed it, but I forgot, and he went to bed early.

In Orange Walk I made a brief stop, on the pretext to McCoigh that I wanted to see the seamstress in the side street. I walked up and back in front of the house where I had seen the woman, but there was no sign of anyone.

As for my absence, Racky seems to have been perfectly content, having spent most of the day swimming off the rocks below the terrace. The insect sounds are at their height now, the breeze is cooler than usual, and I shall take advantage of these favorable conditions to get a good long night's rest.

Today has been one of the most difficult days of my life. I arose early, we had breakfast at the regular time, and Racky went off in the direction of Saint Ives Cove. I lay in the sun on the terrace for a while, listening to the noises of the household's regime. Peter was all over the property, collecting dead leaves and fallen blossoms in a huge basket, and carrying them off to the compost heap. He appeared to be in an even fouler humor than last night. When he came near to me at one point, on his way down to another part of the garden, I called to him. He set the basket down and stood looking at me; then he walked across the grass toward me slowly—reluctantly, it seemed to me.

'Peter, is everything all right with you?'

'Yes, sir.'

'No trouble at home?'

'Oh, no, sir.'

'Good.'

'Yes, sir.'

He went back to his work. But his face belied his words. Not only did he seem to be in a decidedly unpleasant temper; out here in the sunlight he looked positively ill. However, it was not my concern, if he refused to admit it.

When the heavy heat of the sun reached the unbearable point for me, I got out of my chair and went down the side of the cliff along the series of steps cut there in the rock. A level platform is below, and a diving board, for the water is deep. At each side, the rocks spread out and the waves break over them, but by the platform the wall of rock is vertical and the water merely hits against it below the springboard. The place is a tiny amphitheatre, quite cut off in sound and sight from the house. There too, I like to lie in the sun; when I climb out of the water I often remove my trunks and lie stark naked on the springboard. I regularly make fun of Racky because he is embarrassed to do the same. Occasionally he will do it, but never without being coaxed. I was spread out there without a stitch on, being lulled by the slapping of the water, when an unfamiliar voice very close to me said: 'Mister Norton?'

I jumped with nervousness, nearly fell off the springboard, and sat up, reaching at the same time, but in vain, for my trunks, which were lying on the rock practically at the feet of a middle-aged mulatto gentleman. He was in a white duck suit, and wore a high collar with a black tie, and it seemed to me that he was eyeing me with a certain degree of horror.

My next reaction was one of anger at being trespassed upon in this way. I rose and got the trunks; however, donning them calmly and saying nothing more meaningful than: 'I didn't hear you come down the steps.'

'Shall we go up?' said my caller. As he led the way, I had a definite premonition that he was here on an unpleasant errand. On the terrace we sat down, and he offered me an American cigarette which I did not accept.

'This is a delightful spot,' he said, glancing out to sea and then at the end of his cigarette, which was only partially aglow. He puffed at it.

I said: 'Yes,' waiting for him to go on; presently he did.

'I am from the constabulary of this parish. The

police, you see.' And seeing my face, 'This is a friendly call. But still it must be taken as a warning, Mister Norton. It is very serious. If anyone else comes to you about this it will mean trouble for you, heavy trouble. That's why I want to see you privately this way and warn you personally. You see.'

I could not believe I was hearing his words. At length I said faintly: 'But what about?'

'This is not an official call. You must not be upset. I have taken it upon myself to speak to you because I want to save you deep trouble.'

'But I *am* upset!' I cried, finding my voice at last. 'How can I help being upset, when I don't know what you're talking about?'

He moved his chair closer to mine, and spoke in a very low voice.

'I have waited until the young man was away from the house so we could talk in private. You see, it is about him.'

Somehow that did not surprise me. I nodded.

'I will tell you very briefly. The people here are simple country folk. They make trouble easily. Right now they are all talking about the young man you have living here with you. He is your son, I hear.' His inflection here was sceptical.

'Certainly he's my son.'

His expression did not change, but his voice grew indignant. 'Whoever he is, that is a bad young man.'

'What do you mean?' I cried, but he cut in hotly: 'He may be your son; he may not be. I don't care who he is. That is not my affair. But he is bad through and through. We don't have such things going on here, sir. The people in Orange Walk and Saint Ives Cove are very cross now. You don't know what these folk do when they are aroused.'

I thought it my turn to interrupt. 'Please tell me why you say my son is bad. What has he done?' Perhaps the earnestness in my voice reached him, for his face assumed a gentler aspect. He leaned still closer to me and almost whispered.

'He has no shame. He does what he pleases with all the young boys, and the men too, and gives them a shilling so they won't tell about it. But they talk. Of course they talk. Every man for twenty miles up and down the coast knows about it. And the women too, they know about it.' There was a silence.

I had felt myself preparing to get to my feet for the past few seconds because I wanted to go into my room and be alone, to get away from that scandalized stage whisper. I think I mumbled 'Good morning' or 'Thank you' as I turned away and began walking toward the house. But he was still beside me, still whispering like an eager conspirator into my ear: 'Keep him home, Mister Norton. Or send him away to school, if he is your son. But make him stay out of these towns. For his own sake.'

I shook hands with him and went to lie on my bed. From there I heard his car door slam, heard him drive off. I was painfully trying to formulate an opening sentence to use in speaking to Racky about this, feeling that the opening sentence would define my stand. The attempt was merely a sort of therapeutic action, to avoid thinking about the thing itself. Every attitude seemed impossible. There was no way to broach the subject. I suddenly realized that I should never be able to speak to him directly about it. With the advent of this news he had become another person—an adult, mysterious and formidable. To be sure, it did occur to me that the mulatto's story might not be true, but automatically I rejected the doubt. It was as if I wanted to believe it, almost as if I had already known it, and he had merely confirmed it.

Racky returned at midday, panting and grinning. The inevitable comb appeared and was used on the sweaty, unruly locks. Sitting down to lunch, he exclaimed: 'Wow! What a beach I found this morning! But what a job to get down to it!' I tried to look unconcerned as I met his gaze; it was as if our positions had been reversed, and I were hoping to stem his rebuke. He prattled on about thorns and vines and his machete. Throughout the meal I kept telling myself: 'Now is the moment. You must say something.' But all I said was: 'More salad? Or do you want dessert now?' So the lunch passed and nothing happened. After I had finished my coffee I went into my bedroom and looked at myself in the large mirror. I saw my eyes trying to give their reflected brothers a little courage. As I stood there I heard a commotion in the other wing of the house: voices, bumpings, the sound of a scuffle. Above the noise came Gloria's sharp voice, imperious and excited: 'No, mahn! Don't strike him!' And louder: 'Peter, mahn, no!'

I went quickly toward the kitchen, where the trouble seemed to be, but on the way I was run into by Racky, who staggered into the hallway with his hands in front of his face.

'What is it, Racky?' I cried.

He pushed past me into the living room without moving his hands away from his face; I turned and followed him. From there he went into his own room, leaving the door open behind him. I heard him in the bathroom running the water. I was undecided what to do. Suddenly Peter appeared in the hall doorway, his hat in his hand. When he raised his head, I was surprised to see that his cheek was bleeding. In his eyes was a strange, confused expression of transient fear and deep hostility. He looked down again.

'May I please talk with you, sir?'

'What was all the racket? What's been happening?'

'May I talk with you outside, sir?' He said it doggedly, still not looking up.

In view of the circumstances, I humored him. We

walked slowly up the cinder road to the main highway, across the bridge, and through the forest while he told me his story. I said nothing.

At the end he said: 'I never wanted to, sir, even the first time, but after the first time I was afraid, and Mister Racky was after me every day.'

I stood still, and finally said: 'If you had only told me this the first time it happened, it would have been much better for everyone.'

He turned his hat in his hands, studying it intently. 'Yes, sir. But I didn't know what everyone was saying about him in Orange Walk until today. You know I always go to the beach at Saint Ives Cove with Mister Racky on my free days. If I had known what they were all saying I wouldn't have been afraid, sir. And I wanted to keep on working here. I needed the money.' Then he repeated what he had already said three times. 'Mister Racky said you'd see about it that I was put in the jail. I'm a year older than Mister Racky, sir.'

'I know, I know,' I said impatiently; and deciding that severity was what Peter expected of me at this point I added: 'You had better get your things together and go home. You can't work here any longer, you know.'

The hostility in his face assumed terrifying proportions as he said: 'If you killed me I would not work any more at Cold Point, sir.'

I turned and walked briskly back to the house,

leaving him standing there in the road. It seems he returned at dusk, a little while ago, and got his belongings.

In his room Racky was reading. He had stuck some adhesive tape on his chin and over his cheekbone.

'I've dismissed Peter,' I announced. 'He hit you, didn't he?'

He glanced up. His left eye was swollen, but not yet black.

'He sure did. But I landed him one, too. And I guess I deserved it anyway.'

I rested against the table. 'Why?' I asked nonchalantly.

'Oh, I had something on him from a long time back that he was afraid I'd tell you.'

'And just now you threatened to tell me?'

'Oh, no! He said he was going to quit the job here, and I told him he was yellow.'

'Why did he want to quit? I thought he liked the job.'

'Well, he did, I guess, but he didn't like me.' Racky's candid gaze betrayed a shade of pique. I still leaned against the table.

I persisted. 'But I thought you two got on fine together. You seemed to.'

'Nah. He was just scared of losing his job. I had something on him. He was a good guy, though. I liked him all right.' He paused. 'Has he gone yet?' A strange quaver crept into his voice as he said the last words, and I understood that for the first time Racky's heretofore impeccable histrionics were not quite equal to the occasion. He was very much upset at losing Peter.

'Yes, he's gone,' I said shortly. 'He's not coming back, either.' And as Racky, hearing the unaccustomed inflection in my voice, looked up at me suddenly with faint astonishment in his young eyes, I realized that this was the moment to press on, to say: 'What did you have on him?' But as if he had arrived at the same spot in my mind a fraction of a second earlier, he proceeded to snatch away my advantage by jumping up, bursting into loud song, and pulling off all his clothes. As he stood before me naked, singing at the top of his lungs, and stepped into his swimming trunks, I was conscious that again I should be incapable of saying to him what I must say.

He was in and out of the house all afternoon: some of the time he read in his room, and most of the time he was down on the diving board. It is strange behavior for him; if I could only know what is in his mind. As evening approached, my problem took on a purely obsessive character. I walked to and fro in my room, always pausing at one end to look out the window over the sea, and at the other end to glance at my face in the mirror. As if that could help me! Then I took a drink. And another. I thought I might be able to do it at dinner, when I felt fortified by the whiskey.

But no. Soon he will have gone to bed. It is not that I expect to confront him with any accusations. That I know I never can do. But I must find a way to keep him from his wanderings, and I must invent a reason to give him, so that he will never suspect that I know.

We fear for the future of our offspring. It is ludicrous, but only a little more palpably so than most things in life. A length of time has passed—days which I am content to have known, even if now they are over. I think that this period was what I had always been waiting for life to offer, the recompense I had unconsciously but firmly expected, in return for having been held so closely in the grip of existence all these years.

That evening seems long ago only because I have recalled its details so many times that they have taken on the color of legend. Actually my problem already had been solved for me then, but I did not know it. Because I could not perceive the pattern, I foolishly imagined that I must cudgel my brains to find the right words with which to approach Racky. But it was he who came to me. That same evening, as I was about to go out for a solitary stroll which I thought might help me hit upon a formula, he appeared at my door.

'Going for a walk?' he asked, seeing the stick in my hand.

The prospect of making an exit immediately after speaking with him made things seem simpler. 'Yes,' I said, 'but I'd like to have a word with you first.'

'Sure. What?' I did not look at him because I did not want to see the watchful light I was sure was playing in his eyes at this moment. As I spoke I tapped with my stick along the designs made by the tiles in the floor. 'Racky, would you like to go back to school?'

'Are you kidding? You know I hate school.'

I glanced up at him. 'No, I'm not kidding. Don't look so horrified. You'd probably enjoy being with a bunch of fellows your own age.' (That was not one of the arguments I had meant to use.)

'I might like to be with guys my own age, but I don't want to have to be in school to do it. I've had school enough.'

I went to the door and said lamely: 'I thought I'd get your reactions.'

He laughed, 'No, thanks.'

'That doesn't mean you're not going,' I said over my shoulder as I went out.

On my walk I pounded the highway's asphalt with my stick, stood on the bridge having dramatic visions which involved such eventualities as our moving back to the States, Racky's having a bad spill on his bicycle and being paralyzed for some months, and even the possibility of my letting events take their course, which would doubtless mean my having to visit him now and then in the governmental prison with gifts of food, if it meant nothing more tragic and violent. 'But none of these things will happen,' I said to myself, and I knew I was wasting precious time; he must not return to Orange Walk tomorrow.

I went back toward the point at a snail's pace. There was no moon, and very little breeze. As I approached the house, trying to tread lightly on the cinders so as not to awaken the watchful Ernest and have to explain to him that it was only I, I saw that there were no lights in Racky's room. The house was dark save for the dim lamp on my night table. Instead of going in, I skirted the entire building, colliding with bushes and getting my face sticky with spider webs, and went to sit a while on the terrace where there seemed to be a breath of air. The sound of the sea was far out on the reef, where the breakers sighed. Here below, there were only slight watery chugs and gurgles now and then. It was an unusually low tide. I smoked three cigarettes mechanically, having ceased even to think, and then, my mouth tasting bitter from the smoke, I went inside.

My room was airless. I flung my clothes onto a chair and looked at the night table to see if the carafe of water was there. Then my mouth opened. The top sheet of my bed had been stripped back to the foot. There on the far side of the bed, dark against the whiteness of the lower sheet, lay Racky asleep on his side, and naked.

I stood looking at him for a long time, probably holding my breath, for I remember feeling a little dizzy at one point. I was whispering to myself, as my eyes followed the curve of his arm, shoulder, back, thigh, leg: 'A child. A child.' Destiny, when one perceives it clearly from very near, has no qualities at all. The recognition of it and the consciousness of the vision's clarity leave no room on the mind's horizon. Finally I turned off the light and softly lay down. The night was absolutely black.

He stayed perfectly quiet until dawn. I shall never know whether or not he was really asleep all that time. Of course he couldn't have been, and yet he lay so still. Warm and firm, but still as death. The darkness and silence were heavy around us. As the birds began to sing, I sank into a soft, enveloping slumber; when I awoke in the sunlight later, he was gone.

I found him down by the water, cavorting alone on the springboard; for the first time, he had discarded his trunks without my suggesting it. All day we stayed together around the terrace and on the rocks, talking, swimming, reading, and just lying flat in the hot sun. Nor did he return to his room when night came. Instead, after the servants were asleep, we brought three bottles of champagne in and set the pail on the night table.

Thus it came about that I was able to touch on

the delicate subject that still preoccupied me, and profiting by the new understanding between us, I made my request in the easiest, most natural fashion.

'Racky, would you do me a tremendous favor if I asked you?'

He lay on his back, his hands beneath his head. It seemed to me his regard was circumspect, wanting in candor.

'I guess so,' he said. 'What is it?'

'Will you stay around the house for a few days—a week, say? Just to please me? We can take some rides together, as far as you like. Would you do that for me?'

'Sure thing,' he said, smiling.

I was temporizing, but I was desperate.

Perhaps a week later—(it is only when one is not fully happy that one is meticulous about time, so that it may have been more, or less)—we were having breakfast. Isiah stood by in the shade, waiting to pour us more coffee.

'I noticed you had a letter from Uncle Charley the other day,' said Racky. 'Don't you think we ought to invite him down?'

My heart began to beat with great force.

'Here? He'd hate it here,' I said casually. 'Besides, there's no room. Where would he sleep? Even as I heard myself saying the words, I knew that they were the wrong ones, and that I was not really participating in the conversation. Again I felt the fascination of

159

complete helplessness that comes when one is suddenly a conscious onlooker at the shaping of one's own fate.

'In my room,' said Racky. 'It's empty.'

I could see more of the pattern at that moment than I had ever suspected existed. 'Nonsense,' I said. 'This is not the sort of place for Uncle Charley.'

Racky appeared to be hitting on an excellent idea. 'Maybe if I wrote and invited him,' he suggested, motioning to Isiah for more coffee.

'Nonsense,' I said again, watching still more of the pattern reveal itself, like a photographic print becoming constantly clearer in a tray of developing solution.

Isiah filled Racky's cup and returned to the shade. Racky drank slowly, pretending to be savoring the coffee.

'Well, it won't do any harm to try. He'd appreciate the invitation,' he said speculatively.

For some reason, at this juncture I knew what to say, and as I said it, I knew what I was going to do.

'I thought we might fly over to Havana for a few days next week.'

He looked guardedly interested, and then he broke into a wide grin. 'Great!' he cried. 'Why wait until next week?'

The next morning the servants called 'Good-bye' to us as we drove up the cinder road in the McCoigh car. We took off from the airport at six that evening.

Racky was in high spirits; he kept the stewardess engaged in conversation all the way to Camagüey.

He was delighted with Havana. Sitting in the bar at the Nacional, we continued to discuss the possibility of having C. pay us a visit at the island. It was not without difficulty that I eventually managed to persuade Racky that writing him would be inadvisable.

We decided to look for an apartment right there in Vedado for Racky. He did not seem to want to come back to Cold Point. We also decided that living in Havana he would need a larger income than I. I am already having the greater part of Hope's estate transferred to his name in the form of a trust fund which I shall administer until he is of age. It was his mother's money, after all.

We bought a new convertible, and he drove me out to Rancho Boyeros in it when I took my plane. A Cuban named Claudio with very white teeth, whom Racky had met in the pool that afternoon, sat between us.

We were waiting in front of the landing field. An official finally unhooked the chain to let the passengers through. 'If you get fed up, come to Havana,' said Racky, pinching my arm.

The two of them stood together behind the rope, waving to me, their shirts flapping in the wind as the plane started to move.

The wind blows by my head; between each wave there are thousands of tiny licking and chopping sounds as the water hurries out of the crevices and holes; and a part-floating, part-submerged feeling of being in the water haunts my mind even as the hot sun burns my face. I sit here and I read, and I wait for the pleasant sensation of repletion that follows a good meal, to turn slowly, as the hours pass along, into the even more delightful, slightly stirring emotion deep within, which accompanies the awakening of the appetite.

I am perfectly happy here in reality, because I believe that nothing very drastic is likely to befall this part of the island in the near future.

THE FISH-SCALE SHIRT
Ruth Fainlight

THE WOODEN TROUGH where she stood was darkened
and spongy from a constant flow of water that poured
out at an odd twisted angle—like an icicle at the corner
of a roof—through a large brass tap fixed onto the
wall of the boat shed, and the ground below the trough
was always slimy. Moss took hold wherever it could—
though there were few places not sealed against its
advance by a glistening varnish of fish scales, which
gave the whole scene a paradoxical elegance, as if the
barrels and buckets, the baskets into which the cleaned
fish were packed, the trough and puddled yard and
collapsing huts and fences that surrounded it were inlaid

with mother-of-pearl. Ann saw and thought about fish scales all day, dreamed of them every night. Her task was to collect enough to cover the shirt she had to make. She tried to imagine how it would look—a glittering shirt of fish-scale sequins, like chain-mail armour.

She had woken one morning on the shore of a small harbour where fishing boats rose and sank at the horizon with the timeless regularity of waves breaking on the stony beach. Someone must have brought her there, but she had no memory of the journey. The contrast with her previous life was so decisive that she might as well have been shot into space and landed on another planet. An old woman had appeared at her side and given the details of the task, adding that when the garment was ready, Ann would discover who it was intended for. She could never find that woman again among the others.

With them, each day she split and gutted the gleaming bodies tumbled from weed-tangled, barnacle-crusted nets onto the cobbled quayside. The skill and speed of her workmates was astonishing. She watched carefully, trying to see how they managed to open and clean a large fish in what seemed one flowing movement. Her chapped hands and fingers, covered with cuts, smarted from the cold air and salt water. These strong-limbed, full-bodied women, and the tall fair sailors in seaboots and oilskins who looked like their brothers

and husbands, joked together all day long, shining teeth
and glistening lips and tongues in noisy action to speak
a dialect she could barely comprehend. But in spite
of their energetic, friendly presences, they stayed as
unreal to her as she must be to them. Nevertheless,
she studied the men's faces and gestures, and listened
to the different tones of voice, seeking a sign to indicate
that this or that one might become the wearer of the
fish-scale shirt. A few had made tentative yet
unmistakable approaches, but they soon stopped when
she did not respond. None had the special quality that
marked a prince in disguise.

The old woman had shown Ann a broken-down
lean-to behind the fish sheds, and said that was where
she would live. There was a pile of old sacks inside,
which she took to the beach and washed in the foam.
It was a windy, sunny day and they dried quickly, spread
over clumps of seaspurge and marram grass. They would
serve as blanket and towel and pillow. She also found
a tin plate, a chipped enamel bowl and mug, and a
sharp knife. One of the fisherwomen gestured her to
come and share their round loaves of bread and cauldron
of fish soup. Her basic needs were provided. At the
end of a day's hard work and the communal meal, Ann
fell onto the bed of sacks as if it were the most luxurious
divan and slept more deeply than she could remember
ever having done before.

How to gather the fish scales was the first problem.

If her hands and arms were wet from fish juices and sea water, they clung to her skin, impossible to detach. They seemed as fragile and easily damaged as the scales on butterflies' wings. If her hands were stiff from gripping the hard bone handle of the knife and the icy bodies of the dying fish, the scales slid through her clumsy fingers. By trial and error she learned that the best way to gather the scales was to let them dry wherever they landed, and then come back and gently scrape them off with the blunt edge of the knife into the lap of her skirt. It was a slow method, but she could not think of a better one. Day by day, the heap of scales in the corner of the hut mounted higher.

Having decided that none of the fishermen was an enchanted prince the fish-scale shirt would release (so that he in turn could rescue her), Ann looked at the women more closely. There was no reason why her hero might not be a heroine. But although each in her own way was amiable, neither did any of them convince her as the destined one.

'When the time comes, your hero will appear,' a voice half-sang and half-intoned inside her head. 'Just go on doing what you must, gathering the fish scales, and thinking about how you can make a shirt to sew them on, and what you will use for needle and thread.' The voice was her companion. There was something familiar and reassuring about it, like a reminder of childhood. But whether the voice was that of mother or father or nurse or someone else, she could not be sure—nor even if it was her own.

Now the problem had been stated, it did not seem so daunting. She could make a needle from a strong straight fishbone, and pierce an eye through its thicker end with the point of her knife. Splitting open the firm cold bodies and scraping them clean, she wondered if she could use the silvery intestines for thread. But the shrivelled, hardened state of some she had put aside overnight eliminated that possibility.

Every day, cold winds beat rain onto the stone quay and high massed clouds moved steadily across the sky. But between the squalls, sunlight lit their edges with vivid silver and flashed from the encrustations of mica-fine fish scales. On certain evenings the sunset melted crimson, orange and purple bands into the horizon. Either the season was softening, or else she was adjusting to the climate's harshness. One morning, picking up a sacking blanket she had thrown off during the night, it became obvious how the shirt could be made and where the thread would come from. Such practical matters left no time to grieve about her past life or this one. She carefully frayed the rough fabric into the shape of a shirt-body and sleeves, then teased out separate threads to stitch seams down the sides and around the edges. 'I hope my hero won't be too tall or broad,' she mused, holding it against herself. The shirt was hardly larger than her own.

The next step was to sew on the scales, one stitch for each, in overlapping rows. Now the days were longer, rays of sunlight struck through the open door of the hut to the far corner where the glittering heap dazzled like tidewater over wet, bright stones along the shoreline. The slightest current of air would lift a few to skid across the floor or fly upwards then settle on her head like snowflakes or appleblossom. Hunched over a dim, but pungent, fish-oil lamp, she continued working until dawn made the lamplight even weaker. The nearer she came to finishing the shirt, the more Ann wondered why she had been set this task.

One day she walked further inland than ever before. Smooth blackish rocks were scattered on the dark ground—isolated boulders or massive stones piled like cairns built by a race of giants. She noticed a wisp of steam at the base of one where an overhanging shelf of rock sloped back into the earth. Between two black stone lips a hot spring bubbled up in sudden irregular gouts like blood being pumped from a deep wound. Grey scum, brilliant green moss and thick white mineral streaks rimmed the outlet in the shape of something being born from the cleft in the rocks.

The sense of another presence and a movement to one side made Ann turn her head, to be confronted by the speckled yellow eyes and unblinking gaze of a large brown toad sheltering there. This must be the one she had been waiting for, she thought excitedly, the one who had waited here for her. Only a creature under a spell would be in this magical place. And the toad was so repulsive that it must surely become the handsomest prince in the world.

She smiled encouragingly and reached out to touch its head, but at the last moment could not make herself do it. She hoped the toad had not noticed this hesitation, and would not be offended or angry or hurt. Walking slowly backwards she chanted, 'Come home with me, dear toad-prince. Come to my hut. Come and see what I am making for you.' And heaving itself forward with an unpleasant movement and a sound like a paper bag full of water being bumped across a wooden floor, the toad followed. Every few steps she turned to make sure it was still there, and each time the toad stared back with a more intense, significant and intelligent expression.

She must be right to believe the toad was an enchanted prince. No ordinary toad would be so delicate, so considerate. All the stories she remembered about princesses forced to be goosegirls or to take a vow of silence and live in a tree spinning thread from nettles or sorting every poppy seed from an enormous heap of lentils and pebbles ended happily in a transformation scene. By comparison to such tasks, hers was not really hard—and she might have made it easier, she realised, by being more friendly with her workmates and the fishermen. But that would have meant abandoning all hope in the redemptive power of her task, and accepting this existence as permanent.

She had been uneasy about what he might expect, but the toad barely stirred from his place in the furthest corner of the hut, opposite the diminishing heap of fish scales. Ann's first thought when she woke was of him, and her first act was to confirm that the squat warty creature was still there, and meet his insistent yellow stare. She began to appreciate the subtle variations of tone on his mottled back. Her life was different now she knew he would be waiting in the hut at the end of each day. She had no idea how he fed himself. The first few evenings she had brought back some soup in an old bowl and put it down in front of him, but the food remained untouched. She supposed that the toad went outside to drink water and catch flies or whatever else toads eat while she was down at the harbour.

She had sewn the final overlapping row of scales, knotted and bitten off the last length of thread, and held the garment out for them both to admire. The toad seemed to examine it with great interest. Ann thought she might faint from excitement. She moved closer and lifted the shirt high above his head, while she imagined a handsome young man uncoiling from the ungainly body and rising up to meet the garment in mid-air as it settled onto his wide, smooth shoulders. But in the instant between her letting-go of the garment and its collapse onto the dirt floor, the toad hopped away into the furthest corner.

She picked up the shirt and shook the creases out. Some of the scales had been bent to one side and a few had fallen off, but it still looked extraordinary— glinting like metal and yet as delicate as soap bubbles. 'Don't hop away, dear prince,' she murmured, carefully taking the shirt by the seam of each shoulder and raising it above him once more. He had already flexed his back legs in preparation for a leap before she moved, so the shirt did not fall onto the ground again. 'Toad, toad, don't you want to be a prince?' she asked, half laughing with vexation. The toad remained as silent as ever.

After several more attempts at investiture and spell-breaking, Ann had to accept either that her prince preferred to remain a toad, or else was and never had been anything except a simple natural creature. She opened the door and the toad hopped out and disappeared into the darkness. She held the shirt up in front of her own eyes and regarded it ruefully.

She was the one who had been enchanted, in thrall. The shirt was beautiful. She remembered that there had only been enough sacking to make a small one and that it should certainly fit. She pulled it over her head and walked through the open door. Perhaps she had felt a comparable joy and freedom years before, but this seemed quite unlike anything she could recall. The fishwives and the fishermen were drinking and laughing on the quay. She smiled and they smiled back and waved as she strode past. Quite soon she came to a broad highway behind the rise of the land. A silvery car, reflecting the moonlight like the fish scales on her shirt, stood waiting—door unlocked, key inside. She sat down behind the wheel and drove south.

RADIANT HEAT
Robert Drewe

MY MOTHER HEARD it on the radio. They found the boy's body at 4.30 when they were packing up the picnic things, in a metre of water where the bottom of the lagoon shelved suddenly. In the panic it took them twenty minutes to think of counting heads. Then they discovered that another little boy was missing.

The second underwater search in thirty minutes. One child drowned, then another. It's too affecting a beginning, too much to accept. I feel uncomfortable ordering it so definitely. Wise after the event as usual. Full of selective certainties. But I know the second boy was a year younger than the first. Aged six. Lawrence

Barker. I forget the first boy's name but obviously I remember Lawrence's. The compounded tragedy, the coincidences of the same name, age and place—Big Heron Lagoon—even their attending the same holiday child-care centre, saw to that. And my mother's reaction when she heard the news.

I'd told her that it was Peter's and Jenna's week with me. I know I'd said they were staying with Lucy and me down at the coast. They were not with Ellen, not spending their holidays at the child-care centre as usual, they were with me. (Somehow my mother's generation has trouble linking the ideas of 'father' and 'children'.) And 'Lawrence' hardly sounds like 'Peter'. But in the drama of a news bulletin enough connections could be made. I could see her making the leaps of imagination and despair. She knew we'd borrowed a friend's cottage at Bundeena, and Bundeena abuts the Royal National Park where the boys had died. So she had plenty to go on. For a long half-hour she was convinced that her grandson had drowned at a badly supervised children's picnic. When she finally reached me on the phone, I had to repeat to her, 'Mother, I can see Peter from here. He's watching "Inspector Gadget". I'll call him to the phone if you like.'

I never called her Mother but I was terse with her. She didn't believe me. She was babbling. Actually, my hand was trembling on the phone. I felt stunned. Peter was sitting crosslegged on the floor in his pyjamas watching television, and yet this evening there was a drowned boy named Barker, aged six.

Another layer of coincidence was making my hands shake. Only the day before, Lucy and I had taken the kids into the park for a picnic by the same lagoon. While my mother sighed and tutted I was replaying the day in my mind like a film, and recalling every frame. I remembered exactly the way the bottom of the shallow lagoon fell away suddenly in the middle. The water was a quieter, creamier green where the fresh creek met the salty white sand of the ocean beach— where, in winter, the higher tides burst through into the lagoon. I could feel the sandy bottom falling away right then, shifting and oozing around my ankles, the cooler currents around my shins, and I kicked away from the water-filled silence. And while my mother gradually calmed down and I turned the conversation around to Christmas plans, it struck me that my supervision of the children had been less than total. Certainly I watched them while they played in the water, but I read a magazine at the same time. I felt warm and lazy. The sun was bright and heavy on my eyelids; I couldn't swear that I didn't close them once or twice. And when I eventually dived in, the water was so bracing after the thick air that I stretched out and swam for several minutes, around a bend and temporarily out of sight.

Frankly, at the time I knew the risk. It occurred

to me and I swam on. Worse, I anticipated *something*.

I looked at Peter and Jenna, absorbed by the cartoon, amusement flickering on their cheeks. I stared at them. Peter's hair was wet and spiky from his bath; a trickle ran down his neck behind his ear. Now and then he hummed the 'Inspector Gadget' theme. Despite his dead boy's particulars he moved, he spoke. I went over and stroked his head. To keep things fair, I reached over and patted Jenna's too. They didn't notice. A little later I began feeling guilty. Waves of guilt swept over me. But I couldn't dwell on the other parents, on what those families were doing right then. I could imagine, but I tried to put them out of my mind. And I succeeded. I was ruthless. I erased their anguish. I burned it out of the air.

Both my children are good swimmers now. That summer we had them coached, and they still train regularly. Swimming is Peter's only sporting interest. When adults ask his hobbies, he's apt to say, 'My hobby is imagination'. He's one of those sort of ten-year-olds. A sci-fi reader. A dreamy monster-lover. He moons through school classes but knows twenty ancient instruments of torture. He's a 'Dungeons and Dragons' buff. He likes those adventure books where the reader is the hero, and gets to decide which plot strand to follow. Already Peter wants to channel his fate, if only to choose the sword-fight with the skeleton ahead of the possible mauling by the werewolf.

Lucy and I moved to the coast ourselves last year, north rather than south, escaping from city real estate prices as much as other tensions. We bought a cottage at Springstone, a renovated weekender whose high position on Blackwall Hill we believed would compensate for its drawbacks. The views of the bay even made up for the mosquitoes and sandflies which rose from the reeds and mangrove flats at low tide and settled on the house. 'Citronella Heights,' I joked. Lucy is a member of the post-pesticide generation, an advocate of citronella oil as an insect repellent. Last summer we'd spray ourselves before drinks in the garden, before going to the beach, even—especially—before bed. The pungent citronella oil soaked into our clothes, sheets, furnishings, car upholstery. I didn't mind it; the fragrance was nostalgic. It brought back serene times, patchouli oil and incense and women in caftans. But everyone entering our house or car would ask, 'What *is* that smell?'

The children had no faith in citronella. They liked the way pesticides *annihilated* mosquitoes. One Saturday Peter woke with a badly bitten forehead and puffy eyelids. He was struck with awe and admiration for the face in the mirror ('I look like a halfling, a demi-human. I told you that stuff didn't work.'). But his ogre's demeanour had lapsed by bedtime. The first mosquito whine made him frantic. 'They're coming for me!' he yelled. We allowed him dispensation: he was permitted the old poison.

Destruction can be enjoyable, especially with right on your side. It's hard to put more than the broadest Buddhist case for the mosquito. A day I remember from last spring, the Monday of a holiday long-weekend: the arrow on the gauge outside town pointed to Extreme Fire Danger; in the way of city people I was heeding the warning and clearing the bush around the house. What I was doing was really more drastic than clearing. I was hacking into the lantana and scrub with the new Japanese brush-cutter. I was razing things flush to the earth. My blade screamed. Insects flew from the din and lizards scuttled in panic. In the trees above me, lines of kookaburras conspired patiently to swoop on newly exposed centipedes. I was righteous in my destruction: the lantana is an introduced pest, the centipede's bite is painful and poisonous, and so on. I stomped through the scrub wielding the cutter. Rock shards bounced off my heavy-plastic protective glasses, branches snapped underfoot. 'You look like "The Terminator",' Peter said. He approved. He was swinging a scythe. It was too big for him but he swung it anyway. The Grim Reaper, of course, and pleased to be him.

This was the month of unseasonal heat when people in shops and at bus stops first began talking about the Greenhouse Effect. Arsonists were lighting fires in the national parks, and an infestation of Bogong moths, blown by the north-westerlies, descended on the city and coast. The moths had become disoriented on their migration south from Queensland to the alpine country. They turned up in every building. They crawled into cupboards and kettles and shoes, into the luggage lockers in aircraft cabins and the more sinuous wind instruments of orchestras. They flew hundreds of miles out to sea before dropping in the waves. Some made it to New Zealand. Cats and dogs got fat and bored with eating them. (They were big and calorific; on windscreens they splattered into yellow grease.) Everyone had moths, and those places where bottlebrush trees were flowering for spring—the moths' favourite food was bottlebrush nectar—had a hundred times more.

In the hot wind the moths rose in a flurry from our bottlebrushes and showered red pollen on my son's head. Lucy and Jenna had left us to our mayhem. We cut and slashed and raked, but eventually stopped to have a drink. Peter was still charged with an edgy friskiness. While I drank a beer he entertained me with his repertoire of murderous noises and death scenes. He mimed axes in skulls and arrows in throats. He did blow-pipes and bazookas. He lurched about with his red-tinged hair, grunting and gurgling. He switched roles from killer to victim. Bullets ricocheted off rocks, scimitars flashed. He could crumple to the ground a dozen ways, holding his entrails in.

The air on our hill was yellow and smoky. Against the blurry horizon he filled me in on monsters. His favourites were the Undead—zombies, ghouls, wights, wraiths, mummies and skeletons. 'They're *chaotic*,' he said. What he liked about them, and gave him the creeps, was their potential for anarchy. Their evil was disorderly. Despite his patient explanations he lost me after that. The bushfires were on my mind and 'Dungeons and Dragons' is a complex game. But I've flipped through his guidebook, wondering at the attraction. 'A wraith looks like a shadow which flies, and *drains levels* as a wight. A mummy does not drain levels.' I'm none the wiser. I notice they all seem impervious to heroics. 'Ghouls are immune to *sleep and charm spells*. They are hideous beast-like humans who will attack any living thing. Any hit from a ghoul will paralyze any creature of ogre-size or smaller (except elves) . . .'

I knew zombies from those comedy-duo films of the fifties where they chased Abbott and Costello and Martin and Lewis. I knew Malcolm Rydge. This is an easy joke now that I can safely glance out of restaurant windows and not catch him looking in. I can walk the streets and not see him jog past, averting his eyes. I can leave my house suddenly without his car accelerating away. I can return the children to my old house, to Ellen, and not hear his excitable gabble in the kitchen, my name ringing in the air, the abrupt hush, the scramble for the back door.

There was finally a moment, a Friday lunch, when

I looked down from the New Hellas, randomly, between mouthfuls of souvlakia, into Elizabeth Street. Malcolm was standing across the road in Hyde Park staring up at my window seat, my regular table. Our eyes met and held this time, in some sort of recognition. There is always someone who thinks you know the secret. Any secret. The secret of knowing Ellen first. The secret of the window table. Ellen had just thrown him out, he told me on my way out. He was waiting for me. It occurred to me later that he could have had a gun, a knife, in that shoulder bag he always wore. He slipped up in his running shoes and shook my hand as if he liked me. His eyes were distracted. His skin was damp and flickery. She had someone else. The voodoo was over, at least for me.

Lucy doesn't scoff at unquiet spirits. Ellen shuts them all out. She drops the portcullis. Her father went for a walk after lunch when she was twelve and never came back. From the veranda she saw him disappear into the treeline, swinging his stick and eating a Granny Smith apple. No-one ever found anything. Before it was called Alzheimer's Disease, my mother's mother was always trudging into town to hand in her own belongings to the police. 'I found this handbag in Myer's,' she would say. 'Some lass *will* be in a state.' She basked in her honesty as the cops drove her home again. My mother used to examine her own behaviour for early signs. Now that she doesn't any longer, I do.

Is it a sign that she gets younger every year? That since her sixtieth birthday she's been in reverse gear, hurrying backwards from the end? In the nine years since, she's shed twelve—lopping them off like old branches. Soon she'll pass me coming the other way. And this fifty-seven-year-old Elizabeth (who must have given birth to me at fourteen!) has lately turned into Bettina, having arrived there via Betty and Beth. Doesn't she remember the big party, the guests, the witnesses to her turning sixty? That I gave a speech? That we made a fuss of her? 'What's up with Bet?' her old friends wonder. What can I say? Her old friends look seventy. 'Bettina' looks, well, a cagey fifty-eight. She began getting younger in the 1970s with everyone else. In the 1980s, when everyone else started ageing again, she wilfully stayed behind. Is this a sign? The chin lift? The capped teeth? The bag removals? Lots of purple and gold? Sudden yellow hair? Leopard-skin materials? 'Ocelot,' she says firmly. 'Not leopard, ocelot.' What's the difference? It's not as if it's real skin, animal fur. It's only fabric, cotton blend stretch or something. 'It's what leopard skin *stands for*,' my North Shore sister grumbles. 'She's no chicken.'

Why does Penny always bring our father into it, even into the question of the ocelot-print stretch pants, even nine years later? Because our mother began getting younger as soon as he died? Well, she looked old for a month or two, for appearances' sake, then she started going backwards. 'I just know what Dad would say,' Penny says. But she never says what he'd say ('I'd prefer not to see those pants on you, Betty.') 'Maybe he'll let us know,' I could say to Penny. In one of his posthumous letters with the yellow stamps shaped like bananas and a Tonga postmark.

That afternoon the wind carried the sound of fire sirens from the expressway to the coast. They closed the expressway to traffic when the fire jumped the six lanes and surged eastward. From our hill the western sky was a thick bruised cloud fading to yellow. The eucalypts around the house suddenly began to peel. The hot winds had dried and cracked their bark and given the trees a strange mottled look, as if they'd pulled on camouflage uniforms. Now the bloodwoods and peppermints and angophoras were peeling and shedding fast in the wind, dropping sheets of bark all around us, changing their colour and shape before our eyes. Some trees revealed themselves as orange, others were pink, yellow, even purple underneath. All of them seemed moist and vulnerable, membrane instead of wood. They looked as if they'd shiver if you touched them.

All the bushfire-warning literature talks about 'radiant heat'. I'd read that radiant heat was the killer factor in bushfires and I wondered if the trees peeling was some sensitive early-warning system, an early stage of radiant heat. People can't survive more than a few kilowatts of radiant heat touching them. I read that to stand in front of a fire only sixty metres wide was like being exposed to the entire electrical output of the State of Victoria at peak load. Every single metre of this sixty metres beams out the heat of thirty-three thousand household radiators! And now it seemed to be getting hotter even as the sun got lower.

Wary of Peter's vivid imagination, I kept quiet about radiant heat. With the growing clouds of smoke, the trees changing, his eyes were already skittish. 'What holiday is it supposed to be today?' he asked me. Labor Day? I couldn't remember. On rare days things come together: heat, a moth plague, fires, crowds of people. When random factors combine you anticipate more things happening. The drowning tragedy on the news. Maybe the arrival of a letter, mailed from some dozy South Pacific port six months before, from a father five months dead. ('I think the cruise has done me the world of good.') Peter made poison darts fizz through the air, *phht, phht, phht*. 'Let's get out of here,' he said.

In Australia people always run to the coast. Maybe the myth of the bush is a myth. In the car we had less than a kilometre to travel. The heat and the closed windows had activated the citronella oil in the upholstery. It felt like breathing citronella into one lung and smoke into the other.

At the beach we found Lucy and Jenna in the crowd by the rock pool. Everyone seemed to have the same idea. People brushed away moths as they laughed nervously about the smoky wind. Dead moths littered the high-tide line, moths and bluebottles that had been washed ashore. The bluebottles' floats, electric-blue and still full of air, were sharp and erect as puppies' penises. There was a rotting smell from a pile of dead shags. The force of the westerly had flattened the surf; the waves were low and snapping and plumes of spindrift shot away from the beach. People had put up windbreaks and lounged behind them, facing the sea and drinking beer. One group was drinking champagne and giggling.

'What's that red stuff in Peter's hair?' Jenna said.

'Pollen,' I said. 'From the moths.'

'It'll wash off in the sea,' Lucy said.

At sunset the wind dropped suddenly and by the time we needed to leave for the city the expressway was open again. It was early evening. Jenna and Peter had to return to school the next day, back to Ellen's. I was sorry the expressway had reopened. It would have been an excuse to keep them for a while. Maybe they'd have been stuck with me for days, with the road closed, the lines down. We would have been safe enough. We could always run into the sea.

Lucy kissed us goodbye. The narrow road out of

Springstone was clogged with cars, everyone leaving at the same time. On the approach to the expressway the service stations all had fire trucks pulled into the back. Dirty fire-fighters slumped around the trucks, drinking from cans. One man was sitting on the ground trickling water from a hose over his head.

I pulled into the Shell station and filled the tank. I went inside and paid, and bought the kids some drinks. When I came out I noticed how badly the smoky wind and squashed moths had smeared the windscreen. I began to clean it. Just then a small Nissan truck came in fast and braked hard next to our car. A man in his late twenties jumped out of the driver's seat a few metres from me and headed around to the passenger side where a woman was screaming.

The woman was holding a boy of three or four on her lap. She was screaming in his face. 'You're going to die! Do you hear me? Die! Die!'

For a moment the man stood indecisively at the woman's window. He had wavy blond hair and he ran his hands through it and muttered something to the woman, something mild and self-conscious in tone, but she continued to scream at the child that he was going to die. The child looked stunned, as if he had just woken. I was standing there transfixed, with the squeegee in one hand and a wiper blade in the other. The man saw me looking and gave a wink. He took a couple of steps in my direction. 'Sorry, mate,' he said.

I didn't say anything. Through the windscreen I saw Peter's and Jenna's faces staring at the truck cabin. They both had shocked, embarrassed smiles. The man turned to go into the service station office, but the woman began screaming louder and hurling obscenities and he turned back to the truck.

It was no place to be. I was hurrying to finish the windscreen, but—isn't it always the way?—those splattered moths were stuck fast. I seemed to be working in slow motion. Although I was making brisk, fussy dabs at the glass nothing much was improving. I had a sudden inkling the woman was doing something cruel to the boy that the man and I couldn't see. She was dark-haired, dark-eyed, the man's age or a bit older, and the wide spaces between her front teeth showed when she screamed. The boy had her looks and colouring. It's odd hearing a woman calling a man a cunt, over and over. Peter and Jenna weren't smiling any more. Jenna was pale and cupped her hands over her ears. She was near tears, whereas Peter's expression was confused and distant. He looked straight ahead, blinked, tried a silly scowl. His face was off-centre.

'Die, die die!' the woman screamed again, and began to smack the little boy's face. He started to scream, too. The reaction of the blond man to her onslaught was so mild and understated as he leaned in the cabin window that two thoughts struck me: *that's not his child* and *what did he do or say to her just before this?*

'Please don't do that, you're hurting him,' he said as she continued to hit the boy's face. 'You're making him cry.'

I wanted the man to do something. I wanted him to stop shuffling on the driveway and take over. Do whatever's necessary, I willed him. Get tough with her. By now other motorists were pulling in and staring across at the disruption as they filled their tanks. Two teenagers sauntered past, snickering. I could see the lone service station employee peering out from behind the cash register. There was just enough room in the truck cabin for the woman to swing at the boy while she was holding him on her lap, and she began to punch his head.

'Hey!' I yelled. As if he'd been waiting for a complaint from the general public, the man leaned through the window and tried to grab her arm. She hit him with a flurry of punches, and her screeches and abuse rose in pitch. The boy screamed higher. The man stepped back from the truck and ran his fingers through his hair. 'I'm going for those cigarettes,' he announced, and walked inside the service station.

The woman stopped yelling and began rocking the boy on her lap. She stroked his cheeks, murmuring to him, and pulled his head down on her chest. Gradually, he stopped crying. I put the bucket and squeegee back beside the pumps. As I got back in the car she looked up and shot me a defiant glance. She was still glaring at me, muttering something, as we drove off.

Neither the children nor I said anything. My stomach felt queasy. While I was trying to think of something to say my stomach was turning over. Suddenly I couldn't bear the sickly smell of citronella in the car, the way the air-conditioner re-circulated and revived it. I opened my window to get some air. 'Open your windows,' I said. The smell of fire immediately came into the car. Little specks of ash floated in. Trees were smouldering on both sides of the expressway. Even the grass on the median strip was charred and off to the left flames glowed in a gully.

'Look down there!' I said. I was enthusiastic. I welcomed the diversion of the fire. 'It burned right through here, jumped the highway, and there it is now!'

'Wow,' said Peter, in a low voice. In the heavy traffic we were driving in the inside slow lane, well under the limit, peering out at the fire. The firemen had driven it up against a treeless sandstone ridge. It was fading fast without the wind behind it. But then light burst beside us and there was a roar. For an instant I thought *fire!* but it was the Nissan truck accelerating past us on the inside, on the narrow asphalt shoulder, showering us with loose stones. I saw the three profiles as they passed: the man driving with a cigarette in his mouth, the woman with the boy on her knees. The truck swung back on to the road, swerved around three or four other cars, shot into the outside lane and out of sight.

After I took the children home I drove to my mother's flat. Sometimes I stay overnight with her and head back to the coast first thing in the morning. She has a spare bedroom I've been using for emergencies ever since she moved into the flat after Dad died. I was there for a month when Ellen and I broke up. It was after eleven when I got there this time. I was so drained I could hardly think.

She was in her red tracksuit and gold slippers eating toast. She had face cream on her forehead and cheeks. 'Oh, dear,' she said when she saw me. She extracted a tissue from her tracksuit pocket and wiped her face. 'How are you, dear?'

I quickly said I was fine. Often these days she asks me questions and doesn't listen to the answers. I've just begun to answer and she's on to another question. Sometimes I have to say, 'Do you want to hear this or not? It's all the same to me. I'm just answering you.'

'I'm fine, Mum,' I said. 'I just need a brandy and I'll be fine.' I poured us both a drink and carried them into the living room. It's a small room; I sat next to her on the sofa. 'I was thinking of you watching the news,' I said. 'I hoped you wouldn't worry. The fires didn't get near us. Anyway, Peter and I cleared away all the scrub. No need to worry about fires reaching us.'

'What fires?' she said. 'I've been out. I went to see that Meryl Streep film. I thought she looked a bit horsey.'

190

'You always say she looks horsey!' I said. 'She's gorgeous. What do you mean, anyway, horsey?'

'You know, angular. Aquiline features or whatever they are. Equine.'

'Meryl Streep's beautiful! Can't you see that? She's the best film actress in the world.'

'Well, she's not my cup of tea,' my mother said. 'She was playing a booze artist, some Skid Row type.' She sipped her drink daintily. She still drinks alcohol in company like a guilty teenager, as if she's new to it, but there are always a couple of empty Remy Martin bottles when I take her garbage out.

'She was *acting*, Mum.'

'What's this about fires?' she said.

'It doesn't matter.' I took a big sip of brandy and swallowed it. 'The whole central coast nearly went up in flames. But it's under control now.'

'Oh, dear,' she said.

'It was weird. All our trees were cracking and peeling. Hot ash was flying everywhere. We escaped to the beach.'

'You must be careful, living up there.' She got up frowning and padded into the kitchen to make me more toast. 'It's the smoke you die from, not the flames,' she said.

'It's the radiant heat,' I said.

I could hear her out in the kitchen muttering something about smoke. 'Don't worry,' I called out.

She was making familiar kitchen noises. I listened for
her tutting sound, the anxious clicks her tongue made
on her teeth when she did things for us. Things would
come back to her: events, feelings, memories as
organised as snapshots. When she brought me the toast
she would lightly touch me on my head or shoulder.
A little pat or squeeze. I was a war baby. He was
away fighting in the Solomons. For two years it was
just me and her. I sank back into the sofa and called
out again, 'You really don't need to worry!'

UNNAMED ISLANDS IN THE UNKNOWN SEA

Keri Hulme

[*The Contents:*

damned dear. In the last crazy hours before you died, I saw sights through your eyes, sealions tombstoning, albatrosses with weary hearts, eggs with pink yolks. Now I am myself alone again, I must balance what I saw with what I know surrounds me. This reality before the next.

1: the overhang. It juts like the prow of any ship but is massive. It broods over me. One day it will fall but I do not fear that. It has anciently hung here—

remember the bones? Moa you said, and I believe that. They were old old bones, so old the rats hadn't bothered them.

2: the pile of seaweed at the left end. I have rewoven it, more tightly. It makes a ragged screen.

3: your sleeping bag. I washed it, beat it against the rock until all your sweated pain & foulness fled. It is nearly dry. I have rolled it, so it serves me as a backrest. I am undecided whether to sleep in it tonight. I think I might.

4: the rocky floor. It slopes towards the sea. Did it never strike you as odd? The roof rears heavenward and all our floor tries to slip away from us, downwards, outwards, away.

5: the fire—o yes. I haven't let it go out. Even if I go swimming, I want it there to look back to. I feed it dried kelp butts, and twigs from the mikkimik and detritus from the moon, feathers and sundried bladders and a piece of polystyrene float.

6: twelve mussels in their shells. They are placed in an arc by my feet. They make small popping and hissing sounds, as though they had minute mouths that cared to suck air. Kissing sounds. They are tea.

Then there is me clad in my despair & wet clothes; my raw feet; your weatherbeaten seabattered notebook. My notebook. My pen. I hope to God it doesn't run out.

(As you were ultimately your last clear analytic words, so I shall be these pages. And maybe they will be found by someone who doesn't understand, who doesn't read English even, or just can't be bothered reading such stained and faded script, and so burns them. As I burned those poor brown remnants of moa, which had maybe stored all the song of its living in those bones. Did moas sing?)

I have eaten the mussels. Thin meat, mussels. Even the peacrabs don't add much more than crunch. And I used to love them, mussels succulent on a scrubbed shining navy shell, topped with garlic butter or richly robed in melted cheese—

Better to remember Day 2, my feet already butchered by those bloody rocks, and me despairing because you couldn't keep the mussels or limpets down and that was all I could gather. And suddenly the waves flung a fish on the beach. It flopped weakly, one flank deeply gashed—a couta you said. I managed to hit it on the head—indeed hit with a savagery I didn't know inhabited me.

Cooking mussels and limpets had been easy— arrange them carefully in the embers and let them toast. But that red cod? Easy, you said. You sounded very tired, and you were huddled over. That seaweed, that bullkelp? Get some thickish fronds off it and split them and stick the cod inside. Never mind the guts.

You kept down the soft flesh. But it wasn't enough.

Maybe it worsened matters.

I can't remember the order of days after Day 2. It could be as long as 9 days I've been here.

Sometimes during the nights—10? 8?—sometimes during the nights we saw lights far out at sea. Distant ships perhaps, though some grew at a strangely fast rate and others stayed abnormally steady, beacons through the night, winking out at dawn. *We* saw lights? The only time you showed awareness of any of them was that night the waves danced, alive with phosphorescence. Porotitiwai, you whispered, porotitiwai, and I never thought to ask you what that means.

Do you know I have always been scared of the sea? Don't laugh. It is remorseless. There is no humanity in it.

You would have laughed at that.

I am cold and smoked and damp and so alone that I feel all the rest of the world has deliberately gone home, leaving me in the dark. I miss your laughter. O God I miss the way your arms felt either side of me as you paddled. A jaunt you said. Only thirty *k* to that island, and look at the sea. Flat as a pancake. I can get us there and back between dawn and dusk, hell I've paddled Cook Strait! And to my demur you said Think! No-one's set foot on that island for bloody years! Now that's a story! And then added, your eyes full of a wicked glinting glee, That's if you came to get a story and not just see me.

I said very primly that I Am A Journalist Albeit Freelance, and a story was what I came for, and writing about scruffy field assistants cutting transects won't sell *anywhere*, so lead on MacDuff. McLeay actually, you said. From the whisky actually.

This is pointless. The rats'll eat it.

Who's going to come looking for a freelance peripatetic journo?

I don't want to say what bottle I have sent out on the waves—

I used to love reading about islands as a child. Being shipwrecked on one would be heaven. You'd use the materials from your wrecked ship, and feast on the island's provender, and finally when it was getting a little boring, you'd light an enormous bonfire which would hail a passing cruise ship and you'd sail happily home a better and richer man.

God knows when I heard the plane I tried. I grabbed anything I thought would burn and a piece of smouldering kelp and rushed out on the halfmoon of gravel that is the only beach. And the drizzle made everything sodden. The fire was only smoke and a few sullen flickers of flame. Desperate—o how *weak* that reads!—*desperate!* I would have burnt my hair had it been longer, I would have fed my clothes to those flames if they hadn't been wetter than the driftwood! I raced back under the overhang and grabbed my sleeping bag and folded it round the smoulder. I prayed. My feet ached so much from the running I cried. The plane droned away and as it got further and further towards the horizon the sleeping bag suddenly flared into a glorious bonfire. Nobody saw it. Just me.

It has been silent since then, if anywhere near the sea is silent. There were silences before. You would say something, mainly a coherent few sentences—

'Do you know they shake penguins out of their skins before they eat them? Catch them underwater and surface with them and shake 'em so viciously quick that the bird flies out of its skin. Then the leopard seal dines.'

Up until these few days ago I had never *heard* of a leopard seal.

I wanted to ask more but you had closed your eyes and there was another silence that lasted all night.

The days are silent too, mainly. At least, the first few—3? 4?—days. Your belly blackens. The haematoma spreads up to your collar-bones. You bleed to death inside but it all takes silent time. At least, mainly silent.

You start to curl up, going from sitting-up huddle, to lying-down hunch. And as you curl slowly into your beginning shape, you want me to see some other island. You talk against the unremitting pain.

It was a harsh place, this island you loved. A bleak volcanic terrain, sere and disordered. Some subantarctic place where the waters teemed with white pointers and the winds never ceased.

There was mist around our island, closing the world down to just our size.

It was either cliff or swamp, you said, but we had hardwood-plant tracks and so could walk through the headhigh tussock. We could walk past the peat bogs. But if you went off the planks you got quickly lost in the draco . . . and you'd come to a cairn where there was maybe a body underneath, as though the cairn called you. Or arrive at a still inland tarn and there, deep in the water, was an unrusting tripot. We'd been there, people had been there, lots of people, but the land felt *unlived on* and somehow, it wanted people living on it, people as well as the elephant seals and the sealions and the skuas and the albatross.

This Godforsaken rock, *this* island is lived on. It doesn't want us. It already has rats and shags and the mikkimik. The rats live on the shags and each other I think. Presumably the shags live off the sea. They aren't nesting at the moment. The adult birds shuffle but they shuffle faster than I can limp. And the guano burns my feet horribly.

You said weakly, The wind is in my ears.

It is so still outside. The mist hides even the sea.

There is always the wind you say, and nearly always the rain or the snow. 90 knot winds . . . I used to worry about the birds. And how did the cattle stand it? That small shotabout fearful herd—did they crouch into the gullies, die finally in the peaty bogs?

It was then your breathing changed.

Between gasps you say, 'Sometimes there is an unnatural quiet, a threatening calm, as the wind holds still for an hour, deciding its next quarter.'

O God he can't have spoken like that. It got hard. The blood on his lungs. I can do nothing, could do nothing. Collect limpets and mussels and stew the juice out of them and have it ready in the thermos flask so when he is ready he can sup soup. The mist pools on the rocks. We have water. The mist makes it hard to breathe. My own lungs are husking.

But your lungs are heaving in and out harnh harnh every hard intake, the sound pitching higher and higher until you are screaming—

I stay outside for the screaming—

remember thinking, But I screamed too. I screamed, What was it? What *was* it? We lay in a tangle a crush in the froth on shore. You had just laughed and pulled the right side of the paddle down hard. 'Landing!' you yelled. And then the sea lurched. Something sleek and bulky and sinuous, a grey fast violent hulk punched into the kayak punched past me into you fled past us into the onshore surf. I screamed What *was* it? until you had caught your breath. You grunted, 'Leopard seal. Wanted to get out to sea. We were in the way.' You grinned. Your last grin. 'We probably scared it to hell.'

None of the kayak has washed ashore.

I can do nothing now. I fold myself beside you and hold your hand. You say, the screaming finished, the breathing nearly finished, you say in that tired hoarse whisper,

'At new moons there are bigger currents than normal. Huge shoals of fish are swept close inshore. The sharks feed hard. Sometimes they will get in amongst a group of Hooker sealions that are also feeding hard. And then you will see the sealions tombstone— bodies rigid in the water, heads sticking straight out, while the white pointers circle and threaten and crazily decide whether to take one or to take all. They can't take all. Islands don't work like that.'

And somehow I am behind your eyes and I see the cliffs that arrow out of the grey seas to terminate in mean blade edges. I see the sheep, feral Drysdales gone surefooted like goats, gaze fearlessly down on climbing humans. I see the albatross effortfully trudge over a ridge down to the hollow where its chick roosts safely out of the wind. I see it feed the chick. I see a skua pluck a pink-yolked penguin's egg and then hungrily cruise on. I see it take the albatross's chick, a limpnecked vulnerable downy sac. I see the albatross halfway down the ridge, watch; then turn and stagger back up to the top of the ridge and launch into the wind.

And then suddenly the shags outside wave their snaky necks and shoot stinking excrement onto the rocks.

And there is no-one behind your eyes.

But you did say, watching the sad lumbering albatross, you did say, because I heard you there behind your eyes,

'Don't be afraid. We are all islands but the sea connects us, everyone. Swim.'

And I had enough heart and mind left to laugh at a swimming island as you died.

I gave you to the sea. I rolled you down the sloping floor onto a quartermoon of gravel and let the sea take you. The waves toyed with your beautiful black hair, the waves toyed with your scarred strong hands. Then they too rolled you over and swam you out of sight.

I have given my message to the sea, my bottle, my message.

It is unbearable.]

[*The Notebook from the Unnamed Island off Breaksea Sound:*

It is a standard field notebook, issue item 1065, 18 cm × 13 cm, black elastic closure band, 46 double pages lined each side, and divided by a midpage column, with red, waterstained, covers. The standard issue pen is missing from the side holder. The last 10 pages, and the first 2 pages, have been torn out.

The notebook was found inside a plastic sandwich container (Tupperware, item CT 106), which had been wrapped in a light down sleeping bag ('Camper,' manufactured by Arthur Ellis, Dunedin). The sleeping bag, which had been extensively damaged by rats, was found tucked in the far corner on the overhang described in 'Contents'.

There was no other sign of human intervention or habitation on the island.]

[*Conclusion:*

Many people have speculated on the identity of the writer of this notebook since its recovery by two crew members from the fishing boat 'Motu' (Dunedin registration 147 DN). The unnamed 'you' may be Jacob Morehu, a field assistant employed by the DSIR on Resolution Island during the recent blue penguin (Eudyptula minor) counts. Two possible indicators for this identification are:

Morehu was employed during the '84 season on Campbell Island (by the DSIR), and

Morehu disappeared shortly before the now-infamous Skinned Body corpse was discovered at Goose Cove. (Morehu is not implicated. He was an ardent kayak enthusiast, and his kayak vanished at the same time. The area round Breaksea Island is marked 'reputed dangerous' on all charts, and this pertains to the unnamed small island beyond.)

However, it is much more probable the notebook is an obscure joke perpetrated by a person or persons unknown. The indicators for this conclusion, which is that of the Department, are:

a] *nobody else* was reported missing from the *entire South Island* at the time Morehu went missing;

b] the 'Skinned Body' was almost certainly murder, and is thought to have been committed by the eccentric gunship shooter, Mike Corely, who fell into the notorious giant eel tarn in Fiordland National Park two days before the body was discovered;

c] nobody has explained satisfactorily to me why two sleeping bags should be taken on what is described as a *day-trip* in a kayak. A plastic container of sandwiches, yes, but two light sleeping bags suitable only for indoor use?]

GETTING READY

Barry Hannah

HE WAS FORTY-EIGHT, a fisherman, and he had never caught a significant fish. He had spent a fortune, enough for two men and wives, and he had been everywhere after the big one, the lunker, the fish bigger than he was. His name was Roger Laird, better off than his brother, who went by the nickname 'Poot.'

Everywhere. Acapulco, Australia, Hawaii, the Keys. Others caught them yesterday and the weather was bad today and they were out of the right bait. Besides, the captain was sick and the first mate was some little jerk in a Def Leppard tee shirt who pulled in the big grouper that Roger hung because Roger was almost pulled overboard. Then the first mate brought some filets packed in ice to Roger's motel door because Roger was ill with sunburn and still seasick.

Roger had been paying money all day for everything and so when he went to bed, ill, he inserted a quarter for the Magic Fingers.

Something went wrong.

The bed tossed around worse than the boat in four feet of waves.

There was vomit all over the room and when Roger woke up, hearing the knock on the door, he opened the ice chest and looked at the big grouper filets and before he could do anything about it, he threw up on the fish, too, reeling blindly and full of bile back to the bed, which was still on, bucking. His wife was still asleep—but when she heard the new retching sounds from Roger, him trying to lie down, she thought something amorous was up and would have gone for him except for the filthy smell he had.

She crawled away.

Mrs Reba Laird was a fine woman from Georgia, with her body in trim. She had looked up the origin of the Laird name. In Scots, it means landholder. She knew there was an aristocratic past to her husband, for she herself had found out that her side of the family were thieves and murderers brought over by Oglethorpe to populate and suffer from the jungles of Georgia. She thought Roger was a wonderful lover when he wasn't fishing.

Roger eschewed freshwater fishing in Louisiana, where the Lairds lived now, except for the giant catfish in a river near the Texas border. He got a stout pole, a big hook, and let it down weighted with ocean lead and a large wounded shad. He had read all the fishing tips in *Field & Stream* and he knew those giants were down there because there were other men fishing right where he was with stiff rods and wounded live shad.

The man to Roger's right hooked into one and it was a tussle, tangling all the lines out—so Roger felt the mother down there, all right.

When they got the fish out, by running a jeep in and hooking the line to the bumper, it was the weight of ninety pounds.

The jeep backed over Roger's brand-new fishing rod and snapped it into two pieces and ground his fishing reel into the deep muck. Roger saw the fish and watched them wrench it up, hanging from the back bar of the jeep. He was amazed and excited—but the fish was not his. Still, he photographed it with his Polaroid. But when Roger added up the day, it had cost him close to three hundred dollars for a Polaroid picture.

The thing about it was that Roger was not dumb. He was handsome, slender, gray at the temples, with his forehair receding to reveal an intelligent cranium, nicely shaped like that of a tanned, professional fisherman.

Roger watched the Southern teevee shows about

fishing—Bill Dance, others—and he had read the old Jason Lucas books, wherein Lucas claims he can catch fish under any conditions, even chopping holes in the ice in Wisconsin at a chill degree of minus fifty and taking his limit in walleye and muskie. Also, Roger had read Izaak Walton, but he had no use for England and all that olden shit.

It was a big saltwater one he wanted, around the Gulf of Mexico where he lived. On the flats near Isamodorado, Roger had hung a big bonefish. However, he was alone and it dragged the skiff into some branches where there were several heavy cottonmouth moccasins.

He reached for the pistol in his kit. One of the snakes, with its mouth open, had fallen in the boat. Roger shot the stern floor out of the boat. As the boat sank, all his expensive gear in it, Roger Laird kept going down, reloading, firing at the trees, and when he went underwater he thought he saw the big bonefish under the water, which was later, as he recalled, a Florida gar. He could see underwater and could hold his breath underwater and was, withal, in good shape. But the .25 automatic shot underwater rather startled the ears, and the bullet went out in slow motion like a lead pellet thrown left-handed by a sissy. So Roger waded out of the water, still firing a few rounds to keep Nature away from him. Then got his wind back and dove in to recover his radio.

The Coast Guard came and got him.

Roger's father, Bill Laird, was a tender traveler of eighty years in his new Olds 98. Old Mr Laird found remarkable animals all over the land. Behind a service station in Bastrop, Louisiana, he saw a dog playing with a robin. The two of them were friends, canine and bird. They had been friends a long time. Grievously, one day the dog became too rough and killed the bird. The men at the service station were sort of in mourning. They stared at the nacreous eyes of the bird on the counter. The dog was under the counter, looking up sorrowfully at the corpse.

Nothing of this should have occurred.

Roger thought of his father, who had always loved animal life and was quite a scholar on the habits of anything on land that roved on four legs.

Well, where was Roger now?

Roger was at Mexico Beach, thirty miles south of Panama City. He was out of money and had brought only a Zebco 33 with a stiff fiberglass rod. He had no money for bait, and he was just helping pay some of the groceries for George and Anna Lois and their son and stepdaughter, who had a baby. The house was old and wooden, with a screen porch running around two sides; a splendid beach house owned by Slade West, a veteran of Normandy, who had once kept a pet lion there. The lion started chasing cars when the Florida boom hit, and he had to give it to a zoo.

At the moment, Roger was alone in the house. He

was looking out over the ocean at some crows. The crows hung around, although it was not their place. They fetched and quacked in the air and were rolled by sea breezes off the mark.

Somebody's dog from down the way came in and rolled privately in the sea oats. What a lark, all to himself, he was having! Feet in the air and twisting his back in the sand and the roots! But the heavy dangerous trucks going by were just feet from the dog. The dog was playing it very close.

Yesterday, Roger had caught a crab on his line that reminded him of himself. The crab was ageing well and, dumb as hell, was holding on till the very, very last, where Roger might drag him in out of the water if he wanted him. The crab was in the surf, clamped on the shrimp and hook, trying to prove something. While the crab was looking at Roger and deciding on the moment, the dog dashed into the water and tore the crab to pieces with its jaws.

Roger had never seen anything like this. Not only was Roger stunned, he had now caught a dog! So he ran down the beach lickety-split with a loose line— so the hook wouldn't hurt the dog's lips. Roger offered abject apologies, pulling the last ten from his wallet to pay the vet bill.

Next door to the house where Roger was staying was an ugly little brick house fenced in as if somebody would want to take something from it. The owner and occupant was a Mr Mintner, possibly a vampire. Roger had never seen Mr Mintner come out into the sun and all the plant signs around the house were dead and dry. Parked outside was a Harley Davidson golf cart, and at 11 p.m. three nights ago Roger had seen Mr Mintner crank up the golf cart and come back from the Minute Market with several bloody-looking steaks and beef bouillon cubes and some radishes. Roger saw all this in the dim outside light of Mr Mintner's. He saw Mr Mintner in a black golf outfit and black boots, and his arms were pale almost to luminescence. There was a story that his heart had been broken by a woman years ago and that he had never recovered.

Roger had a fascinated aversion to this Mintner and believed that he should be hauled away and made to eat with accountants.

Roger, with no financial resources at the time, cleaned up the house and read some of the *National Geographics* and *Discover* magazines around the place. He had brought along his fisherman's log, in which there was not one entry, only some notes on the last pages where it said NOTES.

He looked out at the green softly rolling ocean again. There were a lot of things out there in 'the big pond,' as McClane's *New Standard Fishing Encyclopedia* called the Gulf. There were things like marlin and sailfish and cobia/ling and bluefish. As for the little ocean catfish, Roger had caught his weight twenty times over of them.

They were trash and insignificant.

Today George and his son Steve were out casting in the surf and catching some small whiting. Roger waded into the water, feeling the warm wash over his sneakers, and then stood straddle legged, arms behind his back, rather like a taller Napoléon surveying an opposing infantry horde from an unexpected country of idiots.

Two-thirds of the world was water, wasn't it?

There were king mackerel out there, too, and big snapper. But Roger had no funds to hire a boat, and all his wonderful gear was back in Louisiana in his garage, every line coiled perfectly, every hook on every lure honed to surgical sharpness, every reel oiled and soundless. As for what Roger had here at Mexico Beach, it was the cheap Zebco with a light–medium-weight rod, the whole thing coming out of a plastic package from T G & Y at a price of twenty-four dollars—such a rig as you would buy a nephew on his eleventh birthday.

Roger's friend George Epworth was having a good time with his son Steve. They were up to their hips in water, casting away with shrimp on the hook. They caught a ground mullet, which Roger inspected. This kind of mullet is not the leaping vegetarian that is caught with a net only. Roger looked on with pursed lips. Then there were some croakers, who gave them a little tussle. It was a fine kid sport, with the surf breaking right around the armpits of the fellows. Steve's wife, Becky, had made a tent over their baby, and Anna Lois, newly a grandmother, was watching the baby and reading from one of Slade West's encyclopedias of sea life. George was a biochemist back at Millsaps College in Jackson. Anna Lois worked for the state crime lab, and their ocean time was precious. They liked *everything* out here and knew a good bit about sea chemistry. Roger envied them somewhat. But he had only a fever for the big one, the one to write home about, the one to stuff, varnish, and mount, whereas none of these fish were approaching a pound, though they were beautiful.

Roger was wondering what in the deuce was so *wrong* with him and his luck now.

Not just the fish.

Not just the fact that his Reba had gone a bit nuts when menopause came on her.

Not just the fact that she bought a new dress *every* day, and from high-priced boutiques, and that she stayed in the bathroom for an hour, making up—but that she emerged in earrings and hose and high heels only to sit on the couch and stare at the wall across from her. Not at a mirror, not at a picture, not at the television, not smoking anymore, not drinking, not reading—which she had loved—just sitting there with a little grieving smile on her face. She wasn't grouchy. She just sat, staring with the startling big gray eyes that had charmed

Roger to raving for her back in college days. They'd just had their twenty-fifth anniversary, Roger and Reba.

Further, his luck with money recently. Why, he'd had near a hundred-fifty thousand in the bank, and they were thinking about living on interest for the first time ever when *bang*, the offshore-drilling speculation in which they had the stock exploded and the money was gone.

It made Roger so tired he had not the energy to track down the reasons.

As for Nature, Roger was tiring, too. He had a weary alliance with Nature—the roses, the wisteria, and the cardinals and the orioles and the raccoons round the deck on the rear of his dutch-roofed little castle. But he was not charmed much now when he went out there and looked.

Were his senses shutting down? He who had never had to use even reading glasses and about whom everyone said he looked a decade younger than he was? At least?

Roger Laird was about to turn and go back to his room, shut the curtains, write in his fishing log *something* that might give him an idea as to what was wrong with him, when something happened out beyond the breakers.

He saw it roll, and he saw a fin of some kind stand up.

Then it rolled again!

A rising shower of small fish leapt up and the gulls hurried over, seconded by the crows, quacking but not knowing how to work the sea as the gulls did.

The big fin came up again!

Roger's eyes narrowed and the point of his vision met on the swirl of water as if on the wrong end of a pair of Zeisses. Given the swirl, the fish was seven to nine feet long at the smallest.

Roger looked slyly around to see if any of his friends, the Epworths, had noticed it. But they were otherwise occupied and had not.

Roger looked again, bending as if to find a nice conch shell like a lady tourist, and the thing rolled again!

The birds were snapping the moiling little minnows, the crows missing and having to move out heavy on the flap because of their sogged feathers.

Then there was no activity.

Roger walked back with the Epworths, helping to carry the bucket of fish they intended to roast over charcoal for lunch. The baby was put to bed. Steve and his wife lay on the divan watching the soap opera 'General Hospital.' The local weather and fishing report came on. The man with big spectacles said the weather was fine but the fishing was no good, apologizing to the world for the ocean this week.

After they had eaten the smoked fish and salad and the oysters Rockefeller, everybody was sleepy except

Roger—who pretended sleepiness and went to his room. It was a half hour he waited there, studying the Zebco outfit in the corner. Then you could hear nothing in the house, and he, despite himself, began making phony snoring noises.

Barefooted, he scooted to the kitchen and found the plastic bowl of bait shrimp. He eased the door to, not even the sound of a vacuum sucking on rubber. Then he put on his sneakers and, holding the Zebco unit, he slipped out into the driveway.

Roger was about halfway down the drive, aiming straight for the sea, when a loud voice from the little ugly red brick house horrified him.

'*You!*'

It was Mr Mintner, shouting from his window.

The pale man was holding the windowsill, speaking with his nose practically against the screen.

'Getting any?' shouted Mintner.

There was a horrifying derisive laugh, like rolling tin, and then the window came down with a smash, Mintner receding into the dark of the room. It was two in the afternoon and the house was totally unlit.

Roger was not certain that there had been a man at all. Perhaps it was just a voice giving body to something waxen and then vanishing.

He had never been a coward. But he was unsettled when he reached the sea. He had some trouble tying on the hook. It was not even a sea hook. It was a thin golden bass hook that came with the Zebco kit. He put the bell weight on and looked out, yearning at the blue-gray hole where the creature had shown.

There was not a bird in sight. There was no whirl and leaping of minnows. The water was as dead as a pond some bovine might be drinking from.

Roger stayed near the water—waiting, getting ready.

Then he cast—a nice long cast—easy with this much lead on the line, and the rig plumped down within a square yard of where he'd seen the fish.

He tightened the line and waited.

There was a tug but small and he knew it was a crab. He jerked the line back, cursing, and reeled in. The shrimp was gone. He looked in the plastic bowl and got the biggest shrimp there, peeled it, and ran it onto the hook, so that his bait looked like a succulent question mark almost to the geometry.

This time he threw long but badly, way over to one side.

It didn't matter.

He knew it didn't matter. He was just hoping that that crab-eating dog wouldn't show up, and he hadn't even tightened his line when it hit.

It was big and it was on.

He could not budge it, and he knew he'd snap the line if he tried.

He forgot how the drag worked. He forgot

everything. Everything went into a hot rapid glared picture, and he was yanked into the sea, past his knees, up to his waist, then floundering, swimming, struggling up.

Then he began running knee-deep and following the fish.

Jesus—oh, thank you, please, please, yes—holy Christ, it was coming toward him now! He reeled in rapidly. He had gone yards and yards down the beach.

It came on in. He could pull it in. It was coming. It was bending the rod double. But it was coming. He had it. Just not be dumb and lose it.

It surfaced. A sand shark. About four feet long and fifteen pounds. But Roger had never seen anything so lovely and satisfying. He grabbed the line and hauled it toward him, and there it was, white bellied and gray topped, and now he had it on the sand and it was *his*, looking like a smiling tender rocket from the deep, a fish so young, so handsome, so perfect for its business, and so unlucky.

By this time a crowd had gathered, and Roger was on his knees in the sand, sweating profusely and with his chest full of such good air it was like a gas of silver in him.

The crowd began saying things.

'I'll kill him with this flounder gig! Everybody stand back!' said one of the young men.

'Ooo! Ugg!' said a young somebody else.

George Epworth was on the beach by then.

'That was something. I watched you through the binoculars. That was something.' George Epworth knelt and watched the shark heaving away.

'Would you unhook him for me?' Roger Laird asked.

George Epworth reached down, cut the line, and pulled the hook out backward through the shank, leaving only a tiny hole.

A man who had been cutting up drift logs for a fire said, 'I'll do the honors. They're good to eat, you know.'

The man was raising his axe and waiting for Roger to move away.

'Not mine, you don't!' Roger screamed, and then he picked up the shark by the tail and threw it way out in the water. It turned over on its back and washed in as if dying for a few minutes, whereupon it flipped over and eased into the deep green.

When Roger Laird got back to Louisiana, he did not know what kind of story to tell. He only knew that his lungs were full of the exquisite silvery gas.

Reba Laird became better. They were bankrupt, had to sell the little castle with the dutch roof. She couldn't buy any more dresses or jewelry. But she smiled at Roger Laird. No more staring at the wall.

He sold all the fishing gear at a terrible loss, and they moved to Dallas, address unknown.

Then Roger Laird made an old-fashioned two-by-four pair of stilts eight feet high. It made him stand about twelve feet in the air. He would mount the stilts and walk into the big lake around which the rich people lived. The sailing boats would come around near him, big opulent three-riggers sleeping two families belowdecks, and Roger Laird would yell:

'Fuck you! Fuck you!'

THE WATER WAS DARK AND
IT WENT FOREVER DOWN
Tim Winton

THE GIRL LEFT her mother in the rented cottage with all the shades drawn and went down to the packed white sand of the beach. She passed the jetty with its whirling braid of gulls and followed the line of the bay. She was tall for her age, but years of training in the pool had taken lankiness from her. Her hair was cropped close. In the summer sun her big nose had gone scabby. She just wished her mother would put the bottles away, raise the blinds, and come outside into the world again, but the girl knew she had a better chance of making the Olympics than changing her mother.

Eight years ago, when the girl was six years old and her father had been gone a year, her mother had a terrible accident. Depressed and drunk, she passed out while smoking in bed and woke in flames. Her nylon nightie crackled and hissed. She beat herself out on the floor and threw a jug of water over the bed, but she did not call out to the girl across the hall. She sat shaking in the dark with a bottle of sherry until dawn when she phoned an ambulance. Because she waited, her scars were hideous. Years later, she told the girl she hadn't wanted to alarm her by shrieking and waking her in the middle of the night looking the way she did, like a charred side of beef. From that moment the girl was convinced that her mother was either stupid or sick.

Down the front of her bikini, the girl saw her tiny breasts and was grateful that her own body was unblemished. Even these days, the sight of her mother caused her teeth to clench. She kicked up a string of kelp and watched it settle back on the sand. This holiday was so boring. There was no one her age. Already she'd run out of books. It was no different to home.

Following the curve of the bay, she saw the small island offshore—low, rocky, spotted with vegetation— and she wondered how far out it was.

She knew her mother was sick and bitter and afraid. She just wished she could pull herself out of it, get a job, stay out of mental hospitals, save for some special surgery, find a man. God, to be *normal*!

All those stupid, recurring statements ran through her head. *'All a person needs is a bit of land,'* her mother would say, *'that's what makes the difference.'* *'Men hate us. They hate our bodies.'* *'God has been cruel to me.'* *'Your father never loved you.'* These came up during TV programmes, at meals; the girl heard them shouted in the night, heard them screeched from their sixth floor window as she slunk home from training. Over and over.

A hot breeze blew off the land, from where the colossal white backs of dunes humped at the edge of town, threatening the place with their shifting weight.

She's gonna send me crazy, she thought.

Every night after school, the girl trained in the swimming squad. It was three hours of blind, busting effort, away from home, and though she didn't love it the way the others did, she knew she couldn't be without it.

The girl stopped walking. It was stupid to walk, she knew. Walking made you think. What she needed was a swim; to be an engine.

By now the island was directly out from her. Crayboats passed it, their motors coming from weird directions in the wind.

An old man on a sailboard skimmed past with a ludicrous smile on his face. With a grunt, she ran to the water and speared into the channel and swam.

She had good style. Her breathing was metrical. She was tuned for it. She swam and thought the thoughts of a machine.

Out in the centre of the channel the water was dark and it went forever down. The island seemed no closer.

She moved all her parts. Everything did its task. She was not tired.

When the water suddenly became warmer, she knew she was there. Standing in the shallows, just out from a little sandy beach, she saw a cloud of birds and heard the blood chug in her ears.

'All a person needs is a bit of land,' she said aloud. She laughed and it wasn't all derision.

She stretched her arms. She noticed that she'd left her watch on. It had stopped. She guessed the swim had taken her fifteen minutes. The easterly was drying her already, leaving streaks of salt on her flesh.

The island was a bird sanctuary. There were signs and warnings. It wasn't a big island. Maybe ten hectares she guessed, or less. She climbed up from the beach and wandered across the island's humpbacked plateau. Seabirds filled the sky; they nested in holes in the ground and limestone nooks; they chased each other in territorial battles and shrieked from places unseen. On the packed sand, scrub and limestone monoliths offered little shelter. The tracks of birds peppered every soft surface. The whole place smelt birdy. On the seaward side surf creased across reefs, and small, sunken lagoons and potholes stood still and full. From the low cliff she could see fish down in the water with birds diving on them. Underfoot, wherever she went, broken eggshells mashed and blew. As she walked, a murmur grew and birds fled before her. One ran blindly from its hole and skidded off her shin. Thousands, thousands of black birds.

In their midst, in the centre of the island, the girl sat down to watch them soar and stitch about her. She wondered why they thrived so. She thought of Biol. class and tried to think. There seemed to be plenty of fish for them to eat. No predators that she could see—no sign of snakes. Just birds, and she didn't even know what kind. Hatching, growing, hunting, mating, dying. There was something relentlessly single-minded about the whole business.

After a time, she stood up and more birds rose with her, taking their atonal music with them. By her foot, she saw the carcase of a small bird. All over the island she found dead birds: whole, mutilated, broken. And shells and feathers. And shit. A constant layer of debris. She felt within the grasp of something important, something she might understand. From Biol. What did that skinny teacher with the tobacco breath call it? That was it—the web of life. She saw it all before her. The sick and the weak died and the young and the strong lived and thrived. It's the way things are, she thought. You need to just *go*, that was it; survive, win.

All you need is a bit of land . . . something solid under you. Ah, what rubbish, especially from her mother. Something solid, and there she was all day in the dark, drinking. A life of fluids. A whole ocean she must have drunk by now and she talked about *land*! Bird sanctuary for a lame duck. She was tired of fighting it all, always always swimming over the top of that sea of grog. Maybe that's why I started swimming, she thought, to stop her drowning me.

She went back down to the sandy beach and she took off her watch and bikini and lay in the sun. Her body was strong and hard. She was young. There was no more room, she decided, for feeling sorry for dead things and dying things and sick things; for her mother or even herself. Now there was only time to live, to survive. Live. Survive. They're the same thing, she told herself quickly. No difference.

She got up and saw that she had left her perfect shape in the sand, and then she cried out in triumph and ran naked down to the water and pierced it and began to swim.

Be an engine. Don't complain. Don't ask. Don't hesitate. Swim, don't think.

Pushing out, she knew that as soon as she was old enough she would leave her mother. There was no room. She had to look after herself, leave her mother to the web. There wasn't time enough anymore for all this swimming through craziness and ugliness and dumbness, sherry, beer, scotch, gin.

Be an engine.

But she faltered.

Don't think, breathe!

She moved her parts. Swimming machine.

Think.

No, you old bitch. I can swim.

She cut through the water and filled up cold with anger and went harder.

I can be a machine. Like a fish, you old bitch. I can swim away.

Harder.

Go.

Do.

Cut.

Harder.

That body thrashed and whitened the water, throttling out, vibrating, parts shearing away, roaring white hot, and all the way down she felt young and strong and perfect in the cold darkness.

REDFISH

Rick Bass

CUBA LIBRES ARE made with rum, diet Coke, and lime juice. Kirby showed them to me, and someone, I am sure, showed them to him. They've probably been around forever, the way everything has. But the first time we really drank them was late at night on the beach in Galveston. There was a high wind coming off the water, and we had a fire roaring. I think that it felt good for Kirby to be away from Tricia for a while and I know that it felt good to be away from Houston.

We were fishing for red drum—redfish—and somewhere, out in the darkness, beyond where we could see, we had hurled our hooks and sinkers, baited with live shrimp. There was a big moon and the waves blew spray into our faces and we wore heavy coats, and our faces were orange, to one another, from the light of the big driftwood fire.

It is amazing, what washes in from the ocean. Everything in the world ends up, I think, on a beach. Whales, palm trees, television sets . . . Kirby and I were sitting on a couch in the sand drinking the Cuba Libres and watching our lines, waiting for the big redfish to hit. When he did, or she, we were going to reel it in and then clean it there on the beach, rinse it off in the waves, and then we were going to grill it, on the big driftwood fire.

It was our first time to drink Cuba Libres, and we liked them even better than margaritas. We had never caught redfish before, either, but had read about it in a book. We had bought the couch for ten dollars at a garage sale earlier in the day. We sank down deep into it and it was easy, comfortable fishing. In the morning, when the tide started to go out, we were going to wade-fish for speckled trout. We had read about that, too, and that was the way you were supposed to do it. You were supposed to go out into the waves after them. It sounded exciting. We had bought waders and saltwater fishing licenses and saltwater stamps, as well as the couch and the rum. We were going to get into a run of speckled trout and catch our limit, and load the ice chest with them, and take them back to Tricia, because Kirby had made her mad.

But first we were going to catch a big redfish. We wouldn't tell her about the redfish, we decided. We would grill it and drink more Cuba Libres and maybe take a short nap, before the tide changed, and we had our sleeping bags laid out on the sand for that purpose. They looked as if they had been washed ashore, too. It was December, and about thirty degrees. We were on the southeast end of the bay and the wind was strong. The flames from the fire were ten or twelve feet high, but we couldn't get warm.

There was all the wood in the world, huge beams from ships and who-knows-what, and we could make the fire as large as we wanted. We kept waiting for the big redfish to seize our shrimp and run, to scoot back down into the depths. The book said they were bottom feeders.

It seemed, drinking the Cuba Libres, that it would happen at any second. Kirby and Trish had gotten in a fight because Kirby had forgotten to feed the dogs that Saturday, while Trish was at work. Kirby said, drinking the Cuba Libres, that he had told her that what she was really mad about was the fact that she had to work that Saturday, while he had had the day off. (They both work in a bank, different banks, and handle money, and own sports cars.) Tricia had gotten really mad at that and had refused to feed the dogs.

So Kirby fed his dog but did not feed Tricia's. That was when Tricia got the maddest. Then they got into a fight about how Kirby's dog, a German Shepherd, ate so much more, about ten times more, than did Tricky Woodles, a Cocker spaniel, Tricia's dog. Good old Tricky Woo.

On the beach, Kirby had a pocketbook that identified fishes of the Gulf Coast, and after each drink we would look at it, turning to the page with the picture of the red drum. We would study it, sitting there on the couch, as if we were in high school again, and were studying for some silly exam, instead of being out in the real world, braving the elements, tackling nature, fishing for the mighty red drum. The book said they could go as much as thirty pounds.

'The elusive red drum!' Kirby shouted into the wind. We were only sipping the Cuba Libres, because they were so good, but they were adding up. They were new, and we had just discovered them, and we wanted as many of them as we could get.

'Elusive *and* wily!' I shouted. 'Red E. Fish!'

Kirby's eyes darted and shifted like a cartoon character's, the way they did when he was really drunk, which meant he would be passing out soon.

'We could dynamite the ocean,' he said. 'We could throw grenades into the waves, and stun the fish. They would come rolling in with the waves then, all the fish in the world.'

He stood up, fell in the sand, and still on his knees, poured another drink. 'I really want to see one,' he said.

We left our poles and wandered down the beach: jumping and stamping, it was so cold. The wind tried to blow us over. We found an ancient, upright lifeguard's tower, about twenty feet tall, and tried, in our drunkenness, to pull it down, to drag over to our fire. It was as sturdy as iron, and had barnacles on it, from where it had spent some time in the sea. We cut our hands badly, but it was dark and cold, and we did not find that out until later.

We were a long way from our fire, and it looked a lot smaller, from where we were. The couch looked wrong, without us in it, sitting there by the fire, empty like that. Kirby started crying and said he was going home to Tricia but I told him to buck up and be a man. I didn't know what that meant or even what I meant by saying that, but I knew that I did not want him to leave. We had come in his car, the kind everyone our age in Houston drove, if they had a job, if they had even a little money—a white BMW—and I wanted to stay, and see what a red drum looked like in the flesh.

'I've an idea,' I said. 'Let's pull the tower down, and drag it over to the fire with the car.'

'Yeah!' said Kirby. 'Yeah!' Clouds were hurrying past the moon, something was blowing in quickly, but

I could see that Kirby had straightened up some, and that he was not going to pass out.

It's been ten years since we were in high school. Some days, when I am with him, it seems that eternity still lies out in front of us; and other days, it seems that we've already died, somehow, and everything is over. Tricia is beautiful. She reminds me of that white sports car.

We kicked most of the sand off our shoes, and got in the car, and it started right up, the way it always did. It was a nice car, all right, and Kirby drove it to work every day—though work was only one-point-eight miles away—and he kept his briefcase in the back seat; but in the trunk, just thrown in, were all of the things he had always kept in his trunk in high school, things he thought he might need in an emergency.

There was a bow and arrows, a .22 rifle, a tomahawk, binoculars, a tire inflator, a billy club, some extra fishing poles, a tool box, some barbed wire, a bull riding rope, cowboy boots, a wrinkled, oily tuxedo which he had rented and never bothered to return, and there were other things, too—but it was the bull riding rope, which we attached to the tower, and to the back bumper of the little sports car, that came in handy this time.

Sand flew as the tires spun, and like some shy animal,

the BMW quickly buried itself, up to the doors.

To the very end, I think Kirby believed that at any moment he was going to pull free, and break out of the sand, and pull the tower over: the engine screaming, the car shuddering and bucking . . . but it was sunk deep, when he gave up, and he had to crawl out through the window.

The Cuba Libres, and the roar of the wind, made it seem funny; we howled, as if it was something the car had done by itself, on its own.

'Let's take a picture and send it to Tricia,' he said. I laughed, and winced too, a little, because I thought it was a bad sign that he was talking about her again, so much, so often, but he was happy, so we got the camera from the trunk, and because he did not have a flash attachment, we built another fire, stacked wood there by the tower, which is what we should have done in the first place.

We went back to get the couch, and our poles and sleeping bags, and the ice chest. I had worked, for a while, for a moving company, and I knew a trick so that I could carry on my back a couch, a refrigerator, or almost anything, and I showed it to Kirby, and he screamed, laughing, as I ran down the beach with the couch on my back, not able to see where I was going, carrying the couch like an ant with a leaf, coming dangerously close to the water. Kirby ran along behind me, screaming, carrying the other things, and when we had set up a new camp, we ran back and forth, carrying the larger pieces of burning logs, transferring the fire, too. We took a picture of the car by firelight.

Our hands and arms had dried blood on them almost all the way up to the elbows, from the barnacles, and we rinsed them off in the sea, which was not as cold as we had expected.

'I wish Tricia was here to see this,' he said, more than once. The wind was blowing still harder, and the moon was gone entirely.

We got a new fire started, and were exhausted from all the effort; we fixed more drinks and slumped into the couch and raised our poles to cast out again, but stopped, realizing that the shrimp were gone; that something had stolen them.

The other shrimp were in a live well, in the trunk, so we re-baited. It was fun, reaching in the dark into the warm bubbling water of the bait bucket, and feeling the wild tiny shrimp leap about, fishtailing, trying to escape. It didn't matter which shrimp you got; you didn't even need to look. You just reached in, and caught whichever one leapt into your hand.

We baited the hooks, and cast out again. We were thirsty, so we fixed more drinks. We nodded off on the couch, and were awakened by the fire going down, and by snow, which was landing gently on our faces. It was just starting. It was beautiful, and we sat up, and then stood up, but didn't say anything. We reeled in and checked our hooks, and found that the shrimp were gone again.

Kirby looked out at the darkness, where surely the snowflakes were landing on the water, and he looked up at the sky, and could not stand the beauty.

'I'm going to try to hitchhike back to Houston,' he said. He did not say her name but I know he was thinking of waking up with Tricia, and looking out the window, and seeing the snow, and everything being warm, inside the house, under the roof.

'No,' I said. 'Wait.' Then I was cruel. 'You'll just get in a fight again,' I told him, though I knew it wasn't true: they were always wild to see each other after any kind of separation, even a day or two. I had to admit I was somewhat jealous of this.

'Wait a little longer, and we'll go out into the waves,' I said.

'Yes,' said Kirby. 'Okay.' Because we'd been thinking that would be the best part, the most fun: wade-fishing. We'd read about that, too, and Kirby had brought a throw net, with which to catch mullets for bait.

We'd read about wade-fishermen with long stringers of fish—the really successful fishermen—being followed by sharks and attacked, and so we were pretty terrified of the sharks, knowing that they could be down there among our legs, in the darkness and under water, where we could not see, following us: or that we could even walk right into the sharks. That idea of them being hidden, just beneath us—we didn't like it a bit, not knowing for sure if they were out there or not.

We fixed a new batch of Cuba Libres, using a lot of lime. We stood at the shore in our waders, the snow and wind coming hard into our faces, and drank them quickly, strongly, and poured some more, raced them down. It wasn't ocean any more, but snowdrift prairie, the Missouri breaks, or the Dakotas and beyond, and we waded out, men searching for game, holding the heavy poles high over our heads, dragging the great Bible cast-nets behind us.

The water was not very deep for a long time; for fifteen minutes it was only knee-deep, getting no deeper, and not yet time to think about sharks.

'I wish Tricia was here,' said Kirby. The Cuba Libres were warm in our bellies; we'd used a lot of rum in the last ones. 'I wish she was riding on my shoulders, piggy-back,' he said.

'Nekkid,' I said.

'Yes,' said Kirby, picturing it, and he was happy, and even though I didn't really like Tricia, I thought how nice it would have been if she could have seen him then, sort of looking off and dreaming about it. I wished I had a girlfriend or wife on my back, too, then, to go along with all the other equipment I was carrying. I was thinking that she could hold the pole, and cast out, waiting for a bite, waiting for the big fight; and I could work the throw net, trying to catch fresh mullet, which we'd cut up into cubes, right there in the water, and use for fresh bait: because the bait had to be fresh.

It was like a murder or a sin, cutting the live mullet's head off, slicing the entrails out, filleting out a piece of still-barely-living meat and putting it on the hook, and then throwing the rest of the mullet away; throwing it behind you for the sharks, or whatever—head, fins, entrails, and left-over meat—casting your hook then far out into the waves and dark and snow, with that warm very fresh piece of flesh on the hook—it was like a sin, the worst of the animal kingdom, I thought, but if you caught what you were after, if you got the big redfish, then it was all right, it was possible that you were forgiven.

I wanted to catch the largest redfish in the world. I wanted to catch one so large that I'd have to wrestle it, maybe even stab it with the fillet knife, like Tarzan with the crocodiles.

Kirby looked tired. He had put on about twenty pounds since high school, and it was hard work, walking with the poles over our heads.

'Wait,' I said. We stopped and caught our breath. It was hard to hear each other, with only the wind and waves around us; and except for the direction of the waves, splashing into our faces from the Gulf, we couldn't tell where shore was, or in which direction the ocean lay.

'I've an idea,' said Kirby, still breathing heavily, looking back to where we were pretty sure the shore was. If our fire was still burning, we couldn't see it. 'There's a place back up the beach that rents horses in the daytime. Some stables.'

'They shoot horse thieves,' I said. But I thought it was a wonderful idea. I was tired, too; I wasn't in as good of shape as I'd once been either.

'I'll go get them,' I said, since I wasn't breathing quite as hard as he was. It was a tremendous picture: both of us on white horses, riding out into the waves, chest-deep, neck-deep, then the magic lift and float of the horse as it began to swim, the light feeling of nothing, no resistance.

Mares, they would be, noble and strong, capable of carrying foolish, drunken men out to sea on their journey, if they so desired, and capable of bringing them back again, too.

'Yes,' I said. 'You stay here. I'll go find the horses.'

Back on shore, walking up the beach to the stables, I stopped at a pay phone, and dialed Tricia's number. The cold wind was rocking the little phone booth, and there was much static on the line.

'Tricia,' I said, disguising my voice, mumbling. 'This is Kirby. I love you.' Then I hung up and thought about how I really liked her after all, and I went to look for the horses. It would be perfect.

We could ride around out in the gulf on the

swimming horses until they tired, casting and drinking, searching for what we were after, pausing sometimes to lean forward and whisper kind things, encouragement, into the horses' ears, as they labored through the waves, blowing hard through their nostrils, legs kicking and churning, swimming around in wide circles out in the gulf, in the darkness, the snow; no doubt full of their own fears of sharks, of drowning, of going down under too heavy of a load, and of all the things unseen, all the things below.

POSTCARDS FROM SURFERS
Helen Garner

'One night I dreamed that I did not love, and
that night, released from all bonds, I lay as
though in a kind of soothing death.'

Colette

WE ARE DRIVING north from Coolangatta airport.
Beside the road the ocean heaves and heaves into waves
which do not break. The swells are dotted with
boardriders in black wet-suits, grim as sharks.

'Look at those idiots,' says my father.

'They must be freezing,' says my mother.

'But what about the principle of the wet-suit?' I
say. 'Isn't there a thin layer of water between your
skin and the suit, and your body heat . . .'

'Could be,' says my father.

The road takes a sudden swing round a rocky outcrop. Miles ahead of us, blurred in the milky air, I see a dream city: its cream, its silver, its turquoise towers thrust in a cluster from a distant spit.

'What—is that Brisbane?' I say.

'No,' says my mother. 'That's Surfers.'

My father's car has a built-in computer. If he exceeds the speed limit, the dashboard emits a discreet but insistent pinging. Lights flash, and the pressure of his right foot lessens. He controls the windows from a panel between the two front seats. We cruise past a Valiant parked by the highway with a FOR SALE sign propped in its back window.

'Look at that,' says my mother. 'A WA number-plate. Probably thrashed it across the Nullarbor and now they reckon they'll flog it.'

'Pro'ly stolen,' says my father. 'See the sticker? ALL YOU VIRGINS, THANKS FOR NOTHING. You can just see what sort of a pin'ead he'd be. Brain the size of a pea.'

Close up, many of the turquoise towers are not yet sold. 'Every conceivable feature,' the signs say. They have names like Capricornia, Biarritz, The Breakers, Acapulco, Rio.

I had a Brazilian friend when I lived in Paris. He showed me a postcard, once, of Rio where he was born and brought up. The card bore an aerial shot of a splendid, curved tropical beach, fringed with palms, its sand pure as snow.

'Why don't you live in Brazil,' I said, 'if it's as beautiful as this?'

'Because,' said my friend, 'right behind that beach there is a huge military base.'

In my turn I showed him a postcard of my country. It was a reproduction of that Streeton painting called *The Land of the Golden Fleece* which in my homesickness I kept standing on the heater in my bedroom. He studied it carefully. At last he turned his currant-coloured eyes to me and said,

'*Les arbres sont rouges?*' Are the trees red?

Several years later, six months ago, I was rummaging through a box of old postcards in a junk shop in Rathdowne Street. Among the photos of damp cottages in Galway, of Raj hotels crumbling in bicycle-thronged Colombo, of glassy Canadian lakes flawed by the wake of a single canoe, I found two cards that I bought for a dollar each. One was a picture of downtown Rio, in black-and-white. The other, crudely tinted, showed Geelong, the town where I was born. The photographer must have stood on the high grassy bank that overlooks the Eastern Beach. He lined up his shot through the never-flowing fountain with its quartet of concrete wading birds (storks? cranes? I never asked my father: they have long orange beaks and each bird holds one leg bent, as if about to take a step); through the fountain and out over the curving wooden promenade, from which we dived all summer, unsupervised, into the flat water; and across the bay to the You Yangs, the double-humped, low, volcanic cones, the only disturbance in the great basalt plains that lie between Geelong and Melbourne. These two cards in the same box! And I find them! Imagine! *'Cher Rubens,'* I wrote. *'Je t'envoie ces deux cartes postales, de nos deux villes natales . . .'*

Auntie Lorna has gone for a walk on the beach. My mother unlocks the door and slides open the flywire screen. She goes out into the bright air to tell her friend of my arrival. The ocean is right in front of the unit, only a hundred and fifty yards away. How can people be so sure of the boundary between land and sea that they have the confidence to build houses on it? The white doorsteps of the ocean travel and travel.

'Twelve o'clock,' says my father.

'Getting on for lunchtime,' I say.

'Getting towards it. Specially with that nice cold corned beef sitting there, and fresh brown bread. Think I'll have to try some of that choko relish. Ever eaten a choko?'

'I wouldn't know a choko if I fell over it,' I say.

'Nor would I.'

He selects a serrated knife from the magnetised holder on the kitchen wall and quickly and skilfully, at the bench, makes himself a thick sandwich. He works with powerful concentration: when the meat flaps off the slice of bread, he rounds it up with a large, dramatic scooping movement and a sympathetic grimace of the lower lip. He picks up the sandwich in two hands, raises it to his mouth and takes a large bite. While he chews he breathes heavily through his nose.

'Want to make yourself something?' he says with his mouth full.

I stand up. He pushes the loaf of bread towards me with the back of his hand. He puts the other half of his sandwich on a green bread and butter plate and carries it to the table. He sits with his elbows on the pine wood, his knees wide apart, his belly relaxing on to his thighs, his high-arched, long-boned feet planted on the tiled floor. He eats, and gazes out to sea. The noise of his eating fills the room.

My mother and Auntie Lorna come up from the beach. I stand inside the wall of glass and watch them stop at the tap to hose the sand off their feet before they cross the grass to the door. They are two old women: they have to keep one hand on the tap in order to balance on the left foot and wash the right. I see that they are two old women, and yet they are neither young nor old. They are my mother and Auntie Lorna, two institutions. They slide back the wire door, smiling.

'Don't tramp sand everywhere,' says my father from the table.

They take no notice. Auntie Lorna kisses me, and holds me at arms' length with her head on one side.

My mother prepares food and we eat, looking out at the water.

'You've missed the coronary brigade,' says my father. 'They get out on the beach about nine in the morning. You can pick 'em. They swing their arms up really high when they walk.' He laughs, looking down.

'Do you go for a walk every day too?' I ask.

'Six point six kilometres,' says my father.

'Got a pedometer, have you?'

'I just nutted it out,' says my father. 'We walk as far as a big white building, down that way, then we turn round and come back. Six point six altogether, there and back.'

'I might come with you.'

'You can if you like,' he says. He picks up his plate and carries it to the sink. 'We go after breakfast. You've missed today's.'

He goes to the couch and opens the newspaper on the low coffee table. He reads with his glasses down his nose and his hands loosely linked between his spread knees. The women wash up.

'Is there a shop nearby?' I ask my mother. 'I have to get some tampons.'

'Caught short, are you?' she says. 'I think they sell them at the shopping centre, along Sunbrite Avenue there near the bowling club. Want me to come with you?'

'I can find it.'

'I never could use those things,' says my mother, lowering her voice and glancing across the room at my father. 'Hazel told me about a terrible thing that happened to her. For days she kept noticing this revolting smell that was . . . emanating from her. She washed and washed, and couldn't get rid of it. Finally she was about to go to the doctor, but first she got down and had a look with the mirror. She saw this bit of thread and pulled it. The thing was *green*. She must've forgotten to take it out—it'd been there for days and days and *days*.'

We laugh with the teatowels up to our mouths. My father, on the other side of the room, looks up from the paper with the bent smile of someone not sure what the others are laughing at. I am always surprised when my mother comes out with a word like 'emanating'. At home I have a book called *An Outline of English Verse* which my mother used in her matriculation year. In the margins of *The Rape of the Lock* she has made notations: 'bathos; reminiscent of Virgil; parody of Homer.' Her handwriting in these pencilled jottings, made forty-five years ago, is exactly as it is today: this makes me suspect, when I am not with her, that she is a closet intellectual.

Once or twice, on my way from the unit to the shopping centre, I think to see roses along a fence and run to look, but I find them to be some scentless, fleshy flower. I fall back. Beside a patch of yellow grass, pretty trees in a row are bearing and dropping white blossom-like flowers, but they look wrong to me, I do not recognise them: the blossoms too large, the branches too flat. I am dizzy from the flight. In Melbourne it is still winter, everything is bare.

I buy the tampons and look for the postcards. There they are, displayed in a tall revolving rack. There is a great deal of blue. Closer, I find colour photos of white beaches, duneless, palmless, on which half-naked people lie on their backs with their knees raised. The frequency of this posture, at random through the crowd, makes me feel like laughing. Most of the cards have GREETINGS FROM THE GOLD COAST or BROADBEACH or SURFERS PARADISE embossed in gold in one corner: I search for pictures without words. Another card, in several slightly differing versions, shows a graceful, big-breasted young girl lying in a seductive pose against some rocks: she is wearing a bikini and her whole head is covered by one of those latex masks that are sold in trick shops, the ones you pull on as a bandit pulls on a stocking. The mask represents the hideous, raddled, grinning face of an old woman, a witch. I stare at this photo for a long time. Is it simple, or does it hide some more mysterious signs and symbols?

I buy twelve GREETINGS FROM cards with views, some aerial, some from the ground. They cost twenty-five cents each.

'Want the envelopes?' says the girl. She is dressed in a flowered garment which is drawn up between her thighs like a nappy.

'Yes please.' The envelopes are so covered with coloured maps, logos and drawings of Australian fauna that there is barely room to write an address, but something about them attracts me. I buy a packet of Licorice Chews and eat them all on the way home: I stuff them in two at a time: my mouth floods with saliva. There are no rubbish bins so I put the papers in my pocket. Now that I have spent money here, now that I have rubbish to dispose of, I am no longer a stranger. In Paris there used to be signs in the streets that said, '*Le commerce, c'est la vie de la ville.*' Any traveller knows this to be the truth.

The women are knitting. They murmur and murmur. What they say never requires an answer. My father sharpens a pencil stub with his pocket knife, and folds the paper into a pad one-eighth the size of a broadsheet page.

'Five down, spicy meat jelly. ASPIC. Three across, counterfeit. BOGUS! Howzat.'

'You're in good nick,' I say. 'I would've had to rack my brains for BOGUS. Why don't you do harder ones?'

'Oh, I can't do those other ones, the cryptic.'

'You have to know Shakespeare and the Bible off by heart to do those,' I say.

'Yairs. Course, if you got hold of the answer and filled it out looking at that, with a lot of practice you could come round to their way of thinking. They used to have good ones in the *Weekly Times*. But I s'pose they had so many complaints from cockies who couldn't do 'em that they had to ease off.'

I do not feel comfortable yet about writing the postcards. It would seem graceless. I flip through my mother's pattern book.

'There's some nice ones there,' she says. 'What about the one with the floppy collar?'

'Want to buy some wool?' says my father. He tosses the finished crossword on to the coffee table and stands up with a vast yawn. 'Oh – ee – oh – ooh. Come on, Miss. I'll drive you over to Pacific Fair.'

I choose the wool and count out the number of balls specified by the pattern. My father rears back to look at it: this movement struck terror into me when I was a teenager but I now recognise it as long-sightedness.

'Pure wool, is it?' he says. As soon as he touches it he will know. He fingers it, and looks at me.

'No,' I say. 'Got a bit of synthetic in it. It's what the pattern says to use.'

'Why don't you—' He stops. Once he would have tried to prevent me from buying it. His big blunt hands used to fling out the fleeces, still warm, on to the greasy table. His hands looked as if they had no feeling in them but they teased out the wool, judged it, classed it, assigned it a fineness and a destination: Italy, Switzerland, Japan. He came home with thorns embedded deep in the flesh of his palms. He stood patiently while my mother gouged away at them with a needle. He drove away at shearing time in a yellow car with running boards, up to the big sheds in the country; we rode on the running boards as far as the corner of our street, then skipped home. He went to the Melbourne Show for work, not pleasure, and once he brought me home a plastic trumpet. 'Fordie,' he called me, and took me to the wharves and said, 'See that rope? It's not a rope. It's a hawser.' 'Hawser,' I repeated, wanting him to think I was a serious person. We walked along Strachan Avenue, Manifold Heights, hand in hand. 'Listen,' he said. 'Listen to the wind in the wires.' I must have been very little then, for the wires were so high I can't remember seeing them.

He turns away from the fluffy pink balls and waits with his hands in his pockets for me to pay.

'What do you do all day, up here?' I say on the way home.

'Oh . . . play bowls. Follow the real estate. I ring up the firms that advertise these flash units and I ask 'em questions. I let 'em lower and lower their price. See how low they'll go. How many more discounts they can dream up.' He drives like a farmer in a ute, leaning forward with his arms curved round the wheel, always about to squint up through the windscreen at the sky, checking the weather.

'Don't they ask your name?'

'Yep.'

'What do you call yourself?'

'Oh, Jackson or anything.' He flicks a glance at me. We begin to laugh, looking away from each other.

'It's bloody crook up here,' he says. 'Jerry-built. Sad. "Every conceivable luxury"! They can't get rid of it. They're desperate. Come on. We'll go up and you can have a look.'

The lift in Biarritz is lined with mushroom-coloured carpet. We brace our backs against its wall and it rushes us upwards. The salesman in the display unit has a moustache, several gold bracelets, a beige suit, and a clipboard against his chest. He is engaged with an elderly couple and we are able to slip past him into the living room.

'Did you see that peanut?' hisses my father.

'A gilded youth,' I say. '"Their eyes are dull, their heads are flat, they have no brains at all."'

He looks impressed, as if he thinks I have made it up on the spot. '*The Man from Ironbark,*' I add.

'I only remember *The Geebung Polo Club,*' he says. He mimes leaning off a horse and swinging a heavy implement. We snort with laughter. Just inside the living room door stand five Ionic pillars in a half-moon curve. Beyond them, through the glass, are views of a river and some mountains. The river winds in a plain, the mountains are sudden, lumpy and crooked.

'From the other side you can see the sea,' says my father.

'Would you live up here?'

'Not on your life. Not with those flaming pillars.'

From the bedroom window he points out another high-rise building closer to the sea. Its name is Chelsea. It is battle-ship grey with a red trim. Its windows face away from the ocean. It is tall and narrow, of mean proportions, almost prison-like. 'I wouldn't mind living in that one,' he says. I look at it in silence. He has unerringly chosen the ugliest one. It is so ugly that I can find nothing to say.

It is Saturday afternoon. My father is waiting for the Victorian football to start on TV. He rereads the paper.

'Look at this,' he says. 'Mum, remember that seminar we went to about investment in diamonds?'

'Up here?' I say. 'A *seminar*?'

'S'posed to be an investment that would double its value in six days. We went along one afternoon. They were obviously con-men. Ooh, setting up a big con, you could tell. They had sherry and sandwiches.'

'That's all we went for, actually,' says my mother.

'What sort of people went?' I ask.

'Oh . . . people like ourselves,' says my father.

'Do you think anybody bought any?'

'Sure. Some idiots. Anyway, look at this in today's *Age*. "The Diamond Dreamtime. World diamond market plummets." Haw haw haw.'

He turns on the TV in time for the bounce. I cast on stitches as instructed by the pattern and begin to knit. My mother and Auntie Lorna, well advanced in complicated garments for my sister's teenage children, conduct their monologues which cross, coincide and run parallel. My father mumbles advice to the footballers and emits bursts of contemptuous laughter. 'Bloody idiot,' he says.

I go to the room I am to share with Auntie Lorna and come back with the packet of postcards. When I get out my pen and the stamps and set myself up at the table my father looks up and shouts to me over the roar of the crowd,

'Given up on the knitting?'

'No. Just knocking off a few postcards. People expect a postcard when you go to Queensland.'

'Have to keep up your correspondence, Father,' says my mother.

'I'll knit later,' I say.

'How much have you done?' asks my father.

'This much.' I separate thumb and forefinger.

'Dear Philip,' I write. I make my writing as thin and small as I can: the back of the postcard, not the front, is the art form. 'Look where I am. A big red setter wet from the surf shambles up the side way of

256

the unit, looking lost and anxious as setters always do. My parents send it packing with curses in an inarticulate tongue. Go orn, get orf, gorn!'

'Dear Philip. THE IDENTIFICATION OF THE BIRDS AND FISHES. *My father*: "Look at those albatross. They must have eyes that can see for a hundred miles. As soon as one dives, they come from everywhere. Look at 'em dive! Bang! Down they go." *Me*: "What sort of fish would they be diving for?" *My father*: "Whiting. They only eat whiting." *Me*: "They do not!" *My father*: "How the hell would *I* know what sort of fish they are."'

'Dear Philip. My father says they are albatross, but my mother (in the bathroom, later) remarks to me that albatross have shorter, more hunched necks.'

'Dear Philip. I share a room with Auntie Lorna. She also is writing postcards and has just asked me how to spell TOO. I like her very much and *she likes me*. "I'll keep the stickybeaks in the Woomelang post office guessing," she says. "I won't put my name on the back of the envelope."'

'Dear Philip. OUTSIDE THE POST OFFICE. My father, Auntie Lorna and I wait in the car for my mother to go in and pick up the mail from the locked box. *My father*: "Gawd, amazing, isn't it, what people do. See that sign there, ENTER, with the arrow pointing upwards? What sort of a thing is that? Is it a joke, or just some no-hoper foolin' around? That woman's been in the phone box for half an hour, I bet. How'd you be, outside the public phone waiting for some silly coot to finish yackin' on about everything under the sun, while you had something important to say. That happened to us, once, up at—" My mother opens the door and gets in. "Three letters," she says. "All for me."'

Sometimes my little story overflows the available space and I have to run over on to a second postcard. This means I must find a smaller, secondary tale, or some disconnected remark, to fill up card number two.

'*Me*: (opening cupboard) "Hey! Scrabble! We can have a game of Scrabble after tea!" *My father*: (with a scornful laugh) "I can't wait."'

'Dear Philip. I know you won't write back. I don't even know whether you are still at this address.'

'Dear Philip. One Saturday morning I went to Coles and bought a scarf. It cost four and sixpence and I was happy with my purchase. He whisked it out of my hand and looked at the label. "Made in China. Is it real silk? Let's test it." He flicked on his cigarette lighter. We all screamed and my mother said, "Don't *bite*! He's only teasing you."'

'Dear Philip. Once, when I was fourteen, I gave cheek to him at the dinner table. He hit me across the head with his open hand. There was silence. My little brother gave a high, hysterical giggle and I laughed too, in shock. He hit me again. After the washing up I was sent for. He was sitting in an armchair, looking down. "The reason why we don't get on any more," he said, "is because we're so much alike." This idea filled me with such revulsion that I turned my swollen face away. It was swollen from crying, not from the blows, whose force had been more symbolic than physical.'

'Dear Philip. Years later he read my mail. He found the contraceptive pills. He drove up to Melbourne and found me and made me come home. He told me I was letting men use my body. He told me I ought to see a psychiatrist. I was in the front seat and my mother was in the back. I thought, "If I open the door and jump out, I won't have to listen to this any more." My mother tried to stick up for me. He shouted at her. "It's your fault," he said. "You were too soft on her."'

'Dear Philip. I know you've heard all this before. I also know it's no worse than anyone else's story.'

'Dear Philip. And again years later he asked me a personal question. He was driving, I was in the suicide seat. "What went wrong," he said, "between you and Philip?" Again I turned my face away. "I don't want to talk about it," I said. There was silence. He never asked again. And years after *that*, in a cafe in Paris on my way to work, far enough away from him to be able to, I thought of that question and began to cry. Dear Philip. I forgive you for everything.'

Late in the afternoon my mother and Auntie Lorna

and I walk along the beach to Surfers. The tide is out: our bare feet scarcely mark the firm sand. Their two voices run on, one high, one low. If I speak they pretend to listen, just as I feign attention to their endless, looping discourses: these are our courtesies: this is love. Everything is spoken, nothing is said. On the way back I point out to them the smoky orange clouds that are massing far out to sea, low over the horizon. Obedient, they stop and face the water. We stand in a row, Auntie Lorna in a pretty frock with sandals dangling from her finger, my mother and I with our trousers rolled up. Once I asked my Brazilian friend a stupid question. He was listening to a conversation between me and a Frenchman about our countries' electoral systems. He was not speaking and, thinking to include him, I said, 'And how do people vote *chez toi*, Rubens?' He looked at me with a small smile. 'We don't have elections,' he said. Where's Rio from here? 'Look at those clouds!' I say. 'You'd think there was another city out there, wouldn't you, burning.'

Just at dark the air takes on the colour and dampness of the sub-tropics. I walk out the screen door and stand my gin on a fence post. I lean on the fence and look at the ocean. Soon the moon will thrust itself over the line. If I did a painting of a horizon, I think, I would make it look like a row of rocking, inverted Vs, because that's what I see when I look at it. The flatness of a horizon is intellectual. A cork pops on the first floor

260

balcony behind me. I glance up. In the half dark two men with moustaches are smiling down at me.

'Drinking champagne tonight?' I say.

'Wonderful sound, isn't it,' says the one holding the bottle.

I turn back to the moonless horizon. Last year I went camping on the Murray River. I bought the cards at Tocumwal. I had to write fast for the light was dropping and spooky noises were coming from the trees. 'Dear Dad,' I wrote. 'I am up on the Murray, sitting by the camp fire. It's nearly dark now but earlier it was beautiful, when the sun was going down and the dew was rising.' Two weeks later, at home, I received a letter from him written in his hard, rapid, slanting hand, each word ending in a sharp upward flick. The letter itself concerned a small financial matter, and consisted of two sentences on half a sheet of quarto, but on the back of the envelope he had dashed off a personal message: 'P.S. Dew does not rise. It *forms*.'

The moon does rise, as fat as an orange, out of the sea straight in front of the unit. A child upstairs sees it too and utters long werewolf howls. My mother makes a meal and we eat it. 'Going to help Mum with the dishes, are you, Miss?' says my father from his armchair. My shoulders stiffen. I am, I do. I lie on the couch and read an old *Woman's Day*. Princess Caroline of Monaco wears a black dress and a wide white hat. The knitting needles make their mild clicking. Auntie Lorna and my father come from the same town, Hopetoun in the Mallee, and when the news is over they begin again.

'I always remember the cars of people,' says my father. 'There was an old four-cylinder Dodge, belonging to Whatsisname. It had—'

'Would that have been one of the O'Lachlans?' says Auntie Lorna.

'Jim O'Lachlan. It had a great big exhaust pipe coming out the back. And I remember stuffing a potato up it.'

'A *potato*?' I say.

'The bloke was a councillor,' says my father. 'He came out of the Council chambers and got into the Dodge and started her up. He only got fifty yards up the street when BA—BANG! This damn thing shot out the back—I reckon it's still going!' He closes his lips and drops his head back against the couch to hold in his laughter.

I walk past Biarritz, where globes of light float among shrubbery, and the odd balcony on the half-empty tower holds rich people out into the creamy air. A bare-foot man steps out of the take-away food shop with a hamburger in his hand. He leans against the wall to unwrap it, and sees me hesitating at the slot of the letterbox, holding up the postcards and reading them over and over in the weak light from the public phone. 'Too late to change it now,' he calls. I look up. He grins and nods and takes his first bite of the hamburger.

Beside the letterbox stands a deep rubbish bin with a swing lid. I punch open the bin and drop the postcards in.

All night I sleep safely in my bed. The waves roar and hiss, and slam like doors. Auntie Lorna snores, but when I tug at the corner of her blanket she sighs and turns over and breathes more quietly. In the morning the rising sun hits the front windows and floods the place with a light so intense that the white curtains can hardly net it. Everything is pink and golden. In the sink a cockroach lurks. I try to swill it down the drain with a cup of water but it resists strongly. The air is bright, is milky with spray. My father is already up: while the kettle boils he stands out on the edge of the grass, the edge of his property, looking at the sea.

SO MUCH WATER SO CLOSE
TO HOME
Raymond Carver

MY HUSBAND EATS with a good appetite. But I don't think he's really hungry. He chews, arms on the table, and stares at something across the room. He looks at me and looks away. He wipes his mouth on the napkin. He shrugs, and goes on eating.

'What are you staring at me for?' he says. 'What is it?' he says and lays down his fork.

'Was I staring?' I say, and shake my head.

The telephone rings.

'Don't answer it,' he says.

'It might be your mother,' I say.

'Watch and see,' he says.

I pick up the receiver and listen. My husband stops eating.

'What did I tell you?' he says when I hang up. He starts to eat again. Then throws his napkin on his plate. He says, 'Goddamn it, why can't people mind their own business? Tell me what I did wrong and I'll listen! I wasn't the only man there. We talked it over and we all decided. We couldn't just turn around. We were five miles from the car. I won't have you passing judgment. Do you hear?'

'You know,' I say.

He says, 'What do I know, Claire? Tell me what I'm supposed to know. I don't know anything except one thing.' He gives me what he thinks is a meaningful look. 'She was dead,' he says. 'And I'm as sorry as anyone else. But she was dead.'

'That's the point,' I say.

He raises his hands. He pushes his chair away from the table. He takes out his cigarettes and goes out to the back with a can of beer. I see him sit in the lawn chair and pick up the newspaper again.

His name is in there on the first page. Along with the names of his friends.

I close my eyes and hold on to the sink. Then I rake my arm across the drainboard and send the dishes to the floor.

He doesn't move. I know he's heard. He lifts his head as if still listening. But he doesn't move otherwise. He doesn't turn around.

*

266

He and Gordon Johnson and Mel Dorn and Vern Williams, they play poker and bowl and fish. They fish every spring and early summer before visiting relatives can get in the way. They are decent men, family men, men who take care of their jobs. They have sons and daughters who go to school with our son, Dean.

· Last Friday these family men left for the Naches River. They parked the car in the mountains and hiked to where they wanted to fish. They carried their bedrolls, their food, their playing cards, their whiskey.

They saw the girl before they set up camp. Mel Dorn found her. No clothes on her at all. She was wedged into some branches that stuck out over the water.

He called the others and they came to look. They talked about what to do. One of the men—my Stuart didn't say which—said they should start back at once. The others stirred the sand with their shoes, said they didn't feel inclined that way. They pleaded fatigue, the late hour, the fact that the girl wasn't going anywhere.

In the end they went ahead and set up the camp. They built a fire and drank their whiskey. When the moon came up, they talked about the girl. Someone said they should keep the body from drifting away. They took their flashlights and went back to the river. One of the men—it might have been Stuart—waded in and got her. He took her by the fingers and pulled her into shore. He got some nylon cord and tied it to her wrist and then looped the rest around a tree.

The next morning they cooked breakfast, drank coffee, and drank whiskey, and then split up to fish. That night they cooked fish, cooked potatoes, drank coffee, drank whiskey, then took their cooking things and eating things back down to the river and washed them where the girl was.

They played some cards later on. Maybe they played until they couldn't see them anymore. Vern Williams went to sleep. But the others told stories. Gordon Johnson said the trout they'd caught were hard because of the terible coldness of the water.

The next morning they got up late, drank whiskey, fished a little, took down their tents, rolled their sleeping bags, gathered their stuff, and hiked out. They drove until they got to a telephone. It was Stuart who made the call while the others stood around in the sun and listened. He gave the sheriff their names. They had nothing to hide. They weren't ashamed. They said they'd wait until someone could come for better directions and take down their statements.

I was asleep when he got home. But I woke up when I heard him in the kitchen. I found him leaning against the refrigerator with a can of beer. He put his heavy arms around me and rubbed his big hands on my back.

In bed he put his hands on me again and then waited as if thinking of something else. I turned and opened my legs. Afterwards, I think he stayed awake.

He was up that morning before I could get out of bed. To see if there was something in the paper, I suppose.

The telephone began ringing right after eight.

'Go to hell!' I heard him shout.

The telephone rang right again.

'I have nothing to add to what I already said to the sheriff!'

He slammed the receiver down.

'What is going on?' I said.

It was then that he told me what I just told you.

I sweep up the broken dishes and go outside. He is lying on his back on the grass now, the newspaper and can of beer within reach.

'Stuart, could we go for a drive?' I say.

He rolls over and looks at me. 'We'll pick up some beer,' he says. He gets to his feet and touches me on the hip as he goes past. 'Give me a minute,' he says.

We drive through town without speaking. He stops at a roadside market for beer. I notice a great stack of papers just inside the door. On the top step a fat woman in a print dress holds out a licorice stick to a little girl. Later on, we cross Everson Creek and turn into the picnic grounds. The creek runs under the bridge and into a large pond a few hundred yards away. I can see the men out there. I can see them out there fishing.

So much water so close to home.

I say, 'Why did you have to go miles away?'

'Don't rile me,' he says.

We sit on a bench in the sun. He opens us cans of beer. He says, 'Relax, Claire.'

'They said they were innocent. They said they were crazy.'

He says, 'Who?' He says, 'What are you talking about?'

'The Maddox brothers. They killed a girl named Arlene Hubly where I grew up. They cut off her head and threw her into the Cle Elum River. It happened when I was a girl.'

'You're going to get me riled,' he says.

I look at the creek. I'm right in it, eyes open, face down, staring at the moss on the bottom, dead.

'I don't know what's wrong with you,' he says on the way home. 'You're getting me more riled by the minute.'

There is nothing I can say to him.

He tries to concentrate on the road. But he keeps looking into the rear-view mirror.

He knows.

Stuart believes he is letting me sleep this morning. But
I was awake long before the alarm went off. I was
thinking, lying on the far side of the bed away from
his hairy legs.

He gets Dean off for school, and then he shaves,
dresses, and leaves for work. Twice he looks in and
clears his throat. But I keep my eyes closed.

In the kitchen I find a note from him. It's signed
'Love.'

I sit in the breakfast nook and drink coffee and
leave a ring on the note. I look at the newspaper and
turn it this way and that on the table. Then I skid
it close and read what it says. The body has been
identified, claimed. But it took some examining it, some
putting things into it, some cutting, some weighing,
some measuring, some putting things back again and
sewing them in.

I sit for a long time holding the newspaper and
thinking. Then I call up to get a chair at the hairdresser's.

I sit under the dryer with a magazine on my lap and
let Marnie do my nails.

'I am going to a funeral tomorrow,' I say.

'I'm sorry to hear that,' Marnie says.

'It was a murder,' I say.

'That's the worst kind,' Marnie says.

'We weren't all that close,' I say. 'But you know.'

'We'll get you fixed up for it,' Marnie says.

That night I make my bed on the sofa, and in the morning I get up first. I put on coffee and fix breakfast while he shaves.

He appears in the kitchen doorway, towel over his bare shoulder, appraising.

'Here's coffee,' I say. 'Eggs'll be ready in a minute.'

I wake Dean, and the three of us eat. Whenever Stuart looks at me, I ask Dean if he wants more milk, more toast, etc.

'I'll call you today,' Stuart says as he opens the door.

I say, 'I don't think I'll be home today.'

'All right,' he says. 'Sure.'

I dress carefully. I try on a hat and look at myself in the mirror. I write out a note for Dean.

> *Honey, Mommy has things to do this afternoon, but will be back later. You stay in or be in the backyard until one of us comes home.*
>
> *Love, Mommy*

I look at the word *Love* and then I underline it. Then I see the word *backyard*. Is it one word or two?

I drive through farm country, through fields of oats and sugar beets and past apple orchards, cattle grazing in pastures. Then everything changes, more like shacks than farmhouses and stands of timber instead of orchards. Then mountains, and on the right, far below, I sometimes see the Naches River.

A green pickup comes up behind me and stays behind me for miles. I keep slowing at the wrong times, hoping he will pass. Then I speed up. But this is at the wrong times, too. I grip the wheel until my fingers hurt.

On a long clear stretch he goes past. But he drives along beside for a bit, a crewcut man in a blue workshirt. We look each other over. Then he waves, toots his horn, and pulls on up ahead.

I slow down and find a place. I pull over and shut off the motor. I can hear the river down below the trees. Then I hear the pickup coming back.

I lock the doors and roll up the windows.

'You all right?' the man says. He raps on the glass. 'You okay?' He leans his arms on the door and brings his face to the window.

I stare at him. I can't think what else to do.

'Is everything all right in there? How come you're all locked up?'

I shake my head.

'Roll down your window.' He shakes his head and looks at the highway and then back at me. 'Roll it down now.'

'Please,' I say, 'I have to go.'

'Open the door,' he says as if he isn't listening. 'You're going to choke in there.'

He looks at my breasts, my legs. I can tell that's what he's doing.

'Hey, sugar,' he says. 'I'm just here to help is all.'

The casket is closed and covered with floral sprays. The organ starts up the minute I take a seat. People are coming in and finding chairs. There's a boy in flared pants and a yellow short-sleeved shirt. A door opens and the family comes in in a group and moves over to a curtained place off to one side. Chairs creak as everybody gets settled. Directly, a nice blond man in a nice dark suit stands and asks us to bow our heads. He says a prayer for us, the living, and when he finishes, he says a prayer for the soul of the departed.

Along with the others I go past the casket. Then I move out onto the front steps and into the afternoon light. There's a woman who limps as she goes down the stairs ahead of me. On the sidewalk she looks around. 'Well, they got him,' she says. 'If that's any consolation. They arrested him this morning. I heard it on the radio before I come. A boy right here in town.'

We move a few steps down the hot sidewalk. People are starting cars. I put out my hand and hold on to a parking meter. Polished hoods and polished fenders. My head swims.

I say, 'They have friends, these killers. You can't tell.'

'I have known that child since she was a little girl,' the woman says. 'She used to come over and I'd bake cookies for her and let her eat them in front of the TV.'

Back home, Stuart sits at the table with a drink of whiskey in front of him. For a crazy instant I think something's happened to Dean.

'Where is he?' I say. 'Where is Dean?'

'Outside,' my husband says.

He drains his glass and stands up. He says, 'I think I know what you need.'

He reaches an arm around my waist and with his other hand he begins to unbutton my jacket and then he goes on to the buttons of my blouse.

'First things first,' he says.

He says something else. But I don't need to listen. I can't hear a thing with so much water going.

'That's right,' I say, finishing the buttons myself. 'Before Dean comes. Hurry.'

THE HANDSOMEST DROWNED
MAN IN THE WORLD

Gabriel García Márquez

THE FIRST CHILDREN who saw the dark and slinky bulge approaching through the sea let themselves think it was an enemy ship. Then they saw it had no flags or masts and they thought it was a whale. But when it washed up on the beach, they removed the clumps of seaweed, the jellyfish tentacles, and the remains of fish and flotsam, and only then did they see that it was a drowned man.

They had been playing with him all afternoon, burying him in the sand and digging him up again, when someone chanced to see them and spread the alarm in the village. The men who carried him to the nearest house noticed that he weighed more than any dead man they had ever known, almost as much as a horse, and they said to each other that maybe he'd been floating too long and the water had got into his bones. When they laid him on the floor they said he'd been taller than all other men because there was barely enough room for him in the house, but they thought that maybe the ability to keep on growing after death was part of the nature of certain drowned men. He had the smell of the sea about him and only his shape gave one to suppose that it was the corpse of a human being, because the skin was covered with a crust of mud and scales.

They did not even have to clean off his face to know that the dead man was a stranger. The village was made up of only twenty-odd wooden houses that had stone courtyards with no flowers and which were spread about on the end of a desertlike cape. There was so little land that mothers always went about with the fear that the wind would carry off their children and the few dead that the years had caused among them had to be thrown off the cliffs. But the sea was calm and bountiful and all the men fitted into seven boats. So when they found the drowned man they simply had to look at one another to see that they were all there.

That night they did not go out to work at sea. While the men went to find out if anyone was missing in neighboring villages, the women stayed behind to care for the drowned man. They took the mud off with grass swabs, they removed the underwater stones entangled in his hair, and they scraped the crust off with tools used for scaling fish. As they were doing that they noticed that the vegetation on him came from faraway oceans and deep water and that his clothes were in tatters, as if he had sailed through labyrinths of coral. They noticed too that he bore his death with pride, for he did not have the lonely look of other drowned men who came out of the sea or that haggard, needy look of men who drowned in rivers. But only when they finished cleaning him off did they become aware of the kind of man he was and it left them breathless. Not only was he the tallest, strongest, most virile, and best built man they had ever seen, but even though they were looking at him there was no room for him in their imagination.

They could not find a bed in the village large enough to lay him on nor was there a table solid enough to use for his wake. The tallest men's holiday pants would not fit him, nor the fattest ones' Sunday shirts, nor the shoes of the one with the biggest feet. Fascinated by his huge size and his beauty, the women then decided to make him some pants from a large piece of sail and a shirt from some bridal brabant linen so that he could continue through his death with dignity. As they sewed, sitting in a circle and gazing at the corpse between stitches, it seemed to them that the wind had never been so steady nor the sea so restless as on that night and they supposed that the change had something to do with the dead man. They thought that if that magnificent man had lived in the village, his house would have had the widest doors, the highest ceiling, and the strongest floor, his bedstead would have been made from a midship frame held together by iron bolts, and his wife would have been the happiest woman. They thought that he would have had so much authority that he could have drawn fish out of the sea simply by calling their names and that he would have put so much work into his land that springs would have burst forth from among the rocks so that he would have been able to plant flowers on the cliffs. They secretly compared him to their own men, thinking that for all their lives theirs were incapable of doing what he could do in one night, and they ended up dismissing them deep in their hearts as the weakest, meanest and most useless creatures on earth. They were wandering through that maze of fantasy when the oldest woman, who as the oldest had looked upon the drowned man with more compassion than passion, sighed:

'He has the face of someone called Esteban.'

It was true. Most of them had only to take another look at him to see that he could not have any other name. The more stubborn among them, who were the youngest, still lived for a few hours with the illusion that when they put his clothes on and he lay among the flowers in patent leather shoes his name might be Lautaro. But it was a vain illusion. There had not been enough canvas, the poorly cut and worse sewn pants were too tight, and the hidden strength of his heart popped the buttons on his shirt. After midnight the whistling of the wind died down and the sea fell into its Wednesday drowsiness. The silence put an end to any last doubts: he was Esteban. The women who had dressed him, who had combed his hair, had cut his nails and shaved him were unable to hold back a shudder of pity when they had to resign themselves to his being dragged along the ground. It was then that they understood how unhappy he must have been with that huge body since it bothered him even after death. They could see him in life, condemned to going through doors sideways, cracking his head on crossbeams, remaining on his feet during visits, not knowing what to do with his soft, pink, sea lion hands while the lady of the house looked for her most resistant chair and begged him, frightened to death, sit here, Esteban, please, and he, leaning against the wall, smiling, don't bother, ma'am, I'm fine where I am, his heels raw and his back roasted from having done the same thing so many times whenever he paid a visit, don't bother, ma'am, I'm fine where I am, just to avoid the embarrassment of breaking up the chair, and never knowing perhaps that the ones who said don't go, Esteban, at least wait till the coffee's ready, were the ones who later on would whisper the big boob finally left, how nice, the handsome fool has gone. That was what the women were thinking beside the body a little before dawn. Later, when they covered his face with a handkerchief so that the light would not bother him, he looked so forever dead, so defenseless, so much like their men that the first furrows of tears opened in their hearts. It was one of the younger ones who began the weeping. The others, coming to, went from sighs to wails, and the more they sobbed the more they felt like weeping, because the drowned man was becoming all the more Esteban for them, and so they wept so much, for he was the most destitute, most peaceful, and most obliging man on earth, poor Esteban. So when the men returned with the news that the drowned man was not from the neighboring villages either, the women felt an opening of jubilation in the midst of their tears.

'Praise the Lord,' they sighed, 'he's ours!'

The men thought the fuss was only womanish frivolity. Fatigued because of the difficult nighttime inquiries, all they wanted was to get rid of the bother of the newcomer once and for all before the sun grew strong on that arid, windless day. They improvised a litter with the remains of foremasts and gaffs, tying it together with rigging so that it would bear the weight of the body until they reached the cliffs. They wanted to tie the anchor from a cargo ship to him so that he would sink easily into the deepest waves, where fish are blind and divers die of nostalgia, and bad currents would not bring him back to shore, as had happened with other bodies. But the more they hurried, the more the women thought of ways to waste time. They walked about like startled hens, pecking with the sea charms on their breasts, some interfering on one side to put a scapular of the good wind on the drowned man, some on the other side to put a wrist compass on him, and after a great deal of *get away from there, woman, stay out of the way, look, you almost made me fall on top of the dead man*, the men began to feel mistrust in their livers and started grumbling about why so many main-altar decorations for a stranger, because no matter how many nails and holy-water jars he had on him, the sharks would chew him all the same, but the women kept piling on their junk relics, running back and forth, stumbling, while they released in sighs what they did not in tears, so that the men finally exploded with *since when has there ever been such a fuss over a drifting corpse, a drowned nobody, a piece of cold Wednesday meat*. One of the women, mortified by so much lack of care, then removed the handkerchief from the dead man's face and the men were left breathless too.

He was Esteban. It was not necessary to repeat it for them to recognize him. If they had been told Sir Walter Raleigh, even they might have been impressed with his gringo accent, the macaw on his shoulder, his cannibal-killing blunderbuss, but there could be only one Esteban in the world and there he was, stretched out like a sperm whale, shoeless, wearing the pants of an undersized child, and with those stony nails that had to be cut with a knife. They only had to take the handkerchief off his face to see that he was ashamed, that it was not his fault that he was so big or so heavy or so handsome, and if he had known that this was going to happen, he would have looked for a more discreet place to drown in, seriously, I even would have tied the anchor off a galleon around my neck and staggered off a cliff like someone who doesn't like things in order not to be upsetting people now with this Wednesday dead body, as you people say, in order not to be bothering anyone with this filthy piece of cold meat that doesn't have anything to do with me. There was so much truth in his manner that even the most mistrustful men, the ones who felt the bitterness of endless nights at sea fearing that their women would tire of dreaming about them and begin to dream of drowned men, even they and others who were harder still shuddered in the marrow of their bones at Esteban's sincerity.

That was how they came to hold the most splendid funeral they could conceive of for an abandoned drowned man. Some women who had gone to get flowers in the neighboring villages returned with other women who could not believe what they had been told, and those women went back for more flowers when they saw the dead man, and they brought more and more until there were so many flowers and so many people that it was hard to walk about. At the final moment it pained them to return him to the waters as an orphan and they chose a father and mother from among the best people, and aunts and uncles and cousins, so that through him all the inhabitants of the village became kinsmen. Some sailors who heard the weeping from a distance went off course and people heard of one who had himself tied to the mainmast, remembering ancient fables about sirens. While they fought for the privilege of carrying him on their shoulders along the steep escarpment by the cliffs, men and women became aware for the first time of the desolation of their streets, the dryness of their courtyards, the narrowness of their dreams as they faced the splendor and beauty of their drowned man. They let him go without an anchor so that he could come back if he wished and whenever he wished, and they all held their breath for the fraction of centuries the body took to fall into the abyss. They did not need to look at one another to realize that they were no longer all present, that they would never be. But they also knew that everything would be different from then on, that their houses would have wider doors, higher ceilings, and stronger floors so that Esteban's memory could go everywhere without bumping into beams and so that no one in the future would dare whisper the big boob finally died, too bad, the handsome fool has finally died, because they were going to paint their house fronts gay colors to make Esteban's memory eternal and they were going to break their backs digging for springs among the stones and planting flowers on the cliffs so that in future years at dawn the passengers on great liners would awaken, suffocated by the smell of gardens on the high seas, and the captain would have to come down from the bridge in his dress uniform, with his astrolabe, his pole star, and his row of war medals and, pointing to the promontory of roses on the horizon, he would say in fourteen languages, look there, where the wind is so peaceful now that it's gone to sleep beneath the beds, over there, where the sun's so bright that the sunflowers don't know which way to turn, yes, over there, that's Esteban's village.

THE CATCH
Nadine Gordimer

His thin strong bony legs passed by at eye level every morning as they lay, stranded on the hard smooth sand. Washed up thankfully out of the swirl and buffet of the city, they were happy to lie there, but because they were accustomed to telling the time by their nerves' response to the different tensions of the city—children crying in flats, lorries going heavily and bicycles jangling for early morning, skid of tyres, sound of frying and the human insect noise of thousands talking and walking and eating at midday—the tensionless shore keyed only to the tide gave them a sense of timelessness that, however much they rejoiced mentally, troubled their habit-impressed bodies with a lack of pressure. So the sound of his feet, thudding nearer over the sand, passing their heads with the deep sound of a man breathing in the heat above the rolled-up, faded trousers, passing away up the beach and shrinking into the figure of an Indian fisherman, began to be something to be waited for. His coming and going divided the morning into three; the short early time before he passed, the time when he was actually passing, and the largish chunk of warm midday that followed when he had gone.

After a few days, he began to say good morning, and looking up they found his face, a long head with a shining dark dome surrounded with curly hair given a stronger liveliness by the sharp coarse strokes of grey hairs, the beautiful curved nose handed out so impartially to Indians, dark eyes slightly bloodshot from the sun, a wide muscular mouth smiling on strong uneven teeth that projected slightly like the good useful teeth of an animal. But it was by his legs they would have known him; the dark, dull-skinned feet with the few black hairs on the big toe, the long hard shaft of the shin tightly covered with smooth shining skin, the pull of the tendons at his ankle like the taut ropes that control the sails of a ship.

They idly watched him go, envious of his fisherman's life not because they could ever really have lived it themselves, but because it had about it the frame of their holiday freedom. They looked at him with the curious respect people feel for one who has put a little space between himself and the rest of the world. 'It's a good life,' said the young man, the words not quite hitting the nail of this respect. 'I can just see *you* . . .' said the girl, smiling. She saw him in his blue creased suit, carrying a bottle of gin wrapped in brown paper, a packet of bananas and the evening paper.

'He's got a nice open face,' said the young man. 'He wouldn't have a face like that if he worked as a waiter at the hotel.'

But when they spoke to him one morning when he was fishing along the surf for chad right in front of them, they found that he like themselves was only on holiday from a more complicated pattern of life. He worked five or six miles away at the sugar refinery, and this was his annual two weeks. He spent it fishing, he told them, because that was what he liked to do with his Sundays. He grinned his strong smile, lifting his chin out to sea as he swung his spoon glittering into the coming wave. They stood by like children, tugging one another back when he cast his line, closing in to peer with their hands behind their backs when he pulled in the flat silver fish and pushed the heads into the sand. They asked him questions, and he answered with a kind of open pleasure, as if discounting his position as a man of skill, a performer before an audience, out of friendliness. And they questioned animatedly, feeling the knowledge that he too was on holiday was a sudden intimacy between them, like the discovery between strangers that they share a friend. The fact that he was an Indian troubled them hardly at all. They almost forgot he *was* an Indian. And this too, though they did not know it, produced a lightening of the heart, a desire to do conversational frolics with a free tongue the way one stretches and kicks up one's legs in the sun after confinement in a close dark room.

'Why not get the camera?' said the girl, beginning to help with the fish as they were brought in. And the young man went away over the sand and came back adjusting the complications of his gadget with the seriousness of the amateur. He knelt in the wet sand that gave beneath his weight with a wet grinding, trying to catch the moment of skill in the fisherman's face. The girl watched quietly, biting her lip for the still second when the camera blinked. Aware but not in the least self-conscious of the fact that he was the subject, the Indian went on with his fishing, now and then parenthetically smiling his long-toothed smile.

The tendrils of their friendship were drawn in sharply for a moment when, putting his catch into a sack, he inquired naturally, 'Would you like to buy one for lunch, sir?' Down on his haunches with a springy strand of hair blowing back and forth over his ear, he could not know what a swift recoil closed back through the air over his head. He wanted to sell something. Disappointment as much as a satisfied dig in the ribs from opportunist prejudice stiffened them momentarily. Of course, he was not in quite the same position as themselves, after all. They shifted their attitude slightly.

'Well, we live at the hotel, you see,' said the girl.

He tied the mouth of the sack and looked up with a laugh. 'Of course!' he smiled, shaking his head. 'You couldn't cook it.' His lack of embarrassment immediately made things easy.

'Do you ever sell fish to the hotel?' asked the young man. 'We must keep a look out for it.'

'No—no, not really,' said the Indian. 'I don't sell much of my fish—mostly we eat it up there,' he lifted his eyebrows to the hills, brilliant with cane. 'It's only sometimes I sell it.'

The girl felt the dismay of having mistaken a privilege for an imposition. 'Oh well,' she smiled at him charmingly, 'that's a pity. Anyway, I suppose the hotel has to be sure of a regular supply.'

'That's right,' he said. 'I only fish in my spare time.'

He was gone, firmly up the beach, his strong feet making clefts in the sand like the muscular claws of a big strong-legged bird.

'You'll see the pictures in a few days,' shouted the girl. He stopped and turned with a grin. 'That's nothing,' he said. 'Wait till I catch something big. Perhaps soon I'll get something worth taking.'

He was 'their Indian'. When they went home they might remember the holiday by him as you might remember a particular holiday as the one when you used to play with a spaniel on the beach every day. It would be, of course, a nameless spaniel, an ownerless spaniel, an entertaining creature existing nowhere in your life outside that holiday, yet bound with absolute intimacy within that holiday itself. And, as an animal becomes more human every day, so every day the quality of their talk with the Indian had to change; the simple question-and-answer relation that goes with the celluloid pop of a ping-pong ball and does so well for all inferiors, foreigners and children became suddenly a toy (the Indian was grown-up and might smile at it). They did not know his name, and now, although they might have asked the first day and got away with it, it was suddenly impossible, because he didn't ask them theirs. So their you's and he's and I's took on the positiveness of names, and yet seemed to deepen their sense of communication by the fact that they introduced none of the objectivity that names must always bring. He spoke to them quite a lot about Johannesburg, to which he assumed they must belong, as that was his generalization of city life, and he knew, sympathetically, that they were city people. And although they didn't live there, but somewhere near on a smaller pattern, they answered as if they did. They also talked a little of his life; or rather of the processes of the sugar refinery from which his life depended. They found it fascinating.

'If I were working, I'd try and arrange for you to come and see it,' he said, pausing, with his familiar taking his own time, and then looking directly smiling at them, his head tilted a little, the proud, almost rueful way one looks at two attractive children. They responded to his mature pleasure in them with a diffusion of warm youth that exuded from their skin as sweat is released at the touch of fear. 'What a fascinating person he is!' they would say to one another, curious.

But mostly they talked about fishing, the sea, and the particular stretch of coast on which they were living. The Indian knew the sea—at home the couple would have said he 'loved' it—and from the look of it he could say whether the water would be hot or cold, safe or nursing an evil grievance of currents, evenly rolling or sucking at the land in a fierce backwash. He knew, as magically to them as a diviner feeling the pull of water beneath the ground, where the fish would be when the wind blew from the east, when it didn't blow at all, and when clouds covered in from the hills to the horizon. He stood on the slippery rocks with them and saw as they did, a great plain of heaving water, empty and unreadable as infinity; but *he* saw a hard greedy life going on down in there, shining plump bodies gaping swiftly close together through the blind green, tentacles like dark hands feeling over the deep rocks. And he would say, coming past them in his salt-stiff old trousers that seemed to put to shame clothes meekly washed in soap and tap-water. 'Over there at the far rocks this morning.'

They saw him most days; but always only in the morning. By afternoon they had had enough of the beach, and wanted to play golf on the closely green course that mapped inland through the man-high cane as though a barber had run a pair of clippers through a fine head of hair, or to sit reading old hotel magazines on the porch whose windows were so bleared with salt air that looking through them was like seeing with the opaque eyes of an old man. The beach was hot and far away; one day after lunch when a man came up from the sand and said as he passed their chairs, 'There's someone looking for you down there. An Indian's caught a huge salmon and he says you've promised to photograph it for him,'—they sat back and looked at one another with a kind of lazy exasperation. They felt weak and unwilling, defeating interest.

'Go on,' she said. 'You must go.'

'It had to be right after lunch,' he grumbled, smiling.

'Oh go on,' she insisted, head tilted. She herself did not move, but remained sitting back with her chin dropped to her chest, while he fetched the camera and went jogging off down the steep path through the bush. She pictured the salmon. She had never seen a salmon: it would be pink and powerfully agile; how big? She could not imagine.

A child came racing up from the beach, all gasps. 'Your husband says,' saying it word for word, 'he says you must come down right away and you must bring the film with you. It's in the little dressing-table drawer under his handkerchiefs.' She swung out of her chair as if she had been ready to go. The small boy ran before her all the way down to the beach, skidding on the stony path. Her husband was waving incoherently from the sand, urgent and excited as a waving flag. Not understanding, she began to hurry too.

'Like this!' he was shouting. 'Like this! Never seen anything like it! It must weigh eighty pounds—' his hands sized out a great hunk of air.

'But where?' she cried impatiently, not wanting to be told, but to see.

'It's right up the beach. He's gone to fetch it. I'd forgotten the film was finished, so when I got there, it was no use. I had to come back, and he said he'd lug it along here.' Yet he hadn't been able to leave the beach to get the film himself; he wanted to be there to show the fish to anyone who came along; he couldn't have borne to have someone see it without him, who had seen it first.

At last the Indian came round the paw of the bay, a tiny black stick detected moving along the beached waterline of black drift-sticks, and as he drew nearer he took on a shape, and then, more distinctly, the shape divided, another shape detached itself from the first, and there he was—a man hurrying heavily with a huge fish slung from his shoulder to his heels. 'O-o-h!' cried the girl, knuckle of her first finger caught between her teeth. The Indian's path wavered, as if he staggered under the weight, and his forearms and hands, gripping the mouth of the fish, were bent stiff as knives against his chest. Long strands of grey curly hair blew over from the back of his head along his bright high forehead, that held the sun in a concentric blur of light on its domed prominence.

'Go and help him,' the girl said to her husband, shaming him. He was standing laughing proudly, like a spectator watching the winner come in at a race. He was startled he hadn't gone himself: 'Shall I?' he said, already going.

They staggered up with the fish between them, panting heavily, and dropped the dead weight of the great creature with a scramble and thud upon the sand. It was as if they had rescued someone from the sea. They stood back that they might feel the relief of their burden, and the land might receive the body. But what a beautiful creature lay there! Through the powdering of sand, mother-of-pearl shone up. A great round glass eye looked out.

'Oh, get the sand off it!' laughed the girl. 'Let's see it properly.'

Exhausted as he was, he belonged to the fish, and so immediately the Indian dragged it by the tail down to the rill of the water's edge, and they cupped water over it with their hands. Water cleared it like a cloth wiping a film from a diamond; out shone the magnificent fish, stiff and handsome in its mail of scales, glittering a thousand opals of colour, set with two brilliant deep eyes all hard clear beauty and not marred by the capability of expression which might have made a reproach of the creature's death; a king from another world, big enough to shoulder a man out of the way, dead, captured, astonishing.

The child came up and put his forefinger on its eye. He wrinkled his nose, smiling and pulling a face, shoulders rising. 'It can't see!' he said joyously. The girl tried it; smooth, firm, resilient eye; like a butterfly wing bright under glass.

They all stood, looking down at the fish, that moved very slightly in the eddy of sand as the thin water spread out softly round its body and then drew gently back. People made for them across the sand. Some came down from the hotel; the piccanin caddies left the golf course. Interest spread like a net, drawing in the few, scattered queer fish of the tiny resort, who avoided one another in a gesture of jealous privacy. They came to stand and stare, prodding a tentative toe at the real fish, scooped out of his sea. The men tried to lift it, making terse suggestions about its weight. A hundred, seventy, sixty-five they said with assurance. Nobody really knew. It was a wonderful fish. The Indian, wishing to take his praise modestly, busied himself with practical details, explaining with serious charm, as if he were quoting a book or someone else's experience, how such a fish was landed, and how rarely it was to be caught on that part of the coast. He kept his face averted, down over the fish, like a man fighting tears before strangers.

'Will it bite? Will it bite?' cried the children, putting their hands inside its rigid white-lipped mouth and shrieking. 'Now that's enough,' said a mother.

'Sometimes there's a lovely stone, here,' the Indian shuffled nearer on his haunches, not touching but indicating with his brown finger a place just above the snout. He twisted his head to the girl. 'If I find it in this one, I'll bring it for you. It makes a lovely ring.' He was smiling to her.

'I want a picture taken with the fish,' she said determinedly, feeling the sun very hot on her head.

Someone had to stand behind her, holding it up. It was exactly as tall as she was; the others pointed with admiration. She smiled prettily, not looking at the fish. Then the important pictures were to be taken: the Indian and his fish,

'Just a minute,' he said, surprisingly, and taking a comb out of his pocket, carefully smoothed back his hair under his guiding hand. He lifted the fish by the gills with a squelch out of the wet sand, and some pictures were taken. 'Like this?' he kept saying anxiously, as he was directed by the young man to stand this way or that.

He stood tense, as if he felt oppressed by the invisible presence of some long-forgotten backdrop and palmstand. 'Smile!' demanded the man and the girl together, anxiously. And the sight of them, so concerned for his picture, released him to smile what was inside him, a strong, wide smile of pure achievement, that gathered up the unequal components of his face—his slim fine nose, his big ugly horse-teeth, his black crinkled-up eyes, and scribbled boldly a brave moment of whole man.

After the pictures had been taken, the peak of interest had been touched; the spectators' attention, quick to rise to a phenomenon, tended to sink back to its level of ordinary, more dependable interests. Wonderment at the fish could not be sustained in its purely specific projection; the remarks became more general and led to hearsay stories of other catches, other unusual experiences. As for the Indian, he had neglected his fish for his audience long enough. No matter how it might differ as an experience, as a fish it did not differ from other fish. He worried about it being in the full hot sun, and dragged it a little deeper into the sea so that the wavelets might flow over it. The mothers began to think that the sun was too hot for their children, and straggled away with them. Others followed, talking about the fish, shading the backs of their necks with their hands. 'Half past two,' said someone. The sea glittered with broken mirrors of hurtful light. 'What do you think you'd get for it?' asked the young man, slowly fitting his camera into its case.

'I'll get about two-pound-ten.' The Indian was standing with his hands on hips, looking down at the fish as if sizing it up.

So he *was* going to sell it! 'As much as that?' said the girl in surprise. With a slow, deliberate movement that showed that the sizing up had been a matter of weight rather than possible profit, he tried carrying the fish under his arm. But his whole body bent in an arc to its weight. He let it slither to the sand.

'Are you going to try the hotel?' she asked; she expected something from the taste of this fish, a flavour of sentiment.

He smiled, understanding her. 'No,' he said indulgently, 'I might. But I don't think they'd take it. I'll try somewhere else. *They* might want it.' His words took in vaguely the deserted beach, the one or two tiny holiday cottages. 'But where else?' she insisted. It irritated her although she smiled, this habit of other races of slipping out of one's questioning, giving vague but adamant assurances of sureties which were supposed to be hidden but that one knew perfectly well did not exist at all. 'Well, there's the boarding-house at Bailey's River—the lady there knows me.

She often likes to take my fish.'

Bailey's River was the next tiny place, about a mile away over the sands. 'Well, I envy them their eating!' said the girl, giving him her praise again. She had taken a few steps back over the sand, ready to go; she held out her hand to draw her husband away. 'When will I see the picture?' the Indian stayed them eagerly. 'Soon, soon, soon!' they laughed. And they left him, kneeling beside his fish and laughing with them.

'I don't know how he's going to manage to carry that great thing all the way to Bailey's,' said the young man. He was steering his wife along with his hand on her little nape. 'It's only a mile!' she said. 'Ye-es! But—?' 'Oh, they're strong. They're used to it,' she said, shaking her feet free of the sand as they reached the path.

When they got back to the hotel, there was a surprise for them. As though the dam of their quiet withdrawal had been fuller than they thought, fuller than they could withstand, they found themselves toppling over into their old stream again, that might run on pointlessly and busy as the brook for ever and ever. Three friends from home up-country were there, come on an unexpected holiday to a farm a mile or two inland. They had come to look them up, as they would no doubt every day of the remainder of the holiday; and there would be tennis, and picnic parties, and evenings when they would laugh on the veranda round a table spiked with bottles and glasses. And so they were swept off from something too quiet and sure to beckon them back, looking behind them for the beckon, but already twitching to the old familiar tune. The visitors were shown the hotel bedroom, and walked down the broken stone steps to the first tee of the little golf course. They were voracious with the need to make use of everything they saw; bouncing on the beds, hanging out of the window, stamping on the tee and assuring that they'd be there with their clubs in the morning.

After a few rounds of drinks at the close of the afternoon, the young man and his wife suddenly felt certain that they had had a very dead time indeed up till now, and the unquiet gnaw of the need to 'make the best'—of time, life, holidays, anything—was gleefully hatched to feed on them again. When someone suggested that they all go into Durban for dinner and a cinema, they were excited. 'All in our car!' the girl cried. 'Let's all go together.'

The women had to fly off to the bedroom to prepare themselves to meet the city, and while the men waited for them, talking quieter and closer on the veranda, the sun went down behind the cane, the pale calm sea thinned into the horizon and turned long straight shoals of light foam to glass on the sand, pocked, farther up, by shadow. When they drove off up the dusty road between the trees they were steeped in the first dark. White stones stood out; as they came to the dip in the road where the stream ran beneath, they saw someone sitting on the boulder that marked the place, and as they slowed and bumped through, the figure moved slightly with a start checked before it could arrest their attention. They were talking. 'What was that?' said one of the women, without much interest. 'What?' said the young man, braking in reflex. 'It's just an old Indian with a sack or something,' someone else broke off to say. The wife, in the front seat, turned:

'Les!' she cried. 'It's him, with the fish!'

The husband had pulled up the car, skidded a little sideways on the road, its two shafts of light staring up among the trees. He sat looking at his wife in consternation. 'But I wonder what's the matter?' he said. 'I don't know!' she shrugged, in a rising tone. 'Who is it?' cried someone from the back.

'An Indian fisherman. We've spoken to him on the beach. He caught a huge salmon today.'

'We know him well,' said the husband; and then to her: 'I'd better back and see what's wrong.' She looked down at her handbag. 'It's going to make us awfully late, if you hang about,' she said. 'I won't hang about!' He reversed in a long jerk, annoyed with her or the Indian, he did not know. He got out, banging the door behind him. They all twisted, trying to see through the rear window. A silence had fallen in the car; a woman started to hum a little tune, faded out. The wife said with a clear little laugh: 'Don't think we're crazy. This Indian is really quite a personality. We forgot to tell you about the fish—it happened only just before you came. Everyone was there looking at it—the most colossal thing I've ever seen. And Les took some pictures of him with it; I had one taken too!'

'So why the devil's the silly fool sitting there with the thing?'

She shrugged. 'God knows,' she said, staring at the clock.

The young husband appeared at the window; he leaned conspiratorially into the waiting faces, with an unsure gesture of the hand. 'He's stuck,' he explained with a nervous giggle. 'Can't carry the thing any farther.' A little way behind him the figure of the Indian stood uncertainly, supporting the long dark shape of the fish. 'But why didn't he sell it?' said the wife, exasperated. 'What can *we* do about it.'

'Taking it home as a souvenir, of course,' said a man, pleased with his joke. But the wife was staring, accusing, at the husband. 'Didn't he try to sell it?' He gestured impatiently. 'Of course. But what does it matter? Fact is, he couldn't sell the damn thing, and now he can't carry it home.' 'So what do you want to do about it?' her voice rose indignantly. 'Sit here all night?' 'Shh,' he frowned. He said nothing. The others kept the studiedly considerate silence of strangers pretending not to be present at a family argument. Her husband's silence seemed to be forcing her to speak. 'Where does he live?' she said in resigned exasperation. 'Just off the main road,' said the husband, pat.

She turned with a charmingly exaggerated sense of asking a favour. 'Would you mind awfully if we gave the poor old thing a lift down the road?' 'No. No . . . Good Lord, no,' they said in a rush. 'There'll be no time to have dinner,' someone whispered.

'Come on and get in,' the young man called over his shoulder, but the Indian still hung back, hesitant. '*Not* the fish!' whispered the wife urgently after her husband. 'Put the fish in the boot!'

They heard the wrench of the boot being opened, the thud of the lid coming down again. Then the Indian stood with the young husband at the door of the car. When he saw her, he smiled at her quickly.

'So your big catch is more trouble than it's worth,' she said brightly. The words seemed to fall hard upon him; his shoulders dropped as if he suddenly realized his stiff tiredness; he smiled and shrugged.

'Jump in,' said the husband heartily, opening the door of the driver's seat and getting in himself. The Indian hesitated, his hand on the back door. The three in the back made no move.

'No, there's no room there,' said the girl clearly, splintering the pause. 'Come round the other side and get in the front.' Obediently the fisherman walked through the headlights—a moment of his incisive face against the light—and opened the door at her side.

She shifted up. 'That's right,' she said, as he got in.

His presence in the car was as immediate as if he had been drawn upon the air. The sea-starched folds of his trousers made a slight harsh rubbing noise against the leather of the seat, his damp old tweed jacket smelled of warm wool, showed fuzzy against the edge of light. He breathed deeply and slowly beside her. In her clear voice she continued to talk to him, to ask him about his failure to sell the fish.

'That catch was more trouble than it was worth,' he said once, shaking his head, and she did not know whether he had just happened to say what she herself had said, or whether he was consciously repeating her words to himself.

She felt a stab of cold uncertainty, as if she herself did not know what she had said, did not know what she had meant, or might have meant. Nobody else talked to the Indian. Her husband drove the car. She was furious with them for leaving it all to her: the listening of the back of the car was as rude and blatant as staring.

'What will you do with the salmon now?' she asked brightly, and 'I'll probably give it away to my relations,' he answered obediently.

When they got to a turn-off a short distance along the main road, the Indian lifted his hand and said quickly, 'Here's the place, thank you.' His hand sent a little whiff of fish into the air. The car scudded into the dust at the side of the road, and as it did so, the door swung open and he was out.

He stood there as if his body still held the position he had carefully disciplined himself to in the car, head hunched a bit, hands curled as if had he had a cap he might perhaps have held it before him, pinned there by the blurs of faces looking out at him from the car. He seemed oddly helpless, standing while the young husband opened the boot and heaved the fish out.

'I must thank you very much,' he kept saying seriously. 'I must thank you.'

'That's all right,' the husband smiled, starting the car with a roar. The Indian was saying something else, but the revving of the engine drowned it. The girl smiled down to him through the window, but did not turn her head as they drove off.

'The things we get ourselves into!' she said, spreading her skirt on the seat. She shook her head and laughed a high laugh. 'Shame! The poor thing! What on earth can he do with the great smelly fish now?'

And as if her words had touched some chord of hysteria in them all, they began to laugh, and she laughed with them, laughed till she cried, gasping all the while, 'But what have I said? Why are you laughing at me? What have I said?'

GREAT BARRIER REEF
Diane Johnson

THE MOTEL HAD smelled of cinder block and cement floor, and was full of Australian senior citizens off a motor coach, but when we woke up in the morning a little less jet-lagged, and from the balcony could see the bed of a tidal river, with ibis and herons poking along the shallows, and giant ravens and parrots in the trees—trees strangling with Monstera vines, all luridly beautiful—we felt it would be all right. But then, when we went along to the quay, I felt it wouldn't. The ship, the Dolphin, was smaller than one could have imagined. Where could sixteen passengers possibly sleep? Brown stains from rusted drainspouts spoiled the

309

hull. Gray deck paint splattered the ropes and ladders, orange primer showed through the chips. Wooden crates of lettuce and cabbages and a case of peas in giant tin cans were stacked on the deck. This cruise had been J.'s idea, so I tried not to seem reproachful, or shocked, at the tiny, shabby vessel. But I am not fond of travel in the best of circumstances—inconvenient displacements punctuated by painful longings to be home. For J., travel is natural opium.

J. was on his way to a meeting in Singapore of the International Infectious Disease Council, a body of eminent medical specialists from different lands who are charged with making decisions about diseases. Should the last remaining smallpox virus be destroyed? What was the significance of a pocket of polio in Sri Lanka? Could leprosy be finished off with a full-bore campaign in the spring? Was tuberculosis on the way back now via AIDS? What about measles in the Third World? I had not realized until I took up with J. that these remote afflictions were still around, let alone that they killed people in the millions. A professor of medicine, J. did research on things that infected the lungs.

He had always longed to visit the Great Barrier Reef, and afterward would give some lectures in Sydney and Wellington, and we planned to indulge another whim en route—skiing in New Zealand in the middle of summer, just to say we'd skied in August and as a bribe to me to come along, for I will go anywhere to ski, it is the one thing. For me the voyage was one of escape from California after some difficult times, and was to be—this was unspoken by either of us— a sort of trial honeymoon (though we were not married) on which we would discover whether we were suited to live together by subjecting ourselves to that most serious of tests, travelling together.

A crewman named Murray, a short, hardy man with a narrow Scots face and thick Aussie accent, showed us our stateroom. It had been called a stateroom in the brochure. Unimaginably small. J. couldn't stand up all the way in it. Two foam mattresses on pallets suspended from the wall, and a smell. The porthole was seamed with salt and rust. Across the passage, the door of another stateroom was open, but that one was a large, pretty room, with mahogany and nautical brass fittings and a desk, and the portholes shone. It was the one, certainly, that had been pictured in the brochure.

'This one here, the Royal, was fitted for Prince Charles, Prince of Wales, when he come on this voyage in 1974,' Murray said.

'How do you book the Royal?' I asked.

'First come, first served,' Murray said. Australian, egalitarian, opposed to privilege.

Up on deck, thinking of spending five days on the Dolphin, I began to be seized by feelings of panic and pain I couldn't explain. They racketed about in my chest, my heart beat fast, I felt as if a balloon were inflating inside me, squeezing up tears and pressing them out of my eyes and thrusting painful words up into my throat, where they lodged. What was the matter with me? Usually I am a calm person (I think); five days is not a lifetime; the aesthetics of a mattress—or its comfort—is not a matter for serious protests. A smell of rotten water sloshing somewhere inside the hull could be gotten used to. Anyone could eat tinned peas five days and survive, plenty of people in the world were glad to get tinned peas. I knew all that. I knew I wasn't reacting appropriately, and was sorry for this querulous fit of passion. Maybe it was only jet lag.

All the same, I said to J., 'I just can't,' and stared tragically at the moorings. He knew, of course, that I could and probably would, but he maintained an attitude of calm sympathy.

'You've been through a rough time,' he said. 'It's the court thing you're really upset about.' Maybe so. The court thing, a draining and frightening custody suit, had only been a week ago, and now here we were a hemisphere away.

The other passengers came on board, one by one or two by two. Cases clattered on the metal gangs. To me, only one person looked possible—a tall, handsome, youngish man with scholarly spectacles and a weathered yachting cap. The rest were aged and fat, plain, wore shapeless brown or navy-blue coat-sweaters buttoned over paunches, had gray perms and bald spots, and they all spoke in this accent I disliked, as if their vowels had been slammed in doors. They spoke like cats, I thought: *eeeoooow*. Fat Australians, not looking fond of nature, why were they all here?

'Why are these people here?' I complained to J. 'What do they care about the Great Barrier Reef?'

'It's a wonder of the world, anyone would want to see it,' J. said, assuming the same dreamy expression he always wore when talking or thinking about the Great Barrier Reef, so long the object of his heart.

I hated all the other passengers. On a second inspection, besides the youngish man, only a youngish couple, Dave and Rita, looked promising, but then I was infuriated to learn that Dave and Rita were Americans—we hadn't come all this way to be cooped up for five days in a prison of an old Coast Guard cutter with other Americans—and, what was worse, Rita and Dave had drawn the Prince Charles cabin, and occupied it as if by natural right, Americans expecting and getting luxury.

Of course, I kept these overwrought feelings to myself. No Australian complained. None appeared unhappy with the ship; no satirical remark, no questioning comment marred their apparent delight with the whole shipshape of things—the cabins, even the appalling lunch, which was under way as soon as the little craft set out, pointing itself east, toward the open sea, from Mackay Harbor.

After we lost sight of land, my mood of desperate resentment did not disappear, as J. had predicted, but deepened. It was more than the irritability of a shallow, difficult person demanding comfort, it was a failure of spirit, inexplicable and unwarranted on this bright afternoon. How did these obese Australian women, these stiff old men, clamber so uncomplainingly belowdecks to their tiny cells, careen along the railings, laughing crazily as they tripped on ropes? Doubtless one would fall and the voyage would be turned back. When I thought of the ugliness of the things I had just escaped from—the unpleasant divorce, the custody battle, the hounding of lawyers and strangers—only to find myself in such a place as this, really unmanageable emotions made me turn my face away from the others.

Dinner was tinned peas, and minted lamb overdone to a gray rag, and potatoes. J. bought a bottle of wine from the little bar, which the deckhand Murray nimbly leaped behind, transforming himself into waiter or bartender as required. We sat with the promising young man, Mark, and offered him some wine, but he said he didn't drink wine. He was no use; he was very, very prim, a bachelor civil servant from Canberra, with a slight stammer, only handsome and young by some accident, and would someday be old without changing, would still be taking lonely cruises, eating minted lamb, would still be unmarried and reticent. He had no conversation, had never been anywhere, did not even know what we wanted from him. Imagining his life, I thought about how sad it was to be him, hoping for whatever he hoped for but not hoping for the right things, content to eat these awful peas, doomed by being Australian, and even while I pitied him I found him hopeless. Even J., who could talk to anyone, gave up trying to talk to him, and, feeling embarrassed to talk only to each other as if he weren't there, we fell silent and stared out the windows at the rising moon along the black horizon of the sea.

There didn't seem a way, in the tiny cabin, for two normal-sized people to exist, let alone to make love; there was no space that could accommodate two bodies in any position. Our suitcases filled half the room. With our summer clothing, our proper suits to wear in Wellington and Sydney, and bulky ski clothes of quilted down, we were ridiculously encumbered with baggage. It seemed stupid now. We were obliged to stow our bags and coats precariously on racks overhead, our duffelbags sleeping at the feet of our bunks like lumpy interloper dogs. J. took my hand comfortingly in the dark, across the space between the two bunks, before he dropped off to sleep; I lay awake, seized with a terrible fit of traveller's panic, suffocating with fearful visions of fire, of people in prison cells or confined in army tanks, their blazing bodies emerging screaming from the holds of ships to writhe doomed on the ground, their stick limbs ringed in flame, people burned in oil splashed on them from the holds of rusted ships, and smells of underground, smells of sewers, the slosh of engine fuel from the hell beneath.

As is so often the traveller's fate, nothing on the cruise was as promised or as we had expected. The seedy crew of six had tourist-baked smiles and warmed-over jokes. There was a little faded captain who climbed out of his tower to greet us now and then, and a sort of Irish barmaid, Maureen, who helped Murray serve the drinks. The main business of the passage seemed not to be the life of the sea or the paradise of tropical birds on Pacific shores or the balmy water but putting in at innumerable islands to look at souvenir shops. J., his mind on the Great Barrier Reef, which we were expected to reach on the fourth day, sweetly bore it all, the boredom and the endless stops at each little island, but I somehow couldn't conquer my petulant dislike.

It fastened, especially, on our shipmates. Reluctantly, I learned their names, in order to detest them with more precision: Don and Donna from New Zealand, Priscilla from Adelaide—portly, harmless old creatures, as J. pointed out. Knowing that the derisive remarks that sprang to my lips only revealed me as petty and complaining to good-natured J., I didn't speak them aloud. But it seemed to me that these Australians only wanted to travel to rummage in the souvenir shops, though these were all alike from island to island: Daydream Island, Hook Island—was this a cultural or a generation gap? I brooded on the subject of souvenirs: why they should exist, why people should want them, by what law they were made ugly—shells shaped like toilets, a row of swizzlesticks in the shapes of women's silhouetted bodies, thin, fatter, fat, with bellies and breasts increasingly sagging as they graduated from 'Sweet Sixteen' to 'Sixty.' I was unsettled to notice that the one depicting a woman of my age had a noticeably thickened middle. I watched a man buy a fat one and hand it to his wife. 'Here, Mother, this one's you,' he said. Laughter a form of hate. It was not a man from our ship, luckily, or I would have pushed him overboard. I brooded on my own complicity in the industry of souvenirs, for didn't I buy them myself? The things I bought—the tasteful (I liked to think) baskets and elegant textiles I was always carting home— were these not just a refined form of souvenir for a more citified sort of traveller?

Statuettes of drunken sailors, velvet pictures of island maidens, plastic seashell lamps made in Taiwan. What contempt the people who think up souvenirs have for other people! Yet our fellow-passengers plunked down money with no feeling of shame. They never walked on the sand or looked at the colors of the bright patchwork birds rioting in the palm trees. Besides us, only the other Americans, Rita and Dave, did this. It was Dave who found the perfect helmet shell, a regular treasure, the crew assured them, increasingly rare, protected even—you weren't supposed to carry them away, but who was looking? I wanted it to have been J. who got it.

Each morning, each afternoon, we stopped at another island. This one was Daydream Island. 'It's lovely, isn't it, dear?' Priscilla said to me. 'People like to see a bit of a new place, the shopping, they have different things to make it interesting.' But it wasn't different, it was the same each day: the crew hands the heavy, sacklike people, grunting, down into rowboats, and hauls them out onto a sandy slope of beach. Up they trudge toward a souvenir shop. This one had large shells perched on legs, and small shells pasted in designs on picture frames, and earrings made of shells, and plastic buckets, and plastic straw hats surrounded with fringe, and pictures of hula dancers.

'I don't care, I do hate them,' I ranted passionately to J. 'I'm right to hate them. They're what's the matter with the world, they're ugly consumers, they can't look at a shell unless it's coated in plastic, they never look at the sea—why are they here? Why don't they stay in Perth and Adelaide—you can buy shells there, and swizzlesticks in the shape of hula girls.' Of course J.

hadn't any answer for this, of course I was right.

I wandered onto a stretch of beach and took off my shoes, planning to wade. Whenever I was left alone I found myself harking back to the court hearing, my recollections just as sharp and painful as a week ago. I couldn't keep from going over and over my ordeal, and thinking of my hated former husband, or not really him so much as his lawyer, Waxman, a man in high-heeled boots and aviator glasses. I imagined him here in these waters. He has fallen overboard off the back of the ship. I am the only one to notice, and I have the power to cry out for his rescue but I don't. Our eyes meet; he is down in the water, still wearing the glasses. I imagine his expression of surprise when he realizes that I'm not going to call for help. What for him had been a mere legal game, a job, would cost him his life. He had misjudged me. The ship speeds along. We are too far away to hear his cries.

It was the third day, and we had set down at Happy Island. Here we had to wade across a sandbar. This island had goats grazing. 'This is the first we've gotten wet,' I bitterly complained. We stood in ankle-deep water amid queer gelatinous seaweed. I had wanted to swim, to dive, to sluice away the court and the memories, but hadn't been permitted to, because these waters, so innocently beautiful, so seductively warm, were riddled with poisonous creatures, deadly toxins, and sharks.

'Be careful not to pick up anything that looks like this,' Murray warned, showing us a harmless-looking little shell. 'The deadly cone shell. And the coral, be careful a' that, it scratches like hell. One scratch can take over a year to heal. We have some ointment on board, be sure to tell one of the crew if you scratch yourself.'

From here, I looked back at the ship, and, seeing the crew watching us, I suddenly saw ourselves, the passengers, with the crew's eyes: we were a collection of thick bodies, mere cargo to be freighted around, slightly volatile, likely to ferment, like damp grain, and to give trouble—difficult cargo that boozed, sent you scurrying unreasonably on tasks, got itself cut on coral, made you laugh at its jokes. I could see that the crew must hate us.

Yet, a little later, I came upon Murray tying on a fishhook for old George, whose fingers were arthritic. Murray was chatting to him with a natural smile. I studied them. Perhaps Murray by himself was a man of simple good nature, but the rest, surely, hated us. The captain, staring coolly out from his absurd quarterdeck, made no pretense of liking us, seemed always to be thinking of something else, not of this strange Pacific civilization of Quonset huts and rotting landing barges and odd South Sea denizens strangely toothless, beyond dentistry, beyond fashion, playing old records over and over on P.A. systems strung through the palms. You felt the forlornness of these tacky little islands that should have been beautiful and serene. I even wondered if we would ever get back to America. Not that I wanted to. America was smeared with horrible memories, scenes of litigation. Why shouldn't J. and I simply stay here? Why, more important, was I not someone who was able, like the lovely goat that grazed on the slope near here, to gaze at the turquoise sea and enjoy the sight of little rose-colored parrots wheeling in the air? Why was I not, like a nice person, simply content to *be*, to enjoy beauty and inner peace? Instead I must suffer, review, quiver with fears and rages—the fault, I saw, was in myself, I was a restless, peevish, flawed person. How would I be able to struggle out of this frame of mind? Slipping on the sandy bank, I frightened the little goat.

By the third day I began to notice a sea change in our shipmates, who had begun in sensible gabardines and print dresses, but now wore violently floral shirts and dresses, and were studded with shells—wreaths of shells about their necks and at their ears, hats embroidered with crabs and gulls. By now I knew a bit more about them. They were all travellers. George and Nettie, Fred and Polly had been friends for forty years, and spent a part of each year, now that they were all retired, travelling in Europe in their caravans. Dave and Rita were both schoolteachers, and Rita raised Great Danes. Priscilla was going along on this cruise with her brother Albert, because Albert had just lost his wife. Mark was taking his annual vacation. Don and Donna were thinking of selling their Auckland real-estate business, buying a sailboat to live on, and circumnavigating the globe. J. told me that George was a sensitive and sweet man who had lived his whole life in Australia, and only now in his retirement had begun to see something of the world. 'And he says that the most beautiful place on earth is some place near Split, in Yugoslavia, and if I take you there, my darling, will you for God's sake cheer up now?' But I couldn't.

Tonight we were dining ashore, in a big shed on Frenchie's Island, a shabby tin building. Music was already playing on loudspeakers. Groups of people from other ships, or hotels, strolled around carrying drinks. A smell of roasted sausages, someone singing 'Waltzing Matilda' in the kitchen at the back. The Dolphin passengers were lined up at the bar and in the souvenir shop. In the big hangar of a room little tables encircled a dance floor, and at one end a microphone stood against a photo mural of the South Seas, as if the real scene outdoors were not sufficiently evocative. The sun lowered across the pink water, setting in the east, and the water in the gentle lagoon was as warm as our blood. 'I wish a hurricane would come and blow it all away,' I said to J.

When the diners had tipped their paper plates into a bin, they began to sing old American songs. Sitting outside, I could hear Maureen singing 'And Let Her Sleep Under the Bar.' Then came canned music from a phonograph, and people began to dance—the ones who were not too decrepit. I tried to hear only the chatter of the monkeys or parrots in the palm trees, innocent creatures disturbed by the raucous humans. J. was strangely cheerful and shot some pool with a New Zealander, causing me all of a sudden to think, with a chill of disapproval, that J. possibly was an Australian at heart and that I ought not to marry him or I would end up in a caravan in Split. His good looks and professional standing were only a mask that concealed . . . simplicity.

It didn't surprise me that people liked the handsome and amiable J.; it didn't even surprise me that they seemed to like me. I had concealed my tumult of feelings, and I was used to being treated by other people with protective affection, if only because I am small. This in part explained why the courtroom, and its formal process of accusation, its focus on me as a stipulated bad person, had been such a shock. It was as if a furious mob had come to smash with sticks the porcelain figure of my self. I had a brief intimation that the Australians, with their simple friendliness, could put me back together if I would let them, but I would rather lie in pieces for a while.

The moon was full and golden. 'What a beautiful, beautiful night,' said Nettie from Perth, the wife of George, coming out onto the beach. Who could disagree? Not even I. The ship on the moonlit water lapped at anchor, resting, awaiting them, looking luxurious and serene. J. came out and showed us the Southern Cross. At first I couldn't see it, all constellations look alike to me—I have never been able to see the bears or belts or any of it. But now, when J. turned my chin, I did see it, and it did look like a cross.

In the night I had another dream, in which the lawyer had said, 'Isn't it true that you have often left your children while you travel?' He had been looking not at me but at a laughing audience. He was speaking over a microphone. The audience wore fringed hats of plastic straw.

'Not willingly, no,' I said. 'Not often.'

'How many times did you go on trips last year and leave them at home?'

'Oh, six, I don't know.'

'That's not often?'

'Just a day or two each time. A man takes a business trip, you don't call it "leaving," or "often."' But I was not allowed to speak or explain.

'We're looking at how often you are in fact away from your children.'

Here I had awakened, realizing that it was all true, it wasn't just a dream, it was what had happened—not, of course, the audience in plastic hats. Even though in the end I had been vindicated in the matter of the children, I still felt sticky with the encumbrance of their father's hate. All I had wanted was to be free, and now I was so soiled with words spoken at me, about me, by strangers, by lawyers I had never seen before, who had never seen me. It didn't seem fair that you could not prevent being the object of other people's emotions, you were not safe anywhere from their hate—or from their love, for that matter. You were never safe from being invaded by their feelings when you wanted only to be rid of them, free, off, away.

In the morning I had wanted to swim, to bathe in the sea, to wash all this stuff off, splash; my longing must have been clear, because Cawley, the other deckhand, laughed at me. 'Not here you don't, love,' he said. 'There's sharks here as long as a boat.'

The captain, Captain Clarke, made one of his few visits. He had kept aloof in the pilot cabin above, though he must have slipped down to the galley to eat, or maybe the crew took him his food up there. Now he invited his passengers two by two to the bridge. When people were tapped, they hauled themselves up the metal ladder, steadied by Cawley or Murray, then would come down looking gratified. Albert, who went up alone, suggested that he had helped avoid a navigational accident.

J. and I were invited on the morning of the fourth day, the day we were to arrive at the reef itself in the late afternoon. I went up despite myself. Captain Clarke was a thin, red-haired man sitting amid pipes and instruments. He let us take the wheel, and showed us the red line that marked our route through the labyrinth of islands on the chart. His manner was grave, polite, resigned. No doubt these visits were dictated by the cruise company.

'But there are thousands of islands between here and the Great Barrier Reef!' said J., studying the charts.

'Souvenir shops on every one,' I couldn't help saying. J. fastened me with a steady look in which I read terminal exasperation.

'These islands are not all charted,' said the Captain. 'The ones that are were almost all charted by Captain Cook himself, after he ran aground on one in 1770. He was a remarkable navigator. He even gave names to them all. But new ones are always being found. I've always hoped to find one myself.'

'What would you name it?' J. asked.

'I would give it my name, or, actually, since there is already a Clarke Island, I would name it for my wife, Laura—Laura Clarke Island—or else for Alison, my daughter.'

'Do you keep your eyes open for one?'

'I mean to get one,' he said.

When we went down to the deck again, Maureen was gazing at the waves. 'It's getting choppy,' she observed, unnecessarily, for the boat had begun to rear up like a prancing horse.

'Right, we probably won't make it,' Murray agreed.

'What do you mean?' I asked, alarmed by the tinge of satisfaction that underlay their sorry looks.

'To the reef. No point in going if the sea's up, like it's coming up—washed right up, no use going out there. If it's like this, we put in at Hook Island instead.'

Astonished, I looked around to see if J., or anyone else, was listening. No, or not worried—would just as soon have Hook Island. They continued to knit and read along the deck, which now began to heave more forcefully, as if responding to the desire of the crew to return to port without seeing the great sight.

'How often does it happen that you don't go to the reef?' I asked Murray, heart thundering. The point of all this, and J.'s dream, was to go to the reef, and now they were casually dismissing the possibility.

'Oh, it happens more often than not. This time of year, you know. Chancy, the nautical business is.'

'Come out all this way and not see it?' I insisted, voice rising.

327

'Well, you can't see it if the waves are covering it up, can you? You can bump your craft into it, but you can't see it. Can you?'

'I don't know,' I cried. 'I don't even know what it is.' But the shape of things was awfully clear; given the slightest excuse, the merest breeze or ripple, the Dolphin would not take us to the Great Barrier Reef, and perhaps had never meant to. I thought in panic of not alerting J., but then I rushed to tell him. He put down his book, his expression aghast, and studied the waves.

The midday sky began to take on a blush of deeper blue, and now that our attention was called to it, the sea seemed to grow dark and rough before our eyes. Where moments before it had been smooth enough to row, we now began to pitch. The report of the prow smacking the waves made me think of cannons, of Trafalgar. In defiance of the rocking motion, the Australian passengers began to move around the cabin and along the deck, gripping the railings, looking trustfully at the sky and smiling. Their dentures were white as teacups.

'Christ,' said Murray, 'one of these bloody old fools will break a hip. Folks, why don't you sit down?' Obediently, like children, the Australians went inside the main cabin and sat in facing rows of chairs. Despite the abrupt change in the weather, the ship continued its course out to sea. J. and I anchored ourselves in the prow, leaning against the tool chest, resolutely watching the horizon, not the bounding deck beneath our feet—a recommended way to avoid seasickness. In twenty minutes the sea had changed altogether, from calm to a thing that threw the little ship in the air. We felt as if we were slithering along the back of a sea monster that was toiling beneath us.

Soon the dread spectre of seasickness was among us. The Captain, rusty-haired, pale-eyed, as if his eyes had been bleached with sea wind, climbed off the bridge and glanced inside the cabin at his passengers.

'Oh, please, they want to go, they'll be all right,' I called to him, but the words were swept off by the wind. The others were so occupied with the likelihood of nausea that they hadn't grasped that the ship might turn back, and they seemed rather to be enjoying the drama of getting seasick. Every few minutes someone would get up, totter out to the rail, retch over it, and return to the laughter and commiseration of the others. The friendly thing was to be sick, so I was contrarily determined not to be, and J. was strong by nature. One of the Australians, Albert, gave us a matey grin as he lurched over our feet toward a bucket. I looked disgustedly away, but J. wondered aloud if he should be helping these old folks.

'Of course, they'll use this as an excuse for not going,' I was saying bitterly. These barfing Australian senior citizens would keep us from getting to the Great Barrier Reef. My unruly emotions, which had been milder today, now plumped around in my bosom like the boat smacking on the waves. J. watched the Australians screaming with laughter and telling each other, 'That's right, barf in the bin.'

'This is a rough one,' Albert said, and pitched sharply against the cabin, so that J. leaped up to catch him. Murray, tightening ropes, called for him to go back inside.

'Tossed a cookie meself.' He grinned at J. and me.

'We don't think it's so rough,' I said.

'I've seen plenty rougher,' Murray agreed. 'Bloody hangover is my problem.'

When the Captain leaned out to look down at the deck below him, I cried, 'Oh, we just have to go to the reef, we have to! Oh, please!'

'What's the likelihood this sea will die down?' J. shouted to the Captain. The Captain shrugged. I felt angry at J. for the first time, as if he were a magnet. It was unfair, I knew, to say it was J.'s fault—the storm, the tossing sea, the Dolphin, and, of course, the rest. J. who had signed us up for this terrible voyage, during which we would be lost at sea, before reaching the Great Barrier Reef, whatever it was, and who had caused the sea to come up like this. All J.'s fault. If I ever saw the children again it would be a miracle—or else they would be saying in after years, Our mother perished on the high seas somewhere off Australia. What would they remember of me? The sight of the boiling waves, now spilling over the bow, now below us, made me think of throwing myself in—just an unbidden impulse trailing into my mind, the way I half thought, always, of throwing my keys or my sunglasses off bridges. Of course I wouldn't do it.

The ship pitched, thrust, dove through the waters. Yet we had not turned back. 'Whoooeee,' the Aussies were screaming inside the lounge. Life was like this, getting tossed around, and then, right before the real goal is reached, something, someone, impedes you.

'J., don't let them turn back,' I said again, for the tenth time, putting all the imperative passion I could into my voice. Without hearing me, J. was already climbing the ladder to the bridge. I looked at my fingers whitely gripping the rope handle on the end of the tool chest. A bait locker slid across the deck, back, across, back, and once, upon the impact of a giant wave, a dead fish stowed in it sloshed out onto the deck. Then, in the wind, I heard Murray's thin voice call out, 'It's all right, love, we're going to the reef! The Captain says we're going to the reef!'

As abruptly as the storm had started, it subsided meekly, the sky once more changed color, now to metallic gray, lighter at the horizon, as if it were dawn. Ahead of us an indistinguishable shape lay in the water like the back of a submerged crocodile, a vast bulk under the surface. The Captain had stopped the engines, and we drifted in the water. 'The reef, the reef!' cried the Australians, coming out on deck. I shouted, too. The crew began to busy themselves with readying the small boats, and the other passengers came boisterously out of the cabin, as if nothing had been wrong. 'Ow,' they said, 'that was a bit of a toss.'

'You'll have two hours on the reef, not more,' the Captain told us before we climbed again into the rowboats. 'Because of the tide. If you get left there at high tide, if we can't find you, well, we don't come back. Because you wouldn't be there.' The Australians laughed at this merry joke.

J. handed me out of the boat and onto the reef. My first step on it shocked me. For I had had the idea of coral, hard and red, a great lump of coral sticking out of the ocean, a jagged thing that would scratch you if you fell on it, that you could carve into formations dictated by your own mind. We had heard it was endangered, and I had imagined its destruction by divers with chisels, carrying off lumps at a time.

Instead it was like a sponge. It sank underfoot, it sighed and sucked. Looking down, I could see that it was entirely alive, made of eyeless formations of cabbagey creatures sucking and opening and closing, yearning toward tiny ponds of water lying on the pitted surface, pink, green, gray, viscous, silent. I moved, I put my foot here, then hurriedly there, stumbled, and gashed my palm against something rough.

'Where should you step? I don't want to step on the things,' I gasped.

'You have to. Just step as lightly as you can,' J. said.

'It's alive, it's all alive!'

'Of course. It's coral, it's alive, of course,' J. said. He had told me there were three hundred and fifty species of living coral here, along with the calcareous remains of tiny polyzoan and hydrozoan creatures that helped to form a home for others. Anemones, worms, gastropods, lobsters, crayfish, prawns, crown of thorns, other starfish, hydrocorals, the red Lithothamnion algae, the green Halimeda.

'Go on, J., leave me,' I said, seeing that he wanted to be alone to have his own thoughts about all this marine life, whatever it meant to him. It meant something. His expression was one of rapture. He smiled at me and wandered off.

I had my Minox, but I found the things beneath my feet too fascinating to photograph. Through the viewer of my camera they seemed pale and far away. At my feet, in astonishing abundance, they went on with their strange life. I hated to tread on them, so stood like a stork and aimed the camera at the other passengers.

These were proceeding cautiously, according to their fashion, over the delicate surface—Mark in his yachting cap, with his camera, alone; the Kiwis in red tropical shirts more brilliant than the most bright-hued creatures underfoot; even the crew, with insouciant expressions, protectively there to save their passengers from falls or from strange sea poisons that darted into the inky ponds from the wounded life beneath our feet. For the first time, I felt, seeing each behaving characteristically, that I knew them all, and even that I liked them, or at least that I liked it that I understood what they would wear and do. Travellers like myself.

I watched J. kneeling in the water to peer into the centers of the mysterious forms. Almost as wonderful as this various life was J.'s delight. He was as dazzled as if we had walked on stars, and, indeed, the sun shining on the tentacles, wet petals, filling the spongy holes, made things sparkle like a strange underfoot galaxy. He appeared as a long, sandy-haired, handsome stranger, separate, unknowable. I, losing myself once more in the patterns and colors, thought of nothing, was myself as formlesss and uncaring as the coral, all my unruly, bad-natured passions leaching harmlessly into the sea, leaving a warm sensation of blankness and ease. I thought of the Hindu doctrine of *ahimsa*, of not harming living things, and I was not harming them, I saw—neither by stepping on them nor by leaving my anger and fears and the encumbrances of real life with them. For me, the equivalent of J.'s happiness was this sense of being cured of a poisoned spirit.

At sunset we headed landward into the sun, a strange direction to a Californian, for whom all sunsets are out at sea. We would arrive at Mackay at midnight—it also seemed strange that a voyage that had taken four days out would take only six hours back, something to do with the curve of the continental shelf. A spirit of triumph imbued our little party—we had lived through storms and reached a destination. People sat in the lounge labelling their film.

Maureen came along and reminded us that as this was our last night on board, there would be a fancy-dress party. When we had read this in the brochure, I had laughed. It had seemed absurd that such a little ship would give itself great liner airs. J. and I had not brought costumes. In our cabin, I asked him what he meant to wear. Since my attitude had been so resolutely one of noncompliance, he seemed surprised that I was going to participate in the dressing up. 'I know it's stupid, but how can we not?' I said. 'It would be so churlish, with only sixteen of us aboard.'

J. wore his ski pants, which were blue and tight, with a towel cape, and called himself Batman. I wore his ski parka, a huge, orange, down-filled garment. The others were elaborately got up, must have brought their masks and spangles with them. Rita wore a black leotard and had painted cat whiskers on her face, and Dave had a Neptune beard. Nettie wore a golden crown, and Don a harlequin suit, half purple, half green. I drew to one side and sat on the table with my feet drawn up inside J.'s parka, chin on my knees, watching the capers that now began. 'Me? I am a pumpkin,' I explained, when they noticed the green ribbon in my hair, my stem. It wasn't much of a costume, but it was all I could think of, and they laughed forgivingly and said that it looked cute.

J. won a prize, a bottle of beer, for the best paper cutout of a cow. I was surprised, watching him making meticulous little snips with the scissors, to see how a cow shape emerged under his hands, with a beautiful, delicate udder and teats, and knobs of horn. I had not thought that J. would notice a cow.

'I have an announcement,' Mark said, in a strangely loud and shaky voice, one hand held up, his other hand nervously twisting his knotted cravat. The theme of his costume was not obvious.

'Excuse me, an announcement.' The others smiled and shushed. 'I've had word from my friend—a few months ago I had the honor to assist a friend with his astronomical observations, and I've just had word that he—we—that the comet we discovered has been accepted by the international commission. It will bear his name, and, as I had the honor to assist, I'll be mentioned, too. Only a little comet, of course, barely a flash in the sky. There are millions of them, of course. There are millions of them, but—'

A cheer, toasts. Mark bought drinks for everybody.

The crew bought drinks for the guests, dishing up from behind the little bar with the slick expertise of land-side bartenders. They seemed respectful at Mark's news. I raised my glass with the rest and felt ashamed at the way I had despised Mark's life—indeed, a nice life, spent exploring the heavens with a friend. How had I thought him friendless, this nice-looking young man?

'Split, Yugoslavia, is the most beautiful place on earth,' George was telling me. 'Like a travel poster. I've been almost everywhere by now, except China, but there, at Split, my heart stopped.' My attention was reclaimed from my own repentant thoughts; for a second I had been thinking that he was describing a medical calamity, and I had been about to say 'How terrible!'

But no, he was describing a moment, an epiphany, the experience of beauty. He had the long, bald head of a statesman, but he was a farmer, now retired, from Perth. I was ashamed that it had taken me so long to see that the difference between Americans and Australians was that Americans were tired and bored, while for Australians, stuck off at the edge of the world, all was new, and they had the energy and spirit to go off looking for abstractions like beauty, and comets.

'Let me get you another one of those,' George said, taking my wineglass, for a pumpkin cannot move.

'How long have you been married?' asked Nettie, smiling at me. I considered, not knowing whether I wanted to shock them by admitting that we were not married at all. 'Two years,' I said.

'Really?' Nettie laughed. 'We all thought you was newlyweds.' Her smile was sly.

I felt myself flush inside the hot parka. The others had thought all my withdrawn unfriendliness was newlywed shyness and the preoccupations of love. They were giving me another chance.

'It seems like it.' I laughed. I would never marry J., I thought. He was too good-natured to be saddled with a cross person like me. And yet now I wasn't cross, was at ease and warm with affection for the whole company. Don and Donna were buying champagne all around, and the crew, now that they were about to be rid of this lot of passengers, seemed sentimental and sorry, as if we had been the nicest, most amusing passengers ever. The prize for the best costume was to be awarded by vote. People wrote on bits of paper and passed them to Maureen, who sat on the bar and sorted them. There was even a little mood of tension, people wanting to win.

'And the prize for the best costume'—she paused portentously—'goes to the pumpkin!' My shipmates beamed and applauded. In the hot parka I felt myself grow even warmer with shame and affection. People of good will and good sense, and I had allowed a snobbish mood of acedia to blind me to it. Their white, untroubled smiles.

In a paper parcel was a key ring with a plastic-covered picture of the Dolphin, and the words 'Great Barrier Reef' around the edge of it. I was seized by a love for it, would always carry it, I decided, if only as a reminder of various moral lessons I thought myself to have learned, and as a reminder of certain bad things about my own character.

'Thank you very much,' I said. 'I'll always keep it. And I'll always remember the Dolphin and all of you'—for I thought, of course, that I would. J. was looking at me with a considering air, as if to inspect my sincerity. But I was sincere.

'I know I've been a pig,' I apologised to him later, as we gathered our things in the stateroom. 'These people are really very sweet.'

'I wonder if you'd feel like that if you hadn't gotten the prize,' he said, peevishly. I was surprised at his tone. Of course, it wasn't the prize—only a little key chain, after all—that had cured me, but the process of the voyage, and the mysterious power of distant places to dissolve the problems the traveller has brought along. Looking at J., I could see that, for his part, he was happy but let down, as if the excitement and happiness of seeing the reef at last, and no doubt the nuisance of my complaining, had worn him out for the moment, and serious thoughts of his coming confrontations with malaria and leprosy and pain and sadness were returning, and what he needed was a good night's sleep.

THE SEASIDE HOUSES
John Cheever

EACH YEAR, WE rent a house at the edge of the sea
and drive there in the first of the summer—with the
dog and cat, the children, and the cook—arriving at
a strange place a little before dark. The journey to the
sea has its ceremonious excitements, it has gone on for
so many years now, and there is the sense that we are,
as in our dreams we have always known ourselves to
be, migrants and wanderers—travelers, at least, with
a traveler's acuteness of feeling. I never investigate the
houses that we rent, and so the wooden castle with a
tower, the pile, the Staffordshire cottage covered with
roses, and the Southern mansion all loom up in the last

of the sea light with the enormous appeal of the unknown. You get the sea-rusted keys from the house next door. You unfasten the lock and step into a dark or a light hallway, about to begin a vacation—a month that promises to have no worries of any kind. But as strong as or stronger than this pleasant sense of beginnings is the sense of having stepped into the midst of someone else's life. All my dealings are with agents, and I have never known the people from whom we have rented, but their ability to leave behind them a sense of physical and emotional presences is amazing. Our affairs are certainly not written in air and water, but they do seem to be chronicled in scuffed baseboards, odors, and tastes in furniture and paintings, and the climates we step into in these rented places are as marked as the changes of weather on the beach. Sometimes there is in the long hallway a benignness, a purity and clearness of feeling to which we all respond. Someone was enormously happy here, and we rent their happiness as we rent their beach and their catboat. Sometimes the climate of the place seems mysterious, and remains a mystery until we leave in August. Who, we wonder, is the lady in the portrait in the upstairs hallway? Whose was the Aqualung, the set of Virginia Woolf? Who hid the copy of *Fanny Hill* in the china closet, who played the zither, who slept in the cradle, and who was the woman who painted red enamel on the nails of the claw-footed bathtub? What was this moment in her life?

The dog and the children run down to the beach, and we bring in our things, wandering, it seems, through the dense histories of strangers. Who owned the *Lederhosen*, who spilled ink (or blood) on the carpet, who broke the pantry window? And what do you make of a bedroom bookshelf stocked with *Married Happiness, An Illustrated Guide to Sexual Happiness in Marriage, The Right to Sexual Felicity,* and *A Guide to Sexual Happiness for Married Couples*? But outside the windows we hear the percussive noise of the sea; it shakes the bluff where the house stands, and sends its rhythm up through the plaster and timbers of the place, and in the end we all go down to the beach—it is what we came for, after all—and the rented house on the bluff, burning now with our lights, is one of those images that have preserved their urgency and their fitness. Fishing in the spring woods, you step on a clump of wild mint and the fragrance released is like the essence of that day. Walking on the Palatine, bored with antiquities and life in general, you see an owl fly out of the ruins of the palace of Septimius Severus and suddenly that day, that raffish and noisy city, all make sense. Lying in bed, you draw on your cigarette and the red glow lights an arm, a breast, and a thigh around which the world seems to revolve. These images are like the embers of our best feelings, and, standing on the beach, for that first hour, it seems as if we could build them into a fire. After dark we shake up a drink, send the children to bed, and make love in a strange room that smells of someone else's soap—all measures taken to exorcise the owners and secure our possession of the place. But in the middle of the night the terrace door flies open with a crash, although there seems to be no wind, and my wife says, half asleep, 'Oh, why have they come back? Why have they come back? What have they lost?'

Broadmere is the rented house I remember most clearly, and we got there at the usual time of day. It was a large white house, and it stood on a bluff facing south, which was the open sea on that coast. I got the key from a Southern lady in a house across the garden, and opened the door onto a hallway with a curved staircase. The Greenwoods, the owners, seemed to have left that day, seemed in fact to have left a minute earlier. There were flowers in the vases, cigarette butts in the ashtrays, and a dirty glass on the table. We brought in the suitcases and sent the children down to the beach, and I stood in the living room waiting for my wife to join me. The stir, the discord of the Greenwoods' sudden departure still seemed to be in the air. I felt that they had gone hastily and unwillingly, and that they had not wanted to rent their summer house. The room had a bay window looking out to sea, but in the twilight the place seemed drab, and I found it depressing. I turned on a lamp, but the bulb was dim and I thought that Mr Greenwood had been a parsimonious and mean man. Whatever he had been, I seemed to feel his presence with uncommon force. On the bookshelf there was a small sailing trophy that he had won ten years before. The books were mostly Literary Guild selections. I took a biography of Queen Victoria off the shelf, but the binding was stiff, and I think no one had read it. Hidden behind the book was an empty whiskey bottle. The furniture seemed substantial and in good taste, but I was not happy or at ease in the room. There was an upright piano in the corner, and I played some scales to see if it was in tune (it wasn't) and opened the piano bench to look for music. There was some sheet music, and two more empty whiskey bottles. Why hadn't he taken out his empties like the rest of us? Had he been a secret drinker? Would this account for the drabness of the room? Had he learned to take the top off the bottle without making a sound, and mastered the more difficult trick of canting the glass and the bottle so that the whiskey wouldn't splash? My wife came in, carrying an empty suitcase, which I took up to the attic. This part of the house was neat and clean. All the tools and the paints were labeled and in their places, and all this neatness, unlike the living room, conveyed an atmosphere of earnestness and probity He must have spent a good deal of time in the attic, I thought. It was getting dark, and I joined my wife and children on the beach.

The sea was running high and the long white line of the surf reached, like an artery, down the shore for as far as we could see. We stood, my wife and I, with our arms loosely around one another—for don't we all come down to the sea as lovers, the pretty woman in her pregnancy bathing suit with a fair husband, the old couples who bathe their gnarled legs, and the bucks and the girls, looking out to the ocean and its fumes for some riggish and exalted promise of romance? When it was dark and time to go to bed, I told my youngest son a story. He slept in a pleasant room that faced the east, where there was a lighthouse on a point, and the beam swept in through the window. Then I noticed something on the corner baseboard—a thread or a spider, I thought—and knelt down to see what it was. Someone had written there, in a small hand, 'My father is a rat. I repeat. My father is a rat.' I kissed my son good night and we all went to sleep.

Sunday was a lovely day, and I woke in very high spirits, but, walking around the place before breakfast, I came on another cache of whiskey bottles hidden behind a yew tree, and I felt a return of that drabness— it was nearly like despair—that I had first experienced in the living room. I was worried and curious about Mr Greenwood. His troubles seemed inescapable. I thought of going into the village and asking about him, but this kind of curiosity seems to me indecent. Later in the day, I found his photograph in a shirt drawer.

The glass covering the picture was broken. He was dressed in the uniform of an Air Force major, and had a long and a romantic face. I was pleased with his handsomeness, as I had been pleased with his sailing trophy, but these two possessions were not quite enough to cure the house of its drabness. I did not like the place, and this seemed to affect my temper. Later I tried to teach my oldest son how to surf-cast with a drail, but he kept fouling his line and getting sand in the reel, and we had a quarrel. After lunch we drove to the boatyard where the sailboat that went with the house was stored. When I asked about the boat, the proprietor laughed. It had not been in the water for five years and was falling to pieces. This was a grave disappointment, but I did not think angrily of Mr Greenwood as a liar, which he was; I thought of him sympathetically as a man forced into those embarrassing expedients that go with a rapidly diminishing income. That night in the living room, reading one of his books, I noticed that the sofa cushions seemed unyielding. Reaching under them, I found three copies of a magazine dealing with sunbathing. They were illustrated with many pictures of men and women wearing nothing but their shoes. I put the magazines into the fireplace and lighted them with a match, but the paper was coated and they burned slowly. Why should I be made so angry, I wondered; why should I seem so absorbed in this image of a lonely and drunken man? In the upstairs hallway there was a bad smell, left perhaps by an unhousebroken cat or a stopped drain, but it seemed to me like the distillate, the essence, of a bitter quarrel. I slept poorly.

On Monday it rained. The children baked cookies in the morning. I walked on the beach. In the afternoon we visited the local museum, where there was one stuffed peacock, one spiked German helmet, an assortment of shrapnel, a collection of butterflies, and some old photographs. You could hear the rain on the museum roof. On Monday night I had a strange dream. I dreamed I was sailing for Naples on the *Cristoforo Colombo* and sharing a tourist cabin with an old man. The old man never appeared, but his belongings were heaped on the lower berth. There was a greasy fedora, a battered umbrella, a paper-back novel, and a bottle of laxative pills. I wanted a drink. I am not an alcoholic, but in my dream I experienced all the physical and emotional torments of a man who is. I went up to the bar. The bar was closed. The bartender was there, locking up the cash register, and all the bottles were draped in cheesecloth. I begged him to open the bar, but he said he had spent the last ten hours cleaning staterooms and that he was going to bed. I asked if he would sell me a bottle, and he said no. Then—he was an Italian— I explained slyly that the bottle was not for me but for my little daughter. His attitude changed at once. If it was for my little daughter, he would be happy to give me a bottle, but it must be a beautiful bottle, and after searching around the bar he came up with a swan-shaped bottle, full of liqueur. I told him my daughter wouldn't like this at all, that what she wanted was gin, and he finally produced a bottle of gin and charged me ten thousand lire. When I woke, it seemed that I had dreamed one of Mr Greenwood's dreams.

We had our first caller on Wednesday. This was Mrs Whiteside, the Southern lady from whom we got the key. She rang our bell at five and presented us with a box of strawberries. Her daughter, Mary-Lee, a girl of about twelve, was with her. Mrs Whiteside was formidably decorous, but Mary-Lee had gone in heavily for makeup. Her eyebrows were plucked, her eyelids were painted, and the rest of her face was highly colored. I suppose she didn't have anything else to do. I asked Mrs Whiteside in enthusiastically, because I wanted to cross-question her about the Greenwoods. 'Isn't it a beautiful staircase?' she asked when she stepped into the hall. 'They had it built for their daughter's wedding. Dolores was only four at the time, but they liked to imagine that she would stand by the window in her white dress and throw her flowers down to her attendants.' I bowed Mrs Whiteside into the living room and gave her a glass of sherry. 'We're pleased to have you here, Mr Odgen,' she said. 'It's so nice to have children running on the beach again. But it's only fair to say that we all miss the Greenwoods. They were charming people, and they've never rented before. This is their first summer away from the beach. Oh, he loved Broadmere. It was his pride and joy. I can't imagine what he'll do without it.' If the Greenwoods were so charming, I wondered who had been the secret drinker. 'What does Mr Greenwood do?' I asked, trying to finesse the directness of my question by crossing the room and filling her glass again. 'He's in synthetic yarns,' she said. 'Although I believe he's on the lookout for something more interesting.' This seemed to be a hint, a step perhaps in the right direction. 'You mean he's looking for a job?' I asked quickly. 'I really can't say,' she replied.

She was one of those old women who you might say were as tranquil as the waters under a bridge, but she seemed to me monolithic, to possess some of the community's biting teeth, and perhaps to secrete some of its venom. She seemed by her various and painful disappointments (Mr Whiteside had passed away, and there was very little money) to have been pushed up out of the stream of life to sit on its banks in unremittent lugubriousness, watching the rest of us speed down to sea. What I mean to say is that I thought I detected beneath her melodious voice a vein of corrosive bitterness. In all, she drank five glasses of sherry.

She was about to go. She sighed and started to get

up. 'Well, I'm so glad of this chance to welcome you,' she said. 'It's so nice to have children running on the beach again, and while the Greenwoods were charming, they had their difficulties. I say that I miss them, but I can't say that I miss hearing them quarrel, and they quarreled every single night last summer. Oh, the things he used to say! They were what I suppose you would call incompatible.' She rolled her eyes in the direction of Mary-Lee to suggest that she could have told us much more. 'I like to work in my garden sometimes after the heat of the day, but when they were quarreling I couldn't step out of the house, and I sometimes had to close the doors and windows. I don't suppose I should tell you all of this, but the truth will out, won't it?' She got to her feet and went into the hall. 'As I say, they had the staircase built for the marriage of their daughter, but poor Dolores was married in the Municipal Building, eight months pregnant by a garage mechanic. It's nice to have you here. Come along, Mary-Lee.'

I had, in a sense, what I wanted. She had authenticated the drabness of the house. But why should I be so moved, as I was, by the poor man's wish to see his daughter happily married? It seemed to me that I could see them standing in the hallway when the staircase was completed. Dolores would be playing on the floor. They would have their arms around each other; they would be smiling up at the arched window and its vision of cheer, propriety, and enduring happiness. But where had they all gone, and why had this simple wish ended in disaster?

In the morning it rained again, and the cook suddenly announced that her sister in New York was dying and that she had to go home. She had not received any letters or telephone calls that I knew of, but I drove her to the airport and let her go. I returned reluctantly to the house. I had got to hate the place. I found a plastic chess set and tried to teach my son to play chess, but this ended in a quarrel. The other children lay in bed, reading comics. I was short-tempered with everyone, and decided that for their own good I should return to New York for a day or two. I lied to my wife about some urgent business, and she took me to the plane the next morning. It felt good to be airborne and away from the drabness of Broadmere. It was hot and sunny in New York—it felt and smelled like midsummer. I stayed at the office until late, and stopped at a bar near Grand Central Station. I had been there a few minutes when Greenwood came in. His romantic looks were ruined, but I recognized him at once from the photograph in the shirt drawer. He ordered a Martini and a glass of water, and drank off the water, as if that was what he had come for.

You could see at a glance that he was one of that legion of wage-earning ghosts who haunt midtown Manhattan, dreaming of a new job in Madrid, Dublin, or Cleveland. His hair was slicked down. His face had the striking ruddiness of a baseball-park or race-track burn, although you could see by the way his hands shook that the flush was alcoholic. The bartender knew him, and they chatted for a while, but then the bartender went over to the cash register to add up his slips and Mr Greenwood was left alone. He felt this. You could see it in his face. He felt that he had been left alone. It was late, all the express trains would have pulled out, and the rest of them were drifting in—the ghosts, I mean. God knows where they come from or where they go, this host of prosperous and well-dressed hangers-on who, in spite of the atmosphere of a fraternity they generate, would not think of speaking to one another. They all have a bottle hidden behind the Literary Guild selections and another in the piano bench. I thought of introducing myself to Greenwood, and then thought better of it. I had taken his beloved house away from him, and he was bound to be unfriendly. I couldn't guess the incidents in his autobiography, but I could guess its atmosphere and drift. Daddy would have died or absconded when he was young. The absence of a male parent is not so hard to discern among the marks life leaves on our faces. He would have been raised by his mother and his aunt, have gone to the state university and have majored (my guess) in general merchandising. He would have been in charge of PX supplies during the war. Nothing had worked out after the war. He had lost his daughter, his house, the love of his wife, and his interest in business, but none of these losses would account for his pain and bewilderment. The real cause would remain concealed from him, concealed from me, concealed from us all. It is what makes the railroad-station bars at that hour seem so mysterious. 'Stupid,' he said to the bartender. 'Oh, Stupid. Do you think you could find the time to sweeten my drink?'

It was the first note of ugliness, but there would be nothing much but ugliness afterward. He would get very mean. Thin, fat, choleric or merry, young or old, all the ghosts do. In the end, they all drift home to accuse the doorman of incivility, to rail at their wives for extravagance, to lecture their bewildered children on ingratitude, and then to fall asleep on the guest-room bed with all their clothes on. But it wasn't this image that troubled me but the image of him standing in the new hallway, imagining that he saw his daughter at the head of the stairs in her wedding dress. We had not spoken, I didn't know him, his losses were not mine, and yet I felt them so strongly that I didn't want to spend the night alone, and so I spent it with a sloppy woman who works in our office. In the morning, I took a plane back to the sea, where it was still raining and where I found my wife washing pots in the kitchen sink. I had a hangover and felt painfully depraved, guilty, and unclean. I thought I might feel better if I went for a swim, and I asked my wife for my bathing trunks.

'They're around here somewhere,' she said crossly. 'They're kicking around underfoot somewhere. You left them wet on the bedroom rug and I hung them up in the shower.'

'They're not in the shower,' I said.

'Well, they're around here somewhere,' she said. 'Have you looked on the dining-room table?'

'Now, listen,' I said. 'I don't see why you have to speak of my bathing trunks as if they had been wandering around the house, drinking whiskey, breaking wind, and telling dirty stories to mixed company. I'm just asking for an *innocent* pair of bathing trunks.' Then I sneezed, and I waited for her to bless me as she always did but she said nothing. 'And another thing I can't find,' I said, 'is my handkerchiefs.'

'Blow your nose on Kleenex,' she said.

'I don't want to blow my nose on Kleenex,' I said. I must have raised my voice, because I could hear Mrs Whiteside calling Mary-Lee indoors and shutting a window.

'Oh, God, you bore me this morning,' my wife said.

'I've been bored for the last six years,' I said.

I took a cab to the airport and an afternoon plane back to the city. We had been married twelve years and had been lovers for two years before our marriage, making a total of fourteen years in all that we had been together, and I never saw her again.

This is being written in another seaside house with another wife. I sit in a chair of no discernible period or inspiration. Its cushions have a musty smell. The ashtray was filched from the Excelsior in Rome. My whiskey glass once held jelly. The table I'm writing on has a bum leg. The lamp is dim. Magda, my wife, is dyeing her hair. She dyes it orange, and this has to be done once a week. It is foggy, we are near a channel marked with buoys, and I can hear as many bells as I would hear in any pious village on a Sunday morning. There are high bells, low bells, and bells that seem to ring from under the sea. When Magda asks me to get her glasses, I step quietly onto the porch. The lights from the cottage, shining into the fog, give an illusion of substance, and it seems as if I might stumble on a beam of light. The shore is curved, and I can see the lights of other haunted cottages where people are building up an accrual of happiness or misery that will be left for the August tenants or the people who come next year. Are we truly this close to one another? Must we impose our burdens on strangers? And is our sense of the universality of suffering so inescapable? 'My glasses, my glasses!' Magda shouts. 'How many times do I have to ask you to bring them for me?' I get her her glasses, and when she is finished with her hair we go to bed. In the middle of the night, the porch door flies open, but my first, my gentle wife is not there to ask, 'Why have they come back? What have they lost?'

A CHANGE OF SCENE
David Malouf

I

HAVING COME LIKE so many others for the ruins, they had been surprised to discover, only three kilometres away, this other survival from the past: a big old-fashioned hotel.

Built in florid neo-baroque, it dated from a period before the Great War when the site was much frequented by Germans, since it had figured, somewhat romanticized, in a passage of Hofmannsthal. The fashion was long past and the place had fallen into disrepair. One corridor of the main building led to double doors that were crudely boarded up, with warnings in four languages that it was dangerous to go on, and the ruined side-wings were given over to goats. Most tourists these days went to the Club Méditerranée on the other side of the bay. But the hotel still maintained a little bathing establishment on the beach (an attendant went down each morning and swept it with a rake) and there was still, on a cliff-top above zig-zag terraces, a pergolated belvedere filled with potted begonias, geraniums and dwarf citrus—an oasis of cool green that the island itself, at this time of year and this late in its history, no longer aspired to. So Alec, who had a professional interest, thought of the ruins as being what kept them here, and for Jason, who was five, it was the beach; but Sylvia, who quite liked ruins and wasn't at all averse to lying half-buried in sand while Jason paddled and Alec, at the entrance to the cabin, tapped away at his typewriter, had settled at first sight for the hotel.

It reminded her, a bit creepily, of pre-war holidays with her parents up on the Baltic—a world that had long ceased to exist except in pockets like this. Half-lost in its high wide corridors, among rococo doors and bevelled gilt-framed mirrors, she almost expected— the past was so vividly present—to meet herself, aged four, in one of the elaborate dresses little girls wore in those days. Wandering on past unreadable numbers, she would come at last to a door that was familiar and would look in and find her grandmother, who was standing with her back to a window, holding in her left hand, so that the afternoon sun broke through it, a jar of homemade cherry syrup, and in her right a spoon. 'Grandma,' she would say, 'the others are all sleeping. I came to you.'

Her grandmother had died peacefully in Warsaw, the year the Germans came. But she was disturbed, re-entering that lost world, to discover how much of it had survived in her buried memory, and how many details came back now with an acid sweetness, like a drop of cherry syrup. For the first time since she was a child she had dreams in a language she hadn't spoken for thirty years—not even with her parents— and was surprised that she could find the words. It surprised her too that Europe—that dark side of her childhood—was so familiar, and so much like home.

She kept that to herself. Alec, she knew, would resent or be hurt by it. She had, after all, spent all but those first years in another place altogether, where her parents were settled and secure as they never could have been in Poland, and it was in that place, not in Europe, that she had grown up, discovered herself and married.

Her parents were once again rich, middle-class people, living in an open-plan house on the North Shore and giving *al fresco* parties at a poolside barbecue. Her father served the well-done steaks with an air of finding this, like so much else in his life, delightful but

unexpected. He had not, as a boy in Lvov, had T-
bone steaks in mind, nor even a dress factory in
Marrickville. These were accidents of fate. He accepted
them, but felt he was living the life of an imposter.
It added a touch of humorous irony to everything he
did. It was her mother who had gone over completely
to the New World. She wore her hair tinted a pale
mauve, made cheesecake with passion-fruit, and played
golf. As for Sylvia, she was simply an odd sort of local.
She had had no sense of a foreign past till she came
back here and found how European she might be.

Her mother, if she had known the full extent of
it, would have found her interest in the hotel 'morbid',
meaning Jewish. And it was perverse of her (Alec
certainly thought so) to prefer it to the more convenient
cabins. The meals were bad, the waiters clumsy and
morose, with other jobs in the village or bits of poor
land to tend. The plumbing, which looked impressive,
all marble and heavy bronze that left a green stain
on the porcelain, did not provide water. Alec had no
feeling for these ruins of forty years ago. His period
was that of the palace, somewhere between eleven and
seven hundred BC, when the site had been inhabited
by an unknown people, a client state of Egypt, whose
language he was working on; a dark, death-obsessed
people who had simply disappeared from the pages of
recorded history, leaving behind them a few common
artefacts, the fragments of a language, and this one

city or fortified palace at the edge of the sea.

Standing for the first time on the bare terrace, which was no longer at the edge of the sea, and regarding the maze of open cellars, Alec had been overwhelmed. His eyes, roving over the level stones, were already recording the presence of what was buried here—a whole way of life, richly eventful and shaped by clear beliefs and rituals, that rose grandly for him out of low brick walls and a few precious scratches that were the symbols of corn, salt, water, oil and the names, or attributes, of gods.

What her eyes roamed over, detecting also what was buried, was Alec's face; reconstructing from what passed over features she thought she knew absolutely, in light and in darkness, a language of feeling that he, perhaps, had only just become aware of. She had never, she felt, come so close to what, outside their life together, most deeply touched and defined him. It was work that gave his life its high seriousness and sense of purpose, but he had never managed to make it real for her. When he talked of it he grew excited, but the talk was dull. Now, in the breathlessness of their climb into the hush of sunset, with the narrow plain below utterly flat and parched and the great blaze of the sea beyond, with the child dragging at her arm and the earth under their feet thick with pine-needles the colour of rusty blood, and the shells of insects that had taken their voice elsewhere—in the dense confusion of all this, she felt suddenly that she understood and might be able to share with him now the excitement of it, and had looked up and found the hotel, just the outline of it. Jason's restlessness had delayed for a moment her discovery of what it was.

They had been travelling all day and had come up here when they were already tired, because Alec, in his enthusiasm, could not wait. Jason had grown bored with shifting about from one foot to another and wanted to see how high they were.

'Don't go near the edge,' she told the boy.

He turned away to a row of corn- or oil-jars, big enough each one for a man to crawl into, that were sunk to the rim in stone, but they proved, when he peered in, to be less interesting than he had hoped. No genii, no thieves. Only a coolness, as of air that had got trapped there and had never seeped away.

'It's cold,' he had said, stirring the invisible contents with his arm.

But when Alec began to explain, in words simple enough for the child to understand, what the jars had been used for and how the palace might once have looked, his attention wandered, though he did not interrupt.

Sylvia too had stopped listening. She went back to her own discovery, the big silhouette of what would turn out later to be the hotel.

It was the child's tone of wonder that lingered in

her mind: 'It's cold.' She remembered it again when they entered the grand but shabby vestibule of the hotel and she felt the same shock of chill as when, to humour the child, she had leaned down and dipped her arm into a jar.

'What is it?' Jason had asked.

'It's nothing.'

He made a mouth, unconvinced, and had continued to squat there on his heels at the rim.

Alec had grown up on a wheat farm west of Gulgong. Learning early what it is to face bad seasons when a whole crop can fail, or bushfires, or floods, he had developed a native toughness that would, Sylvia saw from his father, last right through into old age. Failure for Alec meant a failure of nerve. This uncompromising view made him hard on occasion, but was the source as well of his golden rightness. Somewhere at the centre of him was a space where honour, fairness, hard work, the belief in a man's responsibility at least for his own fate—and also, it seemed, the possibility of happiness—were given free range; and at the clear centre of all there was a rock, unmoulded as yet, that might one day be an altar. Alec's deficiencies were on the side of strength, and it delighted her that Jason reproduced his father's deep blue eyes and plain sense of having a place in the world. She herself was too rawboned and intense. People called her beautiful. If she was, it was in a way that had too much darkness in it, a mysterious rather than an open beauty. Through Jason she had turned what was leaden in herself to purest gold.

It was an added delight to discover in the child some openness to the flow of things that was also hers, and which allowed them, on occasion, to speak without speaking; as when he had said, up there on the terrace, 'It's cold', at the very moment when a breath from the far-off pile that she didn't yet know was a hotel, had touched her with a premonitory chill.

They were close, she and the child. And in the last months before they came away the child had moved into a similar closeness with her father. They were often to be found, when they went to visit, at the edge of the patio swimming-pool, the old man reading to the boy, translating for him from what Alec called his 'weirdo books', while Jason, in bathing-slip and sneakers, nodded, swung his plump little legs, asked questions, and the old man, with his glasses on the end of his nose and the book resting open a moment on his belly, considered and found analogies.

After thirty years in the garment trade her father had gone back to his former life and become a scholar.

Before the war he had taught philosophy. A radical free-thinker in those days, he had lately, after turning his factory over to a talented nephew, gone right back, past his passion for Wittgenstein and the other idols of his youth, to what the arrogance of that time had made him blind to—the rabbinical texts of his fathers. The dispute, for example, between Rabbi Isserles of Cracow and Rabbi Luria of Ostrov that had decided at Posen, in the presence of the exorcist Joel Baal-Shem, miracle-worker of Zamoshel, that demons have no right over moveable property and may not legally haunt the houses of men.

Her father's room in their ranch-style house at St Ives was crowded with obscure volumes in Hebrew; and even at this distance from the Polish sixteenth century, and the lost communities of his homeland, the questions remained alive in his head and had come alive, in diminutive form, in the boy's. It was odd to see them out there in the hard sunlight of her mother's cactus garden, talking ghosts.

Her mother made faces. Mediaeval nonsense! Alec listened, in a scholarly sort of way, and was engaged at first, but found the whole business in the end both dotty and sinister, especially as it touched the child. He had never understood his father-in-law, and worried sometimes that Sylvia, who was very like him, might have qualities that would emerge in time and elude him. And now Jason! Was the old man serious, or was this just another of his playful jokes?

'No,' Sylvia told him as they drove back in the dark, with Jason sleeping happily on the back seat, 'it's none of the things you think it is. He's getting ready to die, that's all.'

Alec restrained a gesture of impatience. It was just this sort of talk, this light and brutal way of dealing with things it might be better not to mention, that made him wonder at times if he really knew her.

'Well I hope he isn't scaring Jason, that's all.'

'Oh fairy tales, ghost stories—that's not what frightens people.'

'Isn't it?' said Alec. 'Isn't it?'

II

They soon got to know the hotel's routine and the routine of the village, and between the two established their own. After a breakfast of coffee with condensed milk and bread and honey they made their way to the beach: Alec to work, and between shifts at the typewriter to explore the coastline with a snorkel, Sylvia and the child to laze in sand or water.

The breakfast was awful. Alec had tried to make the younger of the two waiters, who served them in the morning, see that the child at least needed fresh milk. For some reason there wasn't any, though they learned from people at the beach that the Cabins got it.

'No,' the younger waiter told them, 'no milk.' Because there were no cows, and the goat's milk was for yogurt.

They had the same conversation every morning, and the waiter, who was otherwise slack, had begun to serve up the tinned milk with a flourish that in Alec's eye suggested insolence. As if to say: *There! You may be Americans* (which they weren't), *and rich* (which they weren't either) *but fresh milk cannot be had. Not on this island.*

The younger waiter, according to the manager, was a Communist. That explained everything. He shook his head and made a clucking sound. But the older waiter, who served them at lunch, a plump, grey-headed man, rather grubby, who was very polite and very nice with the child, was also a Communist, so it explained nothing. The older waiter also assured them there was no milk. He did it regretfully, but the result was the same.

Betweeen them these two waiters did all the work of the hotel. Wandering about in the afternoon in the deserted corridors, when she ought to have been taking a siesta, Sylvia had come upon the younger one having a quiet smoke on a window-sill. He was barefoot, wearing a dirty singlet and rolled trousers. There was a pail of water and a mop beside him. Dirty water was slopped all over the floor. But what most struck her was the unnatural, fishlike whiteness of his flesh— shoulders, arms, neck—as he acknowledged her presence with a nod but without at all returning her smile.

Impossible, she had thought, to guess how old he

might be. Twenty-eight or thirty he looked, but might be younger. There were deep furrows in his cheeks and he had already lost some teeth.

He didn't seem at all disconcerted. She had, he made it clear, wandered into *his* territory. Blowing smoke over his cupped hand (why did they smoke that way?) and dangling his bare feet, he gave her one of those frank, openly sexual looks that cancel all boundaries but the original one; and then, to check a gesture that might have made him vulnerable (it did—she had immediately thought, how boyish!) he glared at her, with the look of a waiter, or peasant, for a foreign tourist. His look had in it all the contempt of a man who knows where he belongs, and whose hands are cracked with labour on his own land, for a woman who has come sightseeing because she belongs nowhere.

Except, she had wanted to protest, it isn't like that at all. It is true I have no real place (and she surprised herself by acknowledging it) but I know what it is to have lost one. That place is gone and all its people are ghosts. I am one of them—a four-year-old in a pink dress with ribbons. I am looking for my grandmother. Because all the others are sleeping . . .

She felt differently about the young waiter after that, but it made no odds. He was just as surly to them at breakfast, and just as nasty to the child.

The bay, of which their beach was only an arc, was also used by fishermen, who drew their boats up on a concrete ramp beside the village, but also by the guests from the Cabins and by a colony of hippies who camped in caves at the wilder end.

The hippies were unpopular with the village people. The manager of the hotel told Sylvia that they were dirty and diseased, but they looked healthy enough, and once, in the early afternoon, when most of the tourists had gone in to sleep behind closed shutters, she had seen one of them, a bearded blond youth with a baby on his hip, going up and down the beach collecting litter. They were Germans or Dutch or Scandinavians. They did things with wire, which they sold to the tourists, and traded with the fishermen for octopus or chunks of tuna.

All day the fishermen worked beside their boats on the ramp: mending nets and hanging them from slender poles to dry, or cleaning fish, or dragging octopus up and down on the quayside to remove the slime. They were old men mostly, with hard feet, all the toes stubbed and blackened, and round little eyes. Sometimes, when the child was bored with playing alone in the wet sand, he would wander up the beach and watch them at their work. The quick knives and the grey-blue guts tumbling into the shallows were a puzzle to him, for whom fish were either bright objects that his father showed him when they went out with the snorkel or frozen fingers. The octopus too. He had seen lights on the water at night and his father had explained how the fishermen were using lamps to attract the creatures, who would swarm to the light and could be jerked into the dinghy with a hook. Now he crinkled his nose to see one of the fishermen whip a live octopus out of the bottom of the boat and turning it quickly inside-out, bite into the raw, writhing thing so that its tentacles flopped. He looked at Sylvia and made a mouth. These were the same octopus that, dried in the sun, they would be eating at tomorrow's lunch.

Because the bay opened westward, and the afternoon sun was stunning, their beach routine was limited to the hours before noon.

Quite early, usually just before seven, the young waiter went down and raised the striped canvas awning in front of their beach cabin and raked a few square metres of sand.

Then at nine a sailor came on duty on the little heap of rocks above the beach where a flagpole was set, and all morning he would stand there in his coarse white trousers and boots, with his cap tilted forward and strapped under his chin, watching for sharks. It was always the same boy, a cadet from the Training College round the point. The child had struck up a kind of friendship with him and for nearly an hour sometimes he would 'talk' to the sailor, squatting at his feet while the sailor laughed and did tricks with a bit of cord. Once, when Jason failed to return and couldn't hear her calling, Sylvia had scrambled up the rockface to fetch him, and the sailor, who had been resting on his heel for a bit, had immediately sprung to his feet looking scared.

He was a stocky boy of eighteen or nineteen, sunburned almost to blackness and with very white teeth. She had tried to reassure him that she had no intention of reporting his slackness; but once he had snapped back to attention and then stood easy, he looked right through her. Jason turned on the way down and waved, but the sailor stood very straight against the sky with his trousers flapping and his eyes fixed on the sea, which was milky and thick with sunlight, lifting and lapsing in a smooth unbroken swell, and with no sign of a fin.

After lunch they slept. It was hot outside but cool behind drawn shutters. Then about five-thirty Alec would get up, climb the three kilometres to the palace, and sit alone there on the open terrace to watch the sunset. The facts he was sifting at the typewriter would resolve themselves then as luminous dust; or would spring up alive out of the deepening landscape in the cry of cicadas, whose generations beyond counting might go back here to beginnings. They were dug in under stones, or they clung with shrill tenacity to the bark of pines. It was another language. Immemorial. Indecipherable.

Sylvia did not accompany him on these afternoon excursions, they were Alec's alone. They belonged to some private need. Stretched out in the darkened room she would imagine him up there, sitting in his shirtsleeves in the gathering dusk, the gathering voices, exploring a melancholy he had only just begun to perceive in himself and of which he had still not grasped the depths. He came back, after the long dusty walk, with something about him that was raw and in need of healing. No longer a man of thirty-seven—clever, competent, to whom she had been married now for eleven years—but a stranger at the edge of youth, who had discovered, tremblingly, in a moment of solitude up there, the power of dark.

It was the place. Or now, and here, some aspect of himself that he had just caught sight of. Making love on the high bed, with the curtains beginning to stir against the shutters and the smell of sweat and pine-needles on him, she was drawn into some new dimension of his still mysterious being, and of her own. Something he had felt or touched up there, or which had touched him—his own ghost perhaps, an interior coolness—had brought him closer to her than ever before.

When it was quite dark at last, a deep blue dark, they walked down to one of the quayside restaurants.

There was no traffic on the promenade that ran along beside the water, and between seven and eight-thirty the whole town passed up and down between one headland and the other: family groups, lines of girls with their arms linked, boisterous youths in couples or in loose threes and fours, sailors from the Naval College, the occasional policeman. Quite small children, neatly dressed, played about among rope coils at the water's edge or fell asleep over the scraps of meals. Lights swung in the breeze, casting queer shadows, there were snatches of music. Till nearly one o'clock the little port that was deserted by day quite hummed with activity.

When they came down on the first night, and found the crowds sweeping past under the lights, the child had given a whoop of excitement and cried: 'Manifestazione!' It was, along with gelato, his only word of Italian.

Almost every day while they were in Italy, there had been a demonstration of one sort or another: hospital workers one day, then students, bank clerks, bus-drivers, even highschool kids and their teachers. Always with placards, loud-hailers, red flags and masses of grim-faced police. 'Manifestazione,' Jason had learned to shout the moment they rounded a corner and found even a modest gathering; though it wasn't always true. Sometimes it was just a street market, or an assembly of men in business suits arguing about football or deciding the price of unseen commodities—olives or sheep or wheat. The child was much taken by the flags and the chanting in a language that made no sense. It was all playlike and good-humoured.

But once, overtaken by a fast-moving crowd running through from one street to the next, she had felt herself flicked by the edge of a wave that further back, or just ahead, might have the power to break her grip on the child's hand, or to sweep her off her feet or toss them violently in the air. It was only a passing vision, but she had felt things stir in her that she had long forgotten, and was disproportionately scared.

Here, however, the crowd was just a village population taking a stroll along the quay or gathering at café tables to drink ouzo and nibble side plates of miniature snails; and later, when the breeze came, to watch outdoor movies in the square behind the church.

It was pleasant to sit out by the water, to have the child along, and to watch the crowd stroll back and forth—the same faces night after night. They ate lobster, choosing one of the big bluish-grey creatures that crawled against the side of a tank, and slices of pink water-melon. If the child fell asleep Alec carried him home on his shoulder, all the way up the steps and along the zig-zag terraces under the moon.

III

One night, the fifth or sixth of their stay, instead of the usual movie there was a puppet-show.

Jason was delighted. They pushed their way in at the side of the crowd and Alec lifted the child on to his shoulders so that he had a good view over the heads of fishermen, sailors from the College and the usual assembly of village youths and girls, who stood about licking icecreams and spitting the shells of pumpkin-seeds.

The little wooden stage was gaudy; blue and gold. In front of it the youngest children squatted in rows, alternately round-eyed and stilled or squealing with delight or terror as a figure in baggy trousers, with a moustache and dagger, strutted up and down on the narrow sill—blustering, bragging, roaring abuse and lunging ineffectually at invisible tormentors, who came at him from every side. The play was both sinister and comic, the moustachioed figure both hero and buffoon. It was all very lively. Big overhead lights threw shadows on the blank wall of the church: pine branches, all needles, and once, swelling abruptly out of nowhere, a giant, as one of the village showoffs swayed aloft. For a moment the children's eyes were diverted by his antics. They cheered and laughed and, leaping up, tried to make their own shadows appear.

The marionette was not to be outdone. Improvising

now, he included the insolent spectator in his abuse. The children subsided. There was more laughter and some catcalling, and when the foolish youth rose again he was hauled down, but was replaced, almost at once by another, whose voice drowned the puppet's violent squawking—then by a third. There was a regular commotion.

The little stage-man, maddened beyond endurance, raged up and down waving his dagger and the whole stage shook; over on the wings there was the sound of argument, and a sudden scuffling.

They could see very little of this from where they were pressed in hard against the wall, but the crowd between them and the far-off disturbance began to be mobile. It surged. Suddenly things were out of hand. The children in front, who were being crowded forward around the stage, took panic and began to wail for their parents. There were shouts, screams, the sound of hard blows. In less than a minute the whole square was in confusion and the church wall now was alive with big, ugly shadows that merged in waves of darkness, out of which heads emerged, fists poked up, then more heads. Sylvia found herself separated from Alec by a dozen heaving bodies that appeared to be pulled in different directions and by opposing passions. She called out, but it was like shouting against the sea. Alec and Jason were nowhere to be seen.

Meanwhile the stage, with its gaudy trappings, had

been struck away and the little blustering figure was gone. In its place an old man in a singlet appeared, black-haired and toothless, his scrawny body clenched with fury and his mouth a hole. He was screaming without change of breath in the same doll-like voice as the puppet, a high-pitched squawking that he varied at times with grunts and roars. He was inhabited now not only by the puppet's voice but by its tormentors' as well, a pack of violent spirits of opposing factions like the crowd, and was the vehicle first of one, then of another. His thin shoulders wrenched and jerked as if he too was being worked by strings. Sylvia had one clear sight of him before she was picked up and carried, on a great new surging of the crowd, towards the back wall of one of the quayside restaurants, then down what must have been a corridor and on to the quay. In the very last moment before she was free, she saw before her a man covered with blood. Then dizzy from lack of breath, and from the speed with which all this had occurred, she found herself at the water's edge. There was air. There was the safe little bay. And there too were Alec and the boy.

They were badly shaken, but not after all harmed, and in just a few minutes the crowd had dispersed and the quayside was restored to its usual order. A few young men stood about in small groups, arguing or shaking their heads or gesticulating towards the square, but the affair was clearly over. Waiters appeared. They smiled, offering empty tables. People settled and gave orders. They too decided that it might be best, for the child's sake, if they simply behaved as usual. They ordered and ate.

They saw the young sailor who watched for sharks. He and a friend from the village were with a group of girls, and Jason was delighted when the boy recognized them and gave a smart, mock-formal salute. All the girls laughed.

It was then that Sylvia remembered the man she had seen with blood on him. It was the older waiter from the hotel.

'I don't think so,' Alec said firmly. 'You just thought it was because he's someone you know.' He seemed anxious, in his cool, down-to-earth way, not to involve them, even tangentially, in what was a local affair. He frowned and shook his head: *not in front of the boy.*

'No, I'm sure of it,' she insisted. 'Absolutely sure.'

But next morning, at breakfast, there he was quite unharmed, waving them towards their usual table.

'I must have imagined it after all,' Sylvia admitted to herself. And in the clear light of day, with the breakfast tables gleaming white and the eternal sea in the window-frames, the events of the previous night did seem unreal.

There was talk about what had happened among the hotel people and some of the guests from the Cabins, but nothing was clear. It was part of a local feud about fishing rights, or it was political—the puppet-man was a known troublemaker from another village—or the whole thing had no point at all; it was one of those episodes that explode out of nowhere in the electric south, having no cause and therefore requiring no explanation, but gathering up into itself all sorts of hostilities—personal, political, some with their roots in nothing more than youthful high-spirits and the frustrations and closeness of village life at the end of a hot spell. Up on the terraces women were carding wool. Goats nibbled among the rocks, finding rubbery thistles in impossible places. The fishermen's nets, black, brown, umber, were stretched on poles in the sun; and the sea, as if suspended between the same slender uprights, rose smooth, dark, heavy, fading where it imperceptibly touched the sky into mother-of-pearl.

But today the hippies did not appear, and by afternoon the news was abroad that their caves had been raided. In the early hours, before it was light, they had been driven out of town and given a firm warning that they were not to return.

The port that night was quiet. A wind had sprung up, and waves could be heard on the breakwater. The lights swayed overhead, casting uneasy shadows over the rough stones of the promenade and the faces of the few tourists who had chosen to eat. It wasn't cold, but the air was full of sharp little grits and the tablecloths had been damped to keep them from lifting. The locals knew when to come out and when not to. They were right.

The wind fell again overnight. Sylvia, waking briefly, heard it suddenly drop and the silence begin.

The new day was sparklingly clear. There was just breeze enough, a gentle lapping of air, to make the waves gleam silver at the edge of the sand and to set the flag fluttering on its staff, high up on the cliff where the sailor, the same one, was watching for sharks. Jason went to talk to him after paying his usual visit to the fishermen.

Keeping her eye on the child as he made his round of the beach, Sylvia read a little, dozed off, and must for a moment have fallen asleep where Jason had half-buried her in the sand. She was startled into uneasy wakefulness by a hard, clear, cracking sound that she couldn't account for, and was still saying to herself, in the split-second of starting up, *Where am I? Where is Jason?*, when she caught, out of the heel of her eye, the white of his shorts where he was just making his way up the cliff face to his sailor; and in the same instant saw the sailor, above him, sag at the knees, clutching with both hands at the centre of himself, then hang for a long moment in mid-air and fall.

DAVID MALOUF

In a flash she was on her feet and stumbling to where the child, crouching on all fours, had come to a halt, and might have been preparing, since he couldn't have seen what had happened, to go on.

It was only afterwards, when she had caught him in her arms and they were huddled together under the ledge, that she recalled how her flight across the beach had been accompanied by a burst of machine-gun fire from the village. Now, from the direction of the Naval College, came an explosion that made the earth shake.

None of this, from the moment of her sitting up in the sand till the return of her senses to the full enormity of the thing, had lasted more than a minute by the clock, and she had difficulty at first in convincing herself that she was fully awake. Somewhere in the depths of herself she kept starting up in that flash of time before the sailor fell, remarking how hot it was, recording the flapping of a sheet of paper in Alec's abandoned typewriter— he must have gone snorkelling or into the village for a drink—and the emptiness of the dazzling sea. *Where am I? Where is Jason?* Then it would begin all over again. It was in going over it the second time, with the child already safe in her arms, that she began to tremble and had to cover her mouth not to cry out.

Suddenly two men dropped into the sand below them. They carried guns. Sylvia and the child, and two or three others who must have been in the water, were driven at gun-point towards the village. There was a

381

lot of gesticulation, and some muttering that under the circumstances seemed hostile, but no actual violence.

They were pushed, silent and unprotesting, into the crowded square. Alec was already there. They moved quickly together, too shocked to do more than touch briefly and stand quietly side by side.

There were nearly a hundred people crushed in among the pine trees, about a third of them tourists. It was unnaturally quiet, save for the abrupt starting up of the cicadas with their deafening beat; then, as at a signal, their abrupt shutting off again. Men with guns were going through the crowd, choosing some and pushing them roughly away towards the quay; leaving others. Those who were left stared immediately ahead, seeing nothing.

One of the first to go was the young waiter from the hotel. As the crowd gave way a little to let him pass, he met Sylvia's eye, and she too looked quickly away; but would not forget his face with the deep vertical lines below the cheekbones and the steady gaze.

There was no trouble. At last about twenty men had been taken and a smaller number of women. The square was full of open spaces. Their group, and the other groups of tourists, looked terribly exposed. Among these dark strangers involved in whatever business they were about—women in coarse black dresses and shawls, men in dungarees—they stood barefoot in briefs and bikinis, showing too much flesh, as in some dream in which they had turned up for an important occasion without their clothes. It was this sense of being both there and not that made the thing for Sylvia so frighteningly unreal. They might have been invisible. She kept waiting to come awake, or waiting for someone else to come awake and release her from a dream that was not her own, which she had wandered into by mistake and in which she must play a watcher's part.

Now one of the gunmen was making an announcement. There was a pause. Then several of those who were left gave a faint cheer.

The foreigners, who had understood nothing of what the gunman said, huddled together in the centre of the square and saw only slowly that the episode was now over; they were free to go. They were of no concern to anyone here. They never had been. They were, in their odd nakedness, as incidental to what had taken place as the pine trees, the little painted ikon in its niche in the church wall, and all those other mute, unseeing objects before whom such scenes are played.

Alec took her arm and they went quickly down the alley to the quay. Groups of armed men were there, standing about in the sun. Most of them were young, and one, a schoolboy in shorts with a machine-gun in his hand, was being berated by a woman who must have been his mother. She launched a torrent of abuse at him, and then began slapping him about the head while he cringed and protested, hugging his machine-gun but making no attempt to protect himself or move away.

IV

There had been a coup. One of the Germans informed them of it the moment they came into the lobby. He had heard it on his transistor. What they had seen was just the furthest ripple of it, way out at the edge. It had all, it seemed, been bloodless, or nearly so. The hotel manager, bland and smiling as ever, scouring his ear with an elongated finger-nail, assured them there was nothing to worry about. A change of government, what was that? They would find everything—the beach, the village—just the same, only more orderly. It didn't concern them.

But one of the Swedes, who had something to do with the legation, had been advised from the capital to get out as soon as possible, and the news passed quickly to the rest. Later that night a boat would call at a harbour further up the coast. The Club had hired a bus and was taking its foreign guests to meet it, but could not take the hotel people as well.

'What will we do?' Sylvia asked, sitting on the high bed in the early afternoon, with the shutters drawn and the village, as far as one could tell, sleeping quietly below. She was holding herself in.

'We must get that boat,' Alec told her. They kept their voices low so as not to alarm the child. 'There won't be another one till the end of the week.'

She nodded. Alec would talk to the manager about a taxi.

She held on. She dared not think, or close her eyes even for a moment, though she was very tired. If she did it would start all over again. She would see the sailor standing white under the flagpole; then he would cover his belly with his hands and begin to fall. Carefully re-packing their cases, laying out shirts and sweaters on the high bed, she never allowed herself to evaluate the day's events by what she had seen. She clung instead to Alec's view, who had seen nothing; and to the manager's who insisted that except for a change in the administration two hundred miles away things were just as they had always been. The child, understanding that it was serious, played one of his solemn games.

When she caught him looking at her once he turned away and rolled his Dinky car over the worn carpet. 'Hrummm, hrummm,' he went. But quietly. He was being good.

Suddenly there was a burst of gunfire.

She rushed to the window, and pushing the child back thrust her face up close to the slats; but only a corner of the village was visible from here. The view was filled with the sea, which remained utterly calm. When the second burst came, rather longer than the first, she still couldn't tell whether it came from the village or the Naval College or from the hills.

Each time, the rapid clatter was like an iron shutter coming down. It would be so quick.

She turned away to the centre of the room, and almost immediately the door opened and Alec rushed in. He was flushed, and oddly, boyishly exhilarated. He had his typewriter under his arm.

'I'm all right,' he said when he saw her face. 'There's no firing in the village. It's back in the hills. I went to get my stuff.'

There was something in him, some reckless pleasure in his own daring, that scared her. She looked at the blue Olivetti, the folder of notes, and felt for a moment like slapping him, as that woman on the quay had slapped her schoolboy son—she was so angry, so affronted by whatever it was he had been up to out there, which had nothing to do with his typewriter and papers and had put them all at risk.

'Don't be upset,' he told her sheepishly. 'It was nothing. There was no danger.' But his own state of excitement denied it. The danger was in him.

The taxi, an old grey Mercedes, did not arrive till nearly eight. Loaded at last with their luggage it bumped its way into the village.

The scene there was of utter confusion. The bus

386

from the Club, which should have left an hour before, was halted at the side of the road and was being searched. Suitcases were strewn about all over the pavements, some of them open and spilling their contents, others, it seemed, broken or slashed. One of the Club guests had been badly beaten. He was wandering up the middle of the road with blood on his face and a pair of bent spectacles dangling from his ear, plaintively complaining. A woman with grey hair was screaming and being pushed about by two other women and a man—other tourists.

'Oh my God,' Alec said, but Sylvia said nothing. When a boy with a machine-gun appeared they got out quietly and stood at the side of the car, trying not to see what was going on further up the road, as if their situation was entirely different. Their suitcases were opened, their passports examined.

The two gunmen seemed undangerous. One of them laid his hand affectionately on the child's head. Sylvia tried not to scream.

At last they were told to get back into the car, given their passports, smiled at and sent on their way. The pretence of normality was terrifying. They turned away from the village and up the dusty track that Alec had walked each evening to the palace. Thistles poked up in the moonlight, all silver barbs. Dust smoked among sharp stones. Sylvia sank back into the depths of the car and closed her eyes. It was almost over. For the first time in hours she felt her body relax in a sigh.

It was perhaps that same sense of relaxation and relief, an assurance that they had passed the last obstacle, that made Alec reckless again.

'Stop a minute,' he told the driver.

They had come to the top of the ridge. The palace, on its high terrace, lay sixty or seventy metres away across a shallow gully.

'What is it?' Sylvia shouted, springing suddenly awake. The car had turned, gone on a little and stopped.

'No, it's nothing,' he said. 'I just wanted a last look.'

'Alec—' she began as their headlamps flooded the valley. But before she could say more the lights cut, the driver backed, turned, swung sharply on to the road and they were roaring away at a terrible speed into the moonless dark.

The few seconds of sudden illumination had been just enough to leave suspended back there—over the hastily covered bodies, with dust already stripping from them to reveal a cheek, a foot, the line of a rising knee—her long, unuttered cry.

She gasped and took the breath back into her. Jason, half-turned in the seat, was peering out of the back window. She dared not look at Alec.

The car took them fast round bend after bend of the high cliff road, bringing sickening views of the sea tumbling white a hundred feet below in a series of abrupt turns that took all the driver's attention and flung them about so violently in the back of the car that she and Jason had to cling to one another to stay upright. At last, still dizzy with flight, they sank down rapidly to sea level. The driver threw open the door of the car, tumbled out their luggage and was gone before Alec had even produced the money to pay.

'Alec—' she began.

'No,' he said, 'not now. Later.'

There was no harbour, just a narrow stretch of shingle and a concrete mole. The crowd they found themselves among was packed in so close under the cliff that there was barely room to move. A stiff breeze was blowing and the breakers sent spray over their heads, each wave, as it broke on the concrete slipway, accompanied by a great cry from the crowd, a salty breath. They were drenched, cold, miserable. More taxis arrived. Then the bus. At last, after what seemed hours, a light appeared far out in the blackness and the ship came in, so high out of the water that it bounded on the raging surface like a cork.

'We're almost there,' Alec said, 'we're almost there,' repeating the phrase from time to time as if there were some sort of magic in it.

The ship stood so high out of the water that they had to go in through a tunnel in the stern that was meant for motor vehicles. They jammed into the cavernous darkness, driven from behind by the pressure of a hundred bodies with their individual weight of panic, pushed in hard against suitcases, wooden crates, hastily tied brown parcels, wire baskets filled with demented animals that squealed and stank. Coming suddenly from the cold outside into the closed space, whose sides resounded with the din of voices and strange animal cries, was like going deep into a nightmare from which Sylvia felt she would never drag herself alive. The huge chamber steamed. She couldn't breathe. And all through it she was in terror of losing her grip on the child's hand, while in another part of her mind she kept telling herself: I should release him. I should let him go. Why drag *him* into this?

At last it was over. They were huddled together in a narrow place on the open deck, packed in among others; still cold, and wetter than ever now as the ship plunged and shuddered and the fine spray flew over them, but safely away. The island sank in the weltering dark.

'I don't think he saw, do you?' Alec whispered. He glanced at her briefly, then away. 'I mean, it was all so quick.'

He didn't really want her to reply. He was stroking the boy's soft hair where he lay curled against her. The child was sleeping. He cupped the blond head with his hand, and asked her to confirm that darkness stopped there at the back of it, where flesh puckered between bony knuckles, and that the child was unharmed. It was himself he was protecting. She saw that. And when

she did not deny his view, he leaned forward across
the child's body and pressed his lips, very gently, to
her cheek.

Their heads made the apex of an unsteady triangle
where they leaned together, all three, and slept. Huddled
in among neighbours, strangers with their troubled
dreams, they slept, while the ship rolled on into the
dark.

THE MIDNIGHT LOVE FEAST

Michel Tournier

HE: IT WAS a bright September morning after an equinoctial tide which had given the bay a devastated, frantic, almost pathetic air. We were walking along a shore sparkling with mirrors of water which made the flatfish quiver; a shore strewn with unusual shellfish—whelks, cockles, ormers, clams. But we weren't in the mood for fishing, and spent most of our time looking over towards the south coast, which was shrouded in a milky fog. Yes, there was mystery in the air, almost tragedy, and I wasn't particularly surprised when you drew my attention to two human bodies clasped in each other's arms and covered in sand, about a hundred metres away. We immediately ran up to what we took to be drowned corpses. But they weren't drowned corpses covered in sand. They were two statues sculpted in sand, of strange and poignant beauty. The bodies were curled up in a slight depression, and encircled by a strip of grey, mudstained cloth, which added to their realism. One thought of Adam and Eve, before God came and breathed the breath of life into their nostrils of clay. One also thought of the inhabitants of Pompeii whose bodies were fossilized under the hail of volcanic ash from Vesuvius. Or of the men of Hiroshima, vitrified by the explosion of the Atom Bomb. Their tawny faces, spangled with flakes of mica, were turned towards each other and separated by an impassable distance. Only their hands and legs were touching.

We stood for a moment in front of these recumbent figures, as if at the edge of a newly-opened grave. At this moment a strange sort of devil suddenly emerged from some invisible hole, barefoot and stripped to the waist, wearing frayed jeans. He began a graceful dance, making sweeping arm movements which seemed to be greeting us, and then to be bowing to the recumbent figures as a preliminary to picking them up and raising them to the heavens. The deserted, slack-water shore, the pale light, this couple made of sand, this dancing madman—all of these things surrounded us with a melancholy, unreal phantasmagoria. And then the dancer came to a standstill, as if suddenly in a trance. After which he bowed, knelt, prostrated himself before us, or rather—as we realized—before an apparition that had loomed up behind us. We turned round. To the right, the Tomberlaine rock was emerging from the haze. But most impressive, suspended like a Saharan mirage above the clouds, was the pyramid of the abbey of Mont-Saint-Michel, with all its glistening pink roof-tiles and glinting stained-glass windows.

Time had stopped. Something had to happen to restart it. It was a few drops of water tickling my feet that did it. A foam-capped tongue licked my toes. Listening carefully, we could hear the incessant rustling of the sea that was stealthily creeping up on us. In less than an hour this immense area, now laid bare to the wind and sun, would be returned to the glaucous, merciful depths.

'But they'll be destroyed!' you exclaimed.

With a sad smile the dancer bowed, as a sign of approval. Then he sprang up and mimed the return of the tide, as if he wanted to accompany it, encourage it, even provoke it by his dance. African sorcerers do much the same when they want to induce rain or drive out demons. And the sea obeyed, first flowing round the edges of the depression in which the couple were lying, then finding a breach that allowed through an innocent trickle of water, then two, then three. The joined hands were the first affected and they disintegrated, leaving in suspense stumps of amputated wrists. Horrified, we watched the capricious and inexorable dissolution of this couple which we persisted in feeling to be human, close to us, perhaps premonitory. A stronger wave broke over the woman's head, carrying away half her face, then it was the man's right shoulder that collapsed, and we thought them even more touching in their mutilation.

A few minutes later we were obliged to beat a retreat and abandon the sand basin with its swirling, frothy eddies. The dancer came with us, and we discovered that he was neither mad nor dumb. His name was Patricio Lagos and he came from Chile, more precisely from Chiloe Island, where he was born, which is off the south coast of Chile. It is inhabited by Indians adept in exploiting the forests. He had studied dancing and sculpture at the same time, in Santiago, and had then emigrated to the Antipodes. He was obsessed by the problem of time. Dance, the art of the moment, ephemeral by nature, leaves no trace and suffers from its inability to become rooted in any kind of continuity. Sculpture, the art of eternity, defies time by seeking out indestructible materials. But in so doing, what it finally finds is death, for marble has an obvious funerary vocation. On the Channel and Atlantic coasts, Lagos had discovered the phenomenon of tides governed by the laws of astronomy. Now the tide gives a rhythm to the shore dancer's games, and at the same time suggests the practice of ephemeral sculpture.

'My sand sculptures live,' he declared, 'and the proof

of this is that they die. It's the opposite of the statuary in cemeteries, which is eternal because it is lifeless.'

And so he feverishly sculpted couples in the wet sand just uncovered by the ebbing tide, and both his dancing and his sculpture stemmed from the same inspiration. It was important that his work should be finished at the very moment of slack water, for this must be a parenthesis of rest and meditation. But the great moment was the return of the tide and the terrible ceremony of the destruction of the work. A slow, meticulous, inexorable destruction, governed by an astronomical destiny, and which should be encircled by a sombre, lyrical dance. 'I celebrate the pathetic fragility of life,' he said. That was when you asked him a question of prime importance to us, which he answered in what I considered an obscure, mysterious way.

SHE: Yes, I raised the question of silence. Because according to our customs, dance is accompanied by music, and in one way it is only music embodied, music made flesh. So there was something paradoxical and strange about the dance he was performing in silence round his recumbent sand-figures. But he unreservedly rejected the word silence. 'Silence?' he said, 'but there *is* no silence! Nature detests silence, as she abhors a vacuum. Listen to the shore at low tide: it babbles through the thousands of moist lips it half-opens to the skies. *Volubile.* When I was learning French, I fell in love with that graceful, ambiguous word. It is another name for bindweed, whose fragile, interminable stem twines round the sturdier plants it comes across, and it finally chokes them under its disordered profusion studded with white trumpets. The rising tide too is voluble. It entwines the chests and thighs of my clay lovers with its liquid tentacles. And it destroys them. It is the kiss of death. But the rising tide is also voluble in the childish babble it whispers as it flows over the ooze. It insinuates its salty tongues into the sands with moist sighs. It would like to speak. It is searching for its words. It's a baby burbling in its cradle.'

And he stayed behind and left us, with a little farewell wave and a sad smile, when we reached the beach.

HE: He's a bit mad, your sculptor-dancer, but it's true that by crossing Normandy from east to west, by emigrating from the pebbles of Fécamp to the sands of Mont-Saint-Michel we changed ocean sounds. The waves on the shores of the Pays de Caux smash thousands of stones in a rocky pandemonium. Here, the tide murmurs as it advances with seagull's steps.

SHE: This false silence hasn't been good for you. In Fécamp I loved a taciturn man. You despised all the conventional chit-chat with which human relations surround themselves. Good-morning, good-evening, how are you, very well, and you? what filthy weather . . .

You killed all that verbiage with a stern look. Here, you have become uncommunicative. There are grunts in your silences, grumbles in your asides.

HE: Just a moment! I never despised 'what filthy weather!' I don't think it's a waste of time to talk about the weather. It's an important subject to seamen. For me, weather reports are lyric poetry. But that's just it. The words we use ought to accord with the sky and the sea. The words appropriate to Fécamp don't correspond to the air in Avranches. Here there is something like a soft, insidious appeal, a demand that I don't know how to satisfy.

SHE: Here we are separated by an immense shore of silence, to which every day brings its low tide. The great logorrhoea of May 1968 made me dream of laconic wisdom, of words that were weighed, and rare, but full of meaning. We are sinking into an oppressive mutism that is just as empty as the student verbosity.

HE: Make up your mind! Nowadays you never stop reproaching me for my silence. No attack is too aggressive for you, no matter how hurtful it might be.

SHE: It's to get a rise out of you. I want a crisis, an explosion, a domestic scene. What is a domestic scene?

It's the woman's triumph. It's when the woman has finally forced the man out of his silence by her nagging. Then he shouts, he rages, he's abusive, and the woman surrenders to being voluptuously steeped in this verbal downpour.

HE: Do you remember what they say about the Comte de Carhaix-Plouguer? When they're in company, his wife and he look as if they are the perfect couple. They exchange as many words as are necessary not to arouse curiosity. Though not one more, it's true. Because it's only a façade. Having discovered that his wife was unfaithful to him, the Count communicated his decision never again to talk to her when they were alone—and that was the last time he spoke to her. The extraordinary thing is that in spite of this silence, he managed to have three children with her.

SHE: I have never been unfaithful to you. But I would like to remind you that you sometimes don't even grant me the minimum of words necessary to arouse people's curiosity. On Sundays, we usually lunch together in a restaurant on the coast. There are times when I am so ashamed of our silence that I move my lips soundlessly, to make the other customers think I'm talking to you.

HE: One morning, while we were having breakfast . . .

SHE: I remember. You were deep in your newspaper. You had disappeared behind the newspaper, which you were holding up like a screen. Could anyone be more boorish?

HE: You pressed the playback button on a little tape recorder you had just put down on the table. And then we heard a chorus of wheezing, rattling, gurgling, puffing and blowing and snoring, all of it orchestrated, rhythmic, returning to the point of departure with a reprise of the whole gamut. I asked you: 'What's that?' And you answered: 'It's you when you're asleep. That's all you have to say to me. So I record it.' 'I snore?' 'Obviously you snore! But you don't realize it. Now you can hear it. That's progress, isn't it?'

SHE: I didn't tell you everything. Incited by you, by your nocturnal snoring, I made enquiries. There is always an old student lying dormant in me. I discovered a science, rhonchology, a definition of nocturnal snoring. This is it: 'Respiratory sound during sleep, caused at the moment of inhalation by the vibration of the soft palate, due to the combined and simultaneous effect of the air entering through the nose and the air being drawn through the mouth.' There. I might add that this vibration of the soft palate is very similar to that of the sail of a boat when it's flapping in the wind. As you see in both cases it's something to do with air.

HE: I appreciate this nautical aside, but I might remind you that I have never worked on a sailing boat.

SHE: As for the cures suggested by rhonchology, the most radical is tracheotomy; that's to say, opening an artificial orifice in the trachea so that breathing may be carried on outside the normal nasal passages. But there is also uvulo-palato-pharyngo-plastic-surgery— u.p.p.p.s. to initiates—which consists in resecting part of the soft palate including the uvula, so as to limit its vibratory potential.

HE: Young men ought to be told what they're letting themselves in for when they get married.

SHE: And vice versa! How could a girl ever suspect that the Prince Charming she loves makes a noise like a steam engine at night? Nevertheless, when she spends night after night by the side of a heavy snorer, she works out a rather bitter philosophy for herself.

HE: What does this rhonchological philosophy say?

SHE: That a couple is formed slowly over the years, and that with time the words they exchange take on increasing importance. At the beginning, deeds are enough. And then their dialogue becomes more extensive. It has to become deeper, too. Couples die from having no more to say to each other. My relations with a man are at an end on the evening when, coming back to him from a day spent elsewhere, I no longer want to tell him what I have done, or to hear him tell me how he has spent those hours away from me.

HE: It's true that I was never talkative. But it quite often happens that you interrupt one of my stories because it doesn't interest you.

SHE: Because you've already told it a hundred times.

HE: You made a diabolical suggestion on that subject one day, and I'm still wondering whether you were being serious. You suggested that I should number my stories. From then on, instead of telling you one from beginning to end with all the subtleties of the good story-teller, I should simply state its number, and you would understand at once. If I said 27, you would remember the story of my grandmother's dog which came aboard my trawler by mistake and returned to Fécamp a military hero. 71, and we would both have thought silently of the fidelity of those two gulls I saved and fed on one boat, and which knew how to find me on another vessel. 14, and my grandfather's odyssey during his one and only visit to Paris would have come to mind. So don't reproach me for my silence any more!

SHE: I know all your stories, and I even tell them better than you do. A good story-teller must be able to ring the changes.

HE: Not absolutely. Repetition is part of the game. There is a narrative ritual which children, for instance, respect. They are not concerned with novelty; they insist on the same story being told in the same words. The slightest change makes them leap up in indignation. In the same way, there is a ritual of daily life, of weeks, seasons, feast-days, years. A happy life is one that can cast itself in these moulds without feeling confined.

SHE: You're wrong to think that my idea of numbering your stories was only aimed at silencing you. I could just as well have used it to get you to talk. I would simply have said: 23. And you would straightaway have told me how you lived under siege in Le Havre from September 2nd to 13th, 1944. But I ask myself, honestly: would I have the heart to listen to the same story told indefinitely in the same words? Would I have the childlike imagination needed for that?

HE: I'm quite sure you would. You're lying, or you're lying to yourself. And there's the other point of view:

mine. There's a certain, very dangerous concept which is quite likely to kill off the dialogue between a couple: the concept of the *innocent ear*. If a man changes his woman, he does so in order to find in the new woman an innocent ear for his stories. Don Juan was nothing but an incorrigible braggart, *un hâbleur*—a word of Spanish origin meaning a glib talker. A woman only interested him for the length of time—short, alas, and increasingly short—that she had faith in his *hâbleries*. If he detected the shadow of a doubt in her gaze, it cast a glacial chill over his heart and his genitals. And then he would leave, he would go off to look elsewhere for the exquisite, warm credulity that alone gave their true weight to his *hâbleries*. All this proves the importance of words in the life of a couple. And anyway, when one of the two sleeps with a third person, we say that he 'deceives' the other, which is to situate his betrayal in the domain of language. A man and a woman who never lied to each other and who immediately confessed all their betrayals would not be deceiving one another.

SHE: No doubt. But that would be a dialogue of cynics, and the wounds they inflicted on each other in the name of transparency would quite soon part them.

HE: Then people should lie?

SHE: Yes and no. Betwen the obscurity of lying and

the transparency of cynicism, there is room for a whole range of light and shade in which the truth is known but not discussed, or else is deliberately ignored. In company, courtesy doesn't allow certain truths to be uttered bluntly. Why shouldn't there also be courtesy between couples? You're deceiving me, I'm deceiving you, but we don't want to know about it. The only valid intimacy is of a twilight nature. 'Pull down the shade a little,' as the charming Paul Géraldy said.

HE: Between couples, perhaps, but certainly not between women. There, the crudest cynicism is calmly displayed. Ladies, amongst yourselves, you are appalling gossips! I was waiting at the hairdresser's one day, on the side marked 'Gentlemen', which was only separated from the ladies' salon by a half-partition. I was staggered by the complicity that united stylists, manicurists, shampoo girls and clients in a generalized babble in which the most intimate secrets of bodies and couples were laid bare without the slightest discretion.

SHE: And men in the company of other men keep such things to themselves, I suppose?

HE: More than you think. More than women do, in any case. Masculine vanity, which is generally so ridiculous, imposes a certain reticence on them in such matters. For instance, we aren't too fond of talking about our illnesses.

SHE: It's true that 'intimate secrets', as you so delicately put it, don't amount to much for men. Everything always comes down to figures, with them. So many times or so many centimetres. Women's secrets are far more subtle and obscure! As for our complicity, it's a complicity of the oppressed, and hence universal, because women are everywhere subjected to men's whims. No man will ever know the depth of the feeling of complicity that can unite two women, even when they are perfect strangers to each other. I remember a visit to Morocco. I was the only woman in our little group. As so often in the South, we were approached by a very young boy who spontaneously invited us to come to his house for tea. The father received us, surrounded by his sons—three or four of them, I don't remember exactly. The youngest one must just have learnt to walk. There was a blanket over a doorway which no doubt led to the bedrooms. Every so often it moved surreptitiously, and a black eye could be seen peeping through. The mother, the daughters, the grandmother, the mother-in-law, confined to the inner rooms, were waiting, listening, spying. I remember the way the women had protested when a running-water tap was installed in their houses. For them, that was the end of their trips to the village fountain, and of the long, delightful chats with the other women that these trips occasioned. When we left, I passed a girl on her way home. She smiled at me alone, because I was the only woman, and there was a world of warm fraternity in that smile. And when I say fraternity, I ought rather to say sorority, but the word doesn't exist in French.

HE: Perhaps because the thing itself is too rare to deserve a name.

SHE: It's principally because it's men who construct language. In a strange novel called *The Miracle of the Women's Island*, Gerhart Hauptmann invents his own version of the Robinson Crusoe story. He imagines that after a steamer has been shipwrecked, lifeboats exclusively occupied by women are cast up on a desert island. The result is a women's republic of about a hundred citizenesses.

HE: It must be hell!

SHE: Not at all. Quite the contrary! It's the great sorority. The idea Hauptmann champions is that if women fall out with one another, it's the fault of men. It is men who are the great sowers of discord among sisters, even among the sisterhood of nuns, whose shared confessor is a disruptive influence.

HE: Is that the miracle?

SHE: No. The miracle is that one day, after years of living in their happy sorority, one of the women discovers that she is inexplicably pregnant.

HE: The Holy Ghost, no doubt.

SHE: Everything might still be all right if she had given birth to a daughter. But the malignancy of fate saw to it that she had a son. The knell of the women's island had tolled. The virile virus was about to do its devastating work.

HE: In short, since you and I have the misfortune to belong to opposite sexes, since we have no more to say to each other, the only thing left for us to do is to separate. Let's at least do so with a flourish. We'll get all our friends together for a late-night dinner.

SHE: A *medianoche*, as the Spaniards call it.

HE: We'll choose the shortest night of the year so that our guests will leave as the sun is rising over the bay. We'll serve nothing but the produce of my foreshore fishing.

SHE: We'll talk to them, they'll talk to us, it will be

a great palaver about the couple and love. Our *medianoche*
will be a midnight love feast and a celebration of the
sea. When all our guests have had their say, you will
tap your knife on your glass and solemnly announce
the sad news: 'Oudalle and Nadège are separating
because they don't get on any more. Sometimes they
even have words. Then a disagreeable silence surrounds
them . . .' And when the last guest has gone, we'll put
a notice on the front door: FOR SALE, and we too
will go our different ways.

And so it was. Invitations were sent out for the summer
solstice to all Nadège and Oudalle's friends. Nadège
reserved all the rooms in the three hotels in Avranches.
Oudalle, with two of his fishing friends, prepared a
memorable banquet of foreshore fish.

It was still light when the first guests arrived. These
were the ones who had had the farthest to travel, as
they had come all the way from Arles. Then, almost
immediately, their nearest neighbours rang the bell, and
it was half an hour before the next influx arrived. More
and more came, all through the night, in a constant
balletic flow of cars, just as Nadège and Oudalle had
wished, for they hadn't prepared a formal dinner round
a table but a permanent buffet from which all the guests
could help themselves no matter when they arrived.
To start with, there was poached crab, a consommé
of mussels with croûtons, and smoked eel. Then hermit-

crabs flambéed in whisky, and smoke-dried sea urchins. In keeping with tradition, they waited for the twelfth stroke of midnight to serve the *plat de résistance*—lobster Pompadour garnished with sea cucumbers. Then the night continued with octopus with paprika, paellas of cuttlefish, and a fricassee of wrasse. With the first glimmers of dawn the guests were brought ormers in white wine, sea-anemone fritters, and scallops in champagne. Thus, it was a true marine *medianoche* with neither vegetables, fruit nor sugar.

A group of guests had gathered on the high terrace whose piles reached out onto the shore itself. Neither Nadège nor Oudalle could have said whose idea it was to tell the first story. That one was lost in the night, as no doubt were the second and the third. But surprised by what was taking place in their house, they saw to it that the subsequent narratives were recorded and preserved. There were thus nineteen, and these narratives were sometimes tales which began with the magical and traditional 'once upon a time', and sometimes short stories told in the first person, slices of life that were often raw and sordid. Nadège and Oudalle listened, astonished by these imaginary constructions they saw being built in their own house and which vanished as soon as the last word was uttered, giving way to other, equally ephemeral descriptions. They thought of Lagos's sand statues. They followed the slow work this succession of fictions was accomplishing in them. They had the feeling that the short stories—grimly realistic, pessimistic and demoralizing—were tending to further their separation and the break-up of their marriage, whereas on the contrary the tales—delectable, warm-hearted and tender—were working to bring them together. And while the short stories had at first commanded more attention by their weighty, melancholy truth, as the night wore on the tales gained in beauty and in strength, and finally reached the point of radiating an irresistible charm. In the first hours, Ange Crevet, the humiliated child full of hatred, Ernest the poacher, the suicidal Théobald, and Blandine's frightful father, and Lucie, the woman without a shadow, and a few others—all this grey, austere crowd exuded an atmosphere of morose hatred. But soon Angus, King Faust the Wise Man, Pierrot with his Columbine, Adam the dancer and Eve the perfumed lady, the Chinese painter and his Greek rival, formed the scintillating procession of a new, young and eternal wedding. And it was above all the last tale, the one about the two banquets, that rescued, so it seemed, daily conjugal life by elevating the actions repeated every day and every night to the level of a fervent, intimate ceremony.

The solstice sun was setting the silhouette of Mont-Saint-Michel aglow when the last guest stood up to take his leave after having told, to his hosts alone, the most beautiful tale no doubt ever invented. The incoming tide was flowing under the open-work floor of the terrace. The shellfish caressed by the waves opened their valves and let out the mouthful of water they had been retaining during the arid hours. The thousands upon thousands of parched throats on the foreshore filled themselves with the briny fluid and began to whisper. The shore was stammering in search of a language, as Lagos had understood so well.

'You didn't stand up, you didn't tap your glass with your knife, and you didn't announce the sad news of our separation to our friends,' said Nadège.

'Because the inevitability of our separation no longer seems so obvious to me since all those stories have entered my head,' Oudalle replied.

'What we lacked, in fact, was a house of words to live in together. In former times, religion provided couples with an edifice that was at the same time real— the church—and imaginary, peopled with saints, illuminated with legends, resounding with hymns, which protected them from themselves and from outside aggression. We lacked this edifice. Our friends have provided us with all the materials for it. Literature as a panacea for couples in distress . . .'

'We were like two carps buried in the mud of our daily life,' Oudalle concluded, ever true to his halieutic metaphors. 'From now on we shall be like two trout quivering side by side in the fast-flowing waters of a mountain stream.'

'Your seafood *medianoche* was exquisite,' Nadège added. 'I appoint you the head chef of my house. You shall be the high priest of my kitchens and the guardian of the culinary and manducatory rites that invest a meal with its spiritual dimension.'

LIFEGUARD

John Updike

BEYOND DOUBT, I am a splendid fellow. In the autumn, winter, and spring, I execute the duties of a student of divinity; in the summer I disguise myself in my skin and become a lifeguard. My slightly narrow and gingerly hirsute but not necessarily unmanly chest becomes brown. My smooth back turns the colour of caramel, which, in conjunction with the whipped cream of my white pith helmet, gives me, some of my teenage satellites assure me, a delightfully edible appearance. My legs, which I myself can study, cocked as they are before me while I repose on my elevated wooden throne, are dyed a lustreless maple walnut that accentuates their articulate strength. Correspondingly, the hairs of my body are bleached blond, so that my legs have the pointed elegance of, within the flower, umber anthers dusted with pollen.

For nine months of the year, I pace my pale hands and burning eyes through immense pages of Biblical text barnacled with fudging commentary; through multi-volumed apologetics couched in a falsely friendly Victorian voice and bound in subtly abrasive boards of finely ridged, pre-faded red; through handbooks of liturgy and histories of dogma; through the bewildering duplicities of Tillich's divine politicking; through the suave table talk of Father D'Arcy, Étienne Gilson, Jacques Maritain, and other such moderns mistakenly put at their ease by the exquisite furniture and overstuffed larder of the hospitable St Thomas; through the terrifying attempts of Kierkegaard, Berdyaev, and Barth to scourge God into being. I sway appalled on the ladder of minus signs by which theologians would surmount the void. I tiptoe like a burglar into the house of naturalism to steal the silver. An acrobat, I swing from wisp to wisp. Newman's iridescent cobwebs crush in my hands. Pascal's blackboard mathematics are erased by a passing shoulder. The cave drawings, astoundingly vital by candlelight, of those aboriginal magicians, Paul and Augustine, in daylight fade into mere anthropology. The diverting productions of literary flirts like Chesterton, Eliot, Auden, and Greene—whether they regard Christianity as a pastel forest designed for a fairyland romp or a deliciously miasmic pit from which chiaroscuro can be mined with mechanical buckets—in the end all infallibly strike, despite the comic variety of gongs and mallets, the note of the rich young man who on the coast of Judaea refused in dismay to sell all that he had.

Then, for the remaining quarter of the solar revolution, I rest my eyes on a sheet of brilliant sand printed with the runes of naked human bodies. That there is no discrepancy between my studies, that the texts of the flesh complement those of the mind, is the easy burden of my sermon.

On the back rest of my lifeguard's chair is painted a cross—true, a red cross, signifying bandages, splints, spirits of ammonia, and sunburn unguents. Nevertheless, it comforts me. Each morning, as I mount into my chair, my athletic and youthfully fuzzy toes expertly gripping the slats that make a ladder, it is as if I am climbing into an immense, rigid, loosely fitting vestment.

Again, in each of my roles I sit attentively perched on the edge of an immensity. That the sea, with its multiform and mysterious hosts, its savage and senseless rages, no longer comfortably serves as a divine metaphor indicates how severely humanism has corrupted the apples of our creed. We seek God now in flowers and good deeds, and the immensities of blue that surround the little scabs of land upon which we draw our lives to their unsatisfactory conclusions are suffused by science with vacuous horror. I myself can hardly bear the thought of stars, or begin to count the mortalities of coral. But from my chair the sea, slightly distended by my higher perspective, seems a misty old gentleman stretched at his ease in an immense armchair which has for arms the arms of this bay and for an antimacassar the freshly laundered sky. Sailboats float on his surface like idle and unrelated but benevolent thoughts. The soughing of the surf is the rhythmic lifting of his ripple-stitched vest as he breathes. Consider. We enter the sea with a shock; our skin and blood shout in protest. But, that instant, that leap, past, what do we find? Ecstasy and buoyance. Swimming offers a parable. We struggle and thrash, and drown; we succumb, even in despair, and float, and are saved.

With what timidity, with what a sense of trespass, do I set forward even this obliquely a thought so official! Forgive me. I am not yet ordained; I am too disordered to deal with the main text. My competence is marginal, and I will confine myself to the gloss of flesh with which this particular margin, this one beach, is annotated each day.

Here the cinema of life is run backwards. The old are the first to arrive. They are idle, and have lost the gift of sleep. Each of our bodies is a clock that loses time. Young as I am, I can hear in myself the protein acids ticking; I wake at odd hours and in the shuddering darkness and silence feel my death rushing towards me like an express train. The older we get, and the fewer the mornings left to us, the more deeply dawn stabs us awake. The old ladies wear wide straw hats and, in their hats' shadows, smiles as wide, which they bestow upon each other, upon salty shells they discover in the morning-smooth sand, and even upon me, downy-eyed from my night of dissipation. The gentlemen are often incongruous; withered white legs support brazen barrel chests, absurdly potent, bustling with white froth. How these old roosters preen on their 'condition'! With what fatuous expertness they swim in the icy water—always, however, prudently parallel to the shore, at a depth no greater than their height.

Then come the middle-aged, burdened with children and aluminium chairs. The men are scarred with the marks of their vocation—the red forearms of the gasoline-station attendant, the pale X on the back of the overall-wearing mason or carpenter, the clammer's nicked ankles. The hair on their bodies has as many patterns as matted grass. The women are wrinkled but fertile, like the Iraqi rivers that cradled the seeds of our civilization. Their children are odious. From their gaunt faces leer all the vices, the greeds, the grating urgencies of the adult, unsoftened by maturity's reticence and fatigue. Except that here and there, a girl, the eldest daughter, wearing a knit suit striped horizontally with green, purple, and brown, walks slowly, carefully, puzzled by the dawn enveloping her thick smooth body, her waist not yet nipped but her throat elongated.

Finally come the young. The young matrons bring fat and fussing infants who gobble the sand like sugar, who toddle blissfully into the surf and bring me bolt upright on my throne. My whistle tweets. The mothers rouse. Many of these women are pregnant again, and sluggishly lie in their loose suits like cows tranced in a meadow. They gossip politics, and smoke incessantly, and lift their troubled eyes in wonder as a trio of flat-stomached nymphs parades past. These maidens take all our eyes. The vivacious redhead, freckled and white-footed, pushing against her boy and begging to be ducked; the solemn brunette, transporting the vase of herself with held breath; the dimpled blonde in the bib and diapers of her Bikini, the lambent fuzz of her midriff shimmering like a cat's belly. Lust stuns me like the sun.

You are offended that a divinity student lusts? What prigs the unchurched are. Are not our assaults on the supernatural lascivious, a kind of indecency? If only you knew what de Sadian degradations, what frightful psychological spelunking, our gentle transcendentalist professors set us to, as preparation for our work, which is to shine in the darkness.

I feel that my lust makes me glow; I grow cold in my chair, like a torch of ice, as I study beauty. I have studied much of it, wearing all styles of bathing suit and facial expression, and have come to this conclusion; a woman's beauty lies, not in any exaggeration of the specialized zones, nor in any general harmony that could be worked out by means of the *sectio aurea* or a similar aesthetic superstition; but in the arabesque of the spine. The curve by which the back modulates into the buttocks. It is here that grace sits and rides a woman's body.

I watch from my white throne and pity women, deplore the demented judgement that drives them towards the braggart muscularity of the mesomorph and the prosperous complacence of the endomorph when it is we ectomorphs who pack in our scrawny sinews and exacerbated nerves the most intense gift, the most generous shelter, of love. To desire a woman is to desire to save her. Anyone who has endured intercourse that was neither predatory nor hurried knows how through it we descend, with a partner, into the grotesque and delicate shadows that until then have remained locked in the most guarded recess of our soul: into this harbour we bring her. A vague and twisted terrain becomes inhabited; each shadow, touched by the exploration, blooms into a flower of act. As if we are an island upon which a woman, tossed by her labouring vanity and blind self-seeking, is blown, and there finds security, until, an instant before the anticlimax, Nature with a smile thumps down her trump, and the island sinks beneath the sea.

There is great truth in those motion pictures which are slandered as true neither to the Bible nor to life. They are—written though they are by demons and drunks—true to both. We are all Solomons lusting for Sheba's salvation. The God-filled man is filled with a wilderness that cries to be populated. The stony chambers need jewels, furs, tints of cloth and flesh, even though, as in Samson's case, the temple comes tumbling. Women are an alien race of pagans set down among us. Every seduction is a conversion.

Who has loved and not experienced that sense of rescue? It is not true that our biological impulses are tricked out with ribands of chivalry; rather, our chivalric impulses go clanking in encumbering biological armour. Eunuchs love. Children love. I would love.

My chief exercise, as I sit above the crowds, is to lift the whole mass into immortality. It is not a light task; the throng is so huge, and its members so individually unworthy. No *memento mori* is so clinching as a photograph of a vanished crowd. Cheering Roosevelt, celebrating the Armistice, there it is, wearing its ten thousand straw hats and stiff collars, a fearless and wooden-faced bustle of life: it is gone. A crowd dies in the street like a derelict; it leaves no heir, no trace, no name. My own persistence beyond the last rim of time is easy to imagine; indeed, the effort of imagination lies the other way— to conceive of my ceasing. But when I study the vast tangle of humanity that blackens the beach as far as the sand stretches, absurdities crowd in on me. Is it as maiden, matron, or crone that the females will be eternalized? What will they do without children to watch and gossip to exchange? What of the thousand deaths of memory and bodily change we endure—can each be redeemed at a final Adjustments Counter? The sheer numbers involved make the mind scream. The race is no longer a tiny clan of simian aristocrats lording it over an ocean of grass; mankind is a plague racing like fire across the exhausted continents. This immense clot gathered on the beach, a fraction of a fraction—can we not say that this breeding swarm is its own immortality and end the suspense? The beehive in a sense survives; and is each of us not proved to be a hive, a galaxy of cells each of whom is doubtless praying, from its pew in our thumbnail or oesophagus, for personal resurrection? Indeed, to the cells themselves cancer may seem a revival of faith. No, in relation to other people oblivion is sensible and sanitary.

This sea of others exasperates and fatigues me most on Sunday mornings. I don't know why people no longer go to church—whether they have lost the ability to sing or the willingness to listen. From eight-thirty onwards they crowd in from the parking lot, ants each carrying its crumb of baggage, until by noon, when the remote churches are releasing their gallant and gaily dressed minority, the sea itself is jammed with hollow heads and thrashing arms like a great bobbing backwash of rubbish. A transistor radio somewhere in the sand releases in a thin, apologetic gust the closing peal of a transcribed service. And right here, here at the very height of torpor and confusion, I slump, my eyes slit, and the blurred forms of Protestantism's errant herd seem gathered by the water's edge in impassioned poses of devotion. I seem to be lying dreaming in the infinite rock of space before Creation, and the actual scene I see is a vision of impossibility: a Paradise. For had we existed before the gesture that split the firmament, could we have conceived of our most obvious possession, our most platitudinous blessing, the moment, the single ever-present moment that we perpetually bring to our lips brimful?

So: be joyful. Be Joyful is my commandment. It is the message I read in your jiggle. Stretch your skins like pegged hides curing in the miracle of the sun's moment. Exult in your legs' scissoring, your waist's swivel. Romp; eat the froth; be children. I am here above you; I have given my youth that you may do this. I wait. The tides of time have treacherous undercurrents. You are borne continually towards the horizon. I have prepared myself; my muscles are instilled with everything that must be done. Someday my alertness will bear fruit; from near the horizon there will arise, delicious, translucent, like a green bell above the water, the call for help, the call, a call, it saddens me to confess, that I have yet to hear.

BLUEGILL
Jayne Anne Phillips

HELLO MY LITTLE bluegill, little shark face. Fanged one, sucker, hermaphrodite. Rose, bloom in the fog of the body; see how the gulls arch over us, singing their raucous squalls. They bring you sweetmeats, tiny mice, spiders with clasped legs. In their old claws, claws of eons, reptilian sleep, they cradle shiny rocks and bits of glass. Boat in my blood, I dream you furred and sharp-toothed, loping in snow mist on a tundra far from the sea. I believe you are male; will I make you a husband, uncle, brother? Feed you in dark movie houses of a city we haven't found? This village borders waves, roofs askew, boards vacant. I'll leave here with two

425

suitcases and a music box, but what of you, little boot, little head with two eyes? I talk to you, bone of my coming, bone of an earnest receipt. I feel you now, steaming in the cave of the womb.

Here there are small fires. I bank a blaze in the iron stove and waken ringed in damp; how white air seeps inside the cracked houses, in the rattled doors and sills. We have arrived and settled in a house that groans, shifting its mildewed walls. The rains have come, rolling mud yards of fishermen's shacks down a dirt road to the curling surf. Crabs' claws bleach in spindled grass; dogs tear the discarded shells and drag them in rain. They fade from orange to peach to the pearl of the disembodied. Smells crouch and pull, moving in wet air. Each night crates of live crab are delivered to the smokehouse next door. They clack and crawl, a lumbering mass whose mute antennae click a filament of loss. Ocean is a ream of white meat, circles in a muscular brain. I eat these creatures; their flesh is sweet and flaky. They are voiceless, fluid in their watery dusk, trapped in nets a mile from the rocky cliffs. You are some kin to them, floating in your own dark sac.

Kelp floats a jungle by the pier, armless, legless, waving long sea hair, tresses submerged and rooty. These plants are bulbs and a nipple, rounded snouts weaving their tubular tails. Little boys find them washed up on the beach, wet, rubbery, smelling of salt. They hold the globular heads between their legs and ride them like stick horses. They gallop off, long tails dragging tapered in the sand. They run along the water in groups of three or four, young centaurs with no six-guns whose tracks evoke visions of mythical reptiles. They run all the way to the point, grow bored, fight, scatter; finally one comes back alone, preoccupied, dejected, dragging the desultory tail in one hand as the foamy surf tugs it seaward. I watch him; I pretend you see him too, see it all with your X-ray vision, your soft eyes, their honeycomb facets judging the souls of all failed boys. We watch the old ones, the young ones, the boats bobbing their rummy cargoes of traps and nets and hooks.

I sit at the corner table of the one restaurant, diner near the water where fishermen drink coffee at six A.M. I arrive later, when the place is nearly empty, when the sun slants on toward noon and the coffee has aged to a pungent syrup. The waitress is the postmaster's wife; she knows I get one envelope a month, that I cash one check at MacKinsie's Market, that I rent a postbox on a six-month basis. She spots my ringless hands, the gauntness in my face, the calcium pills I pull out of my purse in a green medicinal bottle. She recognizes my aversion to eggs; she knows that blur in my pupils, blur and flare, wavering as though

I'm sucked inward by a small interior flame. You breathe, adhered to a cord. Translucent astronaut, your eyes change days like a calendar watch. The fog surrounds us, drifting between craggy hills like an insubstantial blimp, whale shape that breaks up and spreads. Rock islands rise from the olive sea; they've caught seed in the wind and sit impassive, totems bristling with pine. Before long they will split and speak, revealing a long-trapped Hamlin piper and a troop of children whose bodies are musical and perfect, whose thoughts have grown pure. The children translate each wash of light on the faces of their stone capsules; they feel each nuance of sun and hear the fog as a continuous sigh, drifted breath of the one giant to whom they address their prayers. They have grown no taller and experienced no disease; they sleep in shifts. The piper has made no sound since their arrival. His inert form has become luminous and faintly furred. He is a father fit for animalistic angels whose complex mathematical games evolve with the centuries, whose hands have become transparent from constant handling of quartz pebbles and clear agates. They have no interest in talk or travel; they have developed beyond the inhabitants of countries and communicate only with the unborn. They repudiate the music that tempted them and create it now within themselves, a silent version expressed in numerals, angles, complicated slitherings. They are mobile as lizards and opaque as those small blind fish found in the still waters of caves. Immortal, they become their own children. Their memories of a long-ago journey are layered as genetics: how the sky eclipsed, how the piped melody was transformed as they walked into the sea and were submerged. The girls and smaller boys remember their dresses blousing, swirling like anemones. The music entered a new dimension, felt inside them like cool fingers, formal as a harpsichord yet buoyant, wild; they were taken up with it days at a time . . .

Here in the diner, there is a jukebox that turns up loud. High school kids move the tables back and dance on Friday nights. They are sixteen, tough little girls who disdain makeup and smoke Turkish cigarettes, or last year's senior boys who can't leave the village. Already they're hauling net on their fathers' boats, learning a language of profanity and back-slapping, beer, odd tumescent dawns as the other boats float out of sight. They want to marry at twenty, save money, acquire protection from the weather. But the girls are like colts, skittish and lean; they've read magazines, gone to rock concerts, experimented with drugs and each other. They play truant and drive around all day in VWs, listen to AM radio in the rain and swish of the wipers, dream of graduation and San Francisco, L.A., Mexico. They go barefoot in the dead of winter and seldom eat; their faces are pale and dewy from the moist air, the continuous rains. They show up sullen-eyed for the dances and get younger as the evening progresses, drinking grocery-store mixed drinks from thermoses in boys' cars. Now they are willing to dance close and imitate their mothers. Music beats in the floor like a heart; movie-theme certainty and the simple lyric of hold-me-tight. I pause on my nightly walks and watch their silhouettes on the windows; nearby the dock pylons stand up mossy and beaten, slap of the water intimate and old. Boys sit exchanging hopeful stories, smoking dope. Sometimes they whistle. They can't see my shape in my bulky coat. Once, one of them followed me home and waited beyond the concrete porch and the woodpile; I saw his face past the thrown ellipses of light. I imagined him in my bed, smooth-skinned and physically happy, no knowledge but intent. He would address you through my skin, nothing but question marks. Instructed to move slowly from behind, he would be careful, tentative, but forget at the end and push hard. There is no danger; you are floating, interior and protected; but it's that rhythmic lapsing of my love for you that would frighten; we have been alone so long. So I am true to you; I shut off the light and he goes away. In some manner, I am in your employ; I feed my body to feed you and buy my food with money sent me because of you. I am very nearly married to you; and it is only here, a northwestern fishing village in the rains, constant rain, that the money comes according to bargain, to an understanding conceived in your interest. I have followed you though you cannot speak, only fold, unfold. Blueprint, bone and toenail, sapphire. You must know it all from the beginning, never suffer the ignorance of boys with vestigial tails and imagined guns. I send you all these secrets in my blood; they wash through you like dialysis. You are the animal and the saint, snow-blind, begun in blindness . . . you must break free of me like a weasel or a fox, fatherless, dark as the seals that bark like haunted men from the rocks, far away, their calls magnified in the distance, in the twilight.

Ghost, my solitaire, I'll say your father was a horse, a Percheron whose rippled mane fell across my shoulders, whose tight hide glimmered, who shivered and made small winged insects rise into the air. A creature large-eyed, velvet. Long bone of the face broad as a forearm, back broad as sleep. Massive. Looking from the side of the face, a peripheral vision innocent, instinctual.

But no, there were many fathers. There was a truck, a rattling of nuts and bolts, a juggling of emergencies. Suede carpenter's apron spotted with motor oil, clothes kept in stacked crates. There were hands never quite clean and later, manicured hands. A long car with mechanical windows that *zimmed* as they moved smoothly up and down, impenetrable as those clear shells separating the self from a dreamed desire (do you dream? of long foldings, channels, imageless dreams of fish, long turnings, echoed sounds and shading waters). In between, there were faces in many cars, road maps and laced boots, hand-printed signs held by the highway exits, threats from ex-cons, cajoling salesmen, circling patrolmen. There were counters, tables, eight-hour shifts, grease-stained menus, prices marked over three times, regulars pathetic and laughing, cheap regulation nylons, shoes with ridged soles, creamers filled early as a truck arrives with sugared doughnuts smelling of vats and heat. Men cursed in heavy accents, living in motor hum of the big dishwashers, overflowed garbage pails, ouzo at the end of the day. Then there were men across hallways, stair rails, men with offices, married men and their secretaries, empty bud vase on a desk. Men in elevators, white shirts ironed by a special Chinaman on Bleecker. Sanitary weekend joggers, movie reviewers, twenty-seventh floor, manufactured air, salon haircuts, long lunches, tablecloths and wine. Rooftop view, jets to cut swelling white slashes in the sky. And down below, below rooftops and clean charmed rhymes, the dark alleys meandered; those same alleys that crisscross a confusion of small towns. Same sideways routes and wishful arrivals, eye-level gravel, sooty perfumes, pale grass seeding in the stones. Bronzed light in casts of season: steely and blue, smoke taste of winters; the pinkish dark of any thaw; then coral

432

falling in greens, summer mix of rot and flowers; autumn a burnt red, orange darkened to rust and scab. All of it men and faces, progression, hands come to this and you, grown inside me like one reminder.

He faced me over a café table, showed me the town on a map. No special reason, he said, he'd been here once; a quiet place, pretty, it would do. One geography was all he asked in the arrangement, the 'interruption.' He mentioned his obligation and its limits; he mentioned our separate paths. I don't ask here if they know him, I don't speculate. I've left him purely, as though you came to me after a voyage of years, as though you flew like a seed, saw them all and won me from them. I've lived with you all these months, grown cowish and full of you, yet I don't name you except by touch, curl, gesture. Wake and sleep, slim minnow, luminous frog. There are clues and riddles, pages in the book of the body, stones turned and turned. Each music lasts, forgetful, surfacing in the aisles of anonymous shops.

Music, addition and subtraction, Pavlovian reminder of scenes becoming, only dreamed. Evenings I listen to the radio and read fairy tales; those first lies, those promises. Directions are clear: crumbs in the woods, wolves in red hoods, the prince of temptation more believable as an enchanted toad. He is articulate and patient; there is the music of those years in the deep well, *plunk* of moisture, *whish* of the wayward rain, and finally the face of rescue peering over the stone rim like a moon. Omens burst into bloom; each life evolved to a single moment: the ugly natural, shrunken and wise, cradled in a palm fair as camellias.

Knot of cells, where is your voice? Here there are no books of instructions. There is the planed edge of the oaken table, the blond rivulets of the wood. There is a lamp in a dirty shade and the crouched stove hunkering its blackness around a fiery warmth. All night I sit, feeling the glow from a couch pulled close to the heat. Stirring the ashes, feeding, feeding, eating the fire with my skin. The foghorn cries through the mist in the bay: *bawaah, bawaah*, weeping of an idiot sheep, steady, measured as love. At dawn I'm standing by the window and the fishing boats bob like toys across the water, swaying their toothpick masts. Perfect mirage, they glisten and fade. Morning is two hours of sun as the season turns, a dime gone silver and thin. The gnarled plants are wild in their pots, spindly and bent. Gnats sleep on the leaves, inaugurating flight from a pearly slime on the windowpane. Their waftings are broken and dreamy, looping in the cold air of the house slowly, so slowly that I clap my hands and end them. Staccato, flash: that quick chord of once-upon-a-time.

Faraway I was a child, resolute, small, these same eyes in my head sinking back by night. Always I waited for you, marauder, collector, invisible pea in the body. I called you stones hidden in corners, paper fish with secret meanings, clothespin doll. Alone in my high bed, the dark, the dark; I shook my head faster, faster, rope of long hair flying across my shoulders like a switch, a scented tail. Under the bed, beyond the frothy curtain duster, I kept a menagerie of treasures and dust: discarded metallic jewelry, glass rhinestones pried from their settings, old gabardine suitcoat from a box in the basement, lipsticks, compacts with cloudy mirrors, slippers with pompoms, a man's blue silk tie embossed with tiny golf clubs. At night I crawled under wrapped in my sheets, breathing the buried smell, rattling the bed slats with my knees. I held my breath till the whole floor moved, plethora of red slashes; saw you in guises of lightning and the captive atmosphere.

Now a storm rolls the house in its paws. Again, men are lost and a hull washes up on the rocks. All day search copters hover and sweep. Dipping low, they chop the air for survivors and flee at dusk. The bay lies capped and draggled, rolling like water sloshed in a bowl. Toward nightfall, wind taps like briers on the windowpanes. We go out, down to the rocks and the shore. The forgotten hull lies breaking and splintered, only a slab of wood. The bay moves near it like a sleeper under sheets, murmuring, calling more rain. Animal in me, fish in a swim, I tell you *everything drowns*. I say *believe me if you are mine*, but you push like a fist with limbs. I feel your eyes searching, your gaze trapped in the dark like a beam of light. Then your vision transcends my skin: finally, I see them too, the lost fishermen, their faces framed in swirling hair like the heads of women. They are pale and blue, glowing, breathing with a pulse in their throats. They rise streaming tattered shirts, shining like mother-of-pearl. They rise moving toward us, round-mouthed, answering, answering the spheres of your talk. I am only witness to a language. The air is yours; it is water circling in like departure.

THE BEACH

Alain Robbe-Grillet

THREE CHILDREN ARE walking along a beach. They move forward, side by side, holding hands. They are roughly the same height, and probably the same age too: about twelve. The one in the middle, though, is a little smaller than the other two.

Apart from these three children, the whole long beach is deserted. It is a fairly wide, even strip of sand, with neither isolated rocks nor pools, and with only the slightest downward slope between the steep cliff, which looks impassable, and the sea.

It is a very fine day. The sun illuminates the yellow sand with a violent, vertical light. There is not a cloud in the sky. Neither is there any wind. The water is blue and calm, without the faintest swell from the open sea, although the beach is completely exposed as far as the horizon.

But, at regular intervals, a sudden wave, always the same, originating a few yards away from the shore, suddenly rises and then immediately breaks, always in the same line. And one does not have the impression that the water is flowing and then ebbing; on the contrary, it is as if the whole movement were being accomplished in the same place. The swelling of the water at first produces a slight depression on the shore side, and the wave recedes a little, with a murmur of rolling gravel; then it bursts, and spreads milkily over the slope, but it is merely regaining the ground it has lost. It is only very occasionally that it rises slightly higher and for a moment moistens a few extra inches.

And everything becomes still again; the sea, smooth and blue, stops at exactly the same level on the yellow sand along the beach where, side by side, the three children are walking.

They are blond, almost the same colour as the sand: their skin is a little darker, their hair a little lighter. They are all three dressed alike; shorts and shirt, both of a coarse, faded blue linen. They are walking side by side, holding hands, in a straight line, parallel to the sea and parallel to the cliff, almost equidistant from both, a little nearer the water, though. The sun is at the zenith, and leaves no shadow at their feet.

In front of them is virgin sand, yellow and smooth from the rock to the water. The children move forward in a straight line, at an even speed, without making the slightest little detour, calm, holding hands. Behind them the sand, barely moist, is marked by the three lines of prints left by their bare feet, three even series of similar and equally spaced footprints, quite deep, unblemished.

The children are looking straight ahead. They don't so much as glance at the tall cliff, on their left, or at the sea, whose little waves are periodically breaking, on the other side. They are even less inclined to turn round and look back at the distance they have come. They continue on their way with even, rapid steps.

In front of them is a flock of sea-birds walking along the shore, just at the edge of the waves. They are moving parallel to the children, in the same direction, about a hundred yards away from them. But, as the birds are going much less quickly, the children are catching them up. And while the sea is continually obliterating the traces of their star-shaped feet, the children's footsteps remain clearly inscribed in the barely moist sand, where the three lines of prints continue to lengthen.

The depth of these prints is constant; just less than an inch. They are not deformed; either by a crumbling of the edges, or by too deep an impression of toe or heel. They look as if they have been mechanically punched out of a more mobile, surface-layer of ground.

Their triple line extends thus ever farther, and seems at the same time to narrow, to become slower, to merge into a single line, which divides the shore into two strips along the whole of its length, and ends in a minute mechanical movement at the far end: the alternate fall and rise of six bare feet, almost as if they are marking time.

But as the bare feet move farther away, they get nearer to the birds. Not only are they covering the ground rapidly, but the relative distance separating the two groups is also diminishing far more quickly, compared to the distance already covered. There are soon only a few paces between them . . .

But when the children finally seem just about to catch up with the birds, they suddenly flap their wings and fly off, first one, then two, then ten . . . And all the white and grey birds in the flock describe a curve over the sea and then come down again on to the sand and start walking again, still in the same direction, just at the edge of the waves, about a hundred yards away.

At this distance, the movements of the water are

almost imperceptible, except perhaps through a sudden change of colour, every ten seconds, at the moment when the breaking foam shines in the sun.

Taking no notice of the tracks they are carving so precisely in the virgin sand, nor of the little waves on their right, nor of the birds, now flying, now walking, in front of them, the three blond children move forward side by side, with even, rapid steps, holding hands.

Their three sunburnt faces, darker than their hair, are alike. The expression is the same: serious, thoughtful, perhaps a little anxious. Their features, too, are identical, though it is obvious that two of these children are boys and the third a girl. The girl's hair is only slightly longer, slightly more curly, and her limbs just a trifle more slender. But their clothes are exactly the same: shorts and shirt, both of coarse, faded blue linen.

The girl is on the extreme right, nearest the sea. On her left walks the boy who is slightly the smaller of the two. The other boy, nearest the cliff, is the same height as the girl.

In front of them the smooth, yellow sand stretches as far as the eye can see. On their left rises, almost vertically, the wall of brown stone, with no apparent way through it. On their right, motionless and blue all the way to the horizon, the level surface of the sea is fringed with a sudden little wave, which immediately breaks and runs away in white foam.

Then, ten seconds later, the swelling water again hollows out the same depression on the shore side, with a murmur of rolling gravel.

The wavelet breaks; the milky foam again runs up the slope, regaining the few inches of lost ground. During the ensuing silence, the chimes of a far distant bell ring out in the calm air.

'There's the bell,' says the smaller of the boys, the one walking in the middle.

But the sound of the gravel being sucked up by the sea drowns the extremely faint ringing. They have to wait till the end of the cycle to catch the few remaining sounds, which are distorted by the distance.

'It's the first bell,' says the bigger boy.

The wavelet breaks, on their right.

When it is calm again, they can no longer hear anything. The three blond children are still walking in the same regular rhythm, all three holding hands. In front of them, a sudden contagion affects the flock of birds, who were only a few paces away; they flap their wings and fly off.

They describe the same curve over the water, and then come down on to the sand and start walking again, still in the same direction, just at the edge of the waves, about a hundred yards away.

'Maybe it wasn't the first,' the smaller boy continues, 'if we didn't hear the other, before . . .'

'We'd have heard it the same,' replies the boy next to him.

But this hasn't made them modify their pace; and the same prints, behind them, continue to appear, as they go along, under their six bare feet.

'We weren't so close, before,' says the girl.

After a moment, the bigger of the boys, the one on the cliff side, says:

'We're still a long way off.'

And then all three walk on in silence.

They remain thus silent until the bell, still as indistinct, again rings out in the calm air. The bigger of the boys says then: 'There's the bell.' The others don't answer.

The birds, which they had been on the point of catching up, flap their wings and fly off, first one, then two, then ten . . .

Then the whole flock is once more on the sand, moving along the shore, about a hundred yards in front of the children.

The sea is continually obliterating the star-shaped traces of their feet. The children, on the other hand, who are walking nearer to the cliff, side by side, holding hands, leave deep footprints behind them, whose triple line lengthens parallel to the shore across the very long beach.

On the right, on the side of the level, motionless sea, always in the same place, the same little wave is breaking.

NOTES ON THE AUTHORS

GLENDA ADAMS was born in Sydney in 1939 and attended the University of Sydney, where she studied Indonesian and Italian. She lived in Indonesia, then New York City, where she taught fiction writing at Columbia University for some years. Her novel *Dancing on Coral* won the Miles Franklin Award and the New South Wales Premier's Award, and another novel, *Longleg*, won the *Age* Book of the Year Award. She is also the author of another novel, *Games of the Strong*, and a book of stories, *The Hottest Night of the Century*.

CANDIDA BAKER was born in London in 1955 into a theatrical and literary family. She visited Australia with the Royal Shakespeare Company production of *The Hollow Crown* in 1975, and emigrated to Sydney in 1977.

Her first novel, *Women and Horses* (1990), was published in Australia and the United States and her story collection, *The Powerful Owl*, will be published by Picador in 1994. The author of the *Yacker* series of interviews with Australian writers, a play, *Personal Effects*, and several stories for children, she has also written for *Time* and the Melbourne *Age*.

RICK BASS, born in 1958, is a petroleum geologist working in Texas, Oklahoma, Kansas, Louisiana, Mississippi, Florida and Alabama, and lives in Montana. His fiction has appeared in *The Paris Review, Antaeus, Esquire, The Quarterly* and other publications. *The Watch*, his first collection of short stories, was published in the U.S. in 1989, followed by a collection of essays, *Oil Notes*.

CHARLES BAXTER is a professor of English at the University of Michigan, Ann Arbor. He has published six fiction titles, *The South Dakota Guidebook, Harmony of the World, Through the Safety Net, First Light, A Relative Stranger* and *Shadow Play*, and a collection of poetry, *Imaginary Paintings and Other Poems*.

PAUL BOWLES was born in 1911 and grew up in New York and New England. He left for Paris to become a writer but after trenchant criticism from Gertrude Stein he turned instead to music and made a name as a composer. He and his wife Jane Bowles became central figures in the transatlantic arts world, living in Mexico and New York before moving permanently to Tangier. There, in 1945, resorting to 'the old Surrealist method of abandoning conscious control and putting down whatever words came from the pen', he began writing stories and novels, including *The Sheltering Sky, Let it Come Down, The Spider's House* and *Up Above the World*. His latest book of selected stories, *A Distant Episode*, was published in 1988.

ITALO CALVINO was born in Cuba in 1923 and grew up in San Remo, Italy. The author of novels, stories, science fiction 'fables' and essays, he has been described as a 'true representative of modern European writing'. His first book, *Il sentiero dei nidi di ragno*, won the Premio Riccione and was published in English as *The Path to the Nest of Spiders*. His mastery of paradox, ironic humour and fantasy are exemplified by the stories *Difficult Loves*, the novels *Invisible Cities, Our Ancestors* and *If on a Winter's Night a Traveller*, and the 'fable' collection, *Cosmicomics*. He died in 1985.

RAYMOND CARVER was born in Clatskanie, Oregon, in 1939. Since the mid-nineteen-seventies he has been one of the world's most anthologised and influential writers of short fiction. In addition to his books of stories such as *Furious Seasons, Will You Please Be Quiet, Please?* and *What We Talk About When We Talk About Love*, he published four collections of poetry. The motto for his fiction might have been, as the narrator says in his story *Mr. Coffee and Mr. Fixit*, 'I've seen some things.' He died in 1988.

JOHN CHEEVER was born in Quincy, Massachusetts, in 1912, and received his only formal education at Thayer Academy. The author of seven collections of stories, most written first for the *New Yorker*, and four novels, his vision of the *haute bourgeoisie* of suburban New York, alternately comically affectionate and darkly satiric, combined with his inventive coining of images and incidents, brought him the National Book Award, the Howells Medal for Fiction from the National Academy of Arts and Letters and the Pulitzer Prize. He died in 1982.

RUTH FAINLIGHT, poet, short story writer and translator, was born in New York in 1931, but now lives in London. She has published numerous poetry collections, including *A Forecast, a Fable, Cages, The Region's Violence, Sybils and Others* and *Fifteen to Infinity*. Her *Selected Poems* appeared in 1983. She has published a collection of stories, *Daylife and Nightlife*, and is a contributor to the anthologies *Caught in a Story: Contemporary Fairytales and Fables, Penguin Modern Stories* and *New Stories 4*.

GABRIEL GARCÍA MÁRQUEZ was born in 1928 in Aracataca, Colombia. He attended the National University in Bogota, became a reporter and worked in Europe and New York as a foreign correspondent.

His books include *No One Writes to the Colonel and Other Stories, One Hundred Years of Solitude, The Autumn of the Patriarch, Innocent Erendira and Other Stories, In Evil Hour, Leaf Storm and Other Stories, Chronicle of a Death Foretold, Love in the Time of Cholera* and *The General in his Labyrinth.* He was awarded the Nobel Prize for Literature in 1982. He lives in Mexico City.

HELEN GARNER was born in Geelong, Victoria, in 1942 and educated there and at the University of Melbourne. Her first novel, *Monkey Grip*, won the National Book Council Award and was made into a film, and her story collection, *Postcards from Surfers*, won the New South Wales Premier's Award. Her novels *The Children's Bach* and *Cosmo Cosmolino* have been widely praised, and she has also published the two novellas, *Honour* and *Other People's Children*, and an original screenplay, *The Last Days of Chez Nous*, directed by Gillian Armstrong.

NADINE GORDIMER was born in 1923 and lives in South Africa. Internationally acclaimed for her short stories and novels embracing the nuances of life in her country, and the subtleties of political and racial tension, she has won many prizes for her literature, including the W.H. Smith Award, the James Tait Black Memorial Prize, the Booker Prize and the Nobel Prize.

BARRY HANNAH was born in Clinton, Mississippi, in 1942 and teaches at the University of Mississippi in Oxford.

He was awarded the William Faulkner Prize for his first novel, *Geronimo Rex*, and the Arnold Gingrich Short Fiction Award for his collection of stories, *Airships*. His other books include a novella, *Ray*, the novels *Nightwatchmen* and *The Tennis Handsome* and the story collection *Captain Maximus*. He has received a Guggenheim Fellowship and been honoured by the American Academy of Arts and Letters.

KERI HULME was born in 1947 in Christchurch and is of Maori, Lancashire English and Orkney Scots ancestry. She is best known for her novel *The Bone People*, which won the Booker Prize, and is also the author of *Lost Possessions* and a volume of poetry, *The Silences Between: Moeraki Conversations*. Her poems and stories have been widely published in magazines and broadcast on radio and television. She is also a painter and whitebaiter, and lives in Okarito, on the west coast of New Zealand, in a house she built herself.

DIANE JOHNSON was born in Moline, Illinois, in 1934, and educated at the Universities of Utah and California. She is the author of five novels, including *Lying Low* and *The Shadow Knows*, a collection of essays, *Terrorists and Novelists*, and biographies of Dashiell Hammett and Mary Ellen Peacock. She also collaborated with Stanley Kubrick on the screenplay for *The Shining*. A frequent contributor to the *New York Review of Books*, she lives in Berkeley, California.

DAVID MALOUF was born in Brisbane in 1934, attended the University of Queensland and now divides his time between Tuscany and Sydney. His first poetry collection, *Neighbours in a Thicket*, won three national prizes and his first short story collection, *Antipodes*, won the Victorian Premier's Award. His novels include *Johnno*, *An Imaginary Life*, *Harland's Half Acre* and *The Great World*, which won the Miles Franklin Award and the Commonwealth Writers' Prize. His most recent novel is *Remembering Babylon*.

IAN McEWAN was born in England in 1948, and lives and works in London. He began writing short stories in 1970 and his first collection, *First Love, Last Rites*, won the Somerset Maugham Award in 1976. His second collection, *In Between the Sheets*, received wide acclaim, as did his novels *The Cement Garden*, *The Comfort of Strangers* (which has been filmed) and *The Child in Time*. He is also the author of an oratorio and the screenplay, *The Ploughman's Lunch*.

FRANK MOORHOUSE was born in Nowra, New South Wales, in 1938. His first book of stories, *Futility and Other Animals*, was published in 1969 while he was working as a reporter in Sydney. His other 'discontinuous narratives', in which characters, and often stories themselves, overlap, include *The Americans, Baby*, *The Electrical Experience*, *Tales of Mystery and Romance*, *The Everlasting Secret Family* and *Room Service*. He won the *Age* Book of the Year Award and the Australian Literature Society's Gold Medal for *Forty-Seventeen*. His most recent book is *Grand Days*.

JAYNE ANNE PHILLIPS was born in 1952 and educated at the Universities of West Virginia and Iowa. Her first collection of stories, *Black Tickets*, was published in 1979. She has published another story collection, *Fast Lanes*, and a novel, *Machine Dreams*. She is regarded as a major figure in the renaissance of American realism, and has been a recipient of two National Endowment for the Arts grants and the St Lawrence Award.

ALAIN ROBBE-GRILLET, the French novelist, film writer and director, was born in 1922. He is regarded as the initiator and spokesman for the school of the 'nouveau roman'. His theories are most tellingly realised in the novels *The Voyeur*, which won the Prix des Critiques, and *Jealousy*. He is equally noted for his film scenario *Last Year at Marienbad*. Of the several films he has directed, *L'Immortelle* won the Prix Louis Delluc.

GRAHAM SWIFT was born in London in 1949. His stories first appeared in *London Magazine*. He is the author of five novels, *The Sweet Shop Owner, Shuttlecock*, which won the Geoffrey Faber Memorial Prize; the internationally acclaimed *Waterland*, which won the *Guardian* Fiction Award, the Winifred Holtby Memorial Prize and the Italian Premio Grinzane Cavour, *Out of This*

World and *Ever After*, and a short story collection, *Learning to Swim*. He also co-edited *The Magic Wheel: An Anthology of Fishing in Literature*.

MICHEL TOURNIER was born in 1924. He studied philosophy and German, and worked as a broadcaster in French radio and television, and in publishing, before turning to writing full time. He won the prestigious Grand Prix du Roman of the Academie Francaise with his first novel, *Friday or the Other Island*, in 1967 and the Prix Goncourt for his second, *The Erl King*, 1970. He has published one collection of short stories, *The Fetishist*, and a book of 'fabulous tales', *The Midnight Love Feast*.

JOHN UPDIKE was born in Shillington, Pennsylvania, in 1932 and attended Harvard College and the Ruskin School of Drawing and Fine Art at Oxford. From 1955 to 1957 he was on the staff of the *New Yorker*, to which he has contributed many short stories, essays and poems. His novels include *The Poorhouse Fair*, *Rabbit, Run*, *The Centaur*, *Of the Farm*, *Rabbit Redux*, *Couples*, *The Coup*, *Rabbit is Rich* (winner of the 1982 Pulitzer Prize for Fiction), *The Witches of Eastwick* and *Roger's Version*. His short story collections include *The Same Door*, *Pigeon Feathers*, *The Music School*, *Museums and Women*, *Your Lover Just Called* and *Problems*.

TIM WINTON was born in 1960 and lives in a small town on the coast of Western Australia. He is the author of five novels, two collections of short stories and two books for children. His first novel, *The Open Swimmer*, won the Australian/Vogel Award and he has twice won the Miles Franklin Award, for *Shallows* and *Cloudstreet*. He has been awarded several senior fellowships by the Literature Board of the Australia Council and a travelling scholarship from the Marten Bequest.

ACKNOWLEDGEMENTS

Acknowledgements are due to the following authors, publishers and agents for permission to include the stories which appear in this book:

'The Hottest Night of the Century', © Glenda Adams 1979, from *The Hottest Night of the Century*, Angus & Robertson.

'Spindrift', © Candida Baker 1994, from *The Powerful Owl*, Picador (Pan Macmillan, Sydney and London).

'Redfish', © Rick Bass 1989, from *The Watch*, W.W. Norton & Co.

'The Cliff', Reprinted from *Harmony of the World* by Charles Baxter, by permission of the University of Missouri Press. © 1984 by the author.

'Pages from Cold Point', © Paul Bowles 1979, from *Collected Stories 1939–1976*, Black Sparrow Press, Santa Barbara; first published in the U.K. by Peter Owen Ltd.

'Big Fish, Little Fish' by Italo Calvino, translated by Archibald Colquhoun, © Giulio Einaudi Editore, Turin. Reprinted by agreement with Aitken, Stone & Wylie Ltd. on behalf of the Estate of Italo Calvino.

'So Much Water So Close to Home', © Raymond Carver 1977, from *Furious Seasons*, Capra Press, Santa Barbara; then *What We Talk About When We Talk About Love*, Collins 1982. Reprinted by permission of Harvill, an imprint of HarperCollins Publishers Ltd.

'The Seaside Houses', by John Cheever, from *The Brigadier and the Golf Widow*, Victor Gollancz, London, 1965. Reprinted by agreement with Aitken, Stone & Wylie Ltd. on behalf of the Estate of John Cheever.

'Radiant Heat', © Robert Drewe 1989, from *The Bay of Contented Men*, Picador (Pan Macmillan, Sydney and London).

'The Fish-scale Shirt', © Ruth Fainlight 1991, from *Caught in a Story: Contemporary Fairytales and Fables*, Vintage, 1992.

'The Handsomest Drowned Man in the World', © Gabriel García Márquez, from *Innocent Erendíra and Other Stories*, English translation © 1978 Harper & Row

Publishers, Inc. Reprinted by permission of Random House UK Ltd.

'Postcards from Surfers', © Helen Garner 1984, from *Postcards from Surfers*, McPhee Gribble and Bloomsbury.

'The Catch', © Nadine Gordimer 1953, from *The Soft Voice of the Serpent*, Victor Gollancz Ltd.

'Getting Ready', © Barry Hannah 1985, from *Captain Maximus*, Alfred A. Knopf, Inc. Reprinted by permission of Houghton Mifflin Company.

'Great Barrier Reef', © Diane Johnson 1992, from the *New Yorker*, reprinted by permission of the Peters Fraser & Dunlop Group Ltd.

'Unnamed Islands in the Unknown Sea', © Keri Hulme 1986, from *Te Kaihau/The Windeater*, Victoria University Press and University of Queensland Press.

'A Change of Scene', by David Malouf, from *Antipodes*, © Chatto & Windus 1985.

'Last Day of Summer', © Ian McEwan 1975, from *First Love, Last Rites*, Jonathan Cape Ltd. Reprinted by permission of Random House UK Ltd.

'Across the Plains, Over the Mountains and Down to the Sea', © Frank Moorhouse 1969, from *Futility and Other Animals*, Gareth Powell Associates. Reprinted by permission of Angus & Robertson.

'Bluegill', © Jayne Anne Phillips 1987, from *Fast Lanes*,

E.P. Dutton. Reprinted by permission of Houghton Mifflin Company.

'The Beach' by Alain Robbe-Grillet, translated by Barbara Wright, from *Instantanes (Snapshots)*, © Les Editions de Minuit, 1962, and John Calder (Publishers) Ltd., 1965.

'Learning to Swim', © Graham Swift, from *Learning to Swim*. Reprinted by permission of Picador (Pan Macmillan Ltd).

'The Midnight Love Feast', by Michel Tournier, from *The Midnight Love Feast*, 1991. Reprinted by permission of HarperCollins Publishers Ltd. First published as *Le Medianoche Amoureux*. © Editions Gallimard, 1989. Translation © Barbara Wright 1991.

'Lifeguard', © John Updike 1962, from *Pigeon Feathers & Other Stories*, Alfred A. Knopf, Inc. Reprinted by permission of Hamish Hamilton Ltd.

'The Water Was Dark and it Went Forever Down', © Tim Winton 1987, from *Minimum of Two*, McPhee Gribble.

Thanks also to Candida Baker, Caroline Baum and Michael Bisits for steering me towards *Water and Dreams: An Essay on the Imagination of Matter*, by Gaston Bachelard (Pegasus Foundation, Dallas), *Haunts of the Black Masseur: The Swimmer as Hero*, by Charles Sprawson (Jonathan

Cape, London) and *Shallow-Water Dictionary*, by John R. Stilgoe, Professor in the History of Landscape, Harvard University (Exact Change Press, Cambridge, Massachusetts).

R.D.